PRAISE FOR "SEARCHING FOR RICK"

"A compelling novel that rises out of the ruins of World War II. The author has written a curious coming-of-age tale that brings together the desperate search for identity with the longing for mentors, the tragedy of war, and the poetry of the peace movement. This book should appeal to both war buffs and fans of warriors-turned-poets."

--Phil Cousineau, author of *The Olympic Odyssey,*
The Hero's Journey, and *The Book of Roads*

"*Searching for Rick* is about idealism, both from a young fighter pilot and later from his young friend who carries on Rick's idealistic crusade as a way of honoring Rick. What follows is Rob's personal journey of discovery from childhood to young adulthood, as told by Cooper in a warm, original, refreshingly traditional tale.

--Philip Kaplan, author of *Big Wings, Two-man Air Force,*
and *Fighter Aces of the Luftwaffe in World War II*

"In *Searching for Rick,* the talented writer Bob Cooper gives us a look at what might have been had fate been changed. Changing fate is no easy task, but Cooper does it artfully. Readers will find *Searching for Rick* just as well-written and enjoyable as his *Serenade to the Blue Lady.*"

--Dan Bauer, author of *The Long Lost Journal of Confeder-*
ate General James Johnston Pettigrew and
The Wartime Journal of B-17 Bomber Pilot Frank Stiles

SEARCHING FOR RICK

A Novel

Marlene,

Old friends are the
best friends. Keep going

Love,

B.S

By

Robert Floyd Cooper

Copyright © 2007 by Robert Floyd Cooper

ISBN 0-7414-4105-5

Published by:

INFINITY
PUBLISHING.COM

1094 New DeHaven Street, Suite 100
West Conshohocken, PA 19428-2713
Info@buybooksontheweb.com
www.buybooksontheweb.com
Toll-free (877) BUY BOOK
Local Phone (610) 941-9999
Fax (610) 941-9959

Printed in the United States of America

Printed on Recycled Paper

Published July 2007

CONTENTS

DEDICATION

To my wife Mary, who has always stood
tall with me in my writing endeavors.

FOREWORD

"Searching for Rick" is fiction. Yet it has a strong basis in fact and this requires explanation. The character of Rick Linden is partially based upon Bert Stiles, a flyer and writer in the World War II era. Before he entered the Air Corps in 1942, Stiles had published a dozen or so short stories when he was still 21 years old. Later, in the "down time" between flying bomber missions, he wrote a powerful novel, "Serenade to the Big Bird," published by Norton and Norton after the war. Bert Stiles died in late 1944 when his plane was shot down over Germany.

The other major character in this book is the young English boy, Rob St. Clair. He is fictitious, as are all the other characters in "Searching for Rick."

Many of the thoughts and philosophies of "Rick Linden" are taken from Bert Stiles' writings. I wish to thank May Stiles Hostetter and Elizabeth Stiles Leffingwell, Bert's sisters, for permission to use this material. Bert's deepest philosophies made sense coming from the mouth of Rick Linden. And I am happy to see them in print.

In addition to his sisters, May and Beth, several friends proofread the final draft: Julia Hunter-Blair, Jack Ele, Dale Ele, Mary Cooper and Jim Lyons. Julia, who is from Scotland and lived in England, also made many suggestions on appropriate English words and terms of the era.

Some might call this an anti-war "message" book, and if this is how it comes across, so be it. But war and politics aside, I found great pleasure in creating scenes and situations involving young men and women in wartime and shortly thereafter.

RFC

PART I

RICK LINDEN

1

BORN TO FLY FIGHTERS

The commanding officer looked at me with steely eyes. I searched those eyes for something simpatico, but couldn't find it.

Ah, well, perhaps any C.O. of a fighter station in England would be equally unsympathetic. He had been poring over my 201 file, so it was no surprise when he asked, "Why should I take a chance on you, Linden, a bomber pilot without any single-engine time? Sell me on yourself, Lieutenant. In five minutes."

I had been preparing for the question for months—ever since I had decided to apply for fighters after finishing my bomber tour. It had not been a difficult decision to make. I had no wife to go home to. There were parents, of course, a sister, a close pal or two, a special girl, but they could all wait. I had been in England for only five months and I wasn't ready to go home. And if I was going to stay, why not fly the P-51 Mustang, a plane I'd long wanted to get to know better.

I'll play this cool, I thought. Not too formal; this was a combat station. But respectful; after all, the guy is commander of a P-51 group.

"Colonel Warren, I was never cut out to be a bomber pilot. I graduated from single-engine Advance Flying School and did fine. It was the kind of flying I was cut out for. I know it. I did well in acrobatics and loved it. I thought I was a lock for combat in fighters, but the luck of the draw put me in the right seat of a B-17. That's what they needed at the time I graduated, and that's what I got. I did my duty and flew the heavies, but it's not too late for me to taste the thrill of fighters."

"Is that what you're looking for—thrills?"

I'd have to watch my choice of words. "Of course thrills are part of it. But, mainly, I'm not through with flying combat. I want to fly another tour, this one in fighters. I know I can make it

3

in '51s, sir. It's what I've wanted to do all my life, what I was born to do." That was laying it on a bit thick, but what the hell, perhaps the Colonel was a romantic.

The Colonel was not a romantic. But he understood, I could tell that. For the record, he said, "No one is born to fly fighters, Linden. You have to work, and work hard, to make it in 51's. Don't ever—ever—take them lightly."

He didn't expect an answer; he was reading my 201 file again. It was all there, the history of my flying life. He looked up at me.

"Hmm. Richard Patrick Linden, age 22, resident of Colorado, graduate of single engine flying school as you said, 30 missions as co-pilot of a B-17, good ratings all around.

"You know, Linden, I'm only eight years older than you. I joined the 98th back in the states when I was barely 21. I'll bet I was even more of an eager beaver than you appear to be. I've been in your shoes and I can sympathize with your desire to fly a Mustang. You wouldn't be the first pilot to fly fighters directly from heavy bombers. In fact, one of my pilots, Lieutenant Morse, is a former bomber jockey. Perhaps you know him."

As it happened I did. Pat Morse and I were friends and fellow co-pilots at our bomber base. Pat had successfully made the transition and had already shot down a German plane. He had been my biggest ally in my own request for a transfer.

The steely eyes were back in place, directly on mine. "We need pilots, it's as simple as that. We have a couple of men who will finish their tours in a few weeks. I don't know when, or if, replacements will come in. So we have you, Lieutenant Linden, volunteering to be one of our pilots. What I don't know is whether your eagerness to fly our planes can readily be translated into the ability to fly them."

"All I can ask is the chance, Colonel. Let me fly a few hours in my old buddy, the AT-6, then a few hours in the P-51, to sort of get acquainted." I paused, thinking I had said enough. My five minutes was long up. I decided to state one thought the C.0., any P-51 commanding officer, would love to hear. "I think the Mustang is the finest plane flying anywhere in the world. I'll take as much training as Operations thinks I need. Then I'll treat the P-51 with as much respect as the plane deserves. And that's a ton."

The Colonel smiled thinly at my pitch. "Linden, you must have guessed why we're short of pilots. We've lost some damned

4

good men in the past months. Good, well-trained pilots. Dead or captured. An untrained man like you would have to work extra hard to keep from becoming another casualty. And I don't like casualties. I want you clear on that."

"Yes, sir."

"I want you to fly at least ten hours in the AT-6. You'd have to pass a stringent cockpit check in the Mustang. And I suggest you get your friend Morse to tell you everything he knows about the airplane you admire so much.

"So I'm going to take a chance on you, Linden."

"Yes, sir."

Then he took me down a couple of pegs. "I would suggest you don't tell your friends that you talked the old man into our private club. Because I wasn't much impressed with your pitch. What's important is our need for pilots, and that's the reason you're about to become a combat fighter pilot." He paused. "Oh, one other thing, Linden."

"Yes, sir."

"You look tired. Hell, you look exhausted. Not surprising, given that you just finished flying 30 missions in heavies. Capt. Stewart at your bomber base told me if you didn't return stateside with your crew, he was going to give you ten days leave. If you are to fly with me, I want you as fresh as possible. Ten days is too long, but, starting at 0800 tomorrow, I'm ordering you to take six days off before you fly any kind of plane again.

"Get away from airplanes. Travel. Get yourself some poontang if that's what you want. Report back to base on September 5th. And if the tired look isn't wiped off your face by then, I may reconsider taking you on as a pilot in my group. That's all, Linden. Dismissed."

I had been christened Richard Patrick Linden in Colorado Springs, my lifetime home. My father was the owner of a small hardware store, my mother a homemaker and part time dress-maker. My only sibling was Jane, three years younger than I, presently a sophomore at University of Denver. Jane was an independent lass, and I was proud of her for that and other attributes.

I was a couple inches short of six feet. My most disting-uishing attribute was my tawny red hair. Before the G.I. scissors crew got me in their clutches, it was a tangled mass, blowing freely in the wind. Now I wore it short, Army style, and lived with it. People said I was a good athlete, and I will agree that could be true in individual sports such as tennis, ice climbing, skiing, and fishing. I fished in the Rockies whenever the season was in and sometimes out of season. I knew every lake and the kind of fish that lived there.

I decided to attend Colorado College in my home town not so much because it was obvious my parents wanted me to (my father was an alumnus) but rather that as a small liberal arts school, C.C. could be helpful in my ambition to become a writer. I had no money to go out of state, and I was too unsure of myself to just strike out on my own. Later, I gained that self-assurance, but now I had just turned 18, my folks had pointed me to the right college, and I went along with the herd. Not that I was unhappy; I just hated following my parents footsteps right down life's path.

After two years of a love-hate relationship with college, I left abruptly and hopped a bus to New York.

I was drawn to the Big Apple because I had begun to take myself seriously about writing. I had written and submitted several short stories during my two years in college. None had been accepted, but some of the comments I'd received had been clearly encouraging. My English teacher in college had given me a letter of introduction to her sister's husband, a literary agent in New York. That was all I needed. I was on my way.

It wasn't a new idea: young artisans of all stripes were all over New York, seeking careers or just a bare living: acting, dancing, composing, painting, and yes, writing. It was heady stuff, particularly since I was still only 20 years old.

I knew my parents were disappointed in my decision to leave college, as was my sister, Jane. But I had decided I wouldn't be deterred by old-fashioned family allegiance. I deserved a chance at independence.

My agent, Timothy Maxwell, turned out to be a swell guy. He really did work on my behalf to entice a few big time editors to read stories I'd submitted. It was tough going but I reveled in it. I grew up in that year of living in New York. And it paid off when *Saturday Evening Post* accepted a story, and then another. And a third. And within four months after that, when I was barely 21 years old, I had sold nine stories. Tim, my agent, wondered aloud if I could crack the Hollywood scene as a writer.

I was back in Colorado Springs on a visit when Pearl Harbor was bombed and America entered the war. I stayed in Colorado and continued to write, but it wasn't the same. I decided I was a latent pacifist—until I started thinking about duty and honor. The clincher was when I realized that military service would provide adventure and viewpoint for a lifetime of writing. I knew I had to find out what a war was all about. I enlisted in the Army Air Corps before the draft could claim me. I was hungry for life. One life was not enough—I wanted to live three lives at the same time, every one of them a different adventure.

I stared at Pat Morse, my fellow pilot who had earlier transferred from bombers. I thought I was the luckiest man alive: an hour ago I had been accepted as a fighter pilot. We were seated across from each other in *The Pussycat and Owl,* a pub in Ridgewell, a mile down a country lane from our fighter base.

"I'm going to have to start giving you some respect," Pat said. "But I'm not surprised: I knew you could do it."

"I just followed your lead."

"Hey, no credit to me. This is your victory, Rick Linden. Savor it."

"I am, believe me, Pat."

Pat and I had met at our bomber base as fellow co-pilots. With a long face and tousled hair the color of wheat, Pat was my best friend in England. I found him one of the few people I had met in the service whom I could talk to.

"You'll have great fun flying this little bird," he said.

"I'd better prove it, buddy. I don't know how many people back home I've written to about my flying fighter planes —my parents, sister Jane, my best friend Rollie, for openers. I wrote them that I was too hot a pilot to come tamely on home. I said that I was needed in fighters in order to close out this war."

We sipped our beers in silence, both deep into our own thoughts.

"Did I ever tell you," I said, "what Capt. Stewart said over at 92nd Bomber, when he realized I might be transferring to fighter aircraft? He said 'Linden, you'll be navigator, radioman, and gunner as well as pilot. The sole pilot. At times I envy you for volunteering for fighters, but most of the time I think you're crazy as hell.'"

Pat fixed his light blue eyes on me in a level gaze. "He may be right, Rick. It's not easy doing everything yourself."

"We've lost so many buddies, Pat. War is stupid. It's criminal. I'm a writer, supposedly. I could write 20 adjectives condemning war, just off the top of my head."

"Tell me again: why did you re-up when you had every right to return home?"

"Just following your lead, buddy. Either we're crazy or stupid. Or perhaps both. But to answer your question: I'm here because it has to be done. Because I love my country, and I'm willing to fight for it. Those are the ostensible reasons.

"Then there's the ethereal viewpoint: I think of the sky, Pat, as a huge canvas spread over our pitiful lives, ubiquitous, changing, mysterious. God, I love the sky. Sometimes I go out into the night and just stand there and look upward with a sense of wonder beyond belief. I let my imagination go wild during these times. I feel a kind of ecstasy, not definable on any level I can express. When I'm flying, these thoughts are magnified and intensified.

"Do you know Saint Exupery, Pat?"

"Sure. *Wind, Sand, and Stars. The Little Prince.*"

"Yes. Among others. I forget which book it was when he wrote something like this: *By the grace of aerial flight, I have known an extraordinary experience and have pondered with bewilderment the fact that this earth that is our home is yet in truth a wandering star.*

"Isn't that good stuff? I wish he were a countryman of mine. Anyway, those are as good reasons as I can come up with for why I fly and fight. The trouble is, there's a lot of dying that goes along with it."

Pat Morse was silent, staring past me at the bartender, so I went right on. "Someone else said, I don't remember who, that airmen are children who never grew up. I subscribe to that, though that means I have to admit to still being a kid at heart."

"Hey, buddy, what's wrong with that?"

2

WANDERING IN SUFFOLK

I changed trains in Cambridge and headed east, settling down to the steady, creaking drumbeat of steel wheels on steel tracks. The sky was overcast, and since it was still cold in the coach, I kept my overcoat on and looked idly through rain-streaked windows at tall willows bordering a wide stream, grazing cows and hedgerows—the sights and sound of rural England.

I'd rolled into train stations in 'Frisco, Philly, Chicago and New Orleans. I'd listened to their shrill whistles in the night, to the sight of a locomotive disgorging black smoke high into the sky, chugging down the line. I wondered sometimes which I liked best: the thought of riding the rails, or actually riding them.

Colonel Warren's orders to take a short leave was like a bright ray beamed to me from on high. It was exactly what I wanted. My destination now was a town on the East Anglia shore where I could watch the waves wash up on the beach or crash into jagged rocks on the headlands.

Then, perhaps back to Cambridge or to Oxford, or to the spas at Cheltenham, even to Shakespeare-land in Stratford. The world was mine for nearly a week and England was the perfect place to be. I was alone on this trip: there hadn't been time to find any of my bomber crew. They were probably in London living the good life. Pat Morse didn't have a leave coming, or he might have been with me.

I was glad to have time on my own, to wonder again why I was returning to the war. Here I was, in England for the duration, when I could be headed home to the Rocky Mountains and freedom from the killing game. I was grateful for this upcoming time in Suffolk, a county I'd like to know better. I painted a picture in my mind: a quiet place by the rolling waves of the North

Sea. Maybe a little old lady would invite me to tea in a lovely, sunny dining room by the sea, and we would talk of many things.

My first glimpse of Felixstowe, a village on the North Sea, was not auspicious. There were no lights on—there was a blackout in effect. It was foggy, the type of throat-gripping fog which clings to your lungs. I looked for the quiet inn by the sea, for the restaurant with pretty waitresses, for a dance or a movie house. What I did see were a group of gray stone houses, a small harbor, some fishing boats bobbing at anchor, and a wharf leading out to sea.

The railroad tracks had ended at Ipswich, a dozen miles from the coast. I probably should have stayed in that mid-sized city—there were restaurants, a movie house, and enough pubs to get by on. But I was so set on staying on the ocean that I took a local bus from Ipswich. Felixstowe sounded like a town to shake hands with.

The timelessness, the loneliness embodied in the tossing surf created a physical ache in my chest, a desire which I wouldn't attempt to define. I sat on a post at the pier's edge until hunger pangs drove me back to the town.

I hadn't looked at my watch for a while and I was surprised that it was 2100 hours—9 p.m. I'd noted at least two pubs in town and I tried the closest. But when I pushed open the heavy doors the assembled company, perhaps 20 in all, looked at me as one. No one spoke and only a few lifted a hand in greeting.

I was in uniform so you'd think they would recognize it as belonging to their staunch American ally.

I approached the bar and asked about food. A few minutes later, I sat at a corner table, wolfing fish and chips, with a large bottle of stout to wash it down. A darts game was going on at one end of the bar, and the players talked in low whispers. There were no women about. Where was the cute, dark-haired waitress or even the little old lady?

I asked at the pub about places to stay and had gotten two addresses. The first was locked tight. At the second address, my rapping finally brought forth an innkeeper who told me the fishing fleet was in; they had no rooms to let. I asked whether he had any suggestions, but he just shook his head. Since it had become cold and windy, my mood quickly turned somber.

I had to find a place to sleep. Even the bus station had closed, or I would have bunked on a bench there.

Ah, the police. They would know. Perhaps the local constable would send me home to meet his buxom wife who would put me in a spare bedroom. A lone corporal of police sat behind a desk. He must have been snoozing because he managed to look guilty and startled at the same time. He looked to be in his late 20s. He was lanky, long-necked, and had freckles splattered all over his face as by a careless paint brush.

"Ah, a flyer." He had noted my wings as I threw open my overcoat.

"Straight from America to Felixstowe," I said, smiling. I asked him about a place to stay and he mentioned the two pubs I'd already tried.

"What's your name, Corporal?"

"Nevis, sir. Ben Nevis."

"Ben Nevis?" I repeated. "I thought that was a mountain in Scotland."

"It is, sir." He seemed proud that I had known about his namesake mountain. "It's the highest in Britain." He leaned towards me and beamed. "And, sir, I climbed it!"

"That's great, Ben." I didn't tell him that I had climbed Longs Peak in Colorado, about 10,000 feet higher than his peak in Scotland. I felt an immediate link with the young man.

"Climb any other mountains?" I asked

"No, sir. Just Ben Nevis."

Again I refrained from telling him about the half-dozen peaks I'd climbed in Colorado, all over 14,000 feet.

"Well, Ben, how would you and Mrs. Nevis like a paying guest tonight? I've eaten so it's just the bed I need. A couch in the parlor would be fine."

He looked at me doubtfully. "We have just the one bedroom, sir."

"How about the couch in the parlor?"

"My wife's aunt is visiting just now. That's where she's bedding—in the parlor. And she snores something awful—it goes right through the walls to our bedroom, it does."

Something about the way he said it, compounded by my growing predicament, made me laugh outright. He smiled slowly and then joined me heartily. I think he enjoyed laughing with a stranger about his wife's aunt's foibles.

We both stared at each other doubtfully. Finally, he said, "You could stay here."

"Here? In jail, you mean?"

"Well now, our cots are pretty soft. You could have your own room, like, with no one to disturb you. And—well, there'd be no cost, like."

I reached across his desk to shake his hand. "It's a deal, Ben. I haven't slept in a jail since one wild night in Denver a few years ago."

He looked at me shyly. "I'm off duty at ten. After that, I'd have to lock you in."

"That's what jails are for. Ben, do you play gin rummy? Or pinochle?"

As the host, he got to pick the game and he chose whist. He taught me the two-handed version which he said he'd invented himself. He beat me four games in a row. It was well after eleven when he showed me my cell, brought me some blankets and bid me good night. "I'll be here at seven," he said, "and brew us some tea. Maybe a crumpet, as well. I'll see what the missus has on hand." With a cheery wave he left me in darkness and closed and locked the door.

The only sound I heard all night was a bass fog horn. I slept deeply.

I didn't even hear him come in the next morning. He tapped me on the shoulder. "I hope you slept well, Mr. Rick. After your wash, come out to join me for tea and the finest fruit pastry in Suffolk."

After a delightful breakfast, I thought I'd better be on my way, and told him so.

"Come back any time you want, Rick. We can usually scare up a bed. And, oh, will you sign something for me?"

I lifted my eyebrows.

"It's a form showed you as a prisoner for overnight. I'll put you down as a drunk. That's to impress the Constable. He likes to keep drunks overnight."

I signed his paper, gave him the biggest smile he would see that day, slapped him on the shoulder, and headed for the bus station. The morning was crisp and clear; the fog had vanished along with the night—good weather for a coastal town in late August. I felt that the tired lines on my face that Colonel Warren

12

had mentioned had begun to disappear, victims of a good night's rest, a tasty breakfast, and a fine day beckoning.

Bury St. Edmunds immediately captivated me. It was the principal town of West Suffolk and dated from Saxon times. Edmund, King of East Anglia, was put to death by the Danes in the ninth century when he refused to renounce Christianity. Later, an abbey was established in his honor.

I had lunch at a small pub on a corner, and found a bed to let upstairs. I booked for two nights and said I might stay for a third. It would depend upon whom I met that was interesting.

I walked down High Street into the country. There was a soft beauty to the fields and hedgerows, with gentle hills in the background. In mid-afternoon, I heard the toll of bells from the town. Perhaps a mass for some aged soul who had died? It was Friday afternoon in the heart of Suffolk and I was glad I'd come.

I'd been told by my parents that I was a good idler and I proved it that afternoon. I was glad I was alone, but I wouldn't mind having company—say for dinner this evening?

However, I dined alone at the nicest café I could find, tucked away on a side street. I put away mutton, potatoes and brussel sprouts and decided it was a pretty good war, after all. Seated near me, facing me directly, was Agatha Christie. Or at least she looked like Agatha should look: tall, perhaps in her late fifties, round polished nose, beautifully coiffured hairdo. She was the woman of my thoughts on the train. I thought she was a cross between my two grandmothers, and I needed some loving grandmotherly attention at the moment.

An older man was with her, and I thought, ah, her husband. Then I noticed his priest's collar and I changed my assumption. She looked directly at me and smiled. I returned the smile. She spoke to her companion for a moment, then he arose and strode my way.

"Mrs. Laughlin was wondering if you'd care to join us for coffee in the lounge after dinner." He was stout, and friendly enough, but it came to me he was carrying out her wishes, not necessarily his own.

I smiled my affirmative at Agatha while he returned to their table. She returned my smile, and it was almost as if she were flirting with me. What a nonsensical idea.

"I need young people around me," she said, after we were seated in comfortable lounge chairs. She looked at her companion. "No offense, Edgar. And if I may speak frankly, young man, you looked lonely."

"I'm glad I did look lonely, Mrs. Laughlin. Do you know, I *was* looking forward to meeting someone tonight."

"Ah, someone special?"

"Yes. Someone like you." I smiled as I spoke, hoping she would take no offense. She leaned back in her chair and laughed aloud.

"I like that, but I don't believe it for a moment."

I told her about comparing her to Agatha Christie, to which she laughed again, and to my grandmothers, which she didn't think was quite so funny.

She told me about her life in Bury St. Edmunds, about her late husband, the loss of a grandson in the RAF, and of her love for everything to do with Suffolk.

"I can't match that," I said. "I haven't lived long enough."

She seemed to find even that funny. I decided I liked this lady. I flitted through some facts about my life. The rector was mainly silent, except to invite me to attend Sunday services at the cathedral church of St. James. I said I would like to if I were still in their town on Sunday.

"You're not staying the full weekend, then?" she asked.

I said I would stay two nights, but perhaps not three.

"Let me suggest places to see tomorrow," she said, and mentioned St. Mary's church, the Norman Tower off the square with its bells of St. James, Abbott's Bridge and the River Lark below it. She also mentioned various shops and historical houses.

"Oh," she added, "you must see the Cloister Gardens. It's dominated by a great copper beech tree. I think you'd like it."

At the conclusion of our coffee, she said, "You now know two residents of Bury St. Edmunds, although we're a bit ancient for you, perhaps. Would you like to meet someone else?"

Simple courtesy required an affirmative reply, but how anxious was I to meet another person their age? I hedged, "Your sight-seeing plans for tomorrow might keep me pretty busy---."

"The person I had in mind is my granddaughter, coming to visit tomorrow at tea time. She just turned 21 years old."

I picked up my broken sentence without a waver, finishing "but I can arrange my tour to be done by mid-afternoon." I tossed another smile her way.

Before we separated, she had changed tea for supper, an early one at five o'clock. She gave me her address and shook hands with me rather formally.

"What's your granddaughter's name?"

"Anne. I think you might like her. She and you have something in common. You can wonder about that overnight."

I'd had experience from my parents and their friends with fixing me up with dates of their choosing. It had never worked out yet and a few times I'd had a miserable experience. But I was so taken by "Agatha" that I thought some of her charm might have rubbed off on her granddaughter.

My first sight of Anne Darby was in the window seat in Lillian Laughlin's old-fashioned sitting room. Guiding me with a firm hand on my elbow, Lillian took me to where Anne was seated. She introduced us and then departed rather abruptly, saying supper duties called.

My first impression of Anne was beauty. And I knew instantly what we had in common. Her red hair, unlike mine, was long; it hung loosely below her shoulders. Her face was clear, and when she spoke her voice was like a bell from the loftiest spire in Bury St. Edmunds. We shook hands and indulged in small talk while her grandmother prepared our supper.

A few minutes later, the other guest arrived, none other than the ubiquitous rector, whose name was Edgar O'Malley. He headed for the kitchen to greet Lillian. That gave us an undisturbed ten minutes to get to know each other.

It came to me that Anne had the sort of class that England used to be noted for, but which had dissipated during wartime. She had a steady boyfriend, she said, who at the moment was "Somewhere on the North Sea, probably standing on the foredeck submarine-spotting." He was a line officer in the Royal Navy. I listened carefully for a note of longing in her voice as she spoke of him, but I couldn't distinguish any. I wondered if I was too late with Anne.

It was a lovely meal, with entertaining talk, fine foods, and toasts to King George and Winston Churchill.

"And to your President Roosevelt," Anne said, her eyes on me. I acknowledged the compliment by lifting my wine glass on high, nodding and smiling. Everyone clapped and I was deeply touched. Suddenly, the evening came into focus: Lillian saving coupons to buy the roast pork, Anne's loveliness, the genial talk, the homilies by the rector, and finally Anne's toast to Roosevelt. At that moment, I wanted more than anything else in the world to end this war, to stop the suffering and killing. I wanted a world without war—so that I could get to know Anne of the long flowing hair.

We talked around the dinner table until Lillian and Anne had cleared the dishes, then I helped the rector with the port, pouring in liberal amounts of the rich dark liquor. No one said nay.

I was feeling mellow and happy, and excited about all of my futures: immediate: would Anne let me kiss her tonight? Intermediate: two or three more days on my charming trip away from war; and longer-run: flying on my personal flying carpet.

It didn't occur to me until later that these thoughts were contradictory: wishing the war over while looking forward to flying a war machine in it.

On the darkened porch I struck gold in my immediate objective. Anne was well ahead of me: allowing the kiss while not overtly encouraging me. I just kept moving in and our lips met in ecstasy. I had known many first kisses, but this one topped them all. Or was it just the most recent one?

I spent the next day with Anne, walking the countryside. Our heads were as one as we dined in her favorite café Saturday night. On Sunday, we attended Father O'Malley's service and the good father caused necks to crane in our direction when he acknowledged our presence in his church. I forgot that I had told my hosts I might not stay a third night. Of course I would.

We hoped for another nice day and we got one, at least until mid-afternoon. We walked into the countryside again until we became pleasantly tired by strolling down country roads, skirting meadows, and through occasional hedgerows. We lay on the riverbank, relaxing and talking. Our lips joined again and again until I sensed I had taken it far enough for this day.

It was inspiring, as we returned to town in mid-afternoon, to hear the bells of St. Marys sprinkling the air with golden notes.

"What's in your future, Anne, after the war?" We were seated on a bench in Cloisture Gardens.

"Oh, university first, then, well, who can tell?"

"And marriage—sooner or later?"

"Oh, sooner, I would think. There's this boy I mentioned, Ian, the naval officer. He may be the one; I just don't know yet." She faced me directly. "I want to be sure, Rick. Marriage is sacred to me."

"I'd like to be in your future, Anne."

"We really don't know each other very well, do we?"

"Not yet."

We talked of love and loss, of a future without a war anywhere around, of lifetime aspirations. Was happiness enough or must there be commitment, as well?

She asked me about my own future.

"I'm just beginning to figure it out. To get some ideas, that is. Now that we can see the end of the war in sight, it's high time I staked out a future." I decided to take it easy with this kind of talk with a pretty girl at my side. But I wanted her to know how I felt about some of the world's ills.

"The world is pretty messed up. It'll take a lot of work by a lot of dedicated people the world over to turn it around. Why not me?"

She looked her puzzlement, so I hastened on. "Just think of the problems that have emerged just in the past few years, Anne. We need to offer universal education. And most important one of all: how to bring permanent peace to the world."

The seriousness of my last few words stopped me abruptly. Any more talk of my future goals would drive her back into Ian's arms. Still, I had challenged her interest, and we discussed the problems of the world for an hour in that romantic setting. My friends at the air base would laugh at me, I thought. What a strange way to woo a girl.

On that last Sunday night in Bury St. Edmunds, my new girl on my arm, I knew I wanted her. But did she want me? I didn't relish any kind of rejection at this point. But my soul demanded a happy ending. If I didn't press her a bit, I might be missing out on one of the supreme sexual experiences of my life. She had a flat in London, near her job. I had her address and telephone number, so I knew I would see her again. In the meantime, should I press my luck?

It was near midnight. We were in a deserted park on a lonely bench, holding hands. Would a class act like Anne go with me to my room—just two blocks down, one block over—and let the lovemaking begin? I didn't know, but I would speak up, take my chances. But then the matter was taken out of my hands.

The bells of St. Mary's Church, just over my left shoulder, tolled twelve times. The noise was deafening. I smiled weakly at Anne and waited them out.

As the last peal died away in the dark sky, Anne rose to her feet. She had used the interval for some hard thinking.

"I must go now, Rick. We could meet in London."

"Oh, yes, London, by all means. But right now, the sky is right, the stars are in my corner, and I want to escort you a few blocks to my little room over a pub."

She smiled as she shook her head, and I was done. The tolling of those damned bells had made the difference. I walked her to her grandmother's house and returned to my pub alone.

I kissed both my girls on the cheek at the station. It was a cold Monday morning and the mood was somber. Lillian surprised me. She drew me to her and I thought she was about to kiss me on the lips. But then she changed course by kissing me on the cheek, a smile hovering somewhere in the background. Then it was Anne's turn. She started to kiss me on the cheek, but at the last moment she switched to my lips, and we hung on to each other for a long moment while I marveled at what might have been—or might still be.

I was happy with my five days away from the war. There had been new people in my life that I prized, Anne and Lillian, and even Ben the jailer. I suspected the interlude had erased my tired lines, as the Colonel had suggested they might.

By the time the train reached Ridgewell hours later, my focus had changed a bit. I was already looking forward again to flying a fighter plane and to the rough-edged male world which surrounded it. Anne was relegated to the back part of my mind. I would see her again in London, and it would be in the laps of the gods as to how I fared. Meantime, it was back to the war.

3

BACK TO THE WAR

Just a month earlier I had flown my final combat mission in a B-17 bomber. And today I would fly my first in a fighter plane. What a difference a month makes.

I'd spent several days chasing clouds in an Advanced Trainer, the AT-6, and checking out in a Mustang. The latter was not routine; the single-seater fighter doesn't provide room for instruction aloft. So I flew solo from the first and had a couple of narrow escapes that I refused to forget. I hoped the lessons learned would help keep me alive.

Then one bright, blustery morning, my name was on the board. A new war was opening up for me. I was thrilled, excited, apprehensive, and to put it plainly, scared as hell.

My friend Pat Morse had told me to take it easy the first few times. My squadron commander, Capt. Marney, said the same. He told me to fly on his wing and observe, observe, observe. Don't try to shoot anyone down, he said. Don't leave the formation. And stay on my wing as if your life depended upon it. It does.

I cherished flying alone. How many times had I dreamed of this? I would no longer depend upon others to keep me safe as I had in a bomber. I was my own best friend and worst enemy. I found I had to make decisions in a split second. Earlier challenges on the football field or ski run I dismissed. Those were games; this was life and death.

The first mission was a cakewalk. I flew left wing off Capt. Marney's lead ship. There were 18 from our group aloft and it gave me a warm feeling to be part of this flying parade. I remembered talks with Pat Morse. War was hell, but if you were going to fight your way through a period of hell, what better place to be than in the cockpit of a plane cruising at 300 miles per hour?

Our mission was in support of two groups of B-24 bombers returning from blasting Berlin. The bombers flew in a high and tight formation and didn't look as if they needed our help. I waved a couple of times when we were close enough to see them, but I couldn't arouse a return wave. Perhaps they were too busy watching their 1,179 instruments.

The bombers were safe, we still had some gasoline in our tanks, and we were ordered to look for targets of opportunity. This was pulse-raising stuff, flying close to the ground, ready to unload our 20-millimeter cannon shells on a train, troops, or anything German. Still flying on Capt. Marney's wing, but much more loosely now, I dove steeply through thin clouds. The ground rose up more steeply than I had expected and I pulled back on the stick a bit too sharply.

"Watch it, Dynamite 6," Capt. Marney said to me.

A troop train loomed up suddenly. Here was my chance.

Under strict orders not to start my own war, I waited for Marney to begin a strafing run. He did no such thing. His words came into my headset loud and clear: "In case you're not aware of it, Linden, that's not the enemy. That's one of our forward troop trains."

God, it would have been so easy to make a mistake, shooting first and regretting later. More likely a court martial.

Our return to the storied land of Britain was routine yet thrilling. As we neared Ridgewell we peeled off into the landing pattern. My touchdown was perfect. I felt like I was on top of the world. Taxiing in, I wondered how it would feel to fire my guns in anger. I had told Pat I was a pacifist in a war. So what would happen? Would I freeze when asked to explode machine gun fire all over the sky, killing everything in sight? I knew I could do it, but would I ever feel right about myself again?

It was early September 1944. Sipping coffee the next morning at the Operations Office, I picked up a copy of *Stars and Stripes,* and read the lead article:

Hitler is on the defensive, fighting for his own homeland. The Soviet army stands poised on the banks of the Oder well within German soil. In the meantime, battle-weary Germans face nearly four times that number under Gen. Eisenhower. Ike has ten times as many tanks as his opponents have, and a significant advantage in planes and artillery. The crushing of Hitler's Reich, which the Fuhrer once boasted would last for 1,000 years, appears to be only a matter of months away.

Still, the Germans were slow to retreat, even after the Allies crossed the River Roer and a bit later, a big prize, the River Rhine. It was evident to me that the Nazis would fight all the way to Berlin—to the end. Until Hitler himself was killed.

Before my fifth mission, Capt. Marney told me this would be my last flight on his wing. After today, he said, he was moving up to lead the Group, quite an honor for him. "You're doing fine, Linden. Just keep your head swinging and your wing tucked in."

We had just reached 25,000 feet on our way to intercept a returning group of B-17s when the attack came. Out of nowhere a gaggle of FW 109s came out of the sun, directly ahead of us. Capt Marney didn't have time to say more than "Bogies at 12 o'clock high" when all hell broke loose. Cannon fire was all over the sky. I saw Marney's Mustang take a massive head-on hit in his cockpit; simultaneously, I knew all the way down to my toes that I had been hit, as well. The drumming on the side of my plane sounded like the worst Colorado hail storm of the season.

My plane was still flying, apparently not yet in serious trouble. And then an FW was in my sights and I poured a burst of .50 caliber machine gun fire at him—the first shots I'd ever fired in anger. The anger was not simulated; I had just watched in horror as my flight leader, Jim Marney, went trailing into a steep dive, cockpit in flames. I saw no parachute; the first bullets had probably killed him. The German fighter I had engaged appeared to be hit, as well, and my adrenaline rose to the red line level. But he disappeared somewhere, out of sight.

Strangely, I was fighting for breath. I realized suddenly that I wasn't receiving oxygen. I must have been hit. I split-essed out of the fight, down through thin layers of clouds. I saw no other planes, ours or theirs. Sometimes that's the way it happened. You're all alone.

I rode my plane, *Long's Lover,* down to the deck, buzzing a small German village, then, when I realized some farmers were taking pot shots at me, I climbed to get out of range. I knew the heading home—270 degrees—and I put the needle there and headed west. Here I was, on my fifth mission, all alone, oxygen out, and probably other damage considering my plane had taken a lot of hits. I was as exhilarated as never before in my life.

Flying at below 1,000 feet over gentle farmland, I figured I had crossed into France. I consulted my map, adjusted my compass heading and flew on, serene and content.

Then my engine began sputtering.

My content vanished like smoke in a strong wind. I looked for a possible emergency landing field, and, amazingly, a field of some sort appeared on the horizon, 20 degrees to starboard. I banked in that direction, eased off on the throttle, and glided along, perhaps losing 300 feet per minute. There was no time to find the windsock, if they used them in France. I continued to let down onto a rough patch of grass opening up in front of me.

It was not my best landing. Perhaps my worst. I had my excuses ready made: damaged plane, grass field, cross-wind landing, and so on. Once the bouncing had ceased I taxied towards a group of buildings. I was about to cut my engine when it cut out by itself. Lady luck had been riding with me this day.

A jeep drove up and an officer and two enlisted men, all armed, got out of the jeep and approached warily. The enemy had been known to fly captured P-51s to Allied bases. I saluted the RAF officer, a first lieutenant, and said, "Lt. Richard Linden. Forced down for repairs. Can you have one of your mechs look over my plane?" By this time there was oil oozing out all over the cowling.

The officer said, "Welcome to Douai Field, Yank. Let me just chat up the maintenance lads." I stood at ease until he'd had a short discussion with a Master Sergeant. He turned back to me.

"We can't do your kite for a day or two. Care to stay over with us? We have tolerable food and we could swap war stories."

An RAF tent was my home away from home. I shared the space with my new friend, Roderick Jeffcoat, and two other pilots. Douai Field, not far from the Belgium border, had only been established for less than a month. As Patton and the other generals advanced, RAF stations moved with them, to reduce the flying time for support of Allied troops. It was the first time I had placed foot on the European continent.

I took over the cot of an RAF pilot who had not returned from a mission. No doubt I was eating his rations at the mess: real English beef, potatoes, and canned beans. And a tart of some sort to top it off. That evening, the four of us huddled around a coal-burning stove in the center of the tent, talked about the war, flying, and what we were going to do on our next leave. I learned that Jeffcoat would stay in flying if he could, perhaps hooking on with a private cargo airline flying to Asia or Africa. One of the other pilots was for going into his father's haberdashery business, and the third RAF flier hoped to study law.

"And how about you, Richard?" Rod Jeffcoat asked.

"Call me Rick."

"Rick then. Anything special in mind?"

I didn't reply immediately. What *was* I going to do? Should I mention my goals for after the war? Nope; too idealistic for the time and place. "Back to college for openers. Travel. And a third possibility: if you'll have me, I'll stay in England, look around a bit more." I told them of my pleasant visit to Suffolk.

Rod Jeffcoat stood up. "That calls for a drink, mate. Right, gentlemen?" He produced a bottle from somewhere and we passed it around. It was half-empty already but it was enough. We talked on into the night of our girl friends, our ambitions, what we'd do when we caught up with Hitler, and the relative merits of the Spitfire and Mustang. We agreed to disagree on that issue.

The only serious moment during the evening was when I described the horrible feeling I'd had seeing my flight leader shot to death before my eyes.

"We've all had that experience, Rick," Jeffcoat said, quietly.

"Well, this was my first. Will you join me in a prayer?" I was ad-libbing it, but I wanted to do it. I lifted my eyes to the top of the tent and said, "To Captain Jim Marney, a fine pilot and gentleman. May you rest in peace, Capt. Jim."

A chorus of "Amens" followed from my fellow pilots.

I talked with the chief mechanic directly after breakfast. He'd just come from looking over my plane and he said I was in luck. They had a "bit of free time" that day and would mend the oil leak and a few other mostly minor problems. "Enough to get you home," he said. "You can have her back by tomorrow, say noon? That soon enough for you, mate? By the way, I guess you know you have a few holes in your kite? We can't patch those. It'll be something to impress your own mates with."

23

My three tent mates were flying and I spent the day more or less alone, reading in the sun in front of the tent. I also did a little exploring around the wooded countryside, but I didn't wander too far. I could see the poster on my bulletin board back at my base:

"LINDEN MISSING IN ACTION. LAST SEEN HIKING IN THE FRENCH COUNTRYSIDE"

My flying horse was ready by early afternoon of the following day. My takeoff was smooth—for which I was grateful since Jeffcoat and his RAF buddies were watching. I flew low over the field and waggled my wings. Then I headed home.

Unfortunately, the timing of my arrival at my base coincided with the return of the day's mission. Somehow, this incensed the Operations Officer. The situation escalated when I came up face to face with him. I regretted I hadn't found the opportunity to make a friend of him in the two weeks I'd been there.

"Linden, you'd better have a good story to tell. You've been reported 'Missing in Action' for two days now. We even had a fellow flyer said he saw you go in. Now, if you don't mind, Lieutenant Linden, what happened?" His tone was sarcastic.

I told him the story: how Capt. Marney had been shot down before my eyes, my mechanical problems with my plane, and how I'd negotiated the repairs from an RAF mechanic in France. I thought he'd pin a medal on me for resourcefulness.

He heard me out. "It checks pretty well, Linden. I want a full report on the loss of Capt. Marney. As his wingman, your report should fill in some pieces. Also, tell us in writing what happened to your aircraft and the corrective steps you took. On my desk by 2000 hours."

"Uh, what day, sir?"

"Tonight, Linden. We're at war, you know." He turned on his heel, even forgetting to return my salute.

It rained all the next morning and the group was stood down. I met Pat Morse at noon mess to tell him of my adventures in France. He said it was all over the base already. He added that they'd lost a man the day before: Ted Lee.

24

"I didn't know him," I said. "But I sure as hell knew Jim Marney. Sounds like we lose a man a day. What kind of killing game are we in, Pat? Only it's not a game."

He had no answer.

"The war is moving along," he said. "We might have Hitler in our grasp by Christmas. Patton has gone crazy with his speed, Simpson's Ninth Army has almost reached Dusseldorf, and Bradley's two armies are in the middle ground. Even Monty is showing signs of catching up."

"I'm torn, Patrick. I want to fly. Geez, I had fun in that little caper of mine. All in one day I shoot at a German fighter, get shot at by small arms fire from rooftops, skim across Germany and France at 100 feet, and then force-land in a small field in France. I want more of that, and yet....I want to live, too. And the only way to assure that is for the war to end, and soon. There are many problems in this world, and I'm going to tackle each of them head on."

The rain petered out late in the day and my spirits picked up. I had noticed a medium-sized stream not far from the east-west runway. Would they have poles, lines, and bait in Supply? They might. The fish might not be biting that well after a rain, but it was worth a try. With luck, I would have my line in the water within an hour and perhaps a couple of fat fish for the mess sergeant to cook for me.

4

A NEW PERSON IN MY LIFE

Supply came through for me, furnishing all the essentials for fishing: rod and line, leaders, and even worms. One of the noncoms who manned Supply, Leon, was a fisherman himself. Of course I had to offer the first fish I caught to him as payment for the supplies. We shook hands on it.

A picture-perfect scene opened up before me: a mossy bank, curving stream, willows as a screen against too much sunlight. The only problem was immediately apparent: there was someone there ahead of me. I would have left him alone except that he was squatting on one of the best fishing holes I had seen since leaving Colorado. He didn't hear me as I approached along the mossy bank.

"How are you doing?" I called out rather loudly. "Catch any?" I was standing barely three feet behind him.

He whirled around to face me, his line shooting up into the overhanging willows where it caught in thick branches.

"Darn," he said, "don't you know enough not to yell like that? Now I'll never catch that bugger down there."

"Sorry, kid. I should know better. I've been fishing all my life. It just slipped out."

He didn't seem to be at all mollified. "Where'd you come from? I thought I had this stream to myself."

"I guess you do have it, on a first-come basis. I'll move on along."

"Stay a minute, if you must," he said, struggling to remain cordial.

I squatted down beside him while he finished untangling his line. "You know, kid, your invitation was about as forced as I've heard recently. But—hey, wait a minute. I'll accept it. We should be friends. I automatically like all fishermen. And I was

26

about to ask you about your stream. For openers, does it have a name?"

He was suffering my presence with barely-concealed impatience. "The River Thom."

"In America, we'd call it a large stream."

He reddened. "If you don't like our rivers in England, go back to America and fish."

I bowed to him. "I deserved that. Again, I know better. My tongue has taken over my good sense today."

I looked him over. He was about 15, and from his talk, a home-grown Limey. He was a well-built boy, with thick and shaggy brown hair. He appeared to be about my height, 5 foot 10 inches. We looked uncertainly at each other, both probably figuring this talk wasn't going anywhere.

"Well, good luck," he said, in a tone which implied the opposite. He leaned over his fishing creel, ready to deal me out of his life.

I've never been one to let well enough alone. Something about the boy caught my interest. Perhaps it was his spark in not letting me ride roughshod over him. Perhaps he reminded me of myself at his age. "Listen," I said, "before we part company forever, I have two candy bars here. Why two? I don't know. Perhaps I divined I would meet someone today I wanted to share with. What say?"

He looked up from his creel and stared at me. I figured he was wrestling with a problem: humor me and have a candy bar, or leave me talking to myself while he found another hole.

A few minutes later we were perched on a log a ways back from the stream, munching our candy bars. As fishermen do all over the world, we talked of bait and leaders and the proper swiftness of running water most likely to lead to success.

"Are you from Ridgewell?" I asked.

"Hmm. At the edge of the village on the far side."

"I'd guess you'd be in about tenth form?"

He nodded without speaking.

"You like sports?"

"Well, fishing. And perhaps football, a little. But I'm no good at it."

"I guess we have a decision to make when we separate. The most painless would for me to go downstream and let you have this hole to yourself."

"Now that you've ruined it for me? No thanks, mister."

I offered him my widest smile. "I don't intimidate you a bit, do I? I like that. In a kid your age, that's kind of remarkable."

He stood up from the log. "That's three times you've called me a kid. I don't like it."

"There you go again—refusing to be intimidated. Bravo. Listen, young man, my name is Rick Linden and I'm stationed at the fighter strip over there." I waved over my shoulder.

"What are you, a mechanic? Or a typist? I heard men do clerk's work there."

"Hey, you know how to hurt a man, don't you? I almost said 'kid' again, but I don't have a name for you, do I? What do I call you?"

"I'm Rob," he said, somewhat reluctantly. "If you're not a clerk or mechanic, what are you?"

"I'm a pilot. I fly one of those fighter planes parked there."

He was looking at me strangely and I could guess what he was thinking: could I be leading him on? Finally, he spoke.

"Your not joking me, are you? You really are a pilot? But you're too ---. He stopped, embarrassed.

"Too short? Too cocky? Too dashing? Not dashing enough? What, Rob?"

He recognized that I *was* joking now. He seemed uncomfortable with trading quips with me.

"I'm sorry, Rob. Well, I am a pilot. In the flesh."

"I've never met a real pilot—and I never knew what they looked like. Except in the pictures."

"We're just ordinary people. I'm an American from a small city in central Colorado. Colorado Springs. I just turned 24 a few weeks ago."

"In September then? I was 15 on the 23rd."

It was my turn to be surprised. "Mine was September 21st. We should have gotten together on the 22nd and thrown a party. Well, maybe next year." I spoke in jest, but he seemed to like the idea. He looked at me with wide-open blue eyes that might have been proud. If so, it might be because an older man was taking him seriously.

I said, "I won't hold your age against you if you won't hold mine against me." Even I didn't know what I meant by that.

It was just me, kidding around. He was probably thinking: *too cocky.*

"Let's check further, Rob," I said. "Do you like reading?"

"Yup. I read all the time."

"So do I, Rob. Do you like to write?"

"It's all right."

"Well, I might as well tell you. I'm a published writer."

"Oh, yes? Maybe I could read a story of yours sometime."

But his voice was flat and his words came out unconvincingly.

I let it go.

I thought of something; it would tell me if he was a romantic. "You know, Rob, we have at least three things in common. We both like fishing, we both have names which begin with 'R' and we both—and here I am sticking my neck out—we both tend to be loners. Or perhaps I have you wrong on that last trait, Rob."

He was silent for a few moments, then he looked at me calmly and said, "I guess I am a loner, Rick."

That touched me, and I decided not to be so glib in my comments and conclusions.

It looked as if my friend and I were locked together by unseen forces, for a half hour later we sat fishing side by side, fishing and talking. When one of us would wander off to try another hole, the other would soon follow. We each caught two medium-sized trout, 12-inches or so. I told him he must be a good fisherman to keep up with the Rocky Mountain champ.

"Were you actually?"

"Yes, I did win it one year. Of course it was limited to kids in my high school. A small triumph, perhaps, but I've never forgotten it."

I could see by his manner that he was beginning to like me. But something was bothering him, and he finally put it into words.

"Why do you bother with me? We've been talking for over an hour now. Wouldn't you rather be with friends your own age? Maybe other pilots?"

I took my time answering. This was a sensitive kid, and I didn't want to turn him off. Still, honesty was called for. "I bother with you, young Rob, because right now you're my best friend.

My best new friend, anyway. I have lots of friends, Rob. Most of my fellow pilots don't do much of anything. They hole up around the coal stove, or drink at the Officer's Club, or write letters home. Or, when they get a day off, they chase girls."

"And you don't do those things?"

He was handing me back some of the wise cracks I'd been feeding him. "Sure I do them. Just not quite so much as most of my friends. And I save time for reading, playing ping pong at the Club, or meeting new friends." I let him see my broad smile as I voiced the last thought.

"Shall we meet again for fishing?" I asked. "It'd give you another opportunity to beat the champ."

He nodded his acceptance at that, but said nothing.

"Now, I've got to go or I'll miss early chow. That's when the choicest cuts of steak are served. But I forgot. I have two fat fish to fry tonight. I owe one to a supply sergeant, but the other will be heaven to eat. Are you going to take your two home to your folks?"

"I will, but my father doesn't like fish. Mum will probably give them to our neighbors."

I never know when to quit sometimes. "Your mom could cook one for each of you, and cook something else for your father."

"She'd never do that. Father wouldn't stand for it."

I was ready to say adieu when I had another thought. I plunged in once again. "Do you know why I like you, Rob?"

"No," he said, in a small voice.

"Because you remind me of the younger brother I never had. I have a younger sister, but that's not the same thing. So you're elected, if you want to be."

He hesitated a long time. "I guess I'd want to be. But—uh, I want to tell you something about me—something you don't know anything about. Something bad. My brother Geoff, a seaman in the Royal Navy, is gone."

"Gone?"

"They say he was washed overboard during a battle. He's probably dead, Rick. And, do you know what? You show up in my life a fortnight after we hear about Geoff. That's what's so weird. I lose him, but then I meet you, and you two are about the same age."

I was stunned to hear that he'd lost a brother. No wonder he had acted so unfriendly for awhile. I could only guess how devastating the loss was to a youngster his age, and how difficult it must have been to speak of it to a stranger.

Tears were in his eyes and I couldn't blame him. He had suffered a greater loss than I had in my lifetime. I blamed myself for being so damned flippant in talking to such an impressionable young man. Never mind that I hadn't known about his brother.

I put my hands on his shoulders. Would he welcome this semi-embrace from someone he'd just met? I could only guess. But if it was me, I thought, I would be glad that someone close by cared.

No longer was I the casual, flippant hotshot of the last hour. I didn't say anything—what can words say at a time like this?—and I thought it might be wise to take my leave.

Just as I turned away, I had a thought which might cheer him up—or perhaps not. "Shall we meet tomorrow at four o'clock? At the same hole?"

For a moment I didn't think he'd even heard me. Or perhaps he was still thinking of his brother. He finally looked at me and stammered, "Oh, that will be all right."

I tossed him a little two-fingered salute, then jogged back to my base, my two trout safely in my creel.

Later that evening I thought of my encounter with Rob. Was it plain dumb of me to make such a big thing about befriending a young lad? Did I really value his company? Was I playing with emotions beyond my control? After a moment, I dismissed the thoughts as unworthy. What harm could come to Rob by knowing me? I would continue to meet him until one or both of us decided it was time to quit. Meanwhile, a fresh-faced young man like Rob was stimulating to be around.

PART II

ROB ST. CLAIR

5

BARELY A LIFE

I can't remember when I first began to hate my father. It was early on, I suspect, when I was about five years old. I hated him for the things he said and did, and even for the long hard stares thrown my way. Were all fathers like this? Perhaps that was the way with fathers. You could expect love from your mother, but your father was different.

He first hit me when I was nine. Hard, that is. I guess there had been taps earlier than that, I don't remember. I was late for supper, something simple, when he caught me and cuffed me on the side of the head. I was off balance and fell to the floor. My father, a big man without an ounce of fat on him, seemed satisfied with the one blow. He left the room without a word. There had been no one else in the sitting room at the time.

Had my brother Geoffrey been present my father would not have dared strike me. Geoff was muscular and large for a 14-year-old. He had taught himself to box and had become a match for my father. Their final fight had been a whopper. I watched from the kitchen while my mother cringed and covered her face. My father had hit Geoff with his open hand, a hard and stinging shot which rocked my brother. He recovered quickly and landed a hard punch to my father's eye. It began to bleed. My father, off balance, confused and chagrined, gave up on that battle, and he never challenged his older son again.

Of course he began picking on me, the slim, undersized younger brother. That first time, when I was nine, I picked myself off the floor and cried a little—not much. He didn't like it that I didn't fight back. I would fight soon enough, I thought grimly, once I put on some weight and learned how to box.

"You should have taken a nailed board to him," my friend Colin said when I told him about it. Colin was my age, though a bit smaller. He told me his own father mostly ignored him. I asked myself: which was worse: to be ignored or beaten up.

"D'you know, Rob," Colin said, "I'd die if my father hit me. Or I'd kill him And I think Pa knows I would, too."

Our family had moved to Ridgewell because my mother was deathly afraid of German bombs. She'd lost her folks and a few friends to the Blitz. For once, she stood up to my Pa and insisted they move to the country. In the end, Reginald St. Clair gave in, though he jeered at my mum for a week. "Can't stand a bit of bombing?" he would say. "If I didn't have a bloody angina problem I'd be fighting the damned Nazis instead of working for low wages in a factory. "

With a wartime manpower shortage, Reginald St. Clair had easily found a job at a sawmill outside of Ridgewell. The work was hard, but then so was my Pa. We moved to Ridgewell and found a small cottage in a new housing scheme at the edge of a large open field.

Ridgewell was set in the middle of green-hued Suffolk. It warmed my heart to see how my mum reacted to the move from the bombs and horror of wartime London to the peace of her small garden. She was a natural gardener. She passed her days there, or at club meetings, and, well, looking after me. She was of medium height but with out-of-proportion breasts bursting the fabric. Later in life, I figured those breasts kept Pa with her.

We'd lived here two years. When I'd arrived I was almost immediately an outcast. The other students had been together since they were toddlers and they didn't take much to the newly-arrived brat from London. Reserved and shy, I could find no way to gain acceptance. I was only fair at football, too small for rugby and not a good cricket player. Some boys are that way. So how do they get along? By personality, I suppose, or perhaps by intimidation. I was stuck with my personality, and I would never intimidate anyone.

My father, noticing my dejection from not making the cricket team, said, "Make your own way in the world, Rob. I won't do it for you." Then he cuffed me on the side of the head before returning to his newspaper.

My parents were not suited for each other. Even I could see that at ten or eleven. They didn't seem to have the spark and vitality, much less the love, of a happy marriage. Colin asked wryly, "What do you expect? Life is not a bowl of cherries." Then he told me some intimate things about his own parents which I would just as soon not have heard. Colin was my only school friend. I'll admit that I was usually fascinated by him, at his disdain for everyone—school masters, students, parents. He heckled them all in equal measure. His mouth was never still. He was everything I wasn't.

Colin was a friend only at school. My father wouldn't allow him in the house. He thought Colin was a "queer." I had not made up my mind about that opinion. It didn't affect me one way or another.

At home, I worshipped Geoffrey St. Clair, my older brother by five years in fact and ten in experience and wisdom. We thrilled together through the Battle of Britain, sitting enraptured by the tube listening to the news-readers from BBC describe the victories by the RAF. That was in 1940 when I was ten years old.

One night I stood on a hill near our house and watched a dogfight, a real no-holds-barred battle between a Spitfire and a German bomber. The Spit peppered the slow bomber and it went down not a mile from our house. I would have run to the crash site had my father not stood in my way. "Not for you, lad," he said, with his usual cuff on my shoulder. Although I was pissed right then, when I was a bit older I admitted my pa might have saved me some horror images.

My brother was in love with going to war. With our country under vicious attack by the Nazi regime, he could barely wait until he was 17 to enlist. He favored the Navy. He enlisted in August 1942 and was assigned to HMS King George. He sailed for the South Pacific at Christmas 1942.

My world was torn to shreds by his departure. Gone was my hero, my protector, my *beau ideal.* Though I had turned 12 and had put on some weight, I would be easy pickings for my father's occasional fits of anger.

"You're what, Rob. Nine stone—ten?" Geoff and I were seated in the back garden on a hot night the summer before he joined the navy. Search lights scanned the sky for the stray enemy bomber, though they had been mostly missing since the RAF drove them from the sky in 1940.

"You know, lad, the old man will probably slug you soon as I'm out of sight. You're strong enough to slug him back. He may even respect you for it. You can't tell with old Reggie. But you're too proud and too special a kid to be his punching bag."

I couldn't find my voice for a moment. "I'll miss you so much, Geoff." I was barely able to keep the tears from my eyes or the quaver from my voice.

"I'm like a father, eh?"

"No, not like a father," I said, missing the irony. "Just the opposite. How can I live without you, Geoff?"

He clapped me on the shoulder. "You'll manage, Bub. You've got some fine stuff in you. Sometimes you keep it well hidden and father and mum don't help you bring it out. But---" and even his eyes misted—"take it from someone who loves you, it's there, Rob. It'll come out and then you're going to set the world on fire. *You're a better man than I am, Gunga Din.*"

Geoff didn't care that my tears were free-flowing now. His eyes were not dry, either.

"You'll probably miss the war," he said the day before he left. "That's probably for the good. War is a tough business."

"You're going in," I said, disputing his logic.

"That's different," was his rejoinder, which didn't make sense, either. "Well, let's hope the war is over by the time you get to be 17. That'd be 1946. That's about when I'll be getting out.

"Listen, Rob, I'll put on my older brother cap for a mon' and chat you up a bit. Remember what the Bible says. Honor your parents. It's tough sometimes, I know, but keep a stiff upper lip. Even so, the sooner you leave home, the better. It should be boarding school for you."

My destiny with a boarding school had been a family topic for years. I was all for it and so was Geoff, but our father was dead against it. "I don't want any bloody headmaster doing the job that mum and I are rightfully doing." He made this outrageous statement without so much as a hint of tongue in cheek.

After Geoff left, looking splendid in his Navy blues, I felt as low as I had in all my life. I was alone and deserted, and bereft of the hero of my life.

There were other things besides bashing his younger son that were on my father's mind. When America entered the war in December 1941, their initial reaction was to send their forces to the Pacific to take on the Imperial Japanese Navy. I thrilled to the exploits of the light bomber raid on Tokyo in April 1942, when 17 B-25s took to the skies from the USS Hornet. I think that, even as young as I was, I realized it was more of a show of determination than to inflict severe damage on the Japanese. It raised morale in America and even in Britain when everyone—friend and foe alike—realized the American entry in the war was going to make a difference.

I think it was that epic mission that raised my consciousness about our new ally across the sea. From that moment, I vowed to live in America after the war was over. While part of that desire undoubtedly came from my unhappy home life, I still admired everything American.

The United States sent an advance contingent to England in 1942 to begin to scout for sites for bases, among other activities. And—a miracle—months later they selected the large open field adjacent to our house. For an airfield.

Our house, a small two-bedroom cottage, was at the edge of a large housing estate. "All we can afford," my father said when mum timidly asked for a larger home for a family of four. "Be happy with what you got, Mildred." No more was said.

In March 1943 the bulldozers came and the building crews went to work, leveling the land, putting up buildings, and, most exciting, building a 4,000 foot runway. Two of them, really, to allow pilots an option when the wind wasn't right.

My dad hated the idea from the start, and actually so did my mother. Mum's complaint was the loss of her view from the kitchen window, which used to be of open fields with rows of barley rustling in the wind. While she took it in stride, my pa was livid with rage by the noise and dust from the construction. He hated the idea of America—who did they think they were?—assigning men and airplanes to their base just right on top of our house. This was English soil, wasn't it? He decided to do something about it, beginning with a complaint to the town council.

We had assumed that bombers would be assigned to Ridgewell. The American thrust was rumored to be bombing Germany to its knees. Other rumors, fanned by articles in the London Times, were that our allies would build some 50 air bases in England. I learned later that U.S. forces did indeed construct some 68 bomber and fighter bases in a comparatively small area of England.

I was thrilled. I didn't care if it was right next to our door. The noise and dust bothered me not a bit, a fact I told my Pa over and over. Now I could talk to him this way with impunity. I had thickened, put on weight, and could hold my own with him. In fact, I could hurt him more than he could hurt me. I had learned to box; my dad knew little of the art.

One day I walked across the field to the runway under construction. I walked up to a man with a roll of maps under his arm. "Sir," I said, "I live in that house right yonder." I pointed to our house. He looked up but said nothing. I asked him what kind of airplane would be flying from this base.

This required an answer and he reluctantly gave me a moment. "Fighter aircraft will be assigned here. That's all I'm going to tell you, kid. I won't even mention that they'll be P-51s." He smiled at his little joke. I walked home in a daze.

Great God Almighty, P-51s. American Mustang fighter planes would be based just across from my house. I was so excited that I forgot to wipe my feet as I entered the sitting room and earned a lecture and a cuss from my father. A kindly look from my mum eased the pain a bit. She was reading her prized copy of *Women's Own.*

That was the beginning of exciting days for me. But I kept my enthusiasm to myself, except for Colin.

"Think of it, Colin," I was sitting on the floor beside his bed. He was standing on his head on the bed. He couldn't quite stay erect without resting one foot on the wall. "A fighter base right outside my bedroom window."

Colin spoke from upside down. "You're frightfully unlucky to be so bleeding close to a noisy flying field."

"You sound like my old man."

"Never that," he said, bouncing upright again. "My pap is pretty sad, but I wouldn't trade him for yours."

It didn't occur to me to be affronted.

"Rob, want to stay the night? There's plenty of room in my bed. I've never crowded you out before, have I?"

I thought of the alternatives: the usual nervous night around my parents in our small sitting room, or an overnight visit when Colin might paw me or even kiss me. I told him I would check with my parents, but my father forbade it.

*   *   *   *

My bedroom was my haven, my place for dreaming, for late reading, and, lately, for the thrill of listening to Mustangs warming up. I moved my bed against the outside window so I could get as close as I could to the warplanes. The room was pretty basic: the bed, a wardrobe, a small chest of drawers, and a tall bookcase crammed with books. The lino floor was an uninviting pale green.

Lying in bed that night, I wondered about my future. With Geoff gone, I felt more alone than ever. We had had a couple of letters from him, and I had received two others addressed to me alone, mailed in care of Colin Leigh-Poulson. Geoff and I had worked out the simple stratagem so that Geoff could share private messages without our parents' knowledge.

In less than two years I would be out of school, ready for either work or university. My father would demand I work, to add to the family's income. My mother would quietly wish for me to further my education. I was on the side of education. I wanted to work with my brain and imagination, not with my hands. I didn't look down on those who did the tough jobs of labor. I just wanted something different. And I would need an education in order to find a job in America.

I had not shared my wish to move to America with anyone, not even Colin. It was too private, too far-fetched.

My mother, in a rare moment of talk over buns and tea in the village, asked me if I wanted to go to university. When I told her I would, she told me not to be too disappointed if it didn't happen. "You mustn't worry if your life is like your father's," she said. "You must make the best of it. I know you are bright enough to aim higher, but the lesson to learn, dear Rob, is to endure. That's what our lot have done for centuries. You seldom can have what your heart desires in this life."

Mum's entire life, and certainly after her marriage, had steeled her to that kind of conclusion. Our talk left me greatly depressed but I appreciated that she had talked plain with me. She had done her best for her sons considering her own lack of education and from always being in the shadow of an overbearing husband.

I remained an unhappy lad living in a barely tolerable home atmosphere. Oh, how I wanted to get away somewhere, war or no war. I had thought of running away from home many times, but it always came to the question of where I could go. My parents didn't have many friends, and those few I might find would never take me against the wishes of my parents.

Relations? My mother had none; her parents had died in an air raid, and she had no siblings. My father had a sister in Manchester. At first it seemed improbable. She was a St. Clair like my father. Take a lad away from her brother? Not quite likely. Then I recalled why we hadn't seen much of Aunt Bea for years: she didn't like her own brother.

Then was she a possibility? I could finish public school in Manchester. I had never been there but I knew it was a large city in the north of England. I would live there until I was old enough to make my own decisions. Such as when to go to America and seek my fortune.

It might work. Geoff had escaped by joining the Navy. I would escape by living with Aunt Bea. I determined I would write to her the next day. I wouldn't tell my parents, not yet. I would write to her secretly, then wait for developments. I felt jubilant that I had thought of the plan; now that I was close to 14 I could out-think him and out-plan him, *and* out-box him.

Aunt Bea, will you take me in, will you take your young nephew for the duration? Oh, I beg of you, auntie, let me come to your house in Manchester and let me be your son for awhile. I'll be a good son. Please, Aunt Bea?

6

PA AND THE MAJOR

The village of Ridgewell was about a mile from our house. The shortest way was across some fields at the edge of the new air base, through a hedgerow, jumping a stream and so to the heart of the village. It was more like a town now, having mostly outgrown a village. There were several pubs, banks on High Street, the post office, a railway station, a few fish and chips shops, and a swimming bath, where I swam when I could. Most of the shops were on High Street, where mum and her friends could browse and shop.

Ridgewell was located in a pretty section of rural Sussex. Cambridge was the nearest city, about 25 miles northwest.

I've counted five churches in the village, each with a distinctive steeple. Pa didn't believe in religion but mum and I attended the High Methodist church occasionally, with Geoff accompanying us sometimes. I used to want to sing in the Youth Choir but something held me back. Perhaps it was because no one asked me to. I didn't know any of the rectors and I was too shy to approach anyone.

My pa didn't want any "false prophets," as he put it, influencing our family. Still, I attended often enough: I was curious about churches and what went on there. I wondered what it would be like to have something—or someone—to believe in. I decided I would find out someday.

By road, the village was a bit further, but I often walked that way. The route was across a bridge over a stream, where lovely fat trout lived. Geoff had taught me to fish when I was quite young. We'd fished there many times, but I also fished alone often enough. The stream was halfway to being a river, so deep and wide it was in spots. I used bait but more often a fly. Brown trout was my specialty and I would often bring mum a special dinner. She was grateful since food rationing was a solid fact of life.

My father wasn't interested one way or the other, though he ate his share of my catchings. I asked Colin to go fishing with me more than once, but he said it was too boring just standing next to a stream, picking his teeth.

As I grew older I realized the main reason I liked fishing was that I could be alone. My house was small and filled with tension. School was all teachers, the headmaster and a group of boys and girls who didn't care about me. At my favorite hole, I was in my element. No one knew where I was, no one bothered me, and there was usually an elusive trout to match wits with. It was the only sport I was any good at. That and swimming.

I had written a wistful letter to my Aunt Beatrice and impatiently waited for an answer. I had asked mum to watch for a letter from her and to hand it straight to me. She had asked why I'd written to her. Not ready for the question, I said I wanted to know more about Manchester. She must have thought it was a weak reason, but she let it go.

It was April 1944 and all the talk in the pubs, and even at school, was when the Allied invasion of the continent would take place. My classmates probably reflected the view of their parents that it would be any time now. My interest had centered on airplanes. I wanted to see a P-51 up close, but I had no idea how to go about it.

American warplanes had been using the field for months now. This was exciting enough. I would watch morning takeoffs from my window, and exult the rest of the day about my luck in living next to an air base. Of course others felt just the opposite. Our neighbors complained about the noise. The old-timers at the *Pussycat and Owl* were not happy to see the influx of young American men, pilots and ground crew alike. I suppose the proprietor, Mr. Stevenson, was. He did right proper with the sudden increase in income. It was said the American boys were loud and overwhelming and sometimes irreverent. I wasn't sure how. Did they swear or tell off-color jokes? But they brought loads of lolly with them and spent freely.

My father was a regular visitor at the *Pussycat and Owl.*

Three or four times a week he went to the pub with his friend from the village, Jim Branch.

"Who the hell do they think they are?" Pa asked no one in particular one night after he had returned early. "I couldn't find a squatting place. I had to wait in line for a pint of Guiness. And the dart board was all loaded with these foreign kids. Me and Jim were shut out. So we just left. That'll teach 'em. Who do they think they are, anyway?"

Reginald St. Clair approached the Town Council. They grew restless under his shouted complaints, and in the end did nothing. This wasn't surprising. What could they do? And why would they want to do anything as long as the pounds kept rolling in? The Council rejected the St. Clair claim with little discussion.

The only recourse left for my father was to visit the base himself—and crack a few heads together, as he put it. He donned clean pants and shirt, and dug out a well-used coat from deep within his closet. I couldn't help smiling to myself as I watched him prepare to overwhelm the enemy. I wanted to go with him, and finally got the nerve up to ask him.

"Come with me?" he roared. "What the hell for? I'm the man of the house. They won't even let you in the gate, a kid like you."

I drew myself up. "I'm 15, Pa."

"Oh, so you've reached that mighty age, have you? Gawd help us all. You'd cramp my style something awful, Rob."

What style was that, I wondered. Aloud I said, "You would be received better with me there. If you go alone you'll just lose your temper, Pa. They would just throw you out. With me along, they will respect you as a father and family man."

It may have been nonsense, but he bought it. He looked at me slyly as he thought it over. "Go get your best clothes on, then. Look sharp or I'll cuff you hard. I've been pretty lenient on you lately, and all I need is an excuse to box your ears right and proper."

We got by the guard—I'd heard the MP on his arm stood for Military Police—at the main gate, just barely. My father finally realized his dominating manner would not work with an American soldier. He showed the sergeant some identification, with the

45

address of our house on it. That finally got us to the office of the commanding officer, which was my father's goal. It was his way to go to the top, not waste time on underlings.

At the C.O.'s outer office, another sergeant listened to my father's pitch, then said that the man to see was a Major Burks, the base PRO—Public Relations Officer.

"Get him in here, then."

"Tuesday's are his day to fly, sir. No telling when he'll be back. I could arrange an appointment---."

"Who's behind that door there?" my father roared, his composure fast disappearing.

"That's the C.O.'s office, sir," the sergeant said. "Colonel Warren."

"Get this Warren out here then."

"I can't do that, sir. I don't know the nature of your business. The Colonel is very busy. I can't interrupt him."

"God damn it, what kind of army are you running here? I live next door to your bloody base and I demand to see the man responsible for all the racket." My father was bellowing loudly now and I wished I had stayed home. Then he made a mistake. He headed for the Colonel's office at a fast clip.

The Sergeant, a small man but solidly built, moved quickly to block his way. At the same time, he unbuckled his side arm. "I wouldn't do that, sir," he snapped.

"What's going on here?" The door had opened from the inside and an older man—he must be at least 30—stood in the doorway glaring at both his sergeant and the visitor. Blissfully, he ignored me.

The Sergeant briefly outlined what had occurred.

"So, Mr. St. Clair," Col. Warren said, "You're a neighbor. We apparently haven't gotten around to you yet—in what I call courtesy calls. We---"

"Courtesy calls? Who in hell said anything about---."

The Colonel, his manner ice cold, interrupted. "I'm not done, Mr. St. Clair. We are good neighbors. My Public Relations Officer is off the base today, but I'll send him over to your house tomorrow evening. Do you have our visitors' address, Sergeant? Well, okay then. You can expect Major Burks tomorrow night."

"Listen, Colonel what's-your-name. I didn't come over here to get thrown out."

"We're not throwing you out. But we will escort you and your son to the front gate." His manner steeled. "Now, will you let my sergeant walk you out of here? Or do you want me to call one of my military policemen?"

My father hated backing down; he'd had scant experience with it. But he had to now and he knew it.

As we left I turned around and gave the Colonel a broad smile, which must have confused him.

I fished the next afternoon, returning about six o'clock. My father was waiting for me and whacked me across the face. I staggered back, surprised and frightened. It didn't occur to me just then to fight back. I had to find out what this was all about.

"What the hell you doing writing to my sister? I got your letter here. What do you mean, asking her to take care of you?"

I faced him directly. "I'm not happy living here right now, sir. I just wanted to know if Aunt Bea would have me for awhile."

He looked at me with contempt. "Well, there's your answer." He tossed a letter on the floor. I scooped it up and headed for my room to read it.

Dear Robbie,

Your letter left me breathless. I'm not surprised that you're unhappy at home. I don't get along so well with your pa, either. I haven't seen him in years, though I keep up with you and Geoff through your mum. Rob, dear, now is a bad time to take you on. I am being married a week Sunday. George is a wonderful man. If you came just now, it would complicate everything. What are you, 15 now?

I dropped the letter and looked blankly at the wall. I was pretty upset: some kind of savior she turned out to be. At least she did know my age; that was good. I took up the letter again:

I don't have the right to do that to George. Rob, try not to hate your pa too much. I did, and I came out the worse for it. God places people like Reginald on earth to test the rest of us. I do love

47

you, Rob, and I wish I could help you. Maybe
someday. Lots of love,

Aunt Bea

Oh, so it would complicate everything, would it? She loves me, but it would be inconvenient just now. I lost my respect for my aunt. In the end, she was just like my pa. A lot smoother and not a bully, of course. But she was no better than he for all of that.

I had one other plan to change my rotten life to something better. It would involve Colin, which in itself was a risk. But before I worked on that, I wanted to hear what this major from the airfield would say to my father's complaints. I hoped my pater was in for another bad time.

The knock on the door came at precisely seven-thirty. I was in my bedroom, but when I heard it I fled to the kitchen. I joined my mum there; she looked at me with pity but no surprise. She had known that I wouldn't want to miss this.

"Ah, Mr. St. Clair," a deep voice easily carried to the kitchen listeners. "I'm glad to meet you. I'm Major Burks, the PRO—that's Public Relations Officer—for the 98th Fighter Group just across the field there."

"I know who you are," my father growled. He didn't offer his visitor a handshake or a chair.

"I won't take much of your time. This is just a neighborly visit. Mind if I sit, sir?" When my father didn't respond, Major Burks seated himself in my pa's favorite chair. I suspected this caused my pa to fume inwardly. And since he seldom fumed inwardly, I expected an explosion imminently.

But the Major forestalled him. "I understand you have a complaint, but let's hold that for a moment, Mr. St. Clair. You know, you're among the last neighbors to receive a call from me. So I'm glad you asked me to drop in on you."

My father finally found his voice. "What in hell is this, anyway? I don't want any friendly call from the likes of you. I have a complaint and I----."

"You're married, I understand. I'd like to meet your wife."

My father glared. He didn't know how to handle a personality as strong as his.

My mother had peeked around the doorway. "Ah, I think I see her in the kitchen. Can you join us, Mrs. St. Clair?"

She didn't wait for an endorsement from her husband. She entered the sitting room and introduced herself. Compared to the slouching man with a bitter look who was her husband, this ruggedly handsome, somewhat older man in crisp green and pink uniform—with wings on his breast—must have made a favorable impression. For the moment, my mother was running things, and I was awfully proud of her.

In answer to the Major's question about a family, she pre-empted my father again. "We have two sons," she said. "Geoff is in the Royal Navy in the Pacific somewhere. And there is Rob, who lives with us here."

"Is Rob home. May I meet him?"

"Now just a damn minute," my father interjected. "I don't want Rob to----."

He stopped abruptly as I entered the sitting room, too. I had easily decided that if my mother could have her way with Reggie, then so could I.

"Get to your room, Robert," my father commanded. He always used my full name when he was especially upset.

The Major continued as if the head of the household had not spoken. "How old are you, Robert?"

"Just fifteen, sir. And I go by Rob."

"Rob it is, then. Do you like airplanes?"

"Do I like them? I do, sir. I like the Mustang best of all the American airplanes."

"Then you don't have any objection to our field next door?"

"No, sir, I'm proud to have a fighter base as neighbors."

This was too much for my embattled father. "Shut your mouth, Rob. Get out of here now. Me and the General are having a private conversation."

My new hero, the major, didn't intervene as I hoped he might.

It was a time of decision for me. Years of obedience took its toll. I left the sitting room, detouring through the kitchen so that I could take up my position by the door. My mother joined me.

"Now let's get down to the bleeding business," my father began. I knew what was coming: the noise, the dirt, crowded pubs—the lot. The American Army had to do something—now!

And from Major Burks: we have over 50 bases right now in your country. And we'll add a few more, no doubt. Let me tell you we're damned grateful for the use of your land that much closer to Germany. We're bombing hell out of the Nazis, sir. A little inconvenience is natural. But other communities are cooperating with us with grace.

Implied was the lack of grace exhibited by one Reginald St. Clair. I thought it was well put by the American. But it was as if my father hadn't heard him, let alone understood his viewpoint. My father went on and on, and the major heard him out until there was nothing more to say. My father had the last word.

"You haven't heard the last of this, Major. We live here, by God, and you Yankees don't have the right to just kick us around. Now get the hell out of here before I lose my temper."

It seemed to me he already had.

I lay in bed, proud of the American Army Air Corps, and happy that my father had been bested again. I knew there was no chance, none, that Reginald St. Clair could win this battle. The Americans needed the bases and that was the end of it.

I had a ridiculous thought: would the 98th Fighter Group adopt me as a mascot? I could wash planes, or more likely dishes, and in return I would have a bunk over there. I had a last sleepy thought: how would it be to have a father like Major Burks?

7

A LIFE IN TURMOIL

I had turned 15 with no fanfare. It was September 1944 and the greatest invasion in history had proven successful after some anxious moments. The Allies had dug in on the continent, moving towards Berlin. Few thought the war would be over soon, but the mood was optimistic throughout the free world.

Mum fixed my favorite dish: liver and bacon and onions with mashed potatoes and peas. I wondered how much she had sacrificed to acquire so many good things. The meal was the only recognition that it was a special day for me. Colin asked me over to stay all night, but my father forbade it.

There was a new girl in school, with silken black hair and a perky nose. She seemed an outsider, too. Perhaps I would get to know her. I was certainly interested in girls, but I didn't know how to approach them. I couldn't think what we'd talk about.

On the next Friday, I thought of asking Lydia, the new girl, to the next day's matinee. They were showing *Thirty Seconds Over Tokyo,* the story of the Doolittle raid. Spencer Tracy and Van Johnson were starring in it.

· It would be splendid if Lydia would accompany me to the film. Would I hold hands with her? I didn't know, but the thought gave me goose pimples. I could never find her alone to ask her during the day but on the way home I bumped right into her.

"Why, Robert," she said. She didn't know me well enough to call me Rob. I remarked how well she had done on the math test that day and she blushed. We were getting on famously. I lost my reticence and asked her to the film on Saturday afternoon.

"Actually, Robert, that's a lovely idea. I'll just have to ask my mum." Then she was embarrassed for a moment and I couldn't think why. "Well, actually, Henry Bragg asked me to go swimming with him tomorrow. I had forgotten. You could ask me again sometime."

She skipped away, unaware she had broken my heart. I knew Henry slightly. He was the best cricket player in school, and the slickest looking boy, as well. What chance did I have against Henry the charmer?

At home my life didn't improve. My pa still taunted me whenever he chose to. He began something new—repeating whatever I said, always in sarcastic tones.

"I wrote a good essay in school today, mum," I might say.

"Oh, so my boy wrote a good essay in school?"

Or I would kiss my mother's cheek. "I'm going to bed, mum. I want to read my book. It's so good."

"Oh, so little Rob is going to bed early. He wants to read his book. It's so good."

I did my best to ignore him, but it was trying. I wondered whether I could last two more years of schooling, when I could join the services or go to University. I had not given up hope of getting away somewhere. I had talked to Colin about it off and on for months. Then, the Monday after my birthday, Colin told me to come to his house after school. He had a plan.

"It's a simple plan," he began. He had grown taller but was just as slim as ever. His voice had not changed much; he sounded like a 12-year old boy and he was nearly 15. He was the same Colin, one half crazy, one quarter sly, and one quarter plain dishonest. Yes, dishonest. It didn't bother him to lie, cheat, tell half-truths, or simply make something up. Still, I liked him. I had not made any other special friends.

"I have this aunt and uncle," he said. "They're even older than my folks. Uncle Tim had a stroke or something and they decided to retire. Know where they chose?"

"How the hell would I know?" I asked. I now used a few swear words. They were so common around my house that it was hard *not* to get in the habit.

"Well, it's Bishop's Stortford."

I shrugged. "What then?"

"We're going to burrow in with my aunt and uncle in B.S., Rob. We'll be Edward G. Robinson and James Cagney, on the run, snug in our hideout."

"Do your aunt and uncle know about this?"

I had learned how to be sarcastic and it felt good when I used it with Colin.

"Well, no, but they'll put up with us. My aunt hasn't spoken to my mother for years."

Hmm, I thought, is this the way it is in every family?

"We'll leave here next Friday night, Robbie. We'll go by bus, or maybe walk. Depends upon how much lolly we have."

"Colin, it sounds barmy. So we walk through the night and half the next day and then just drop in on Uncle Tim and Aunt Whoever. And they cheerfully put up with us? Then what?"

Nonchalantly, he said, "We stay there a fortnight, until the heat is off. Robinson and Cagney will be forgotten. We'll be written off as permanent runaways. It happens all the time—I read about it in the papers. A lot of kids leave home, live on the street, whatever. Even with the war on."

His mention of war reminded me that we hadn't heard from Geoffrey for two weeks or so. The post from the other side of the world was unpredictable. Geoff had been writing to me almost weekly through Colin.

We talked on about his plan. I thought it was a crazy plan for two young teenagers, especially since one of them was Colin. But it wasn't any more crazy than my life at home just now. Later, we would go to London, he said, where he knew his way around. We would find jobs as waiters at a hotel, or working on a rubbish lorry, or anything else that came up.

"We would have to rough it a bit, Rob. But you're game for that, right? I am. You can count on me."

That worried me. I couldn't think of anyone I could trust less than Colin.

I told him I'd think about it. I wasn't ready for the idea but the alternative of staying home was even worse. Perhaps I would die somehow and that would solve my problems. I gulped at the thought of a wished-for death, but I didn't shy away from it.

Colin had told me that teenagers were always killing themselves. Couldn't get along at home or girl trouble. I wrenched myself away from such thoughts as I walked home.

My father met me at the door. "Where the hell have you been?"

I stood up to him now. I was about his height, but I weighed at least four stone less than he. I forced myself to look at him level-on, determined to give him straight answers.

"I was at Colin's."

"In his bedroom?"

"Yes, father, in his bedroom. That's the only place we can talk without being spied on."

"Be careful in his bedroom. He's a homo, remember."

"That's your idea, pa. I don't worry about it."

"Did he kiss you or feel you up or anything?"

I looked coldly at him and said no he most definitely had not. But it occurred to me that if I ran away with Colin, and was alone with him, something like that might happen.

"What did you talk about all afternoon?"

"It wasn't all afternoon. It was just for an hour after school."

"So instead of playing football or cricket, you and your mate talk dirty in his room."

I usually had a low boiling point, but this was too much.

"What we talked about is none of your damn business."

When he shoved my shoulder hard, I struck his hand right off my shoulder, surprising him. It was time to leave. I went to my bedroom door and shoved a chair under the knob. I would have locked it with a key but my father would not allow it. "A father has a right to know what his son is up to," he said.

Now, infuriated, he pounded on the door and yelled at me.

The house eventually quieted down. I opened the window a crack so I could hear the flow of traffic at the airbase. There had been regular flights over Germany—missions they called them—for several months. The continual noise, which I reveled in, never gave my father a chance to forget that he hated it, especially from an American base just at his shoulder.

My father was not an easy forgiver. He would carry on indefinitely about his opinion of airplanes and Americans. I didn't help. As often as possible, I reminded him that I *liked* airplanes and Americans. Of course this just made it worse for mum and me. It had become nearly unbearable at home, which explained why I would even consider Colin's crazy scheme to run away.

After supper the head of the household went off to the *Pussycat and Owl*. Mum knocked lightly on my door a few minutes later and said, "Come out to my kitchen, Rob. I want to show you the two letters that arrived today. Mrs. Leigh-Poulson brought them over. Both are addressed to you. I read the one from Geoffrey, if you don't mind. A mother needs to know."

I read that one first; the other, from Aunt Bea, I didn't care that much about.

Dear Rob,

This will be a short note tonight. So you are still in trouble with pa. Well, he can't beat on you like he used to, but he can pester the daylights out of you, which we both know. But hang on tight, Robbie. Don't do anything foolish like running away.

I can't tell you where I am because of the censors, but the temperature is a lot like Cornwall. Remember when we went there for a holiday? Our ship—I can't say what kind—is large and is my home now. Take care of mum, Robbie. And bear the cross you must.

Geoff

I had to duck away from mum for a moment while I dried my eyes. My heart was filled with pride and love that I had a brother like Geoff. My longing for him was like a knife cutting through my guts. If he were here now, he would know what to do. I was bothered about his specific warning not to run away. Should I let that guide me? I didn't know.

I picked up the other letter with much less enthusiasm. Why even read another letter from my selfish aunt? I still hadn't admitted to myself that she was right—with a new husband, it was exactly the wrong time to have a young lad come live with you.

My dear Rob,

I think you are old enough to know that a newly married couple likes their privacy. Being married to George is something special. I want you to meet him. Just hang on there and have patience.

Will you do that for me, Rob?

55

There was a bit more but I didn't bother with it, throwing it down on my bedroom floor for picking up later. I said good night to mum and lay on my back in the dark, thinking strange thoughts. I felt as though I was cornered in a room without doors, without windows. If I stayed at home, would I go mad? Would I kill my father? What would happen to me?

As sleep overtook me, I had made the decision to go off with Colin, to try a plan that might not work but was still better than staying home with a hated father and a cowed mother.

At school I told Colin what I had decided. We would leave late that night. He had decided we would hitch a ride. He seemed sure that two young boys like us, ostensibly out for an end-of-week fling, could talk a lorry driver into taking us 30 miles (it had been 20, now it was 30). If we couldn't, then we would have to hoof it. "That's as may be, Rob," he said.

I returned home for supper that fateful day in early October. I was unhappy about running away from my mother. It was a terribly mean thing to do. She would have to put up with my father all by herself. I almost dropped the whole idea as I entered my house. Soon the decision was taken out of my hands.

I had thought to be cheery that evening so as not to give out any hints as to my plan for that night. In the sitting room, my father was sitting in his favorite chair, staring blankly at the opposite wall. He didn't look up.

"Hello, pa. You're home early today."

He showed no sign that he'd heard me. Well, I thought, this is a new phase for the old man: giving me the silent treatment. Then I heard queer noises from my parents' bedroom.

It didn't sound like my mother. I entered cautiously and found her lying on her bed, fully clothed, and sobbing her eyes out. She threw her arms out to me and I, wondering, went to her side. She reached for me and drew me down to her on the bed. She sobbed in my ear and I was bewildered. Had the world gone crazy?

"Oh, Robbie," she cried in my ear. "It's Geoffrey. He has been lost at sea. He is"—she had trouble speaking—"presumed dead. Oh, Rob, what are we going to do?"

It was like a thunderbolt had struck me: I couldn't see, couldn't think, couldn't talk. I was blinded with tears. What I wanted to do most was cry my eyes out in my room. But I also wanted to comfort mum. I put my arms around her and held her tight. We lay like that for at least 30 minutes, until I gently pulled myself away from her. "How did you hear about it, mum?"

"On the dresser," she mumbled.

I picked up the telegram and read:

Mr. and Mrs. St. Clair,

We deeply regret to inform you that your son, Seaman Second Class Geoffrey Alistair St. Clair, has been reported Missing in Action and presumed dead as a result of enemy action in the Pacific. As soon as further details are available, we will contact you again.

It was signed by a Navy Captain. The house was like a tomb. I lay on my bed and gave myself over to feeling sorry for myself. Later, mum entered my room with supper on a tray. Her life would have to continue, serving the two men left in her family. She was a true hero, and I felt nearly as badly for her as I did for myself.

Oh Geoff, where have you gone? Are you lying dead at the bottom of the sea? Does "presumed dead" simply mean they don't know for sure? Oh, Geoff, you were my life, my savior. Will I ever see you again?

I forced myself to think what my life would be like now. Of course I couldn't go off with Colin. I wanted to console mother, to help her deal with father.

I opened my window to stare at the airfield. A moment later, I saw a plane coming in for a landing. It was a P-51: I knew its lines well, even in the dusk. I watched it safely in to its parking space; then I closed the window abruptly.

My life had turned. I was at the lowest point in my life. My brother missing in action and probably dead, my Aunt Bea not interested in me, my mother forlorn, my father still the same rotten bastard. Could my life descend any further into hell?

8

A NEW PERSON IN MY LIFE
(REVISITED)

The next morning, a Saturday, I stayed in bed late. What was the use of getting up? Nothing I might do made any sense to me. My thoughts ranged widely, but mostly they centered on Geoff, on the things we had done together and would never do again.

We were mostly silent at breakfast, although I felt mum wanted to talk about her elder son. She and I talked a bit while my father sat stone-faced, eating mechanically. I finally decided I might as well tell Colin our runaway plans were cancelled, and why. I put on my coat and cap which brought my father abruptly to life.

He said sharply, "Where you going?"

"To see Colin." I hoped this might upset him.

It did, and I stood there for a few minutes on the receiving end of a torrent of verbal abuse. I ran out the door, slamming it, and headed for my friend's house. On the short walk there, it occurred to me Colin might be upset that I hadn't kept the tryst the night before. Now it was just not important.

The news about Geoff was still capable of stunning me. I felt as if I had the worse head cold of my life. I wondered if Geoff was watching me from his place at the right hand of God.

I needed something more uplifting than that thought. Perhaps even now he was in a ship flying the colors of the United Kingdom or the United States. Or he could have been picked up by a Japanese fleet ship and headed for a prisoner of war camp. I refused to think that he lay dead somewhere in far-away waters. Or blown to bits by the heavy guns of the Japanese Navy.

*   *   *   *

After I left Colin's house, I decided that he was not my best friend anymore. He was mostly interested in when we would make another attempt on his runaway scheme. He cared more about that than he was in Geoff's fate.

I had nowhere to go but home. I wondered what I would do if I were to run into Lydia again. Could I tell her the news about my brother without breaking up? I'll bet she would hug me to her. What I desperately needed at this moment in my life was that kind of reaction from a young girl, preferably Lydia, but practically anyone would do.

I stood at the main gate to the air base and asked the military policeman there how I could find Major Burks. It was Monday morning and I had skipped school for this special mission. My folks knew nothing about it. I had asked my father the day before how we could find out what had happened to Geoff. He had said he had no idea. From his manner, he wasn't going to try to find out. I decided to put feeling sorry for myself on hold while I enquired about my brother. I knew one man at the air base: Major Burks. I would ask him.

My pa had told me the previous night, "Don't go thinking to take advantage since you're the older son now. You'll never replace Geoff, Rob." The strange thing was that I didn't feel insulted.

Now, in my best clothes. I stood waiting for the MP to respond. He was perplexed. This civilian, a young kid, wanted to see their PRO? Well, he must have reasoned, that's what PRO's are for. He picked up the phone, got Major Burks on the line, and described me by name and appearance.

The MP's next move surprised me. "Hop in my jeep there, kid. I'll take you over myself." He motioned to another MP to take his place at the gate.

Five minutes later, I was sitting facing Major Burks in his office. The major, a cigar planted in the center of his mouth, reminded me of Edward G. Robinson. He ordered morning tea; I was surprised it wasn't coffee. Didn't all Americans drink coffee?

59

He had no idea why I was in his office. I told him in halting terms about our bad news, and showed him the telegram.

He came out from behind his desk and came over to where I was sitting. "I'm awfully sorry, Rob. I know your older brother must have meant much to you." He allowed me several seconds to compose myself. "And you think I can help find out what happened to him? Well, perhaps I can. I don't know who could do better than a supposedly crack PRO officer. I'll ring Eighth Air Force headquarters and have them get on to the Royal Navy. We'll take it one step at a time.

"Do you have a telephone? You don't? Well, ring this number"—he wrote on a piece of paper and handed it to me—"early next week. I may not know anything by then, but I could. If not, you can try calling me later in the week.

"You said the other night you were 15 years old. That right?"

"I just turned 15, yes, sir."

"Well, I have sons 14 and 16. You'd fit right in between. That's something, eh? I also have a daughter, but she's 18 and already off to college."

I returned his smile. He was trying to be nice and he was succeeding.

"'Missing in Action' is an overused phrase," he went on. "He may have been washed overboard and picked up by another ship. Perhaps one of your own or an American. He may be safe even as we speak."

My heart lifted but then I realized that he was just trying to buck me up.

"Are there many Japanese ships in the Pacific?"

He knew where I was headed. "Well, yes there are. That's their waters, actually."

I didn't want to think about this. I had read about the atrocities at Japanese prison camps.

I telephoned on Monday. Major Burks had news for me. "Can you get over to my office again? I'd drop by your house but I really don't want to run into your father. Let's just keep this between the two of us for now. Get yourself to the main gate and I'll have an MP bring you to my office. Like last time. At 1500 hours, then. Right, Rob."

Major Burks quickly told me about the results of his investigation. "Your brother's heavy cruiser, the *King George*, was torpedoed off the northeast coast of Australia, in the Coral Sea. The ship went down, Rob, but reports from other Allied ships in the area were that a great number of sailors got off the ship and into the water. No knowledge yet of rescues by either friend or foe. Was your brother a deck sailor or did he work below decks?"

"He was a deck sailor, sir." I knew this from my brother's coded letters.

"Then I think he would have had a better chance of getting off into a lifeboat than if he'd been below decks. So you can hope, Rob."

Maybe not too much, I thought but did not say. Above deck he might have been killed outright by enemy fire.

For reasons I could not define, I didn't tell my parents about the information Burks had gotten for me. I don't quite know why. Perhaps it was because the major had two sons in my age bracket. Maybe it was because he'd said, "This is just between us." I wondered again what it would be like to have Major Burks as a father.

The following day it rained some but it cleared in the afternoon and I decided to go fishing. The River Thom beckoned.

Running water had its usual calming effect upon me. I'd often had the incongruous thought I'd still fish a stream even if I knew it had been fished out.

I trekked upstream about one hundred yards to the hole I'd decided was my favorite. I picked my way across the mossy bank so as not to disturb any big ones napping there. I threw line in water, a juicy worm from mum's garden hiding a deadly hook. Although I could feel the awful weight of my brother's loss, still I shivered with anticipation as I awaited the result of the cast. It was as if the trout was waiting for me. Almost immediately I felt a strike.

Just at that moment someone within a few feet of me yelled, "Catch any, kid?" Feelings of disappointment and hatred flooded me. Yes, hatred. The fish was lost, my line in the willows, and I whirled around to tell this newcomer how stupid I thought he was.

It was a young red-haired man and he carried his own pole and equipment. I was ready to do battle. I could see he was probably from the air base since he was wearing what the army called fatigues. Although he was several years older than me, I chewed him out. "Darn," I said, "don't you know enough not to yell like that?"

A few minutes later we were eating candy bars together and I even missed a chance to dismiss him from my life when he offered to find another hole. What had prompted me to grasp the straw of friendship that was held out to me by this unknown American? Was I seeking a replacement for my brother? Was I just recognizing the worth of someone who was nice to me? I didn't know the answers, but I discovered one thing: the next few minutes changed my life. There was no hope before I met Rick Linden. After I did, hope came inching in, even if was accompanied by heartbreak.

PART III

RICK LINDEN

9

GETTING TO KNOW MY
NEW BROTHER

Slanting rain pelted the tin roof of our Quonset hut. It was early and my two roommates were asleep. I lay there on the cot, arms clasped behind my neck, and thought of my new acquaintance. He was just a boy of 15; why had I told him he was my best friend? With dozens of pilots my age all around me, and with girls readily available—Ah, Anne of the flowing red hair, I must get to London to see you—why had I picked up on a young Brit?

Purely chance, I concluded. We were both at the same fishing hole at the same time and it would have been unusual if we hadn't talked. But become friends? I could imagine what I offered him: the romantic pilot image, an American, and, most important, a temporary replacement for a lost brother. But what did he offer me? Oh, get off it, Linden, do you have to weigh what a fellow offers before you can decide to be his friend? You're a better man than that, Linden.

Did he remind me of myself at that age? No, not really. He was a serious kid; I never took myself or my life too seriously. He was sort of a sad boy—but who wouldn't be after losing your brother? Had I ever been sad in my life? If so, I couldn't remember when. To me, life was a breeze, a challenge, a love affair. On short acquaintance, Rob seemed to have had more bad days than good. So, Linden, what's going on?

What's the big deal: he was just a kid I'd met fishing. I might never see him again. Oh, yeah? Then why did you tell him you'd see him tomorrow at the fishing hole? I decided then and there not to look any deeper than that. And just in time: my dreamy introspectives were smashed by a pillow in my face,

65

courtesy of my roommate, Al Rankin, and a loud fart from Ken Smith, my other roommate. "Come on, out of bed, Linden," Smith said. "It's your turn. Fire up the coal stove. Get some heat in this here igloo."

This was a non-mission day. That much we knew well before breakfast. I was thinking of a good book in a corner chair of the Officer's Club, when a fellow pilot, Joe Bailey, slid in next to me at the chow table.

"I can beat you now, Linden," he said. Since arriving at the base three weeks earlier I had quickly established myself as the man to beat in ping pong. Bailey was one of those types who always needed to be the best at everything—flying, romancing, ping pong, whatever. To my way of thinking, he hadn't reached any of those pinnacles. But he had to keep trying.

I put him off until eleven o'clock. He would have two or three buddies with him. I wanted to line up Rankin, Smith, and Pat Morse to root for me. We settled on the best three out of five games. The bet was $10.

He gave me a long look. "You're going to be surprised, Linden. I know your game—defense and then more defense. I'm going to smash my way past your best defenses on my way to the club championship." Of course there was no club championship except in Bailey's mind.

I quickly lined up my supporters, then, with an hour to spare, I found my favorite chair and retrieved my book from under the chair. It was *Martin Eden* by Jack London. I settled back while outside the rain intensified. I knew Bailey was in the Game Room practicing his drives. I wouldn't lower myself to join him. My game would have to be good enough or I would be out ten bucks.

About 10:45, Major Burks, a cigar sitting squarely in his mouth, stopped by my chair.

"Too early for a drink, Rick?" I had known the PRO for only three weeks, and he was already a friend. He was by way of being a hero of mine: a command pilot with a Distinguished Flying Cross and two purple hearts.

"No thanks, Major. I have a match in ten minutes." I told him about the ping pong challenge. "But I'll join you in an hour or so—win or lose."

"Either a victory drink, or a 'drown your sorrows', eh? Okay, see you."

He ambled to the bar, where he had a tab going. A pre-lunch drink before eleven was a bit much for me, but I would be glad to join him around noon.

Bailey was perspiring; he had been hitting balls with a buddy. He looked warmed up and confident. I asked to hit a few and he gave me five minutes.

He was an aggressive player, more so than me. He was also competent enough at defense. His smash was on and he won the first game, 21-14. I had played almost exclusively defense, but it was hard to stay cool when his drives were so accurate.

"Ha. Got you," he said as we exchanged sides.

His words mobilized me. Not so much the words but the sneering tone he used. I didn't want to lose to this guy.

I changed tactics. I smashed everything, from both sides, but my drives were a bit rusty. He won, 21-18.

I called for a water break, using the time to decide what to do. I'd lost at both defense and offense. Could I win today? I should go with my best, I concluded as I took paddle in hand. For the first time, I was taking the match as seriously as he was.

I won the third game, 21-13, with an impeccable display of defense. It must have demoralizing to him to see his best drives returned with impunity.

Quite a crowd had gathered, perhaps 20 in all. I caught a glimpse of Major Burks, standing in the doorway, cigar in one hand, drink in the other, a bemused smile on his face. I gave him a long wink, but he didn't acknowledge it.

I repeated my success in the fourth game, with a solid defense. But it was close, 24-22.

This time he asked for a break while he conferred with his posse. I gave my friends a chance to comment, but only Pat Morse had anything to say. "Back to offense," he mouthed.

I wandered over by Burks. He spoke with the cigar still in his mouth, and I caught his words: "Smash 'em, son."

Disregarding both Morse and Burks, I played defense again. He would expect me to continue my winning ways with more offense. I watched his desperation shots go wild, while I calmly returned shot after shot. I could almost see him lose heart. The game and match were mine, 21-12. I pocketed ten dollars.

I joined the major at the bar. My mouth was dry and it was time for a drink. Burks had left the match after I was well ahead in the final game.

"That give you any pleasure?" he asked, flicking a cigar ash my way.

"Not much. It helped that Bailey is an asshole."

"No comment." He gave me a long look. "What does a fly boy like you do on a rainy afternoon?"

"I haven't given it much thought. Long lunch, one drink after lunch—just one—then back to reading, letter-writing, kidding around with the boys. If the weather clears a bit, I might throw line in water in late afternoon."

"Do you fish alone?"

"Usually. But, a funny thing, I met a local kid there yesterday. I have a feeling he may be there again today. Actually, I hope he is. He reminds me of the younger brother I never had."

"That doesn't make any sense, Rick."

"How could I be reminded of someone who never existed? You are so right, Major."

He looked bemused, but made no further comment.

He was standing under a tree trying to keep dry. "Hello, Rick," he said. "I wondered whether you'd come today."

"It's a terrible day for fishing." The rain increased in intensity, and we crowded under a tree together, watching and listening to the rain pound the streams and banks.

"Isn't that a beautiful sound?" I said, after a minute. "The sound of rain coming down hard. It reminds me of times I've been caught in a hail storm in the Rockies. There's something romantic about it."

"Isn't romantic something between a lad and a lass?"

I told him there was more than one meaning to the word. I wasn't certain he had grasped the difference. "Tell me about your brother, Rob."

For a moment he looked stricken and I held my breath. Then he unwound and told me how Geoff had always stood up for him. As youngsters, they had joined forces to defeat, or at least neutralize, their father. They'd had secret codes, and in fact, had communicated by codes in the last letter Geoff had written. He stopped talking abruptly, and his eyes filled.

"Have faith, Rob. Sometimes that's enough."

In a moment he went on. "Do you know a Major Burks, Rick? He's been very nice to me."

I was amazed. He knew just one man on my base besides me, and it was Burks. Perhaps there was something going on here, some trick of fate, which was working towards bringing us together. I didn't share this thought, but I did tell him that yes, I did know Burks, and in fact we had lunched together.

I told him about growing up in Colorado Springs, my college life, my love of skiing. He asked about my parents.

"They're swell, Rob, usually more like an older brother and sister than parents. Of course they know where to draw the line between friend and parent." I told him about dropping out of college and my parents' strong negative reaction to it. I told him about my sister Jane. "She gets tired of my happy-go-lucky take on life," I said. "She's a serious girl. Right now she's being very serious about a college education."

While I was talking I noticed that Rob's eyes never left my face. Perhaps it was simply that he was glad to be talking about someone else's family.

The rain stopped and we moved to our favorite log, wet as it was. Again, I produced two candy bars. "Looks like I'm destined to keep you supplied with G.I. candy bars for the duration," I said. I asked him what his interests in life were.

When he mentioned "America" and "flying," I was vain enough to wonder if that had anything to do with me.

"What do you think is the toughest year in growing up?" he asked. "I know mine."

"Thirteen," I answered without hesitation. "It was a bad year for me."

He was looking at me, mouth open. "Mine was 13, as well."

What was going on here? Were our stars in alignment?

I said, "You should come to America after the war and I'll show you around. I could help you find the right college."

My young friend's face turned red, then pale, and finally, a big grin flushed across his face.

"Oh—that would be grand." He was silent a moment, then asked, "Uh, Rick, what are you going to after the war?"

"Oh, I'll be continuing my writing career. I have a lot of things I want to write before I'm done."

"Can I read something you wrote?"

"The main thing I've done lately is an autobiography of my life in your country. Flying bombers. I finished it a month or two ago and sent it to my agent in America. Hmm. I do have a carbon copy, but a friend of mine, Jeanne, is reading it just now."

"What's the name of your book?"

"*Trail of the Bombers.*" He stared at me with intensity. "It's charged my soul to get my thoughts on paper, Rob. Scene 1, little kids standing openmouthed in doorways, craning scrawny necks to watch us. Quite a sight: seven or eight hundred bombers high in the sky. Scene 2: Tons of bombs dropping on their heads, their houses, their schools. I know, Rob. I was there. And finally, Scene 3, a horrifying sight for an eight year old, watching his family die before his eyes."

Rob was staring at me with unbelieving eyes. He said nothing.

"I'm still trying to come to terms with understanding war, with how civilized people can kill and maim other people in the name of—God knows what. I don't. Sometimes I think the dark forces of the world have taken over the universe. Sorry about the morbid lecture, Rob. I'm usually more light-hearted than that."

He looked stricken and I realized he must be thinking of his brother's fate. How crude of me, especially on short acquaintance, to burden him these kinds of thoughts.

It wouldn't have surprised me if he had not wanted to meet again. But he seemed eager to. We set a date for the following Friday on the River Thom.

As late October faded into oblivion, the war news turned good. Allied armies had smashed forward to cross the Somme River and into Belgium. Brussels had fallen to British and Canadian troops a few weeks earlier. The emphasis was to knock out V-2 rocket-launching sites near Antwerp. V-2s had done severe damage and lowered morale considerably since June, when flying bombs had first landed on London.

As winter closed in, our long-anticipated march to Berlin was delayed by the German army, who put up a fierce struggle. The Battle of the Bulge was about to begin.

I began to believe that I would finish my missions before the war ended. Was this good? Was this bad? I didn't know.

I met Rob two or three times a week. I wondered if he began to think of me as a surrogate for his brother. I couldn't decide if this were good for him or not. Within a few months, my missions would be complete, I'd be out of his life, and he'd be alone again. On the other hand, he so obviously needed support now, and I was nearly always available to offer it, that it seemed a shame not to stay connected.

He understood this perfectly well. On one of our late afternoon meetings (during which we'd had bites but no fish) he asked me how many missions I had to fly.

"Fifty, Rob. I don't know whether the war will be won first, or I'll be finished before then. I have twenty odd now. At the rate I've been flying I'll be out of here by February."

I could see, immediately, that I had done it again. The stricken look on his face was painful to see. He spoke softly:

"What am I going to do after you leave? I'll be alone again."

10

CONVERSATION IN A TEAROOM

"I'll bet you'd rather have a beer at the *Pussycat and Owl,* Rick."

I admitted it then added, "Tea is okay."

We were seated in the sunniest corner of a small tearoom in the center of Ridgewell. Lace curtains, checkerboard table-cloths and quaint chalk paintings of country scenes provided a pleasant backdrop for a cozy chat. Most patrons were elderly ladies. It was 4:30 and tea was part of the national pastime at that hour.

I'd returned from a flight two hours earlier. Flying was still at the center of my mind. I thought I'd share my feelings about it. "Flying fighters is the most exciting thing I've ever been involved in," I said. "I don't need to shoot down a German plane to prove my competence or virility. It's enough to be flying a Mustang and helping to win a war."

"When can I look over a P-51 up close?"

"Any time, Rob. Well, not just any time. I'll pick the time and let you know."

"What I'd really like to do is fly with you, Rick."

"Difficult in a single-seater airplane. I'll think about it." I wanted to give him hope that it might happen, although I could think of no way it could. Rob looked troubled for no reason I could discern.

"The thing I can't understand," I said a moment later in a conscious attempt to lighten the mood, "is why they call these things biscuits." I fingered a round, sugared cookie. "Why don't they call them cookies? Isn't that what they are?"

He smiled. "Biscuits they've been for hundreds of years, and biscuits they'll remain. A visiting American flyer can't expect to change our traditions that easily."

In the past two weeks we had been fishing, taken a bicycle ride twice, and drank my yearly quota of tea. Beer was out, I thought; Rob had told me his father forbade it.

"Rick, can I show you something?"

"Sure."

"It's a letter from my aunt. Do you want to read it?"

"Sure. You read it aloud, Rob."

My dear Rob,

I have been worried about you living there with my brother. Listen, Rob, I wrote a selfish letter to you which I regret. I should never put a bit of inconvenience above my nephew's welfare. I talked to George about you. He was great. He said if it means so much to you and your nephew, well bring him on. Rob, talk to your mother. If she thinks it's the right thing to do, then do come and live with us. You could finish schooling here. Let us know soonest.

Love, Aunt Bea

"Wonderful letter," I said. "Sounds like a great lady. Do you want to, Rob?"

"I don't know if I can stand two more years at home. My mum isn't much help."

I poured fresh tea. "Well, then, young Rob, perhaps you should move out. War brings a lot of changes. Two years in Manchester might be a lark. It'd certainly be different than Ridge-well. A big city, near surf fishing, lots of girls---."

I stopped abruptly when I noticed tears forming in his eyes. "I'd miss you, Rick," he said, softly.

"Still, it might be for the best. I'll borrow a jeep and come to see you after I finish my missions. We'll go fishing and---."

I stopped again as tears did appear in his eyes.

"Don't you see, Rick? I can't leave you now. You're like a brother, you *are* my brother. You make my life worth living. To know you're around, just next door to my bedroom window, to watch you take off, to be your friend, is enough."

I said, "It's your decision, Rob. If having your father and me both in your life isn't too bad, then stick around. If it's too much, then head north, young fellow. Gosh," I added, "your father must be an ogre. Someday I'd like to see for myself."

He managed a small smile. "Don't bother."

"Let's move out," I said a bit later. "I'll walk you home. Will your dad be there this time of day?"

"Not likely."

"I love your country, Rob. I think sometimes of the history that took place here. Of kings and peasants. Of Shakespeare and Sherlock Holmes. Of Sir Walter Raleigh and Rudyard Kipling. Of Oliver Twist and Beau Geste. So many great names, so much history, so many creative accomplishments. Yes, I love your country."

"And I love yours. I want to visit America after the war. I'd go right now if there was a way."

"If you want to come over, Rob, you will. There aren't many great things that haven't started with a dream."

We passed through the brick streets of Ridgewell. Shopkeepers were closing their shops. A lowering sun, red on pink, was sinking swiftly towards the distant hills.

"You know what else I believe in?" I went on. "Beauty. Life should be as beautiful as we can make it. Beauty is happiness. I don't know which is truer. And beauty lies in the eyes of the beholder, in the ears and the touch and in all the other senses. I always seek it out, Rob. Beauty. I've found it in many places. One moment I am in the dumps, no beauty around, and the next instant I find it, and for that instant I am completely happy."

"Are you happy now?"

"Totally. There's something beautiful about the two of us walking down this pastoral road in Ridgewell." I toasted the air around us with my two-fingered salute. "You know where I find beauty? In making someone happy."

"Like—with girls?"

"Sometimes. But there's more to beauty than just a pretty face, to paraphrase rather badly. If you accept my theory that beauty is an end in itself, and making someone happy is beautiful, then love is the highest thing in life.

"I've been in love with a score of girls and in each there was a glimpse of something so lovely that it left me gasping. But it eluded my eyes. Someday I'll find it all, complete in one girl. As long as you're searching for love, then all else becomes of lesser import. Without love, one is no better than a walking corpse."

A blush began to flood his face. Uh, oh. I had gone too far again. We stopped for a moment and I put one hand on his shoulder. "You don't have to pay any attention to me, Rob. I'm just spouting forth, trying out ideas."

"I want to hear you ideas. I don't get any at home and precious few in school."

"That gives me leave to try one other on you. The biggest crime in civilization, I think, is that there are only a tiny percentage of people do what they have fun at, what is beautiful for them."

"Can't we do something about that, Rick?"

"We might. It comes about from tradition and the way education is set up, and from the people themselves. If a man can conceive of nothing more than making a pot of money, then he deserves to be enslaved and to live a life of ugliness. But if he can create a life of doing things he loves and can laugh at, then he has at least a fighting chance for true happiness."

Our random walk had taken us to a housing scheme. Suddenly I spied a big man on the porch on the last house on the street. Beyond was my air base. I had a premonition.

Rob spoke urgently. "We can't talk any more."

"I see what you mean. G'night, Rob." I strode off rapidly the way we'd come.

"Hey, you, stop right there, damn you."

His father had seen us in the darkening skies. He walked rapidly into the street and up to me. I stopped in my tracks.

I decided to face up to him. "You must be Mr. St. Clair."

"Damn right I am. And who are you?"

Rob came up to stand by me. Out of the corner of my eye I saw a few curtains fluttering. The neighbors were interested in the proceedings.

I took the older man by the arm and steered him back to his front stoop. This infuriated him. I spoke directly to him, quietly but distinctively. "My name is Rick Linden and I'm a pilot from the base. I met Rob fishing and we've become good friends. That's all."

His father glared at me. "What does an older man see in this kid? And you an American. What are you after, Lincoln?"

"Nothing, sir. And the name is Linden."

"Linden, Lincoln, who cares? You're probably filling my boy with all sorts of trash—bad words, smoking, talk of girls, who knows what else?"

Rob spoke up quickly. "There's none of that, Pa. Rick hasn't used bad words or anything." He trailed off, uncertainly.

"Stay out of this, Rob. This is nothing about you."

"It *is* about me, father. Rick is my friend."

He gave Rob a hard shove on the shoulder. I tensed. I knew it would be havoc if I interfered between father and son, and yet how I wished I had one free punch.

Rob surprised me by taking the lead. "So long, Rick. We're going into supper now." I left without another word, waving at Rob behind his father's back. Of course St. Clair had to have the final word.

"Don't you come around here any more, damn you," he yelled. "You pester my son again and you'll get beat up real bad."

I ignored him and kept walking.

It was important that Rob know I was still his friend. I walked to the creek on Friday. We'd had an easy mission that day, but now it was 1600 hours and I was on my own.

When I was 30 feet away, I squashed out my cigarette and yelled, "Catch, Rob," at the same time tossing him a candy bar. He caught it neatly and flashed me a smile.

I got right down to it. "How's your father?" We were sitting on our favorite log. His mouth was full of candy.

"I've been ignoring him since the other day," he said. "I'm sorry, Rick."

"That's okay. I'll just have to accept that not everyone likes me. Maybe I'll take it as a challenge to win over your dad."

"Don't bother."

"You know, it'd be a lot easier for you if I just bowed out of your life. What say you, Rob?"

He was stunned. For a long moment he just stared at me. Then he said, "Crikey, Rick, I'd rather have my father out of my life than you."

"Thank you, I think. I'll have to be more discreet about when and where we meet."

"I would like you to meet mum," he said. "She's nothing like father. You don't ever have to talk to him again."

"On balance, I'd just as soon not."

"Rick, are we still friends?"

I clapped him on the shoulder. "What could possibly make me cross you off my list of friends? Nothing ever will. Count on it, Rob."

His look almost embarrassed me.

Before we separated, I pulled a book out of my pocket and handed it to him. "I brought this for you. I read it just last night. *The Bridge of San Luis Rey* by Thornton Wilder. It's a short read, but a real gem. One of the protagonists, Uncle Pio, tells of his three passions, at age 20. First, the need for independence and adventure. Next, his desire to be near beautiful women. And last, his love for literature. I won't give it away any more. Interested?"

"Wizard. Thanks." He put the book in his pocket. His face beamed suddenly. "You know who else that describes?"

"No, who?" But I thought I knew.

"Rick Linden, that's who."

"Thanks, buddy. That makes my day complete. Hey, let's see that book again. I want to read you something." I flipped to the last page. "Listen to this:

> There is a land of the living
> And a land of the dead,
> And the bridge is love,
> The only survivor, the only meaning."

"What does it mean?" he asked.

"I'm not sure, but I like the sound of it."

"So do I, Rick."

11

A LIFETIME AHEAD OF US

We rested after a half hour of steady hiking on Roans Peak. The view of meadows and hedge rows below was expansive. A companion peak, round-topped like Roan, was partially obscured by filmy clouds in the near distance. I told Rob that this peak was totally unlike the tall and majestic Rocky Mountains I was so familiar with.

During the jeep ride to the base of the mountain, I told him that I badly needed a day away from the war, from flying. "Off hand," I said, "I can't think of any of my fellow pilots who would hike up a mountain on their day off."

We perched on rocks on opposite sides of the rocky trail, legs stretched out in front of us. "Tell me about your aunt in Manchester."

"I think she's a decent type," he said. "But I hardly know her so I can't really say. I haven't seen here for three or four years. I think she told mum a long time ago that she wouldn't waste petrol to come visit us. And my father would never go there, either." He paused, then continued, guardedly, "But if you leave, I may decide to live with her."

"Do you have other relatives?"

"I used to have three first cousins. On my mother's side. Older ones. Two boys died early in the war, one in the blitz on London, one in Africa. The third one, Lynn, married and moved to Australia. I never knew any of them very well."

I told him of my own relatives, most of them in Colorado or Wyoming, with frequent visits and a plentitude of love. I wondered if he might be comparing my family with his.

"Rob, the Bible tells us to honor our parents," I told him. "Sometimes it's not easy. But keep trying. I've seen a gain in your confidence just since I've known you."

"Righto, Rick. I'll try. But I can't wait to get away some-where, anywhere."

"That reminds me of me at your age. I used the same words to my parents, to anyone who would listen."

We began climbing again at the same brisk pace as before. "Did you ever have fights with your folks, Rick?"

"Oh, yes. Not too often, but once in awhile they were really doozers."

"Doozers?"

"Formidable. Awesome. They're great people. Fair, firm, understanding. But, like I've said before, they can come down hard. Especially so when I was quite a bit younger, when I thought I knew what made the world go around."

"How old were you before you could do anything you wanted, whether they approved or not."

"Good question. Years ago, I suppose. I was—maybe 15. Hmm, your age. I was feeling my oats and I didn't want to take their word on much of anything. I didn't finish college, Rob, but I wouldn't advise that for you. I was into writing so much that I just had to try my luck in the Big Apple—New York. And that didn't sit well with them. I let them know, in a nice way I hope, that as soon as I finished high school I had left their domain."

I was leading him up the trail. He talked to my back. "That gives me hope. If only I was older and ready for university. I can't wait to grow up."

"Hey, kid, enjoy it while you can. Time moves fast. Have you decided where you want to go to university?"

"Yes, Cambridge. I went there last year for a visit. With Colin and his parents. It looked just right for me."

I stopped and turned around. "That's another connection between us. I spent a few days there with Pat Morse a few months ago. I fell in love with Cambridge. I was really impressed with the choir at Kings College. Pat and I sat spellbound at a rehearsal. Hey, if you're going to Cambridge, I'll come back after the war and meet you there. If they'll have me—a Yank with only average grades."

His eyes were sparkling. "That would be great. We could go to school together. Except you might have graduated by then."

"I'd let you catch up. I'll go home first, Rob. Take a year at Colorado College, maybe, then I'd be ready try Cambridge. I haven't gotten my fill of England, anyway."

"Is that true blue, Rick? I'd go to Cambridge if you did."

"Hey, great. I love your country. Just thinking of it raises my arm hairs sometimes. I've read a lot of English history. I can close my eyes, when I'm lying in bed, and hear the soft thunder of war horses going into battle. Or the sound of steel clashing. Plumed helmets, fluttering pennants, great battles. Reading about your country, strange and mysterious passages sometimes come back to me out of nowhere."

He did not respond.

"The old-time wars were acceptable—depose one king and set up another. It seemed romantic to my young eyes. But it doesn't change my opinion about war now that I've seen it up close."

We walked on in silence. We could see the top of Roans Peak now, beyond huge boulders.

A bit later, stopping again, I said, "Listen, kid, if we both don't go to Cambridge, you could go to college in Colorado." My remark, so casually stated, left him staring at me again.

"That's what I want to do, Rick. Wizard."

We ate our lunch at the summit, huddled under a huge sloping rock. The wind had risen and a few drops of rain fell, foreboding worse weather. We had not brought rain gear.

"Is this a mist or a light rain?" I asked. "Or is there a special name for it?"

"We invented this kind of weather," he grinned. "If I go to America, will you teach me American football? And baseball?"

"Those sports, for sure. And also skiing. You've got to try it. When I'm on skis I'm no longer a man: I'm a god. I guess that's my element. Then there's tennis and golf and climbing and all the rest. And maybe sometime you can teach me the rudiments of cricket. I've never figured it out.

"Sure, come to America. As soon as you're out from under your parents' yolk. You can stay with us. I want you to meet my family. See Pikes Peak, the ski runs at Vail, climb Longs Peak with me." I paused. "Interested?"

"Gosh, yes."

I got warmed up. "Room with me for awhile if it suits you. I have the basement to myself. Of course by that time I might be wandering the world, or back in New York writing, or maybe in

Hollywood punching out screen plays. That's what so exciting about the postwar, Rob. Anything can happen. If I wasn't there, my folks would care of you. To quote a line of my mothers': 'Any friend of Rick's is a friend of ours.'"

He looked at me with wonder and hope.

We stayed in the shelter of the rock for an hour, enjoying the sound of wind sweeping over our hilltop. The view from our 2,700-foot perch was sweeping: fields, meadows, small farms, winding roadways, a lake in the distance. With an abruptness that surprised me, a flight of three fighter planes—I told Rob they were P-47s—flew low overhead, probably headed for the continent and the war. It was a vivid reminder that the war was still on. As soon as tomorrow, I'd be back in the sky, myself.

"I've got something I want to talk over with you, Robbie. Sorry, but you're a captive audience. I've mentioned this to only one other fellow, Pat Morse. Now it's time to see what a proper Englishman thinks. No offense.

"I want to get back to the states and start to work on this agenda. Well, that sound's stuffy. Goals? That's even stuffier. My great projects. My life's work."

I had the complete attention of my young protégé.

"I want to finish college, where I don't know yet. Perhaps Colorado College. More likely Chicago or Stanford. The world is my oyster: I can go anywhere my finances and grades will take me. But this period is going to be short. I want to get to work, and work hard, at several things. Maybe I can attain some level of success at two or three."

I stopped momentarily. We were both shivering but I don't think it bothered either of us.

"About me, Rob. I'm a romantic and an idealist, as well. Now those are two very difficult attributes for a man to come to terms with. It complicates my life, but I glory in it. I'm not a simple person. And yet I like simple things, friends, girls, mountains, sports, good food, family. But most of all I love freedom. It might even be more precious than love.

"This flying combat has done something to me. It's changed the way I look at things, made me want to use the next 40 or 50 years to try to accomplish a few things. Now that's a helluva conceited thought for someone just turned 23. And me with no real education yet, or other qualifications. But, hey, I do have one qualification. Writing. I seem to be able to put down stuff on paper which interests, amuses, and hopefully influences people. And that's a talent I intend to put to good purpose."

We were both hugging our knees. "Let's start down, Rob. It's too cold for sitting still."

We jogged down the trail. We were halfway down before he yelled at my back, "Let's stop. You have more to say, and I want to hear it."

His words warmed me. We sat on a huge rock; the wind had died down at this lower altitude. Our bodies were warm from the recent exertion. Facing us, across a half mile of empty space, was a vertical wall of slate some 300 feet straight down.

"The short fiction I've published was written to entertain. But it doesn't go deep enough. I do go deeper in my full length book, *Trail of the Bombers*. It's supposed to be a serious description of how I feel about war. If it gets published, it's intended to influence a few people. That's a start. Now—or rather after I get back to Colorado—I want to research and write about other subjects I feel strongly about: education, poverty, injustice, inequality of the races, and some other things. We can do better, Rob, in America and in the world. I intend to do something about it. Boy, that sounds conceited. But being able to write is my God-given talent and I'm going to use it to the hilt."

My companion couldn't hide his wide-eyed look of wonder, and—I guessed—admiration. I must have seemed like a young god to him, standing there outlined against a dark and troubled sky, spouting forth my ideals.

"Education. So important. A prime goal of mine. Why not universal education for everyone? Everyone. Good teachers. What a difference a good, caring, compassionate teacher makes.

"What the degree is in is not important. Me, I'll probably end up with a Bachelor of Arts in Humanities, something like that. I intend to use my energy and my writing ability to influence the powers that be—at whatever level, city, county, state, federal, school board, whatever—to give money and emphasis to educate every citizen of the country. Because that's the only way we're going to survive this world of wars we've stumbled into. It should be every youngster's birthright to learn about their world, then be able to do something about it."

Rob hadn't said much. When I didn't go on immediately, he said, solemnly, "I'm going to help you, Rick."

"That's great, but—you're kidding, aren't you?"

"What better way to put my aimless life into something worthy—like your ideas?"

That drew a solemn look from me. "Rob, let's talk over your future soon, when it's not so damn cold. For now, just remember this. You don't have an aimless life!"

We started down the trail at a fast trot.

I wanted to get it all out there. "Continuing to write is a must and a no-brainer." I threw the words over my shoulder. "Working on education is another no-brainer. It'll take time and the influence of a lot of important people I'll cultivate.

"Rob, let's stop a minute. It's too hard to talk while we're running." We perched on adjacent boulders.

"What you've said is chipper, Rick. Back there I think you said there were three main goals. What's the third one?"

"The third project, maybe the most important, is a life's work in itself: promote peace. Outlaw against war, legislate against it, wrestle with it constantly. But do something, or a number of things, that will make the atrocity of war a thing of the past. Simply stated, very difficult to get a handle on. But someone has to try it, and keep trying. Why not me?"

"And me," he added.

We ran down the trail for five minutes while neither of us tried to talk. Then, at a protected wide place on the trail, we stopped again. It was still raining lightly. The wind had abated.

"Did you write about these ideas in your book, Rick?"

"Some of it. I'm going to write a lot more when we get this war over."

"I'll remember this day forever, Rick. Hiking a mountain with my best friend, who is also my new brother. For the first time, I feel I really know you and understand you. It's a great feeling."

Boy, had he ever matured. This was a Rob I hadn't recognized or appreciated until now. Maybe he *could* help me.

My new friend wasn't quite through. "I want to remain your friend throughout my life," he said. "After you go back to America, I'll come, as well." He wasn't embarrassed by the words. On the contrary, he seemed proud of them.

"It's a deal then," I said. "A lifetime ahead of us."

12

THE BOY WITH LATENT SPUNK

By the first of December my mission count was up to 27 and, as I told Pat, I, too, was a veteran. Newer pilots have asked me the same questions I had asked a couple of months earlier. Of course this added to my self-confidence, never a bad thing.

"The ground troops are slogging their way towards the Rhine River," I said. We were sitting in the mess hall over coffee, just like a couple of civilians during peace time. There was a mission on today, but we had not been included. Pat had the *Stars and Stripes* open in front of him. "Listen to this," he said:

> The Germans showed they were not ready to concede even a hard-nosed victory to the Allies. Under cover of heavy fog, 38 German divisions struck along a 50-mile front. The mechanized Nazi units overran several First Army positions in Bastogne in the southern Ardennes. Fighting in the intense cold, the Allies suffered major casualties.

"Doesn't sound so good, does it, Rick?"

"Sounds terrible. They're calling it the Battle of the Bulge."

"Not a very attractive name."

"Wonder how it will affect we flyboys?"

"We'll be flying every day from now on. We'll be up tomorrow, odds on."

The war had entered a new, unexpected phase. I was in total admiration for the Infantry units battling attacks, cold, disease, and the loss of pals.

"We fly and fight and return each night to our snug beds in our little Quonset hut." I said, "while the ground troops slog their way to death or glory." I cast a level look at Pat and added, "I wouldn't be here now if that was the way I had to fight a war. I'd have gone back to peaceful Colorado, and right now I'd be wrapping my arms around some chick."

"Okay, enough of this. You want to play ping pong?"

"You want to take on the base champ?"

"I'll go easy on you." We walked over to the Game Room and there was Lieutenant Bailey practicing his offense against one of his pals. He was facing away from us and didn't see us. We backed out of the room. I didn't want any part of Bailey today.

"Pat, you know you're the only guy I can talk to in the whole Group. Maybe if I got to know Burks better he'd also be a good guy to talk with."

"What do you want, an ear for some of your wild ideas?"

"I'm fresh out, Pat. But I appreciate the offer. These other guys—like Bailey and his pals—they're surface guys. They're pretty much smart-ass, into drinking too much, chasing dames, and maybe stealing a jeep now and then."

"I hate to disillusion you, Lieutenant Hot-shot Linden, but you are among the best at those particular activities yourself. Some would say you are *the* best."

"Oh, I know, I know. No excuse, sir. Right now I think I'll chase on back to the barracks and finish a letter to my folks I started last night. What are you going to do?"

"Oh, I'll be around. See what's happening in the club. Maybe try a bit of poker or bridge. Write letters myself. I owe a lot of letters to people back home. Got to keep their spirits up."

"Then I'll see you, Pat."

I liked writing to my parents. I had asked them to save all my letters so that I would have the basis for a war memoir someday. Or even a short story about how it was to fly in fighters in an all-out war.

I reviewed what I had written and found it was not so hot. Too lazy to re-write, I simply added a few words:

To everything there is a season, a time of war and a time of peace. That is from Ecclesiastics and it is cool and true. Some day soon it will be the time for peace again---and time for love. But time does not flow, it stands still in patches. There is love and there is peace. It is like being a little kid again and then growing old in an hour and then being thrown into the middle. And there are no good answers.

Still in the writing mood, I wrote three more letters: to my best lady friend Bo, to my tennis partner Rollie, and to a gal I'd been writing to off and on since we'd met at a dance pavilion in Pecos, Texas. She'd fallen for me, I guess, and she wasn't letting go. I thought of my letters to her as "bucking up" the home folks.

It'd been three or four days since the hike up Roans Peak. I hadn't been down to the fishing hole. I had some vague thought that perhaps I was too much an influence in Rob's life. But, after finishing my letter-writing, I wanted to get out of the dumb tin hut and do something. A thought occurred to me: what if he was waiting for me? What if he had waited every day?

He was there, looking cold and lonely. God, what a life Rob had. I decided not to press him on whether he was going to move in with his aunt. I hoped he would, although that meant I would lose him as a friend.

"I forgot the candy, Rob."

"Do you think I care about that? I don't come here for sweets, Rick."

"I never thought you did, fella. Did you decide anything about your immediate future?"

"I'm staying here, Rick. Father is not so bad. I just ignore him. If he hits me, I hit him back. It's hard on mum, but I can't help that." He looked away from me for a moment. "I'm staying because you're here. I want to know you as long as I can. Do you mind my saying that?"

Usually I'm unflappable but he was reaching me now. I would be careful with my response. "Actually, I'm flattered. Thanks for putting it that way. But—well, I'll level with you. Here I am, a 23-year-old happy-go-lucky type of guy, and you probably think of me as a pseudo parent or an older brother."

"What's wrong with that?"

"Nothing. I kinda like the job. But don't you have a friend of your parents, or a pastor, or a teacher, someone who could give you a better perspective on how to live life than me. Someone who knows you better than I do, for openers."

"There's no one who knows me better than you do, Rick. And there's no older person to talk to. Except you."

That led to a void in the conversation. Neither one of us cared to pick up on where we were. But emotion was everywhere around.

I quickly changed the subject. "I was finally issued a pair of silk gloves and a pair of chamois to wear over them, then a pair of gauntlets to wear over that. And I have a G-suit and my name is on the board about every other day. I now know all about the wild blue yonder I've been singing about since cadet days. Conclusion: I'm a happy flyer."

"If you're happy, then I'm happy, too," he said. But his eyes were bleak.

Before we separated, I told him I'd arranged for a jeep for the next afternoon. "So—four o'clock here. I've always wanted to find out how fast these neat little vehicles go. We'll whiz around your countryside with abandon."

The cloudy look on his face disappeared in a trice. There was nothing wrong with this kid that some treat like riding a jeep with his best friend couldn't fix. But, I realized, this was only a temporary fix.

The evening meal was over and we'd wolfed down the steak cook had been promising for two weeks. My stomach was filled, my spirits were in the mid-levels, and I decided to look for Major Burks.

He was sitting at a table by the window with our C.O., Col. Warren, apparently in an intense discussion. I certainly didn't want to interrupt all this brass, but the Colonel, apparently just leaving, saw me, and guessed my desire to talk to Burks. He waved me over.

"Hello, Linden," he said, cordially. "I hear good things about you from Squadron. Keep it up." He smiled and strolled out of the club, no doubt aware that his presence in an officer's club probably inhibited most of the inhabitants. Oh, the lonely life of a commander.

Burks was his usual self, cigar centered in his mouth, drink handy. "Hello, Rick." It was only the second time he'd used my given name. "Have a seat."

I joined him, slouching in one of the deepest chairs in the lounge. He usually preferred to be alone but now he seemed friendly and perhaps ready for a talk.

I needed his advice but I didn't want to blurt it right out. I'd let things develop.

"So, Lieutenant Linden. What are you up to tonight?"

"Killing time, Major. At 2000 hours I want to check the board to see if I'm flying tomorrow."

"I remember those days, Rick. In World War I. I was just a 19-year-old, but I learned how to kill and drink and a few other things, all before I turned 21."

"Sounds like some things don't change much over the years. If you're comfortable about it, sir, I wanted to ask you something."

"Do a favor for me first, will you? Get me another cigar, same brand, then fill my glass with brandy. Same for you, including the cigar. On my tab."

"I'm not much of a smoker, sir."

"You're going to have a cigar tonight or I'm not going to answer any of your questions."

"What makes you think I have questions?"

"I know you have something to talk about or you wouldn't be here."

I smiled. "You haven't lost your touch, sir. I'll be right back."

We sipped brandy and smoked good cigars in silence until he finally looked me in the eye. I noticed for the first time that his face was slightly scarred from some ancient combat wound. For the first time he looked his age, which I put at about 45. "So what did you want to know?"

"I've heard that you make it a point to meet our neighbors around the perimeter, Major."

"Yes, I've met nearly all of them by now, Linden. Complaints, mostly, about noise, smoke, danger. Some of them think we have no right to be here. Others are swell, of course. Whom are you inquiring about?"

"Why do you think I'm inquiring about anyone?"

"Spare me the naivete, Linden. Let me guess: the town grouch, St. Clair."

"That's pretty psychic."

"Give me some credit, son. I've been around. You're interested in the St. Clair family. House on the end of the tract about opposite the eastern end of Runway 22-40. I had a chat with the father. Been here two-three years. Moved here from London."

"What do you think of him?"

"A jerk of the first water. Pompous, bombastic, mean-tempered. Let's see, what else? Treats his wife and son like dirt."

"And the wife, Major?"

"Scared of the old man, as who wouldn't be? Keeps peace in the family. Stays out of the way."

"And the son?"

He looked at me in silence. "You know, Linden, I've been spouting off here pretty regular. I'm usually the one who asks questions. You're pumping me pretty good. Now if I didn't know your reputation with the fair sex, I'd start to wonder. You're interested in this young man, and it's my turn to ask a question. Why?"

"It's just that I've become his friend, sir. What do you think of him?"

He looked at me for several long seconds, puffing away on his cigar. "Believe me, Linden, you won't get out of here tonight without some answers for *me*. I'll give you my take on the kid. He's clearly under his father's yoke. Not quite old enough to stand up to him. He'd like to run away but he's probably scared to. Or perhaps he has no place to go. His mother can't help him. I'd say he has some spunk around somewhere. Latent spunk." He cocked his head. "But something tells me you already knew all that."

"You're a regular detective, Major."

"Is that all you're going to say, or do I start my intensive grilling technique?"

I smiled. "Well, Rob and I have become pretty good friends. I like encouraging him. I like helping him. He's a decent kid and he's so unhappy it hurts. So I spend a little time with him."

"Yeah, tea in the village. Climbing a mountain. And doing a lot of fishing, in season or not."

"Are all PROs' as observant as you?"

"None that I know of. What's this all about, Rick? Where does it lead?"

"I don't know, sir. I'll just keep on being a big brother to him."

"Nice of you—I guess. Remember, Lieutenant, you're a combat pilot. Anything that takes your mind off flying Mustangs is suspect. And dangerous."

"Come on, Major Burks. I go to London every chance I get. There are two girls there who say they want to marry me. What's the harm in being friendly to a neighbor boy?"

"I didn't quite say there was anything harmful in it. Just keep your mind on flying combat."

"Believe me, Major, I'm going to do the best flying I'm capable of for the next 20 or so missions, then it's back to the Rocky Mountains for me."

"Where does that leave young St. Clair?"

"He's maturing rapidly. He'll be all right."

We talked of other things then and I let him buy me one more drink, my limit since I didn't know if I'd be flying the next morning. The thing about Major Burks was that he always insisted on buying. "I'm on flight pay, too, you know," he said, "and I'm not getting shot at. So let me do this." He flicked a cigar ash my way. "Just don't let the word get around the base that the PRO can be had that easily."

I flew my 30th mission in the morning and took Rob for a jeep ride in late afternoon. His doldrums from the previous day disappeared with the exhilarating experience of fast driving in an open air vehicle along narrow country roads, supper by a creek that reminded me of the River Thom, and fleeting views of a late fall day in rural Sussex.

That whole day I had carried a letter in my pocket from Anne. She invited me to visit her in London when I could get a short leave. I'd brought it along to show to Rob, but something held me back. Would he be jealous? Life already had all the complications I needed. I decided to read him the poem she had signed off with. It was a sort of prayer which, she said, had been on the cover of her church bulletin the previous Sunday:

This is my song, O God of all nations
A song of peace for lands afar and mine
This is my home, where my heart is,
Here are my hopes, my dreams, my shrine,
But other hearts in other lands are beating
With hopes and dreams as high as mine.

13

THE CALL OF LONDON

Three days after my talk with Major Burks, the 98th Group flew halfway to Berlin to meet returning Eighth Air Force bombers. The Luftwaffe had nearly disappeared from the skies, but there was always flak. The pellets of death scared the hell out of me. Our group flew four days in a row while losing just one plane. The killing game was unpredictable, but it was always deadly.

I had placed my plans on hold to meet Anne in London. I counted on the brass giving us a short leave to help us recover from those consecutive days of flights. Somewhat amazingly, they did, and I telephoned Anne to see if the following Monday would work out for her. It did. I would draw a 48-hour pass, which meant I would have two nights with Anne. I didn't know how it would turn out, but I could hope. Perhaps the old Linden charm, successful in America, would work here, too.

I wanted to let Rob know my plans—no more waiting at the creek for a friend who didn't show. Since it was raining lightly I jogged the distance. Why did it always rain on our off day? He wasn't there. It occurred to me that he had a life outside of me—perhaps a project at school or with his crazy friend Colin—but then I dismissed that thought. He'd told me I was the only life he cared about, except for his mother.

Then Rob arrived on the run, neatly snaring the candy bar I tossed him. I told him about my coming trip to London.

And it was a mistake. I thought I knew why. He wasn't in the mood to share me with anyone, even with Anne, whom I'd told him about. I could tell by his short answers, his lack of interest, and his sullen looks that he was at least envious, maybe jealous?

His demeanor soured even more when I asked him if he had heard anything further about his brother. He told me that our mutual friend Major Burks has found out a bit about Geoffrey.

"Amazing that you've met—and liked, too, huh?—the PRO. Looks like he's a friend to both of us."

"We're still doing it, Rick. Finding things we have in common."

"We have so many now I can't keep track of them. That's destiny at work again."

That drew a loud "Hah" and I felt he was his old self. We didn't talk long this day; he said he'd better get home.

I did some quick figuring. "Then I'll see you Wednesday. The usual time—four o'clock."

"I'll be here, Rick." His face fell again and I figured he had just remembered that I was leaving him to spend a few days with someone other than himself.

While Anne prepared dinner I selected several of my favorite records, hoping they'd be hers, as well. I came up with *Stardust, Moonlight Cocktails, I'll Get By—* the sweet romantic tunes of the early 40s.

Anne was simply ravishing. She had cut her hair shorter and I didn't see how it could have looked better, never mind the length. I told her how happy I was to see her and she asked me how my life as a fighter pilot was doing.

"Funny thing, Anne. I love it and I hate it. Flying a plane like the P-51 is pure joy, though it's work, as well. Being in sole command of a streaking airplane, seeing the world from a new angle. But I have to keep reminding myself, I'm not up there joyriding. I'm there for a purpose. To kill the hated Germans. My machine gun bullets kill people just as dead as those from bombers or battleships. And it makes me sad as hell."

I could see that Anne felt the same as me. Enough said. I was determined to get off war and flying and talk about some of the joyful things of life—Suffolk, her grandmother, the odd things that happened during London blackouts, trips we would make after the war, when Noel Coward's new play was due.

We dined at a tiny table in front of a glowing coal stove. It was about as romantic as you could expect in wartime London. The sweet music helped. We talked of her early life in Bury St.

Edmunds and mine in Colorado Springs. We decided our two cities, about the same size, would get along with each other.

I had noticed a fold-up bed in the sitting room of her tiny flat. I pictured myself there before long, after we'd tired of music and talk. And the picture, when the lens was opened wide, would include Anne.

Late in the evening we danced to *Stardust,* playing for perhaps the fourth time. It was pure heaven sharing cheeks with a beautiful girl. The lights were low and romantic music stroked our ears from the background. We kissed long and passionately.

A little later, I said, "Getting sleepy, Anne?"

She knew what I meant and she didn't hesitate. She placed her hands on my shoulders. "I don't want you to sleep here tonight, Rick. I'm still Ian's girl. But," she held a long shrug, "His ship is in port and I have a dinner date with him tomorrow night. We're going to talk. I honestly don't know what the outcome will be."

I took it philosophically. My destiny with Anne was in other people's hands. What will be will be. I left a bit before midnight with little idea of where I was going to sleep. I found out rather quickly that there are places in London where the underground doesn't run. At least not directly. So I decided to walk—about five miles, I estimated—to a Red Cross Club. I enjoyed the walk in the darkness. Frustration and anticipation balanced about equally.

The next morning I looked for a gift for Anne. The best I could find was a white silk scarf. I had no idea whether this was a proper gift for my girl; I never had been good at buying gifts. With Anne at work I had the day to kill. I picked out a book from the club library, *Sky Pilot in No Man's Land,* because I liked the title. I didn't care for the writing, however, and gave it up. I had lunch at the club then watched several boys play a kick-ball game in the street. I wondered what game they were playing.

A scruffy-looking 12-year-old came up to me and asked if I wanted to play football. I figured he meant soccer. It was a sport I had not tried but they needed me to even up the sides and I figured I could sort out the rules in short order. I spent a pleasant hour with the group of nine youngsters, kicking, bouncing, running, passing, and trying to keep my feet under me.

I grew careless. Caught up in the pace of the game, I kicked the ball hard—and it wasn't there. Down I went on my butt. I managed to skin my arm and a leg, too. Just like I used to on the streets of Colorado Springs when I was their age. The kids snickered a bit to see this grown man make a fool of himself, but I got up and went on with the game.

I even scored a goal, I think. The kids cheered me, so I must have.

"Want to play tomorra?" the kid who'd asked me to play said when we quit.

"Sorry, I can't. I've got a train or maybe a plane to catch tomorrow." The boys stared at me in awe and then waved as they ran off in several directions.

I walked all the way back to Anne's flat. It didn't help that I got lost along the way. No map; poor planning, Linden. It was five o'clock when I arrived. I saw a note on the front door.

I hope you are enjoying yourself in my town. Don't get lost. I'm off for an early dinner with Ian. I should be back about 8:30 or 9:00. I don't know how it will work out, Rick. I don't even know how I want it to work out.

The last line bothered me a bit, but you can't change fate, can you?

I had a few more hours before she could be expected to arrive. I remembered seeing a pub a block or two away and I whiled away an hour or so playing darts with a couple of old-timers. I limited myself to two beers. I wanted to be at my best pending how my girl would decide my fate. I picked up some daisies at a flower shop and drifted back to her flat. As I walked up the front steps, a taxi, small and black and nondescript, arrived.

I watched nervously as Anne paid the fare. Then she turned to me while a most delightful smile lit her face. She rushed towards me and I opened my arms as she flew into them.

She whispered in my ear. "I was wrong in my note. I knew how I wanted it to turn out, and it did, Rick. Ian and I have broken our engagement."

I couldn't remember ever hearing any sweeter words.

We repeated our actions of the previous night: supper, music in the background, flickering candlelights. But we hastened through dinner without a lot of talk. The time for talk had passed. The fold-up bed got some well-planned use that night.

The train arrived at Ridgewell station about 5:30. I had been gone exactly 51 hours. And what a time it had been. I could face combat again as soon as tomorrow morning. Then I thought of facing something else—or someone else—and I nearly detoured to the creek. But surely Rob wouldn't be there this late. I had told him my schedule.

I was sick the next day. I had not been scheduled for a mission, anyway, so there was no harm done. Major Burks came to my hut. "Did a little poon-tang make you sick to your stomach?"

"My lord, Major Burks, you have the best network of spies of anyone I've run into."

He laughed. "That was a pure guess. But your red face sort of serves up the answer."

"In civilian life, you'd be a crackerjack detective."

"I came over to talk about Rob St. Clair. You're pretty close to that kid. Have you thought this out? What if you 'bought the farm' as we used to say in the Great War? I seriously doubt if he could handle it."

"I'm not going down, Major. I know it. Once I get aloft, I'm untouchable."

"That's nonsense and you know it. Listen, I'm old enough to be your father...."

"I doubt that."

"...and so I feel justified in giving you a bit of fatherly advice. Ease off a bit with young St. Clair. He's got a brother missing, probably dead, you know."

"He told me about it."

"If he lost you both, he'd be in a bad way, indeed."

"I suppose that's true, but why talk about me dying? I love the sky, Major Burks. The sky would never harm me. I've only got 20 or so missions to go then I'll be on my way home in a month, month and a half."

"All right, forget your imminent death. You're too ornery to die, anyway. But when you go home, it'll be the same result for St. Clair. He'll miss you terribly."

"Of course that's occurred to me, sir. I know Rob will think I've deserted him. So maybe I won't be in a hurry to go. I'll stay on. Perhaps for several months. They're going to need pilots on the continent. For re-building, helping refugees, hauling food in, ferrying the troops home. I'll volunteer for any or all of it.

96

That'll keep me flying the plane I love, and also keep me within shouting distance of Rob."

"You said the other night at the club that you could hardly wait to see the Rockies."

"I say a lot of things. Some are true, some are not."

"Don't parry words with me, Linden. But if you mean you'd put the welfare of a lost 15-year-old over your natural desire to go home, then I tip my hat to you."

There didn't seem to be anything to say to that, and a moment later Burks stood up and put on his cap. "Well, I'm glad you're not seriously sick. I've said what I came over to say. But think about what I said."

"Yes, father."

It was a facetious thing to say to a superior officer, friend or not, but he only turned back and said, "You're incorrigible, Linden." He left without another word.

I was just down for a day. I figured it was the food at the Red Cross or on the train that had felled me for a short time. It certainly wasn't Anne's cooking.

It wasn't until Saturday afternoon that I saw Rob again. I told him that I hoped he hadn't waited for me the past two days.

"Three," he said. He looked sad rather than upset. I think he must have thought he was beginning to lose my friendship.

I counted aloud. "Wednesday, back late from London. Thursday, mission and didn't return until after five. And yesterday I was sick. There was no way I could get word to you."

His countenance cleared up immediately. "I'm sorry you were sick."

"I'm okay now. Hey, want to hear about my trip to London?"

The downcast look re-appeared but I ignored it. "Anne kicked me out the first night and I had to walk five miles to find a place to sleep." I told him I'd played a little football and fell on my butt. "The kids tried not to laugh but they couldn't hold it back."

He grinned widely. "I think it was great of you to play with a bunch of kids. They probably didn't know that you were a famous author and fighter pilot."

"Forget the famous. Just call me lucky."

97

He was quiet for a long moment, then he suddenly asked, "Did you walk to the Red Cross Club the second night, as well?"

I took my time answering, "No—I stayed at her house the second night."

He came out of the blue with "Did you fuck her?"

His words and manner stunned me. My mouth fell open. "That's not an appropriate question, Rob. I didn't think you used that word."

"I don't use it, except in fun with Colin."

"Rob, forget that word and what it means. Your time will come. Meanwhile, let's just have fun and talk about our futures. Both our futures."

"Are you going to answer my question?"

"Nope."

"Why not?"

"Because some things are best not discussed even between friends. And because you're pretty young. I have a relationship with Anne. Nothing serious yet. She's a delightful person. That fair enough, friend?"

"You think I'm too young to be your confidant?"

"Hey, Rob, let's get off this. You *are* my confidant. Haven't I told you that several times? Haven't I invited you to school, to live with me and my parents. If you *want* to."

"I want to," he said, softly. "Even if you won't answer my question. I'm—I'm sorry, Rick It's just that—that I need to know everything about you, everything."

"You never know everything about another person, even a close friend."

We were both silent and I began to think of how I could end this encounter.

He got up suddenly. "I better get home."

"Okay, Rob. We're still friends, right? Listen, I have a ferry job tomorrow to France. We'll be back late. I don't want you to hang out here waiting for me again. How about if we make it Monday at four o'clock?"

"Roger, Rick." It tickled me that he used Air Corps slang now and then. "S'long."

14

RICK THE SECOND IS BORN

I was on board for a mission on Monday, December 20th. The previous day had been a breeze, a milk run. Six of us ferried new P-51s to an advanced American base in France. There was no flak, no enemy aircraft, no excitement. We flew in loose formation; it was a joy not to worry about the Krauts shooting at us. We talked back and forth by radio, practiced a few slow rolls en route and landed at the base in France. Then we took a nap. Yes, a nap.

Our leader, Capt. Daniels, told us we were to be picked up by a C-47 dispatched from England to return us to Ridgewell. He opined that it wouldn't be in for an hour or more, so he told us to relax. Sleep if you want to. You'll hear the Gooney Bird come in.

We took his suggestion to heart and lay on hammocks set up outside the barracks. I closed my eyes and thought of the troops slogging it out on the road to Berlin. I thanked God again for putting me into a fighter plane with no one to look after except myself.

I had meant what I told Major Burks about staying in England for awhile. But I wanted to get to the states, as well. I would spend time with my folks, my girl Bo, my best friend Rollie, and sister Jane, along with a few others. I would visit my old fraternity and say hello to a few 18-year-olds who might be hanging around. And I would contact my agent, Glenn Fox, to see how my book was doing. I hadn't heard from him lately, but he had said it was good enough to find a publisher. Hmm.

Before I left England, I would have to decide whether to return. That would depend on a lot of things: whether I was called to duty in the Pacific, how my book was coming, my attitude about England from across the ocean, and my updated opinion about two people I cared about. Anne was special to me; she possessed what I had always admired in girls: beauty, charm, and intelligence. And Rob St. Clair. If I could get him out of the trap of his life, I would almost literally be saving his life.

Thinking of Rob reminded me that I had told him I wanted to change the world. Wow, Linden. *Change the world.* What kind of crazy, conceited thoughts were these? But I hadn't been talking nonsense to Rob on Roans Peak. I meant to do some things— perhaps great things—before I was done with this world.

God, Linden, you've bitten off a horrendous chunk of goals. Life's work, indeed. Well, I would try damn hard and see what happened. I had always been a devotee of "Nothing ventured, nothing gained."

I dreamed on for a few more moments until I fell asleep. An hour later we heard the drone of an incoming C-47 cargo plane and knew our short respite from war had ended.

The mission the following day was something else. My name was on the board to fly my 37th mission, escorting B-24 Liberators to Berlin. It sounded like a bitch of a mission—long, boring, tiring, with flak coming up to meet us in forever quantities.

Rob was there at the fence to wave as I lifted off just opposite him. I waved back. It had become a ritual of sorts, not every time I flew, but many times. We departed at 0800 hours to allow the bombers time to drop their bombs. We would escort them home. Another fighter wing had escorted them inbound on their way to Germany.

The sky was clear and, because there were no clouds to dodge behind, menacing, as well. But no enemy fighters challenged us and I was not surprised. Perhaps the Luftwaffe was grounded for the duration. The anti-aircraft boys had not retired, though, and random shards of steel came winging up to meet us.

One of the Liberators took a massive hit in a vital spot. The huge bomber headed for the ground at a moderate pitch. The pilot was working hard to get his men out, and he was succeeding. I saw five parachutes blossoming beneath the stricken plane, but five other men were still aboard, centrifugal force probably keeping them glued to their positions. God, to die in a plunging plane during the last few months of the war. What a way to go. I silently renewed my vow to work towards peace for the world. This kind of scene did not have to happen.

We were just about out of Germany when one of our fighters caught a burst. He was flying two flights over, in another squadron, and I doubted I knew the pilot. But then I had a premonition—that it was Pat Morse, my best buddy. I don't know why I thought so, I just did.

I radioed our squadron leader, Dynamite Three, asking for permission to see if I could help the Mustang in trouble. He responded to proceed with caution and to return to our formation within a few minutes. I snapped out a "Roger, Leader," and peeled off to the right, out of fighter formation.

It *was* Pat in *Little Eva;* his plane was destined for mother earth. But Pat was apparently alive and in at least some control, because he was holding his plane relatively level. I shoved the throttle to the hilt and soon caught up to him.

"Get out of there, Pat," I yelled into the radio. There was no response. Then I saw a flash of flames, a new and deadly threat. *Come back, Pat. I want to have long talks with you, I want to visit you in Connecticut, I want you to visit me in Colorado. Don't die this way, Patrick.* My thoughts were spinning and wild and meaningless. There was no way I could help him. Then I prayed to God, and *He* helped my friend.

Pat's Mustang flew straight and level for no more than 20 seconds, but it was enough. I watched as he climbed out of the cockpit. He lifted an arm. I thought he saw me, perhaps recognized me: he was close enough. He had no time for fraternizing. In a moment he was clear of the cockpit. I watched with thankfulness as his parachute blossomed. *Thank you, God.*

I flew home in a happy daze. I would see Pat again. He would probably return to our base tomorrow or the following day. I expected that I would be scheduled tomorrow also, probably because I'd had that wonderful two-day pass. I set the plane down in a perfect landing, perhaps my best yet. I was a bit tired, a bit proud, and very thankful for Pat's life.

We sat on the same log as when we'd first met and exchanged reports on our recent past. He told me of trouble at school, of the shenanigans of his wacky buddy Colin, and of his relentlessly unhappy life at home. And I told him about sleeping in the sun in France, which drew a smile from him. Then, since he'd met Pat on two or three occasions, I told him of his stricken P-51 and his miraculous bail-out over friendly territory.

Rob looked steadily at me; tears formed at the edge of his eyes. "That could have been you, Rick," he said in a low voice. "You're still in danger. Do you have to keep flying?"

I told him the war wasn't over until Hitler was dead, and he was kicking the last time I'd heard. "There's not much danger any more. It's like a Sunday ride in a roller coaster—a great feeling. I wouldn't pull myself off the roster even if I could."

Rob had no answer to that. Then, since his parents were out until about eight o'clock, I suggested we go into Ridgewell for supper. I told him there was something serious I wanted to talk to him about.

"That's a wizard idea, Rick."

"When you come to Colorado," I began, to remind him he had a future with me, "you'll meet my parents. You'll like them. Everyone does. Ruth. Sweet, caring, loving, a good mother. And old Alex, my dad. He doesn't lose his temper often but he lets you know when you've done something that doesn't square with his way of thinking. But deep down he's a pushover. You'll see.

"And Jane, my sis. She has a mind of her own, does she ever. But we've done a lot of things together. I taught her to play tennis and now she can beat me. Well, once in awhile. She did beat my record up Longs Peak. She has a scholarship to Stanford going. Got a guy, I heard."

He was listening wide-eyed. I thought he was comparing my All-American family with his own. He spoke for the first time in several minutes. "When I come to America I want to be your younger brother. I could change my name to Linden. Rob Linden: how does that sound?"

I did a double-take. "That's a bit far out. But sure, join the family. Be a Linden in all but name, anyway. Hang out with us. But—you would need your parents' approval."

He made a sour face at that but he was too exhilarated to let it stay on for long.

By this time I was on my third beer and he on his second cup of tea. He told me, his face glowing, that he had never felt as excited about his life as at this moment. He said there was real promise now that things would change for him. "And I remember full well our discussion on Roans Peak. I know what your passions are, Rick: peace for the world, writing and influencing people, and educating everyone."

"Good memory, Rob. Yes, those are my lifetime goals. As I see this god damned war ending—sorry, I told your father I didn't use bad words—I'm getting closer every day to doing something about them. And I am going to do some things, Rob, that maybe will make your hair curl. It's going to be my life. I've had my fun—flying a Mustang, romancing English girls, roaming England, getting on intimate terms with a war, writing a book. Meeting some great people, present company *included.* When the war is over, a new world will have to be built up from the ruins of the old. I want to be a part of it. A big part.

"A year from now I'll be somewhere exciting, in Colorado or New York or Timbuktu—and I'll remember these days in Ridgewell as being sort of mad and gay and horrible, all at the same time. And by that time I'll be on my way, according to my grand plan."

Emotion was running high on both sides of the table. I took the time to fill my glass, raise it on high, and wink at Rob. He winked back, tears in his eyes. I had talked pretty big for ten minutes. Now I waited for Rob to have his say.

"Rick," he began, and he waited while I fixed my blue eyes on his brown ones. "You can't do this alone. You'll need helpers, disciples, just like Jesus Christ had."

"Whoa!" I looked at him thoughtfully; he had apparently just compared me to Jesus. "I wouldn't use the word 'disciple' in that sense. But you have the general idea. I'll need people who believe as I do, and are willing to do what it takes to get the job done. I could never do it alone."

He looked at me eagerly. "Then, don't you see, Rick, you have your first disciple—sorry, follower. Because I believe in those goals, too. Since you do, I do."

I set my mug down and looked directly at him. I spoke clearly and slowly, heedless of the bar noises in the pub. "Listen, kid, and this is important. Don't follow me because *I* believe the way I do. Follow me because you believe that way, too, assuming you do."

He took a deep breath and said, "I'm too young to have such ideas and goals. I might never have them. I need someone like you who does. I'll follow you anywhere. Don't you see—I'm too inexperienced and too emotional to accomplish anything like you said. I just want to string along with you, help you in a small way. And I'll give you a lifetime of loyalty."

That kind of loyalty prickled my skin. This was some kid. His eyes, brown and wide and soul-searching right now, bore into mine. I thought about playing it down, telling him he should finish school, then let me know if he was still interested. But I knew, intuitively, that this would break his heart. I took my time, downed my ale, and waved at Mac the bartender for another. I fixed my best steely look on him. I wanted him to know that I wasn't just talking in a noisy pub, that I meant what I was about to say, that this was serious business, indeed.

"Okay, Rob, I hear you loud and clear. If you were drinking beer like me I would put it down to the liquor talking. But tea? Can't be done. So I know you're serious and I respect that and I'm very flattered. But, Robbie, when you're older your values and interests will undoubtedly change. I'm a friend who's in your life now, but I won't be for long. You'll go to university, meet all sorts of interesting people, and hopefully some inspiring teachers along the way. Your ideas two years from now may be completely different than they are at this moment."

He stared at me, tears in his eyes, heedless of the pub's chatter and smoke. "I'm ready now, Rick Linden. Now. I'm going to be 16 next birthday and I know my mind. I don't care if you go back to America and I don't see you for a year. I'll never forget you.

"Rick, Rick, I don't want to be put off like a little kid who asks for one treat too many. I want to---" he stopped, unable to go on. I was embarrassed for him and disgusted with myself. I should never have let it go this far. Then, before I could form the right words, he added, "I want to be *Rick Linden the Second*."

He certainly had the capacity to stun me. I knew he was watching for my reaction, and I immediately dismissed rejection of the phrase. It would break his heart. I decided I must speak from *my* heart. And very carefully.

"Hmm. You've just coined a new phrase, you know that? It's terribly complimentary. I rather like the sound of it: Rick Linden the Second."

He brightened immediately and his tears disappeared. Neither of us could speak. I didn't know where this was headed. Then the romantic, impulsive Rick Linden surfaced, and I thought of something which might be the perfect climax to this very unusual conversation.

"Let's commemorate the occasion, lad. The occasion being that we'll work together after the war on the lofty goals we've both expressed. And we want to do this with ceremony." I spotted the bartender. "Hey, Mac, got any champagne? Yeah, two mugs of the best right over here. Thanks, mate."

I poured the champagne into both mugs and handed him one. "Your father will have to forgive me, but this is a special occasion. Drink up, Rob, but no more than half of it. I have something else in mind."

I drank deeply from my mug, watching him sip from his. "Ah-h-h, great stuff. Have you had a good taste? I have a surprise for the rest of the bubbly, and a proper one, if I do say so. So, young man, will you bow your head?"

He bowed, wonder in his eyes. I took his mug from his hand and poured the remainder of the champagne over his head and face. It was a deliberate and rather foolish act, and he looked at first startled, then angry, before a dawning happiness marched across his flushed face. He did not speak.

"Sorry, Robbie, that was a bit much. But it's done and can't be undone. So, here we go: *I hereby christen you Rick the Second, second-in-command, Executive Officer, and Adjutant to Richard P. Linden, Esq.* Do you accept the honor, Robert J. St. Clair?"

He regained his tongue quickly. "Yes, I do, sir," he said, solemnly. "I am hereby your slave forever in this great endeavor." He bowed his head again, then looked up slyly at me with a charming smile.

I felt I had over-dramatized the gesture, but he didn't. Not when the sly grin had turned into a broad smile, and a long wink sprinkled delightfully across his face.

We left soon afterwards, after I'd called for a towel so he could dry his hair. "It's seven o'clock and I've got to get back to the base. I'm on a mission tomorrow. It'll be an easy one, a milk run." And me with three beers and a half of bottle of champagne under my belt. "Are you ready to move out?"

A few minutes later I dropped him off at his parents' cottage. They were still out, thank God, so there was no scene. I didn't think his parents would catch the small whiff of champagne on their son's breath, but his elation would be hard to hide. I said as much to Rob.

"I'm going directly to my room and put a chair under the knob. I don't want to share this feeling with anyone."

Still, he didn't go inside, and something about his manner drew me to him. I hopped out of the jeep, strode up to the door and embraced him. This had happened only once before. He seemed slightly embarrassed and I drew back. To cover the possibly awkward moment, I looked up at the sky. "You know, Rob, the night sky is wonderful. Whenever I need power or to get through some ordeal, or just for inspiration—like now—I look up at the sky. It has a life of its own. To me the sky spells mystery and mysticism, and strength. Somehow, it's a symbol of the equality of man, everywhere. We all use the same sky.

"*'Someday, in that dark sky, the men of all nations will learn the true meaning of brotherly love.'* I read that somewhere and I've never forgotten it." My skin was prickling and Rob surprised me again.

"Is your skin prickling like mine is?" he asked. He rested his right hand on my shoulder. "It'll be our special slogan. I want to get it right. 'Someday, in that dark sky, the men of all nations will learn the true meaning of brotherly love.' I'll never forget it."

There was nothing more to say. I got behind the wheel of the jeep. He was still standing there, alternately looking at the sky and at me.

"Takeoff at eight tomorrow," I said. "Will you be there to watch me take off?"

He said softly, "I'll be there, Rick the First."

"So long, Rick the Second." My words were solemn and forever. I tossed him a two-fingered salute and drove off into the night.

PART IV

ROB ST. CLAIR

15

I KNEW IT IN MY BONES

It was seven o'clock on a cold December morning and I was wide awake. I could hear my father's snoring coming from my parents' bedroom. I left the house, closing the front door softly, then walked the 400-odd meters to the barbed wire fence separating our house from the air base. I began to appreciate why my father put up such a fuss about noise. It was deafening: the cacophony of sound from many planes warming up on a fighter base. Nevertheless, I gloried in the sounds; it made chills run up and down my spine.

Rick would be flying one of those warplanes, white scarf swirling around his neck, gloved hands manipulating throttle and stick, eyes wide open in concentration on the exciting maneuver. He had told me about it.

"Most people seem to think the landing is the most thrilling time during a flight. I find it during takeoff. You're at full power, much faster than at landing, concentrating on that powerful engine in front of you. You have to keep the plane straight and you have to be constantly alert. Of course, if I ever got on the tail of an ME-109 with a chance to shoot it down, I might change my mind. But for now, give me a full-power takeoff for the best of all thrills."

I didn't watch the flotilla of planes take off unless I knew Rick was flying. On this Tuesday, Rick was to take the air. So he has said last night, just before our emotional farewell. *Some day, in that dark sky, the men of all nations will learn the true meaning of brotherly love.* The phrase, already engraved on my memory, would remind me of Rick forever, when we were separated, when we were together. I still glowed at the memory of the raw emotion of last evening, of our kinship, of Rick the First. And now I was *Rick the Second*, and always would be.

I put one foot on the second barbed wire from the bottom, my hand on the top of the steel post. I looked hard at the lineup of P-51s awaiting takeoff. They were using the runway closest to my house because of the prevailing south wind.

There were 18 planes going aloft this day; I had counted the ones with propellers spinning. In only a moment's time, Rick's plane would appear opposite me. I knew I would easily recognize his aircraft, *Long's Lover* (after his favorite mountain, Longs Peak). An orange ring had been painted around the single engine. I had asked him what the circle meant.

"I dunno," he had answered. "I just liked it."

Four, then five Mustangs had roared by me, full power on in their takeoff runs, before I spotted the orange ring. He was the seventh plane in line. That's as it should be, I thought, seven being my lucky number.

Then Rick's plane was fast approaching my place on the fence and I could see the orange circle, the name *Long's Lover*, and even his name stenciled beneath it, Lt. Rick Linden. I looked hard at the cockpit, and there was Rick and he saw me at the same instant. He looked directly at me and gave me his little two-fingered salute. Then, tail up, his plane gained the power it needed to lift off and it seemed to float upward in a perfect takeoff.

The next few moments blurred and intermingled before my unbelieving senses. I heard a faltering in the powerful Merlin engine, then saw a red flare come shooting out of the tower, at the same time realizing there were no other planes taking off. Some plane was in trouble, and it could easily be—had to be, actually— Rick's Mustang. My heart was beating so rapidly that I thought it would burst my chest open.

Oh, Rick, Rick, what's going on? What's happening to you?

Regardless of regulations, regardless of any possible danger, I hopped the fence and ran out into the middle of the runway. A military policeman spotted me and started for me at a hard run.

It was Rick's plane, it was headed to the ground. His engine had failed, but good pilot that he was, Rick had kept his plane nearly level and was going in for a straight-ahead crash landing. The plane seemed under control, and I knew gratefulness beyond measure. God, God, thank you!

The MP reached me and grabbed me around the waist as I yelled desperately, "Let me go! That's Rick Linden, my friend." I had to see him safely on the ground again. His mission would be aborted and he could tell me about it himself within an hour or so.

The MP seemed to relax for a moment and we both squinted down the field with widespread eyes. Rick had retracted his landing gear at takeoff, and his plane plunged into the ground in what was the best crash landing—or worst normal landing—of his life. A cloud of dust obscured everything—by this time he was off the paved runway.

My heart sang with joy. He was on the ground. He was safe. Then, with an abruptness that was like a physical blow to my whole being, I saw flames reaching for the sky and a moment later heard an explosion that was beyond my wildest imagination. Rick's plane, loaded with high-octane gasoline as well as explosives, had simply disintegrated in front of my eyes.

I began to run to the stricken plane, but the MP brought me down with a lunging tackle. He man-handled me to the fence, then perhaps realizing that something extraordinary was going on, rather gently lifted me over the barbed wire fence.

"Go home, boy," he said. "This is no place for you. We have an emergency alert going on and you shouldn't be here. Go on home. That clear, kid?"

I don't know how I got home. Perhaps I walked, perhaps I crawled. Then I was there and my parents were there, too. Awakened by the explosion, they stood outside the front stoop, amazed to see me coming from the air field.

"Rob, what in holy hell are you doing out here? Get to your room now. No breakfast. Get in there, damn it."

I couldn't keep the tears from spilling, but I was so shocked and sad that I wasn't even embarrassed. I dashed to my room, unable to look at either one of them, unable to think beyond one single thought: Rick was dead. My friend was gone forever. And my life was as good as over, too.

A few minutes later my mother knocked on the door and peeked in. "Rob, can I help? Why are you so upset, dear? Listen, I'll bring you some breakfast. Never mind what your father says."

I summoned all my stretched resources and said, "Mum, I just want to be alone. I don't want breakfast. I don't want anything. I'm—I'm sick, mum. I'm feeling terrible. I just want to sleep all day. Will you do that for me, mum, if you love me?"

What mother could turn down that kind of plea? She said, softly, "All right, dear, I'll look in on you later."

She had hardly closed the door before I was out my window. Why had I so quickly accepted that it had been Rick's plane? Oh, lad of little faith. Perhaps it wasn't his plane. Or it if was, perhaps he had been thrown clear and survived. My heart pounded in my chest, painfully so.

The base was a bee-hive of activity. Fire trucks roared by, an ambulance was just disappearing in the direction of the crash, and military policemen were everywhere. I leaned over the fence and waved frantically at an MP—not the same one—and he finally came over.

"What is it, fella? We're awfully busy here."

"I—I live just over there. What happened?"

"Listen, I'm just going to tell you once, then I gotta get back to work. One of our planes lost power on takeoff and went in. It exploded. The pilot died in the crash." He started to turn away.

"Sir, sir." I yelled. "What was the pilot's name?"

"I can't tell you that, kid. Even if I knew. Now, get ---."

"My friend was flying one of those P-51s. His plane had an orange ring on its nose, and he was the seventh one off."

He looked a little more kindly at me. "I can tell you just one more fact. Then I want you out of here. Okay?" After I nodded, he added, "I understand six fighters got off okay but the seventh one went in."

I'd known it was Rick—I'd never had any real hope. But I had to try. Now I knew, and my life was over. I didn't want to continue without Rick Linden.

I couldn't go home. At first I walked aimlessly, but then my steps took me to the little stream where Rick and I had spent so many pleasant hours. I sat on the log where we'd shared a candy bar that first day, and many a talk since. Tears streamed down my face; I made no attempt to stop them.

How could this happen to Rick? How could God take him to His kingdom when there was so much to do in this one?

I slipped off the log and lay face up on the mossy bank. I felt as if I were looking down on a stricken soul from some faraway place. That couldn't be me down there absorbing this terrible news. I couldn't swallow; I couldn't talk. I turned onto my stomach and lay face down on the mossy bank, thinking of Rick. I counted each time we had met—I remembered 26 times, and I probably missed a couple. I had been with him 26 times in the 90 odd days of knowing him. It was supposed to be a lifetime but it had been only a handful of days.

A little later I heard the church bells chime nine times. I remembered lying in bed the previous night when I had the certain feeling that my life was about to change drastically. I had thought it was my destiny to go to America, but instead it was Rick's death that changed my life. The unfairness of it was painful. The certainty last night that our destinies were to have been joined had been so strong that I wondered now if that destiny was still meant to be. Perhaps I would join Rick in heaven. I stood overlooking the deepest pool, the one where the elusive trout lived, and thought a terrible thought: perhaps I should tie the heaviest boulder I could find to my body and just jump in. *Rick and I would be joined forever in heaven.*

I had always been a loner. Now I felt like one more than I ever had before. I wandered for hours, nearly all day. I walked into Ridgewell, sat on a bench in the center of town, walked out a lonely road to a park I knew, and watched a cricket match with absolutely no interest in the game. I sat on the grass, my back against a tree, for a long time. Unbidden, a line from a poem we had been studying—Keats, Shelley, I didn't remember—fled into my mind.

Eyes so bright with futile hope,
So dulled by the cloudy onrush of death.

I had felt sorry for myself all day. Now I needed to do some planning. I had no desire to return home. This was the time, I quickly concluded, to run away at last. But I needed to talk to someone about it—I was just not thinking clearly enough to decide anything by myself. The only friend I had now was Colin. I walked to his house and tapped on his bedroom window. He was there and a moment later I was through the window of his bedroom. He had met Rick two or three times and he knew my relationship with him. He had already heard the news and his first gesture embarrassed me: he hugged me to him.

Although about my age, Colin was smaller than I was by three inches and lighter by two stone. His freckles were what you noticed about him first. And his infectious grin. My mum was probably right in calling him unprincipled. But I wanted to confide in him now. I needed his quick mind. He was going to tell me what to do.

"That's easy as pie, Rob. We'll go back to my plan. Hitch to Bishop's Stortford for a fortnight, then off to London. I'll take care of you, Rob. I'll take Rick's place in your life."

The thought of Colin replacing Rick repelled me, and I left immediately without saying goodbye. Was this the best I could expect from my only school friend?

It was after four. I walked the short distance to my house with trepidation. I would face my parents down.

My father was livid, having waited all day to chew me out. My mother was loving but quiet and introspective. It was only her presence that kept my father from striking me, as old as I was. "I hear the pilot killed was that American you brought by one time. Linville, Linfield, whatever."

"His name was Rick Linden and he was my best friend," I said, tiredly. "I don't want to talk about it—not with you—and I'm going to my room."

"What do you mean 'not with me'?" he yelled. "And you're not going to your room. You sit right down there—there on the settee—and we'll damn well talk about it."

I was too dispirited to fight back.

"Reginald," my mum started, "Now is not a good time---."

"I'll handle this," he snapped, without looking at her. "I'm going to have it out with this disobedient, ungrateful son of yours right now." I sat on the edge of the settee and watched him warily. "Listen, Rob, this—pilot—was a god damned American. And much older than you. You won't even remember his name a month from now."

I lifted a tear-streaked face. "That's not true! I'll never forget him. He was like a brother. He understood me. He was my friend."

He stared at me. He probably couldn't believe I was defying him so openly.

I was on my feet, ready to dispel further hot words in defense of my friend, when there was a knock on the door. We all froze in our positions like statues.

"Damn it to hell, who could that be?" my father shouted.

I was amazed and happy to see Pat Morse on our doorstep. Ignoring the charged atmosphere in the room, he gave me a quick hug, then stepped back. "I'm so sorry, Rob. I understand your loss and I share it. Rick was one of the best people I ever met."

"Thank you, Mr. Morse. Rick—Rick told me about your bailing out. I'm—I'm glad you came back to us." I was happy about Pat's survival, but I was thinking of Rick.

My father, who had been standing there open-mouthed, finally got back in control. "Who the hell are you?" he asked Pat. "Who asked you into our house? If you're a friend of that dead pilot, that's reason enough to boot you out of here."

I could see that Pat Morse could hardly believe his ears. He had come over to pay his respects to me and instead took a blasting from the head of the household. After a moment of charged silence, he faced my father and said, "You're Rob's father, I assume. I'll leave in a minute. But I want you to know that if you were 20 years younger, I'd ask you outside and beat the hell out of you."

After Pat Morse left, I wanted no further part of the evening's events, although I didn't know there was to be one more act. I ran into my only haven, my bedroom, and put a chair under the knob. I lay down on my bed—to think, to cry perhaps, and even to scare up a small grin. My father's face had been so *purple.*

About two hours later, after seven o'clock, unbelievably there was another knock on the door. While my father went to answer it, I quickly took down the chair and sneaked into the kitchen, from where I could see and hear everything. My mum was there and I put a finger to my lips. I had a feeling I would want to know who the visitor was and what he had to say.

An Air Corps major stroke into the room, uninvited. He addressed my father. "Remember me? I'm Major Burks, PRO of the base you hate so much." He paused while my pater gaped.

"Now, usually public relations implies getting along with people. It means making friends. Well, I'll tell you, St. Clair, I was sitting fat, dumb, and happy in the Officer's Club an hour ago. I was sad because one of our pilots, a man I liked, was killed this morning. To partially offset the loss, another pilot was returned to us today from Belgium—Pat Morse, a close friend of Lieutenant Linden's. I invited Morse to have a cigar and brandy with me. We talked about Linden and Linden's friendship with your son." Major Burks' voice deepened. "And finally, after some probing from me, he told me the gist of what you said about Linden here in your house a couple of hours ago."

Father's face was red again, and he could barely stand still. "What the hell are you saying, and what the hell are you doing in my house?"

It amazed me how calm the major could be in this highly charged atmosphere. "I'm coming to that, St. Clair. Morse told me he would have knocked your block off except for the fact that you had twenty years on him. Well, St. Clair, I put us at close to the same age. So I'll just do it for him."

Without another word, Major Burks raised his right hand and slapped my father across the face. It was a powerful blow and my father staggered under the impact.

"If you want to do anything about that, we'll go outside. I don't want to mess up Mrs. St. Clair's living room with your blood." I could see the major was furious, and father saw it, as well. For once, he backed down. But he did have something to say.

"I'll have you kicked out of the army, you bastard. After I see your commanding officer tomorrow, he'll ship you right out to the front lines."

The major headed for the door. "I've done what I came to do. If you do see our C.O., I don't think you'll find him very sympathetic to your side of the story. Lieutenant Linden was a friend of his. But, if you're right, so be it. We'll leave that to fate." He left the house, slamming the door.

I quickly kissed my mum and went back to my bedroom. I wanted no part of father that evening. Or perhaps forever.

My father pounded on my door several times. I ignored him. He couldn't get past the tilted chair. I heard him muttering threats to me and to the American Air Corps. I lay on my bed and thought harder than I had in all my life. The easiest choice would be to stay home. But every atom of my being argued against that. I was sick of my life at home.

My hands clasped behind my head, I decided to see what my lost friend would say. I needed a sign.

Staring at the ceiling, I said aloud, *Rick, Rick, what should I do? I put my faith and future in you. And now you are gone.*

You advised me to stay at home. But that was when I had you as a friend. I could take it if you were here as my friend. Now you are—dead—and I am alone again. Rick, tell me what to do! Lying there in the dark, I experienced the most absolute sense of loss and helplessness in my life. Loss, because I'd seen Rick die that morning. Helplessness, because I knew Rick could never answer my urgent query.

And then he did. A late-flying fighter plane, returning from somewhere well after dark, buzzed the runway nearest our house. The sound was like a banshee gone wild. It made me start, shiver, and thrill all at the same time. That was Rick up there, or Rick's surrogate, answering my question. I had no hesitation on how to read the P-51 buzz job—which had never happened before.

You want me to change my life, don't you Rick? Away from my parents, from school, from Colin, from the airbase next door, even from constant memories of you. I read you well, Rick: take up Aunt Bea on her offer. Now. Run away from home.

A kind of peace came over me. I would act on it right away, tomorrow, as soon as my father was at work and my mum out of the house on one of her errands. I would leave everyone in my life without as much as a goodbye. I'd write a letter to mum from Manchester.

Exhausted both physically and mentally, I fell asleep.

It wasn't Rick who came into my dreams that night. That would come on other nights, when I had built up sufficient stamina to withstand them. But I did have one dream in which I saw the whole fabric of my life and all that had gone into making me. I felt the presence of my childhood, but then it faded away. I was a child no longer.

16

JOURNEY TO THE NORTH

It had been naïve to think I could leave the next day. I needed to get my money together, including two pounds I had loaned to Colin. I wanted to say goodbye to Pat Morse. And I needed to decide how I would take leave of my mother.

As for Rick Linden, one consoling thought helped me keep my sanity. He would be my friend forever. He would never drift away like other friends might—like even Rick might have if he'd lived. He would always be my buddy. What I couldn't take was the attitude of my parents. My mother seemed to have forgotten who he was, while my father reacted in the opposite manner: he delighted in bringing up Rick's name.

"Who?" my mother would say when I mentioned Rick. "Oh, you mean that American flyer? Well, we hardly knew him, did we?" And she would change the subject. My father was more direct: "Your Yankee friend is gone for good, eh? Now you won't have any more high and mighty ideas about moving to America. Yeah, I knew that's what him and you were thinking about. He might have become a god damned obsession."

He is an obsession, father, and damn your eyes.

Another time he said, "Lincoln came along and disrupted your life and ours. You should have listened to me."

I'll never listen to you again, father. And it's Linden.

Both times I left the room abruptly. It occurred to me that my pater was jealous of my friendship of Rick. He knew I had never shown that kind of passion with *him.*

These kind of contacts with my parents made it easier for me to leave home, perhaps forever.

*   *   *   *

A total surprise was a note pinned to the front door.

I thought you might like to have some of Rick's belongings. If you can meet me where you fished with Rick, I'll be there both today and tomorrow about four o'clock.

Pat Morse

His note thrilled me. It was already three o'clock. I said something to mum, then left for our old meeting place. The closer I got the worse I felt. It hit me again: I would never see red-haired Rick, with his welcoming smile and candy bar, waiting for me by the River Thom.

Pat arrived a few minutes after I did. We were both early.

We shook hands. I didn't think he would bring up Major Burks' visit to our home the evening before. He didn't, so I mentioned it and let him know how proud I was about Burks taking my father down a peg or two. He seemed surprised, but happy, with my reaction.

"I have some things for you, Rob," he said. He handed me a large package with Rick's spare flight cap, properly crushed as fighter pilots like them, a training manual on the P-51, a pair of gauntlets, and a shoulder patch with 8th Air Force on it. The prize of the lot was a pair of wings and silver first lieutenant's bars.

I took the package with a look of gratitude at Pat. It must have been hard for him to put this together.

"How are you doing, Rob? How are you *really* doing?"

I wished he hadn't put me on the spot. I decided to tell the truth. "Not very good," I said, looking at the ground to hide any tears that might surface.

He put his arm around my shoulder. "I want you to let me know if I can be of help, Rob."

"I will, Mr. – Pat. But I'm going to Manchester to live with my aunt. I may not see you again."

"When are you going?"

"Tomorrow."

"Then I won't see you. Perhaps we'll meet in America. Something tells me you'll be coming to my country someday. I'm going to give you my parent's address in Connecticut." He wrote on a piece of paper and handed it to me. "They can always find me." He smiled, clapped me on the shoulder again, scrambled up the bank and disappeared.

Somehow I got through the evening. I helped my Mum with the supper things and pretended to do homework in the sitting room with my father sitting ten feet away. I said good night to both of them about eight-thirty. There was no mention of Rick Linden by any of us. Before going to my bedroom, I doubled back to the kitchen and caught my mother around the waist. "Good night, Mum," I said, and kissed her on the cheek. She looked slightly surprised, slightly confused, but in the end she just patted me on the shoulder and said good night. What I would have liked to have said was "Good bye, Mum." But I couldn't do that; I was living in secrecy with everyone—parents, Colin, even Aunt Bea, who didn't know I was coming.

In bed, I could scarcely believe it was only yesterday morning that a fiery explosion had changed my world. Thus, the narrow sphere of my few years in Ridgewell would soon be abruptly breached while the greater world beckoned me with the promise of change and adventure. And continued heartbreak.

I would have to be careful on the way north so as not to look like a boy of fifteen on the run. I left for school at the regular time, but instead detoured to the station and purchased a one-way ticket to Manchester. I had packed the night before and left my suitcase outside my window so my parents wouldn't discover my flight. They would know about it soon enough.

The train whistle thrilled and depressed me. The shrill tone evoked a yearning in me that was hard for me to define. As I boarded, single bag in hand, I thought of far-away places and I knew my life would never be the same again. I had a bun and tea and called it a meal. I wished with all my heart that Rick was sitting beside me.

Beatrice St. Clair Horley was five years younger than her brother Reginald. They had been the only children in a family who seldom spoke a lighthearted word, who didn't take holidays, who co-existed with indifference. Then their father had disappeared, never to reappear again. Some said he had found another woman; some that he had simply grown tired of his family; and one wild rumor had it that he had been murdered and his body disposed of. His wife never looked far for him.

Reginald and Bea were never close. There was the age difference, there was the family tradition, and—most important— there were marked personality differences. He left for London at an early age, after a bare goodbye to his mother and 13-year-old sister. As I tried to get comfortable on the rumbling train, it hit me hard: I hadn't even said a proper goodbye to my mother and none at all to my father. Was I following in my father's footsteps?

I alighted from the train in Manchester with trepidation and loneliness. What was I doing here? Aunt Bea might send me back after a bare overnight stay. She was married and who knew what kind of person her husband was. I only knew his name: George Horley. Had Bea said he was an English or American serviceman? My parents had never mentioned that Bea had married again. Did they even know?

Bea's letter of invitation had been received a month earlier. I had not answered her, not wanting to accept because of the presence of Rick in my life, yet not wishing to turn her down and thus burn an important bridge.

The station was busy; Manchester was an important rail center. British servicemen, and Americans, as well, were everywhere. A light rain cast a pall over my arrival. In the station house, I asked about transport. I had my aunt's address but I didn't know where it was. I found it on a map, but there didn't seem to be any buses heading quite that way. Well, I would walk.

Three hours later, often consulting the map I had picked up at the station, I found Aunt Bea's house. It was early afternoon. During the long walk I rehearsed what I was going to say to her. I hadn't seen her in two or three years, the last time being at the funeral of her mother, a grandmother I barely knew. Would Bea truly welcome me? Or would she have little to do with her brother's son?

And yet my few memories of her were positive. She told funny stories, made fun of herself, and laughed a lot. Too much, my parents had said. Just right, I had thought at the time. Maybe she hadn't changed at all; maybe she was still lighthearted, still friendly. Maybe she liked me. Well, I would soon find out.

I had gotten keyed up for nothing; there was no one at home. I had little choice but to camp on her doorstep, suitcase by my side. My morale was low. What was I doing here in a large city in Northern Britain, where I had never been before, where I knew no one except a little-seen aunt?

Why couldn't I stick it out at home? And an intriguing question: what would Rick have advised?

"Well, what's this?" The voice, loud and piercing, was spoken directly into my ear. I scrambled to my feet, embarrassed that I had fallen asleep on her doorstep.

"Hello, Aunt Bea," I said, quietly. "Remember me?"

"Remember you? Of course I do, Rob. How could I ever forget you? One of my favorite people in the world."

With those words, all of my fears and worries evaporated. I had a new home.

She served me black bean soup, tea, and hard bread. That was for tea. A couple of hours later, for supper, she dredged up fish and chips, more tea, and a crème tart. Of course she didn't wait that long to pick my brains. Over the first tea, she said, "Talk youngster. Eat and talk at the same time, I don't care."

I vaguely remembered she said crazy things like that. I decided to see if she was shock-proof. "I ran away from home, auntie. Just like that."

She threw up her hands as if in supplication to the gods. "Oh-h-h, Robbie," she screamed, "how quaint."

I thought her choice of words strange but I had no time to think further about it; she went right on.

"I'm not surprised, Rob, except perhaps that you waited this long. How old are you? No, I know that. Fifteen this past September, wasn't it? Am I right?"

I nodded, touched that she had remembered my age and birth month.

"You are the best of them, Robby."

"The best---." I stopped, confused.

"Of your family. Reginald and I are on different planets. Always have been. And your mother—well, I never got to know her well. She never made much of an impression on me. Sorry I put it that way, Rob. Well, I did forget Geoff. He and you are tied at the top rung. How is Geoff? I suppose he's in the service?"

I was surprised—and saddened—that she did not know that my brother was missing in action. How could my parents not have told her? I told her what I knew and that filled the time before supper. My aunt was much moved by Geoff's fate.

Later, she said, "Listen, tomorrow being Christmas Eve, we must do something special. George will be home tomorrow and we'll plan Christmas Day around you. There's not much petrol, so we can't drive to the shore, but what we could do is have a few neighbors over. Some of them have youngsters. I want to have a crowd of people around to meet my nephew and play some games and drink some punch. I'll get on to them tomorrow and see what we can arrange. How does that sound, Rob?"

"It sounds—strange, auntie." I was telling the truth. My parents hardly knew their neighbors and had never had a party at our house during the time we lived in Ridgewell.

"You must tell me your plans," she said still later. "Or"— and she chuckled loudly—"perhaps your lack of them. In the meantime, you're to stay with us for as long as you want. I don't suppose you want me to let your parents know you are safely in your aunt's care?"

"No, not really, Aunt Bea."

"How long have you been gone?"

"Just since yesterday mid-day."

"We have a lot to talk about and a lot of time to talk. Listen, your parents will soon enough figure out you are here. Do you have other relatives, on your mother's side?"

"No, just you." It sounded so forlorn that we both quickly formed tears. A full body hug quickly took care of that.

123

17

LIFE WITH AUNT BEA

"My man George should be home this afternoon," Bea said over kippers and eggs. "How was it on the settee? I'm afraid it'll be there every night. You have it to yourself after we go to bed, and that's a blessing." She fixed drawer space for me in the lav for my personal possessions, such as they were. For meals, the kitchen table would accommodate three, if barely.

I had no idea how her husband would react to me. What would he say to an unknown boy moving in while he was gone? How would my life be in a small house with a woman I barely knew and her unknown husband?

Bea guessed my thoughts. "George will like you, you can bet on that. He loves to talk American football. Do you know anything about the game?"

"No, but I can read up on it and pretend I do. Bea, I won't be hard to find. What will we do then? Will they have the county constable take me back with them?"

"Before we plot on that one, Rob, tell me whether you are sure you want to stay up here. Do you miss your parents?"

"Yes and no," I said. "I don't want to ever live at home again."

"My, you do have a case. Well, then, we'll fight like hell for you, and pardon the language. I've been thinking that you might be happiest at a boarding school. You'd make a new set of friends. We'd have to be careful on the cost, though. We have a bit of money to spare and the rest will have to come from your parents."

"No chance there."

"Your parents will be no match for George. He loves a good fight. Once he's convinced you should stay here in Manchester, he won't stand for your parents taking you back. And he is a good salesman. He can extract money from anyone, for anything. I'll help, Rob, but really your best ally will turn out to be George."

"If he likes me," I said, barely audibly.

"He will, he will. I know him pretty well. I know a few things I wished I didn't. You should know or you might wonder. I know George loves me; a woman knows. But he is not a one-woman type of person. He has womenfolk in other ports. I don't cry about it—as long as he comes home to me. And he has for two full years that we've been together."

"And he married you, not them."

"Righto. That was his chance to escape, and he didn't."

"Isn't this, well, jolly hard on you?"

"Yes, it is. But if I want George, that's the way it is. And I want George."

There seemed no answer to that.

She told me he was an American, a sergeant in the Motor Pool at the U.S. base outside Manchester. He was a truck driver of heavy army vehicles, his duties taking him out of Manchester every week or so, delivering goods, or ferrying jeeps sometimes. He liked England, seldom spoke of returning to America, and she thought she had him forever.

Nothing is forever, I thought. Look at Rick. Look at Geoff. Look at me.

In the afternoon we walked around her rural neighborhood while she called upon a few neighbors to come to her house for a huge tea on the following day, Christmas 1944. People would come over in the early afternoon, bringing food and small gifts.

Aunt Bea told me about her own job as a clerk in a small accounting office in Manchester. She took a bus there and back. She didn't care much for the job, but the pay was good and she lived for the weekends. She was supposed to be working a half day today, but she had telephoned to say she wouldn't be in. She didn't want to leave me on my own. I was touched.

It happened that George had parked an army jeep at his house for a few days. "Let's take a ride," my aunt said.

It felt strange riding in a military jeep with my aunt driving. I had ridden with Rick, but this was different. Now I expected to be stopped by every policemen I saw, especially the American military police. But nothing happened. Bea wore one of George's coats and caps and, if we were noticed at all, she was likely taken for a WAC delivering a jeep somewhere with her son along for the ride.

I knew Manchester was a large city but I learned it was the fourth largest city in England, nearly 2,000,000 people in the metropolitan area. It was connected with the Irish Sea and the city of Liverpool by the Manchester Ship Canal. My aunt told me that Manchester was the center of one of the greatest manufacturing districts in the world. Cotton, rubber goods, oil, chemicals and dyes were primary products. I saw debris piled high ready for hauling, whole sections of buildings not yet cleared, and other evidences of the horror of the German bomber raids. Again, I thought of what Rick had said over and over: modern war is hell. With a jolt of pain, I thought of Rick's desire for peace in the world. Standing at the edge of a pile of rubble in the center of the city, I again vowed to carry on his goals. But how long would it be before I could do something about it?

George Horley, Staff Sergeant with the U.S. Army, walked into his house late that afternoon. He had been built up so much that I thought there might be a let-down. There wasn't: he was larger than life.

After a long embrace with Bea during which he lifted her off the floor and swung her around, he turned his attention to me, as if he hadn't noticed me when he first came in. "What's this?" he asked. "Bea, you been dallying while I'm away? He's kinda young for you. You know what you're doing, lass?"

I couldn't keep a flush from flooding my face. Bea cuffed her husband on the shoulder and said, "This is my long-lost nephew, Georgie, and he's going to stay with us for a bit of time. That is, if you don't mind."

"Mind? Of course I mind. A good-looking young guy taking up residence in my own house? You're a bit skinny, though," he said, his attention shifting to me. "We'll have to put some army beef into you." George stood six feet three inches and weighed about 16 stone. I must have looked puny to him.

He looked me over closely. "Hmm. Not a bad build for a youngster. Wiry arms. You ever do any arm-wrestling? I'll tell you what, I'll take you on with my left arm, your right. Okay? We'll do that after supper. Do you play American football?"

"No," I said, not yet warming to this big man.

"You want to learn?"

"I guess so."

"Do you play cricket? Do you know the rules of that dumb game?"

"Yes, I do."

"Then you can teach 'em to me in return for the football lessons. I like cricket far as I can tell. I just can't seem to understand the damn rules." He thought for a moment. "Do you want to learn to drive a two-ton army vehicle?"

"I've never even driven a car."

"How old are you?"

"Going on sixteen."

"Then it's high time you did. We don't own a car so you'll just have to learn on a two-tonner. That okay with you?"

"Okay with me, Mr.---". I couldn't remember his last name.

"Call me George. Another thing, fella. Your aunt and I like to—well, make a bit of hay in the bedroom. It might get noisy at times. Any problems?"

It was difficult to force a smile. "That's all right. I can always stuff pillows around my ears."

George grinned. "I already like this guy."

Our neighbors overflowed the house at Christmas Tea. Bea and George were genial hosts and no one paid much attention to me. We drank spiked punch, ate crumpets, played a few parlor games, then sang Christmas carols with Bea leading us by standing on a stool and waving her arms wildly. I tested out my newly-developed baritone. It was my first Christmas away from home.

By the time George Horley left the day after Christmas to deliver jeeps to other areas, I had arm-wrestled him (losing), driven the army truck (lots of problems) and caught a football a bit awkwardly. After I explained the rules of cricket, he still had trouble with it. I ended up liking him. I hoped he didn't have a lady friend where he was headed this week.

Before she left for work that day, Bea brought out an old banjo which she said had been gathering dust in a cupboard. "I didn't know you were so musical, Rob. Here—teach yourself to play the banjo. It will give you a lot of pleasure. There's a manual around here somewhere." While she was gone I did some elementary playing on the instrument and decided I was pretty good.

"I want to tell you why I'm here, Auntie," I said over supper that evening. "It has to do with an American flyer named Rick Linden. And my parents are part of the story."

"Let me fill your mug, then tell away."

So I told the story of a lonely boy with only a brother and a friend named Colin. "Maybe it was my fault," I said, "for not making friends and for letting my father get under my skin."

"Listen, Reggie got so much under my skin that I thought he lived there."

I told her of a flashy, friendly boy-man named Rick who befriended the lonely boy, offering a rich taste of hope and style and, most important, friendship. I told her of his adoption of me as his "best new friend," our long talks, our personality traits in common, and the things we did together during the last three months of his life.

"Auntie, Rick was very important to me. I'll never forget him." My eyes began to mist just talking about my friend. "There will never be anyone more special than Rick in my life. And this is the amazing thing, Auntie. I think he felt the same way about me. Destiny at work, Rick would have said."

I wasn't ready to tell Bea about Rick's lifetime goals and ideals. For now, I just wanted her to know about him.

I thought my parents would not let me out of their lives so easily. My father would feel bested, my mother sorrowful. And he would resent Bea stealing his son away—even though he hadn't done much to keep that son happy at home.

They wrote, they telephoned and they said they had hired a solicitor. Whether they did or not I never knew. Aunt Bea was wonderfully firm, saying to him things like "You've had your chance and you botched it," and "Rob is one of the best and it's a shame you didn't realize it in time."

I told my father on the telephone, quite bluntly, that I was where I wanted to be, appreciated and loved. When he threatened to take legal action I motioned for George to take over the phone. I found out he could match, or top, my father's bluster, swear words, and threats.

I also talked with my mother on the telephone and we had a nice cry together. She said she was sorry that she hadn't paid more attention to me and said I would always be welcomed home. That touched me. I said I would return someday. I told her I loved her. I asked about news of Geoff, but they hadn't heard anything further.

I wanted to tell my aunt more about Rick and his ideas for the future. I found the opportunity after supper one evening as we huddled over the kitchen stove—the only heat in the house. George was gone on a trip for a few days.

"It's not just that I lost a friend in the war. There's more to it than that."

My aunt was all ears. She liked a good story.

"Rick had these ideals," I continued. "He was just 23 years old. He wasn't just fighting a war over here and waiting to go home. He had grand plans for after the war."

"College, marriage, finding a good job?"

"Yes, those things. But I'm really talking of something much more important—important to the world and to the future of civilization."

Bea's puzzled look told me she didn't have any idea what I was talking about.

"Rick wasn't just a pilot doing his job." I told her about his goals. My aunt's frown reflected major problems with Rick's idealistic dreams. But she did me the courtesy of taking me seriously. I told her briefly that he had written an anti-war book not published yet. "Don't you see, Auntie, the things he wanted to work on after the war are all related—writing, peace, education. He could do it if anyone could.

"I haven't told you the exciting part yet." This was hard for me. I could sense my aunt's doubts about what she probably thought was the hero-worship of an American pilot by an English teenager. Not so unusual in our country.

"I'm going to carry on for him. I'm to work on things he was going to. He asked me to America after the war to live at his parent's house and help him in these great endeavors. Now I'll go on my own. It'll be hard without him, but I have to."

It must have been my phrase 'great endeavors' which set my aunt off. I didn't blame her. At her house was a 15-year-old runaway, and this youngster was spouting forth ideas about changing the world on behalf of a dead American flyer.

She chose her words carefully. "I have no wish to disillusion you, Rob. But these are awfully big plans for you. Best that you find a school, finish your education, and then see what you want to do with your life."

"That does sound right," I said, slowly. "But I've been christened *Rick the Second* to aid him with his great tasks."

Aunt Bea blanched when she heard "Rick the Second," and I think she stopped taking me seriously from that moment. But, bless her, she didn't say anything further. I knew I must make my case better than I had so far.

Life at Maston Boarding School on the north environs of Manchester was not a part of my life whose memory I would treasure. Since I roomed and boarded there, I saw Bea and George only about twice a month, at most. Maston was moderately costly but somehow this problem had been solved, if barely. George and Bea contributed and my parents did, to a limited extent. George never told me, but I think he threatened them with abandonment if they didn't cooperate. I contributed by working in a grocery store. I made it a point of honor to spend as little as I could. I couldn't afford to date girls who attended a nearby girl's school. I think everyone at Maston's put me down as a miser. About right.

The war was winding down. In March 1945 George handed me a copy of *The Stars and Stripes*, the American military newspaper. I read it at their house on a gloomy Sunday afternoon:

Hitler is on the defensive. The Soviet army stands poised on the banks of the Oder River, well within German soil. In the west, a million battle-weary Germans face nearly four times that number under General Eisenhower. The crushing of Hitler's Reich, which the Fuhrer once boasted would last for 1,000 years, appears to be only a matter of weeks or months away.

My fellow students didn't seem to follow the war. They were more interested in staying on the good side of the Masters and learning all they could about sex. And playing pranks. I stayed out of their way. I was still a loner and it came to me that I would always be.

Then one magic day in early May, the war in Europe ended. Hitler was dead; and the Germans signed an unconditional surrender on May 7, 1945 at Allies Headquarters in Reims, France.

Bea and George and I drove an army jeep all over Manchester and as far as Liverpool. We watched seemingly millions of English soldiers and civilians, joined by American military personnel, drink and carouse and shout and sing and generally behave as if their lives had changed forever. We joined them at times, and it was a rousing, fantastic experience. I had been about ten years old when the war started and here I was going on 16. I had lived well over a third of my lifetime during wartime. It was not something I'd forget very easily.

After we had returned from our jeep trip, I took a long walk around my aunt and uncles' neighborhood. Aunt Bea didn't ask me why I wanted to be alone. I needed to think and dwell on the events that had brought me to Manchester. I took stock. I had no money. I had parents who didn't seem to care much for me. I had no clear plans for the future, except for one general plan which kept nagging at me. No, two plans, really. The first was to go to America and the second, closely related, was to become Rick Linden the Second and to live my life the way I thought he would have lived his.

But there was another person in my thoughts—my brother Geoff. With the war over, he could be coming home any time. I knew I would never leave England until I found out what had happened to him. I imagined my reunion with Geoff; it would be fantastic. A brilliant idea dominated my thoughts for all of one day: maybe Geoff would want to go to America with me. What an idea!

Going to America, with or without my brother, was a strange thought for a lad of my age. And with no money. If I had discussed them with my aunt, or the Headmaster at Maston, or with practically any adult, I would have earned blank stares and gratuitous advice. I would have been advised to "grow up first" and "don't make this an obsession," or "live your own life"—and similar advice. Advice I didn't want.

So I didn't discuss my hopes and aspirations, not even with Aunt Bea. No one would see my viewpoint. Well, let's think about this, St. Clair, I said to myself. Is it possible everyone else is right and you are wrong? You concede you are young and inexperienced. Aren't you also being unrealistic? And too stubborn? My whole being cried out "No" to these unfair indictments. I would carry on because I *had* to. If I didn't make a spirited attempt to carry out Rick's goals, I would not be able to live with myself. Certainly I could fail. Certainly I might alienate friends, relatives, and strangers. But if I didn't try, it could never happen. If I tried and succeeded, it would be the high point of my life. And it would validate Rick's life, as well.

So I would put my head down for a year or so and then, school out of the way, go as hard as I could towards my goals. How and when and at what cost were barriers I simply could not fathom now. I suppose I had confidence that I would experience an epiphany at just the right time that would keep me glued to the ideals I had set for myself.

Had he lived, Rick would probably be in Colorado now and that's where I wanted to be, as well. England held nothing for me now. I couldn't think of anything more important in my life than to follow his lead, his plan, his absent leadership.

18

GOODBYE TO ALL THAT

In February 1946, with the war over for nine months, I received the news I had been dreading. My brother was dead. My mother had telephoned Aunt Bea, who called me at school and asked that I come to their home for the night. She had not told me over the telephone, but she did burst out with the news as soon as I entered the house. It was not a surprise. I figured someone had died, either mum or father—or Geoff.

For a week I was in a daze, although I returned to school. Mum wanted me to come home to Ridgewell. I didn't really want to face either of them right now. Aunt Bea thought the best place for me was in school; I would at least have something to do there. But it was worse there: no one knew Geoff—they hardly knew me—and I became more of a loner than ever. In due course, I learned that Geoff had died in a Japanese prisoner camp.

My life had bottomed out again. The thought of a lifetime without Geoff was devastating. The loss of my two brothers, a real one and an emotional one, was nearly too much to bear. Bea told me years later that I was difficult to be around during this time.

And yet, just a long fortnight after the Red Cross had confirmed the death of Geoffrey St. Clair, a miracle occurred. It was just in time to save my sanity, perhaps my life. Bea and George were going to America. He was being mustered out.

Within a heartbeat I said, "I'm going with you." She tossed me a long look. "Why am I not surprised? You'd leave your school in mid-term, leave your country, leave your parents?"

"Yes, I would. There's nothing to keep me here now, except," and my voice dropped to a whisper, "my mother. But, well, she told me one time, in a tea shop in Ridgewell, that I should do what my heart told me to do. I think she will understand. About pa, I don't know."

I had made up my mind. Aunt Bea could help me or not. I would go alone if need be. With Rick and Geoff both gone, I had no guide in my life except a dead friend whose ideals and goals I had adopted. No, that wasn't quite right: he had *given* them to me. I couldn't carry on for him in this country. It had to be in America, where I had always planned on going, anyway.

When Bea and George realized I was serious about going with them, they did their best to help me. George had received the necessary travel permit for his wife. But a nephew? George talked with a friend he played rugby with. The friend, a solicitor, advised him to secure a letter of consent from my parents, then state in writing that Bea and George intended to adopt me as soon as we reached the United States. George thought it could work out. Who would care? The American authorities wouldn't—they had enough to do shipping their troops to all parts of the United States, than to worry about some G.I.'s English teen-aged nephew.

George pulled off a magician's trick and got the army to pay for my travel costs, as well.

"Georgie," Bea said, "how are we ever going to get Reginald and Mildred to sign a letter letting us take their son off to another country?"

"They already have," he answered, a smirk on his face.

"I can't believe it. The only way you could do that would be to forge it."

He was silent but the smirk remained.

"Sometimes I can't believe you're for real, honey."

"Anyway, it's done. By the time Rob's parents find out what's going on, we'll be in America. What would they do, extradite him? The worst that can happen—and it won't—is that Rob would have to return to the U.K. and live with his parents until he's 18. And that's only a year or so from now. The red tape would take that long."

I sat listening to this exchange with a wide mix of emotions. Elation was at the top of the list, but sadness was there, too: I would not be able to say a proper goodbye to mum. I loved her, and although I wouldn't let her stop me from going, I wanted her blessing and a proper goodbye.

In the end, I rationalized that as soon as I reached America, I would write her the most loving letter she'd ever received—but from America.

I would not, could not, lose this opportunity to move to America so soon, and with Bea and George, at that. While I was gaining independence quickly, I had not been looking forward to the inevitable loneliness I would experience if I went abroad alone. Now I would stay with them until I finished high school, then take off for Colorado Springs to the biggest adventure of my life.

We sailed on the U.S.S. *Woodrow Wilson,* and a lovely ride it was. I had never been on the high seas before and it was all new and exciting. Never before had I stood on a rocking deck, open seas all around, reveling in the breeze in my face, watching the sailors performing their task to near perfection.

I had my own cabin to the delight of all three of us. My aunt and uncle still acted as if they were newly-married, spending much time in their cabin. That left me the freedom of all the decks I could roam on. It was May 1946 and the war had been over for a year. The world was recovering from a six-year war, and all sorts of changes: re-building bombed–out areas, electing and appointing new officials, and shifting to a peace-time economy. There were old problems and a whole set of new ones and people on both sides of the Atlantic set to with a will to solve them.

I had at least a half year of school to finish somehow, somewhere, before I could strike out on my own. I would be ready for it.

"Let's talk, Auntie," I said as we stood by the rail one night. George was playing poker in the main lounge. "I know I'm the third person in a two-person family. I don't enjoy that. I want you to know that I won't burden you much longer."

"Burden? I don't accept that word in connection with you, Rob. Listen, we'll rent a two-bedroom house in Morro Bay or San Luis Obispo."

"Yes, that would be jolly. It'll be Manchester all over again, except for more room. Auntie, do they have summer school in California?"

"I have no idea. But you can probably work something out with the school people. Are you so anxious to finish school? You'll not be 17 until September."

"If I can get the credits I need this summer, then I can depart for Colorado on my birthday."

We had both been facing the dark seas, enjoying the stiff breeze. Now she turned to face me, and I could sense an inquisition coming.

"Have you given much thought to this decision, Rob? Running off by yourself to an unknown area of America, chasing a rainbow? With no job and no money and no plans? Are you that set on following the memory of Rick Linden halfway across a country you know nothing about? Where you know no one and no one knows you, much less cares about you."

"Auntie, listen. I haven't talked much about Rick for several months now. But he's been on my mind, and in my heart, all of this time. I want to be Rick Linden. I don't want to just copy him. Rick is gone but he had such wonderful ideals that it would be a disservice to mankind if I did nothing to carry on his great goals."

"Oh, dear, you put it so grandly. How can I disagree with such an appeal? But there must be people with experience and money and influence that could do it—well, better than you. And why Rick? The world lost millions of young men and women."

"Yes, I know. But I only knew one of them, and he had to be one of the best. I can't just lead a normal life and forget I knew him. Maybe it will be ineffective, and wasteful of my own life. But it *is* my life Do you see my point? You're adventurous yourself. Look at what you're doing now—giving up your country to go live on the California coast."

"I suppose I couldn't talk you out of it no matter how long and hard I tried."

"You couldn't." I looked at the near full moon over the sparkling waters. "That's a fine moon up there, Bea. Why don't you rescue George from losing his money and show him the moon?"

San Luis Obispo, near the central California coast, looked nothing like any part of England I knew. The small city, which I knew from the map to be about halfway between San Francisco

136

and Los Angeles, was nestled among several small peaks. There were seven of them between San Luis Obispo and Morro Bay, each one about a mile apart. They looked like good hiking and one of them, Bishops Peak, resembled Roans Peak where I had first learned of the great plans of a young poet-warrior.

San Luis Obispo was close to three beaches—Morro Bay, Pismo Beach, and Avila. The latter had the best body-surfing conditions and became my favorite. I rode my bicycle, bought second-hand. I was a novice at surfing but learned quickly and spent many an hour there, usually alone.

Bea and I had visited the school district administrator's office in San Luis Obispo and were given a series of courses designed for high school seniors that would graduate me within six months, if I applied myself. It was mostly summer courses. I would be taking 18 units, a challenge for me, although I had done reasonably well in school. One thing was in my favor: I had the strongest of motives.

We rented a small house in Morro Bay with a view of sand dunes and the Pacific Ocean through tall eucalyptus trees. My courses were all in San Luis Obispo so I usually hitch-hiked the nine miles both coming and going. Often, I rode with a classmate who lived in Cayucas, up the coast from Morro Bay.

George retrieved his job as a truck driver and resumed his old habit: disappearing for days at a time as he drove as far as Kansas City or Dallas delivering goods. Bea, knowing no one in Morro Bay, talked to me more often than she normally would have. Then she would remember my studies and reluctantly take up a book or tend her garden. She was looking for a job that was right for her.

My experience with girls had been nil. At Ridgewell I was too immature; at Maston School for Boys in Manchester there were none; and I had been on the move since. I was well aware of the attraction of the opposite sex, but just now I didn't have time. I was studying most of the time and I was preparing to leave town. Not the best of times to go romancing.

Then Erin found *me*.

She was from my school and she was not hesitant to tell me I was the boy of her dreams. I told her she was crazy; I had just met her, how could she know? She laughed that off and wangled a date or two with me. She hinted she would like to know me better, as well as a girl could know a boy.

It was mid-July and the weather was perfect. She was older than me, 17, and she had a driver's license. We drove her parents' car to the beach at Avila. We walked on soft, white sands, dug for the occasional clam, and climbed the cliffs at the south end of the beach. Around the most southern point was a small beach about the size of two soccer fields plotted together. It was reachable only when the tide was out. Known as King Kong Beach, it was becoming notorious because some school kids swam there at times without the benefit of swim suits.

We found the tide out now (had Erin researched the tidal charts and arranged a visit for this particular time?) and dashed around the jutting rocks to the deserted beach. Erin took her clothes off while I was looking over rock-climbing possibilities on the far side of King Kong Beach. When I turned around, I was stunned.

I gaped at her. I had never seen a naked girl in my life, not even in magazines. She wasted no time. "Take 'em off, Rob," she said, and advanced on me. I was willing, yet the fact that she had taken the lead so quickly and possessively bothered me a bit.

I led her on for a few minutes, trying to convince her that the English had a law against swimming in the nude. Finally, I grinned and stripped my clothes off. We had a good time as we frolicked in the ocean hand in hand. Then three college kids, two girls and a boy, came dashing around the headland and soon took their clothes off, as well. Our minor adventure ended with barely getting back to Avila before the incoming tide could trap us.

Erin tried her best with me, and she was a likable, cheerful flirt of a girl. But my need to get on with my life in barely two months won out. I took her hands in mine. "Erin, you should go to Cal Poly right here in town. Find yourself a football player with a winning smile. That would suit you better than me—a displaced English lad who is leaving town soon. What do you see in me?"

Erin was at her loveliest when she smiled. "I see a boy with a lovely build, smart as a whip—I can't believe you're taking 18 units—and as sexy as any American boy I know. Then there's that English accent."

"I'm not classy enough for a girl like you, Erin. Forget me. I'm just a ship passing in the night."

Aunt Bea did her best to change my mind. Why not stay here on the lovely California coast? San Luis Obispo would grow, prosper, and I could go to Cal Poly, and maybe get a job in a bank?" (She had heard that Erin's father was president of a Savings and Loan). "You could move out of our house if you preferred your privacy, you know. You love the ocean, and there are no oceans near Colorado that I know of."

"Auntie, I'm going to Colorado because I promised myself one night a long time ago, that it was my destiny to do so. I want to meet Rick's parents and sister, and perhaps some of his friends. That says it all."

"You don't *have* to follow the ghost of your friend."

"Yes, I do. And please don't call him a ghost. I believed in him when he was alive and I believe in him now that he has gone, maybe even more. He's as real to me as you are, Auntie. No offense. That's just how strongly I feel."

19

STRANGER IN A STRANGE LAND

I had never hitch-hiked in England, but here I found it exhilarating to do so. It was an activity mostly for the young and penniless, although older people with at least some money could be found on the road, as well. My aunt offered to pay for bus fare but I wouldn't hear of it.

It was a strange way to travel, actually, sticking your thumb into the open air and jerking it back and forth. People stopped often enough. I don't think I was ever stranded on the road for as long as an hour. I quickly learned some of the rules of hitch-hiking: never turn down a ride, don't insult the driver or the car, listen rather than talk, and try not to be dropped off at a lonely place. And don't get into the position of morally having to buy your driver lunch or breakfast. These rules were well tested and some broken in the next few days.

An older lady, driving alone, took me as far as Paso Robles, 30 miles north of San Luis Obispo. She was a delightful person, with the unlikely name of Louisiana Dart. She told me of her activities in Paso Robles, her children who had flown the nest, and even described her husband's favorite meal. I was sorry to lose her after such a short trip.

The next drive was much longer, as far as San Francisco, but it was nerve-wracking all the way. The driver was a man in his 60s, the car a Packard sedan, and the conversation was nil. This would have been fine with me, except that he reached over to the glove compartment (funny name for an area which seldom held gloves) and withdrew a pint bottle. He would take a long swig, then wipe his mouth with the back of his hand while the car swerved alarmingly, finally settling down to stare at the road ahead. Cars on the two-lane highway going in the opposite direction roared by within five feet of us. I wondered what he'd do if I threw the bottle out of the window. Throw me out, too, no doubt. I finally decided to show some gumption. "Do you mind not drinking so much?" I asked. He glared at me, thought for a moment, then said, "Do you want to be dumped right here?" Since we were in an isolated spot on Highway 101, I said I'd shut up. "You'd better." Later he muttered, "All the thanks I get."

He did dump me in South San Francisco. I had a bite to eat at a roadside diner, emerging into a dense fog. Immediately two girls, who had been eating inside earlier and had apparently waited for me to finish, asked me which way I was going.

I told them I wanted to get across the Bay Bridge and then up to Sacramento. "That's just where we're going," the driver said. She was a slim girl with a mop of red hair. I wondered if she spoke the truth. But I climbed into the old model Chevrolet and, at their invitation, sat between them in the front seat. "Plenty of room," the driver said.

The girls were twins, I found. They apparently liked my accent, and perhaps other things about me, too. For they asked me questions for the next two hours: my age, where I was from, where I was going, did I have a girl friend, what popular ballads I liked, had I seen any good shows lately, and so on. Why people want to know, even need to know, details about a stranger has always escaped me.

Finally, just before we reached their destination in West Sacramento, the driver asked me the ultimate question: "Are you a virgin?" The question didn't stun me; I had almost expected something like this. But I had trouble deciding how to answer. Her sister, a slightly more sensible type, said, "That's not right to ask him that, Vera. Don't answer, Rick." I silently thanked her.

And so it went. I had a few perfectly normal rides, as far as I could judge Americans. One couple was friendly and not inquisitive (perfect), while another was argumentative during a long ride across Nevada on Highway 50. Thankfully, they didn't bother much with me, dropping me in Green River, Utah, where I stopped to eat.

Again, I was picked up by fellow diners. They seemed like an all-American couple, young and happy with each other, and driving a Ford sedan. It would have been a fine ride had it not been for the dog. He sat in the back seat with me and obviously resented sharing his favored seat. I endured 50 miles of intermittent growling, broken occasionally when he would grab

141

my sleeve and tug. Once he went for my neck, and I thrust him away violently.

The young lady happened to be looking at me when this occurred, and she snapped out, "Watch yourself, young fellow. He's our dog and you're just a free-loader. John, let's drop this joker in Glenwood Springs." The man turned to glare at me and added, "We should let you out right here on the highway. If you try to hurt Harold again, that's it, buster." He added to his wife, "I never did like foreigners, anyway." So much for the all-American couple.

A trucker took me down Highway 70 to Denver. Not quite, actually. As he told me two or three times, he lived in Idaho Springs, west of Denver. He said he would leave me there. "I'll drop you at a great little café. The wife and I go to dinner there once a week or so. But not tonight. The old lady will be waiting up for me and she has only one thing on her mind when I blow into town. Know what I mean?" And he leaned clear across the cab to nudge me in the ribs. I grinned back at him as if I knew all about a wife's needs.

The trucker had caught on to my British accent. "Our war was much shorter than yours," he said. "You guys fought for several years, didn't you?"

His words cheered me. I was proud of my new country, Rick's country. My chest throbbed painfully as I thought of my new identity. For I had been "Rick" during all the rides, eight of them. I borrowed Rick's name during these few days of anonymity. Of course I couldn't use it in Colorado Springs where Rick was too well known. But using even his first name gave a feeling of closeness, of bonding, with him. I knew it was a silly thing to do, immature, ingenuous. There was no one to hold me back, to counsel me differently, to call me a fool or worse. I felt thrilled to be on my own in a strange land.

The cafe was nearly empty; it was approaching midnight. I slipped into a booth and ordered fried eggs, ham, and chips. Fries they called them here. Solid American food. I had hoarded my dollars. I figured I could eat only one hearty meal per day until I had a job somewhere. I glanced around the café: a long narrow counter, two weary-looking waitresses of uncertain age, hand-printed food advertisements tacked on the wall. I might have to stay the night here unless another friendly trucker came along.

I had barely begun my meal, wolfing it down, when I heard the air brakes of a truck pulling in. But instead of a solitary truck driver I might have found a ride with, dozens of passengers filed in. Cross-country bus.

It was a night for traveling. There was barely enough room in the café for the newcomers. First, an older couple, he in overalls, she in a gingham dress, sat opposite me in the booth. They nodded but didn't speak. Blessedly taciturn, I thought.

A moment later, a rumpled-looking blonde with bangs sat next to me. I figured her for 25, perhaps older.

"Sorry—have to share," she said and her smile revealed white teeth which transformed her face from average to, well, a bit above average.

She nodded at the couple opposite then gave her full attention to me. "I'm Louise," She said, smiling. "I didn't see you on the bus, and I don't miss good-looking young guys very often."

I grinned back. "I wasn't on the bus. I'm a hitchhiker. Between rides right now. I'm Rick." I decided I wanted her to know me by my stolen name.

"You don't much look like a hitchhiker. You don't sound like one, either." She snapped her fingers. "Got it. Australian. Seeing our country for the first time, right?"

I was determined to tell the truth as often as I could though I knew I'd have to lie occasionally. "I'm English. I came over here with my aunt and uncle. Now I *am* seeing your country." I told her of my recent move to America and my newly-developed plan to see her country.

"And that would be—college or high school?"

"College." I smiled. "Actually, I graduated from high school last week, and turned 17, as well."

"How about *that?* Did your parents give you a big send-off?"

"Not exactly."

We finished our meal and I found, as tired as I was, that I had enjoyed the interaction with an American girl, although she wasn't an outstanding looker, and was older.

The bus driver came in from outside, stamping his feet against the late September cold. "Denver bus leaves in five minutes. All aboard."

Louise looked at me rather shyly. "Sure you want to try your thumb again tonight?"

I picked up on her smile, wide and honest, and decided I liked this woman. I even accepted her droopy bangs which virtually obscured her pale forehead. If you squinted your eyes and put your imagination to work, she could have passed for Veronica Lake.

I raised my eyebrows and she added: "There's room on the bus. You can pay cash to the driver. And I'm sure I can get the old gent seated next to me to move, if I asked him real nice. So join me."

I was easily hooked. If this was how you met girls in America, I was for it. Five minutes later we were on the bus telling each other our life stories. I nearly forgot that 20 minutes earlier I had only wanted privacy and silence.

She was a waitress at a café in Pueblo, south of Colorado Springs. She admitted she liked college boys down that way. And in Denver. And in Colorado Springs. She had been married, no children. She had a boy friend now, sort of, but Chuck had become too possessive. She wanted to go back to school, get out of waiting on table, but she never did anything about it. Perhaps she would marry again, to some nice man. Not to Chuck.

She was returning from Grand Junction for the wedding of her sister. Chuck had wanted to drive her there, but she'd made an excuse. She hadn't wanted to encourage him just before getting rid of him. The bus was an expensive alternative, but worth it. She finished her story, linked her arm through mine, and said, "Your turn."

I told her the truth: born in London in 1929, my father a manual worker, my mother a housewife. I told her about my lone friend Colin, about how I lived with my aunt and uncle, and how I had just left them in California.

"I swear, Rick, you have a past. And you just turned 17."

"I was a pretty unhappy lad for a few years." She squeezed my arm and snuggled against me, making me acutely aware of her femininity. "I had only a few friends, mostly this chap Colin. Then I met Rick."

"A special friend, eh? And the same name as yours?" Something clutched at my heart; she had found me out already.

"We were great buddies. But then—he died in the war."

She had no response to that—except that she snuggled closer to me.

I was anxious to finish the story. "I was still young but I decided to run away from home—it's a long story—so I stayed with this aunt. In Manchester, in the north of England. Then I came to California. Another long story." I was surprised at myself, telling a stranger my life story. I realized it was just bus talk. "This is going on too long, Louise."

"You *do* have a past, Rick."

Although it was dark outside I could tell we were in some sort of mountain pass. The bus was laboring along in a lower gear, and I caught flashes of trees and mountains on both sides of us. We must be in a gorge, I thought. We stopped at Glenwood Springs, had a root beer there, then climbed back aboard. Louise wasn't quite ready to leave my story.

"Have you decided what you're going to do now?"

"That's an even longer story." I wasn't about to mention Rick again. Or my vows to him. I'd said enough already.

I was thrilled to be linking arms with this young American girl in a cozy bus rolling through the mountains of Colorado. We had found that we both had the same destination: Colorado Springs, following a transfer in Denver. She suggested we find seats together after Denver. I was surprised this older woman found my company that desirable. As for me, I was content to stay the course.

Story time was over. Still hanging on to my arm, she closed her eyes. "I like Englishmen," she said, softly. "Young ones. And with brown hair. And with accents."

She must have been as tired as I was, for she settled down quickly and soon fell asleep. But I—who had had only a few snatches of sleep in assorted cars in the last 36 hours—lay awake and stared out the window past Louise's mop of blonde hair. God, I thought, what am I doing on a Greyhound bus, halfway through Colorado, on my way to where Rick Linden grew up? And me with no plan of action—other than to check into a YMCA, look for a rooming house, find a job. But they were such utilitarian things. How would I fare when the choices got tougher?

145

I wanted to meet Rick's parents, his sister, some of his friends. Talk to them about Rick. My chest throbbed as I thought of my friend, dead now for 21 months. It was time—it was past time—to begin to carry out Rick's oft-expressed drives, his dreams, his *life work*.

It might be good to learn the things Rick loved. Skiing, writing, flying, fishing and hiking in the Rockies. Wasn't it logical that if I did, I would begin to think like him in other ways? I had shelved the identity of Rob St. Clair back in England. Now I would be Rick, a poor substitute, but even so a second Rick Linden appearing magically on the scene. *Rick the Second.*

Finally, my eyes closed involuntarily. While tired of analyzing, I was well aware of the proximity of my seat partner. Her head had drooped onto the middle of my chest. Then her hand, which had been resting on my breast, dropped into my lap.

My insides wound up as tight as when Erin had been naked before me. Her proximity challenged all my natural physical responses. My agitation was breathtaking. I was afraid to breathe, wanting out of the moment, but wanting it prolonged, as well. Slowly, I relaxed, my breath slowing to an even gait again. I stared at her hand in my lap, willing it to explore a bit. Her hand was small and white and still. She was asleep.

Enjoy the moment, Rob. It was something Rick had said often. I felt drowsy, but at the same time vividly aware of the power of sexual desire. Slowly, my sensual self unwound and I fell asleep even as I had decided I would never do so tonight.

At four o'clock on a dull Monday afternoon the bus station in Colorado Springs was nearly quiet. Louise spied her boyfriend Chuck as we walked down the aisle. "Oh, Gawd," she whispered to me. "He came up to the Springs to meet me. He must have got his car out of hock. Well, Rick, it's been nice, really nice. With Chuck here, you'd better disappear. He's the jealous type, I mean he really is. Leave me right here. Please, Rick."

I'd be damned if I would. Instead, I helped her off the bus while continuing to hold her arm snugly. I suppose I had asked for it. But the fury and power of his blow to my face stunned me. I fell back against the bus and slumped into a sitting position, wondering if I wanted to be an embarrassed coward or a beaten-up fool. I decided on the heroic fool's role. Rick had taught me that.

But by the time I was on my feet ready to charge, there was a burly bus guard watching me closely. Louise and Chuck were on their way out of the terminal. The wink from Louise—whether real or imagined—salved some pride. I was beaten up a bit, but I was here, I was *here*.

I checked the narrow cot, single wash basin, scarred chest of drawers, and the crooked mirror poised above it—and shivered.

What a welcome to the state of Colorado and to Rick Linden's hometown. I checked my swollen eye in the mirror. There was also a cut on my chin and my thick brown hair, which my new friend Louise had so recently admired, was in disarray. I was lucky the desk clerk had rented me a room. I turned the mirror's face against the wall and headed down the hall to the bathroom. It was occupied; it was the way my new life was going.

Later, lying in bed, the strangest feeling came over me: it was my fate, my destiny, to be here in Colorado Springs at this moment. And I was happy despite the black eye.

The last thought I had before sleep took me was that I had been called Rick for the past two days. It had sounded perfectly natural. This led to the corollary question: was I Rob St. Clair, or was I on my way to becoming Rick Linden? The Second.

20

DUMB ENGLISHMAN AT LARGE

A dull and lifeless day greeted me in the morning. I had slept later than I'd planned. I parted the drapes of the room's single window. A slanting rain was beating against the pane. I lay back in bed to think things over. I closed my eyes.

I would have fallen asleep again if my guilt feeling had not been overpowering. I dressed quickly. It was so cold out that I thought it might snow—but snow in mid-Colorado in late September? I didn't think so. I ate a lonely, hasty meal at the Y counter. Now I was ready. But—it *was* snowing. I remembered we were above 5,000 feet, higher than most of England.

My resolve quickly fell apart. I hadn't taken the time to formulate a plan on what to say to Rick's parents. Well, it could wait until tomorrow. But today I could explore a bit; I wanted to know Rick's hometown.

I walked through the business district, past the Roxie Theater, peeked inside the Antlers Hotel, strolled along Monument Creek on a trail winding towards the Colorado College campus, Rick's school. Near campus, I sauntered into the Art Center as if I belonged there. I found Murray's Drug Store, where Rick had no doubt taken his dates for cokes. In the afternoon, I focused on the campus. I identified buildings I had heard him mention: Shove Memorial Chapel, Lennox Hall, Cutler Hall, the library. I stood for a long time across the street from the Phi Gamma Delta fraternity where Rick had lived.

I had lunch at Murrays, ordering ham and cheese on rye and a vanilla milk shake. Wasn't that what people ate here in America? I would learn to like it as much as any American would. I had no coat (poor planning) and went into the Roxie Theater to stay warm. It was playing *Since You Went Away* which I'd seen, but I watched it anyway. Shivering, I jogged back to the YMCA. I was furious with myself. I hadn't accomplished anything. I had toured the city and the campus as if I was a tourist. It was close on to six o'clock and most of the city's citizens were hurrying somewhere where they were loved or needed. I wasn't loved or needed. No one even knew where I was.

I took off my still-wet clothes, threw a blanket from the bed around me and walked down the hall to the bathroom. I had to wait in the hall: another resident was entrenched in the tub. I could hear him splashing. When my turn came, I soaked for a long time, until the soapy water was on the freezing side of lukewarm. I had forgotten my towel so I scampered back to my room with the blanket, scratchy and stiff, barely covering my torso.

After I'd toweled, I lay on my bed and stared unblinkingly at the ceiling. Time for a reality check. I'd left my parent's house with ill grace, and somehow had arrived where I wanted to be. Yet I was feeling sorry for myself.

Well, I'd do what Rick would have done: write. Throwing off my towel, I dove into bed, found my notebook, and looked for a pencil. None in sight. I got up again, searched my luggage, the dresser drawers, even under the bed. Nothing. Is that it? Is someone trying to tell me to give up, forget this pilgrimage, go home? But where was home?

Angrily, I threw on my wet clothes and took the stairs to the lobby two-three at a time. I borrowed a pencil from the desk clerk, and because there was a steaming radiator in the small lobby with an empty chair beside it, I decided to write downstairs, my clothes drying on my body. Then, of course, not having expected to stay downstairs, I hadn't brought my notebook. So back upstairs at a run, grab my notebook, then back downstairs before someone took my chair by the radiator. No one had. Ah, my first break of the day.

At the boarding school in Manchester, I had vowed I would live in Colorado Springs and search for Rick. Now, here I was, ready to look for him. So far I had spent the better part of two days without accomplishment, except to become familiar with the town and campus.

At 17 I had expected to be organized, self-confident, and motivated. Motivated I might be, but it was unfocused. As for the other two attributes, I was a failure.

I remembered the climb on Roans Peak in the wind, when Rick had first described what he intended to accomplish when the war was over. It was over for him and I was selected—yes, selected by Rick himself—to carry on for him. I knew his goals, which were mine now. Helping tremendously in the pursuit of them was to write meaningful, thoughtful, hard-hitting, persuasive articles. Even books. Ergo: I must learn to write well enough to be a force in this new world.

I had so much on my mind that I was suddenly overwhelmed by passion, with love, with desire—and with the need to get on with the job.

Sitting tamely in a chair by a crackling steam radiator was not consistent with my expansive mood. I scrambled to my feet, notebook and pencil tumbling to the floor. Pacing nervously in the overheated lobby, I found I couldn't stay put. I had to get out-of-doors, where I could see the sky—which Rick had loved so much. I dashed outside, coatless—and stopped dead. It was dark, damn it, and it was still snowing, double damn it. I couldn't even see the sky.

Reality checked in again. Who am I? The answer was loud and clear: *An immature kid playing at a game way over my head. All right, you were appointed to be the surrogate for Rick Linden. That's as may be. But what qualifications do you have, Mr. St. Clair? You're young, inexperienced, untrained in war or writing or education or any other discipline I could name.*

My adrenaline kicked in just as loud and twice as clear. *Sure I'm young. I may be a dumb Englishman at large but I have a high school education and I'm healthy, and most of all, I'm dedicated. And no one is holding me back—not parents, not aunt, not anyone in the world.*

Reality snapped back. *And you think those are assets? Dumb Englishman is right, anyway. What can you do at your age except earn a dollar an hour, if you're lucky, then go to school, if they let you in. But can you take care of yourself? You brag about being beholden to no one. Don't you realize, you dumb Englishman, that this means no one is beholden to you? No one cares about your self-termed great quest, except a dead man.*

And where are you going to work? Do they require work permits in America? What about your silly English accent? And how will you get into college, with no address, no parents you want to acknowledge, no transcript, no pedigree, no nothing?

My adrenaline lost the contest. I fell silent.

And suddenly all I wanted to do was run hard, become physically exhausted. Still coatless, I raced on skidding feet down the sidewalk, heedless of the slippery, icy pavement, dodging cars and pedestrians alike. I ran swiftly for several blocks, not waiting for the silly lights to change, not caring whom I might run down. Finally, tiring, I settled into a fast walk, eventually sitting on the curb, chest heaving, knowing I had tears on my face, probably *freezing* on my face.

I sat there for a long time, sobbing quietly, uncaring about my appearance. Then I arose, walked across the street to where a coffee shop was still open. Inside, I looked bleakly at the silver-haired waitress.

"Coffee?" she asked.

I looked at her uncomprehendingly.

"Do you want coffee, dearie?"

Instinct kicked in. "I'd like tea, please." But this was America, Rick's country. "No, no, I want coffee."

Something made me look to the far end of the counter. And there he was. It was Rick! I leaped to my feet, then sank back slowly, stunned. Of course it wasn't Rick. The young man there had the same red hair, the same rather sculpted face, the same dark blue eyes, even the same assured expression. And he was reading a book, like Rick would be doing. Conscious he was being watched, the young man stared at me for a long moment, frowning slightly. Then he lowered his head to his book again, oblivious of the silly young Englishman's unwelcome inspection.

I sat there a long time, staring at the dregs in my coffee cup, expecting nothing more from this day and wishing it were over. Perhaps I would dream of Rick tonight and he would give me a sign of approval, of understanding—or something.

As I trudged the dozen or so blocks to the YMCA, a flash of maturity surfaced, enough for me to realize I had run a gamut of emotions. I certainly didn't want that to happen every day. But, for all my suffering and embarrassment, I was no closer to a plan on how to even start my Rick quest. Suddenly, I longed for the sound of my own name spoken by someone I knew, who knew *me.*

I almost wished Louise was waiting for me at the "Y". If she were I'd try my best to lose my virginity tonight. That was a measure of how much I was starved for human contact.

*   *   *   *

I lay on my back on my bed, exhausted both mentally and physically. Intuitively, I knew I would have to endure this kind of emotional roller coaster every once in awhile—until I had figured things out. If there was one thing I had learned from the night's adventures, it was that I would not give in to despair or indecision or even, if I could manage it, immaturity.

As I turned out the lights, I remembered I had left my notebook and pencil downstairs. I threw on pants and shirt, took the stairs in a series of jumps, and retrieved my belongings from the darkened lobby. In my room, it was clothes off again, a leap into bed shivering violently until the wool blankets warmed my body. I thought about the past day, the first full day of my life in Colorado Springs, and I realized I had accomplished nothing. Absolutely—nothing. The time I'd wasted in Rick's hometown carried a strong burden of guilt. There was an ache in my soul.

Rick told me at the pub that he intended to make a difference in the world. But how do I, the new Rick, go about doing that? I'm no Rick. I'm a fraud. My goals are not formed and perhaps never will be. I want to be what he named me: Rick the Second, but how can I, with 17 years of Rob St. Clair inhibiting me?

I woke up or I never fell asleep. I never did know whether the words came from me or from a dream. My morale was at an all time low. My first step in the morning should be to meet Rick's parents. But what was I going to tell them? How to explain my sudden appearance in their lives, a lad from England whom, I would say, knew their son? I desperately needed to think this through. I should have done this months earlier. Was this a propensity for failure, or merely more immaturity?

21

TEARS IN THE DARKNESS

I had put off meeting Rick's parents so long that it had become a sick joke. If I couldn't mobilize myself for this opening step, I might as well call the whole thing off, return to San Luis Obispo, flirt with the banker's daughter and go to college there. I realized, in a moment of terrible clarity, that if I couldn't take this first step—now—then the whole enterprise would fail and my life's goals—and Rick's—would be in shambles.

By mid-morning I sat hunched on a rear seat of the city bus, traveling north on Cascade Street. I knew their address: 1115 Curtis Street. But I was not prepared. I had not rehearsed my approach. I was nervous, the nervousness fed by apprehension, the apprehension fed by the prospect of failure, of rejection, even of ridicule. I arose and walked towards the exit door; I would return to the "Y" and think it over. The driver was watching me in his rear view mirror. Did he, too, sense my failure?

Procrastinator, quitter, coward. Get on with it, Rob.

Earlier that morning I had written a few lines in my note-book: "Meet Rick's parents," "Move out of the 'Y'", "Find a job," then "See about college." That's all I had written, not much for nearly two years of preparation. Yet I couldn't even get going on the first of those steps. As I waited for the bus to stop and let me off, my spine stiffened and I did an abrupt about-face. I re-seated myself near the exit door, and remained on the bus.

At Cache la Poudre, the campus stop, I did exit the bus. I would walk the campus again, soak in more of the atmosphere that had helped form Rick Linden. I mingled with American students, some of whom had probably known Rick. I wondered if this was a typical campus, filled with bright-eyed students. Some, I knew, were slightly older men who had returned from fighting a war in Europe or the Pacific.

By now I should be knocking on the door of the Linden home, beginning a crusade. Crusade? Who was I kidding? What a travesty. My deeper self, the honest one, whispered to me that I was putting off meeting the Lindens because I was a coward and therefore not worthy of the entire enterprise. My surface self responded that I was just doing the necessary groundwork, that I would rise to the occasion when I had to.

Despite my inner turmoil, I was impressed with the overall appearance of the campus: mature oak trees, athletic fields, imposing two-story buildings, a relaxing ambience. This was Rick's school, and it was important, I told myself, to get the feel of the place. That feeling included money, maturity, and purposefulness. I was short on all those things; I would never fit in here.

I could feel my dreams and ambitions fade away with the last vestiges of my self-confidence.

I bought a cheese sandwich and a bottle of milk for 50 cents and was still hungry. Consulting a map, I walked north on Cascade Street. All the while I was planning what my opening words would be to the Lindens. "Hi, I knew your son," or "I was with Rick right up to his last flight," or "You know, Rick and I got along famously." It all sounded so trite, so presumptuous, so vapid.

A few minutes later I stood across the street from a small-ish one-story house. Number 1115. I was drawn to it, yet afraid. This was where Rick had lived! I noted the comfortable covered porch and the appearance of a well-lived-in house.

I hesitated. I imagined Rick were here now, slightly amused, writing a theme about his young friend Rob: *And so, at the age of 17 years and one month, height five foot ten, weight one hundred sixty five pounds, dressed in brown corduroys, plaid shirt, gray jacket and brown and white saddle shoes, Robert Jeffrey St. Clair, also known as Rick the Second, stands on Curtis Street at three o'clock in the afternoon and stares across the street at my old house. Why doesn't he ring the bell, meet my mother, and tell her all about my last months on earth?*

Well, St. Clair, that was fun: Rick might have written thoughts like these. But he's dead, he's gone, and I am on my own. I was just a kid who had known a wonderful man; how could I approach that man's closest relatives so casually, so unprepared? But I was going to do it. I crossed the street, up on the sidewalk, to the front walk. That's it: No. 1115. Righto.

And I couldn't go on. It was as if a glass wall was standing solidly between me and their house. I couldn't do it; I wasn't ready. Ah, an idea, a saving grace: check out Rick's high school; it was close by. Didn't I need to get the complete picture of his neighborhood?

I studied the campus of North Springs High School from across the street. I stared at young students—my age—coming and going, boys flirting with girls, studious types carrying a load of books, some bigger boys coming out of the gymnasium. And, to prove that I wasn't gutless, I walked casually into the entrance, mingling with students, peering into classrooms, then out the rear door to the athletic fields. I walked into the gym where I figured Rick had thrown many a basketball.

My next diversionary step was to seek out Lincoln Park. Rick had told me that as a four-year-old, he used to wade in the shallows of that lake.

It was a game now. I asked myself how else I could delay meeting the Lindens. Ah, I have it, his church. During one of our talks on spirituality, Rick had told me the location of the first Methodist Church. Further north, on the far side of the park. I would check it out. Churches welcomed everyone. I walked the halls, nodding at two older ladies as if I knew them, and looked right through a young pastor who scared me by looking at me quizzically. I pretended to read the bulletin board, glancing at the notices. And I saw the way out. The announcement, displayed prominently in the center of the board read:

Potluck dinner – Friday night, October 6th – 6:30 pm.
A variety of food offered – games for the youngsters—
and a brief and inspiring message from Pastor.
Come one, come all. Welcome to everyone!

I had stumbled across the perfect way to see Rick's parents. See them, not meet them, a vast difference. I would have someone point them out to me, then feel my way through the evening. And, most important, I would have a few more days to prepare for that meeting. My ego grasped at this valid-sounding reason to give up meeting them today.

*   *   *   *

Two nights later, I still wasn't ready to meet them. Well, I didn't have to. I would see them from across a large room, then plan the actual meeting with assurance. Or so I told myself. I strolled nonchalantly about the room, never standing still, trying to blend with the group. I talked casually with a young lady, not introducing myself, with an older lady, and with two giggling teen-aged girls. I had brought some hard rolls as my contribution to the potluck, and I deposited them on a long table with the other food. I decided to wait until after dinner to inquire about the Lindens—of course they might not even be here—when a lady in her late forties tapped me on the shoulder. "Pardon me, young man, we haven't met. You must be new here. I'm Ruth Linden."

I stared at her. My tongue refused to respond to my brain. Finally, I gulped "Hello" and a moment later, "I'm Rob"—then I lapsed into a stunned silence.

Mrs. Linden, aware that her new acquaintance had a problem of some sort, didn't let it deter her from extending her hospitality. "Rob," she said, grabbing my elbow. "I'll bet you don't have a table yet. No? Let's find one—there'll be a mad dash in a moment." And she steered me along with her.

By the time I had been introduced to Alex Linden, I had found my voice. Barely.

Sitting between Rick's parents, it seemed like I was in an aberrant world. I felt as if I was looking down on myself from outside my body. Who was that stricken soul down there? When I spoke it was in strangled gasps. I suppose I summoned up the presence of mind to be polite. And then it struck me: I hadn't told them, as I certainly planned to, that I had known their son in England. Could I blurt it out now?

Could I say, *"By the way, Mrs. Linden, I knew a young man in England whose name was also Linden. Rick Linden. Any relation?"*

Or *"How do you spell your name? L-i-n-d-e-n? By any chance, did you have a son who was a pilot in the American Air Corps? Who was killed in December 1944?"*

God, help me. Intuitively, I knew I couldn't do it. I had let the opportunity slip away. I would have to bring it up later. I was so nervous about it, so disturbed, that I was barely able to respond to the natural questions the Lindens had about their new acquaintance.

What part of England was I from? Are you just a visitor to our town, or do you live here? Going to school here? Are your parents here in Colorado Springs with you? Perhaps you'd like to make First Methodist your church home?

Then came the question from Ruth Linden which I had been alternately eagerly anticipating and desperately dreading. "Were you in England during the war?"

"Uh—oh, yes, Mrs. Linden."

"You were too young to have been in it, of course. We lost a son in that war. He was a pilot. We think of him every day."

So do I, Mrs. Linden, so do I.

"Our daughter Jane has left home now. We're empty-nesters in our house a few blocks from here."

"Yes, I know, Mrs. Linden."

Then, after the conversation from across the table broke the chain of thought for a few minutes, Mrs. Linden spoke again. "Where do you live, Rob?"

"Well—uh—I'm staying at the YMCA. Temporarily."

"If you don't mind my saying this, Rob," Mr. Linden said, speaking for only the second time, "that's not a place to spend much time in. I go by it every day—it's not far from my store." He had short iron-gray hair, wore glasses, and looked like a middle-class business man, which of course he was.

"I hope to move out soon," I said. "it's too expensive.'

"You'll probably be moving to a dormitory at Colorado College then?" He had assumed I was attending his son's college.

As for me, I had no idea where I was going.

"Not for awhile." I was in control of myself now, but aware I was headed for dangerous ground. "I won't start there until next year."

"Then where will you move?" Mrs. Linden asked.

"Somewhere cheap," I said. Mr. Linden gave me an amused glance.

There were games for the children, a talk by the pastor, and a half-hour of songs led by the choir master. Desserts of all kinds were spread before us, introductions of guests (Mrs. Linden claimed me as a special guest from England) and more talk. I thought desperately that no one seemed interested in leaving. Except me.

I was torn between a deep desire to get to know Rick's mother and father, and an equally deep disgust of myself for being so spineless, so deceiving.

When the Lindens were finally ready to go, I could hardly wait to separate myself from them. I had some serious thinking to do. I needed to analyze my abrupt introduction to Ruth and Alex Linden. I wanted to come to terms with my new specialties: liar, phony, hypocrite. Bogus said it best.

It was snowing lightly as we exited Fellowship Hall. I was out the door ahead of them, flinging back words of parting. "Nice to meet you folks. I hope we meet again. Thanks for everything."

But Mrs. Linden was closer behind me than I'd thought. "Rob," she said, quickly, "how are you going to get back downtown?"

I felt sheepish for my anxiety to be out of their sight. "I guess by bus," I said. "It's the way I came out here." At least that much was true.

"My husband will take you back, won't you, Alex?"

"Of course," he said.

I had thought I was out of the situation. My emotions were a tangled mess. I couldn't think fast enough to come up with a logical reason to refuse. I felt guilty again: the Lindens must have noticed my desire to get away.

Ruth Linden asked to be dropped off at her home. As she emerged from the front seat, the snow seemed to intensify. A thought struck her: I was to find out she was a woman of quick and independent ideas followed by appropriate action.

She leaned back into the front seat to address me. "Rob, I don't like Alex to drive in the snow. Not so late at night. I'm sure the last bus has departed. So, young man, why don't you stay the night with us? We'll give you breakfast in the morning, then you can catch a bus downtown."

Stunned anew, I couldn't move or speak.

Undeterred, Ruth Linden continued. "You can sleep in our son Rick's old bedroom in the basement. I think I may have a pair of his pajamas, as well."

*　　　　*　　　　*　　　　*

What is happening to me? I've wanted to meet Rick's parents for a long time—but not this way. I feel cheap, tawdry, manipulative. They're such nice people and I'm so bogus. What should I tell them? When should I tell them? How can I tell them?

God, St. Clair, you're such an asshole.

I lay in the dark, on my back, in the double bed in the basement bedroom. I was in Rick's house, Rick's bedroom, Rick's bed, wearing Rick's pajamas. Mrs. Linden had found a toothbrush, still in its wrapper.

"Rick bought this to take overseas, but he forgot it," she said, and I practically bawled in front of her.

No, I couldn't tell them. I had thought about it again—I had thought of little else since meeting them—when Mr. Linden had shown me a photograph of Rick in his uniform.

Oh, was that your son? Well, what do you know, I knew him. Yes, it was while he was flying fighter planes. We used to go fishing together. So you're Rick's parents?

I knew I didn't have the guts. I was too broken up to trust my voice, to trust any decision I might make now. I had looked at Rick's picture without comment, returning it after only a moment. Then, after a cup of cocoa ("Rick used to have cocoa with us late at night") and a quick tour of the house ("Rick loved this old house") it was time for everyone to call it a night. Thank God. I couldn't take any more of my double-dealing.

Lying there in the darkness, I couldn't hold back my tears. I didn't want to. I wanted—I demanded—to live these nocturnal moments thinking of Rick Linden. I realized I had never been closer to him since he had been lost to me.

22

LIVING AT RICK'S HOUSE

I slept soundly enough until I heard a gentle rapping on the bedroom door. It was nine o'clock and breakfast was waiting. I was more composed as I joined my hosts for the meal. I didn't want to talk about their son. My emotions were too near the surface.

While we ate, Mr. Linden told me he was going to the store for a short while. He said he often did, on a Saturday. Did I want a ride downtown with him? Yes, I said, as gracefully as I could manage. I had run out of ways to escape the Linden household, while intensely aware that I didn't want to. It was just that there was pressure all the time, pressure to tell the whole truth.

Neither of us spoke for several blocks. I sensed there was something on Mr. Linden's mind. He was more reticent than his wife. He kept his eyes on the street ahead.

"You know, Rob, we've missed Rick so much. Ruth said last night how much you reminded us of him. Not in any obvious way. You're younger, more heavily built, and with brown hair and---." He went on for a moment more.

I didn't dare look at him. How much more could I take? Why was he talking to me like this? I was just a kid he'd met last night. Unless—my breath caught. *Unless some part of their son's character has been transferred to me. Destiny?*

"What I'm getting at, Rob, is, well, Mrs. Linden and I have talked it over—and, well, why don't you move in with us, until you find a place to live? We'd—we'd like to have you. You could have Rick's room just as you did last night. You could board with us, to. We wouldn't charge you for the room, though perhaps you could help a bit towards the food."

My state of paralysis had not escaped Mr. Linden's notice. While having no idea what was causing it, he had no wish to press me, thank God. "No need to respond now. Think about it. If you want to stay with us, I could pick you and your belongings on my way home any night, as early as tonight, if you wished."

And, finally, Alex Linden had turned an inquiring face my way, shrugging his shoulders slightly the same way Rick used to. I couldn't meet his eyes. After a moment I said, "I'll think about your—k-k-kind—offer, sir." He dropped me off at the YMCA and gave me a little salute like Rick used to. My God.

I lay on my face on my cot at the "Y," waves of feelings sweeping over me: guilt, gratitude, love. But, most of all, an unworthiness to be on the same planet as Alex and Ruth Linden. I knew immediately that I would accept. I *couldn't* turn it down. I wanted to live with the Linden family. What a great opportunity to get to know them, to learn more about Rick, meet his sister, perhaps a friend or two. And yet, and yet...I had been dishonest, non-forthcoming, ungracious, a classic heel. The word that best described me was *bogus.*

I wrestled with the problem the rest of the morning and into the afternoon. I skipped lunch; I felt like I didn't deserve it. At two o'clock I called Mr. Linden to say I would be happy to live with them for a week, maybe two, until I found a permanent place to live. I was relieved but still deeply troubled. But my bogus feeling was overwhelmed by exhilaration. *I was going to live at Rick's house. God almighty.*

.

I had told Mr. Linden that I would come out on the bus on Monday. I didn't want further conversation with him just now.

When I came in from a lonely dinner the next night, a Sunday, the night desk clerk hailed me.

"Mr. St. Clair. Your sister and I looked for you a half hour ago. She said she'd be back this evening."

I stood dumbly in front of him. Had the world gone mad? "My—sister? I don't have a sister—who, uh, lives anywhere near here. What did she look like?"

"Blonde, rather longish hair, built—well---."

"Thanks, uh, thanks." My heart leaped. Louise had been here. My insides tightened at the thought.

I lay on my bed, waiting. Would she come again? A bit
later came a knock on the door. I jumped from my bed quickly.

"Hello, young Rickie," she said. My heart was thumping
like a punch-drunk fighter. I had spent a lonely afternoon, not
wanting to treat myself to a movie. I felt I didn't deserve any
treats. Now here was the biggest treat of all.

"How have you been, Rick? I'm sure glad you were still at
the Y. I couldn't get up here from Pueblo any sooner. My job, you
know. I thought you might want to see me."

It seemed like the devil had taken my tongue prisoner. We
both knew why she was here. I said, finally, "It's a small room.
Nothing much here but the bed."

"That's all we'll need."

"You were so cute last night," she said in the morning.

"First time, eh? For awhile you were tensed up something
awful, then you relaxed and we played great music together."

I wondered what Rick's first time had been like. I wondered what he had said then, what he would say now. "It was one
of those things that had to happen," I said, finally. The world
seemed suddenly different. "You can't imagine how happy I feel
now, Louise. Is that how it is every time?"

I realized I'd spoken my assumption that she was an experienced girl in the ways of sex. She smiled wryly. "Every time is
different."

A few minutes later she leaped from the bed. "Hey, I've
got to catch the nine-thirty bus," she said as she dressed. "I'm on
at noon at the restaurant."

I had not gotten up, content to just lie there, hands clasped
behind my head. She leaned over me, planted a lingering kiss on
my lips and said, "You're better than Chuck, Rick," and she was
gone, leaving behind her a sad emptiness in my soul. It wasn't for
a minute or two that I realized she had called me by a name which
didn't belong to me. I felt both proud and ashamed, too.

I lived with the Lindens for two weeks. I ate every meal
with them, I shopped with Ruth Linden, I picked vegetables with

Alex Linden, I got to know their neighbors and a few of their friends. I was a regular at their church.

There were days of rain, days of snow, nights of stars and dreaming. And I communed hourly with someone who had been dead for close to two years. Rick's room was now my room, his clothes were on my back, I read his books, I looked at photo albums of him from birth onward. And still I didn't tell my hosts that I had known their son.

How could I—now? How could I excuse the obvious duplicity in my sudden arrival at their church potluck that night, of my ready acceptance of their offer to live with them? Of taking advantage of their hospitality, their friendship?

Most of the time I simply hated myself. I was a weakling, a stunted boy with no guts, no pride, no ideals. I had distanced myself from the memory of my friendship with Rick. I wasn't fit to be even a dim shadow of Rick Linden. There was a hole in my soul.

At the end of two weeks I could stand the deception no longer. I had practiced my speech until I had it down.

"You've been awfully nice to me," I said after dinner in their dark-paneled dining room. "It's time to get on my own. I am going to Foothill"—naming a junior college at the south end of Colorado Springs, at least three miles from the Linden's residence.

"I'm going to live down that way, as well. They've accepted me for the winter session. Before then, I want to study and make some money. I have a job hashing at a restaurant near school."

Was that three lies or four? I told lies easier than I told the truth. I couldn't tell the difference between the two.

I turned away from the hint of a hurt look on Mrs. Linden's face. She asked me a few questions, handing me a chance to tell more lies. I wondered if she recognized by now how phony I was. She probably thought I was bored with them. *Not true, Mrs. Linden. You're great, both of you. I just can't stand playing you for fools any longer.*

Mr. Linden's questions were less searching, more practical. Did I need a loan? If I ever wanted to buy a car, let him know. He was pretty good with cars. Did I need a reference?

I was close to breaking down and I guess I looked it. I nearly told them everything. But I couldn't do it. Choked up, close to tears there at the dining room table, I pleaded weariness, saying I had better get in some reading about the college I was going to.

"I have some pamphlets from school," I began, then stopped talking abruptly, simply not able to keep on lying. But then a strange feeling came over me. I had found something I was good at: lying. Fooling people. Becoming an imposter. Was I crazy? Good liar or not, I certainly wasn't enjoying it. My primary feeling was profound disgust with myself.

In Rick's basement room, I flopped on his bed, tears flowing freely.

When the knock came on my door an hour later, I hadn't read anything. I had just been lying naked on my bed, staring at the ceiling. I tore the blankets back and leapt into bed, drawing the sheet up almost to my chin.

"Who is it?" I asked in as normal a voice as I could muster.

"It's Mrs. Linden, Rob. May I come in for a moment? Are you decent?"

"Yes, come in, come in," I said, and the words came out as if I were being strangled.

She entered the room and seated herself on the room's only chair. "I won't stay but a moment, dear, but Mr. Linden and I thought something was wrong, that we could help you. You can tell us your troubles, you know. Your parents are far away, but we're parents, too. Will you talk to me, Rob?"

I looked at her through bleak eyes. I had no thoughts, no words. Nothing would emerge from my tortured lungs.

Ruth Linden continued, as if she hadn't asked a question gone unanswered. "You know, this is exactly what I did many times with Rick. He would be in that very bed, and"—smiling—"usually without a pajama top, or bottom, either, for all I knew. And we'd talk. Talk about his goals, his girl friends, his love of writing, his plans for the next day, his ideas about---,"

Her kind face was above me, smiling down, and I noticed the network of tiny wrinkles there. "Mrs.—Mrs. Linden," I croaked finally, "I—wish—you wouldn't—talk about your—your son right now. I can't stand it—can't talk tonight." I closed my eyes and willed her to leave.

Seemingly undisturbed by my words and attitude, she rose to her feet. "I do go on and on about Rick, I know. If you'd known him, you would understand. I'm sorry, Rob. May I say one more thing?"

My eyes still closed, I could only barely nod.

"At times Rick would act just the way you are now—not wanting to talk, willing me out of the room. But, usually, the next day he'd seek me out and we'd have that talk. Will you remember that, Rob? I'll be here, upstairs in my kitchen, all day tomorrow, if you want to talk. I'd be so happy if you did. Good night, Rob." She closed the door softly.

As I brushed my teeth later I looked with disgust in the mirror. The bloodshot eyes (from crying), the stubbled jowls (not knowing how to shave), the unsteady hands (too much emotion), and the silly look on my face. I hated that face.

I left the Linden's house the next morning without a talk with Rick's mother. I promised her I'd let her know where I lived, I said I was grateful for the kindnesses of both she and her husband. I plotted the words carefully. No emotion was anywhere around.

Mrs. Linden, a wise woman, let me go without further mention of a talk.

I lay on my bed at the YMCA, where I had returned to live. I forced myself to think of my future. I had to decide things for myself; I hadn't made an independent decision for weeks, not even my recent night with Louise. So, what is it to be, St. Clair—give it up, go back to Aunt Bea's house and forget all of this nonsense? I could live a normal life as a freshman at a junior college—Cuesta College in San Luis Obispo—but what was the point of living in California?

I had come to America to follow Rick's leadership, to follow in his footsteps, to accomplish things in his name. I was in precisely the right place: Colorado Springs. Get on with it, St. Clair. Rick had not been a quitter and I wouldn't be one, either.

I was deeply ashamed of my lies about going to college and finding a hashing job there. But wait: I would erase the lies by doing just that; it was what I'd planned to do, anyway. For I was going to college—the best way to begin fulfilling lofty goals. To that extent, I hadn't lied to Rick's parents. I would go to school in the south of town, away from the emotional influence of the Lindens.

I would find work and lodging as far away from the Lindens as I could. Later, I could decide how to approach them again.

But they might have written me out of their lives; I might never see them again. The thought saddened me. I truly liked them aside from their being Rick's parents.

The next morning I walked the south area. And soon came across a café with a "Dishwasher wanted" sign in the window. I would set table, clear table, stock supplies, help in the kitchen. It was exactly what I wanted and needed: penance through manual labor. And an income, too.

On the same walking trip I found a large first-floor room in a rooming house a few blocks from the restaurant. I would share a bath with two others. I was relatively content: on my own in a city I was beginning to like and I would be starting my higher education in a few months. And there were a lot of girls in this college neighborhood.

I lay in the bathtub down the hall. It was midnight and I shouldn't be disturbed at this hour. I asked myself what I could do to reverse the consequences of my horrible beginning with Rick's parents. I still wanted—badly—to become Rick the Second, to follow his postwar quests. And while an education and some emotional maturity were mandatory, I wouldn't have to wait to finish college to get started. I could launch into that while still in college. The thought cheered me immeasurably.

I felt good about my work/living/college decisions, all of which I had made on my own. Not that most college freshmen didn't do the same every day.

I turned the hot water valve to "Hot", ignoring the sign about "seconds" on the hot tap.

As I had often since Rick's death, I asked myself how the flyer would have handled a given situation. And it came to me that if Rick hadn't wanted to face a problem in person, he would have written about it. It was his natural medium.

In my room again, I penned a letter to the Lindens:

I'll bet you didn't expect to ever hear from me again. You probably hoped you never would. I left because I couldn't face you. I'm going to tell you what was going on with me.

I wrote on, describing briefly how I had met Rick, how we had shared so much, and how I had wanted to—had to—carry on the lifetime ideals of their son.

Why Rick allowed me, a 15-year-old kid, to be his friend, I will never know. But I will always be grateful for it. You may be wondering why I followed him to his home, and why I forced myself on his parents under false pretenses. I'm deeply sorry for that and someday I'd like to talk to you about it.

I'm living in the south part of the Springs now, like I said I would, and I'm happy. I'll call you someday, although I wouldn't be surprised if you didn't want to talk to me.

I ended it simply: Sincerely, Rob

I had written the letter straight from the tub, by the weak light of my bedside lamp. I re-wrote it three times, and I still wasn't terribly happy with it. But I vowed I would mail it in the morning, without a return address, and then, like my letter said, get on with my life.

23

GIFT FROM A DEAD SON

My life steadied as I succeeded in reducing the emotional strain thrust upon me. I thought of myself, finally, as a "normal" college freshman away from home for the first time. I aimed to fit in with other boys my age, my thoughts, like theirs, centering mainly on grades, living somewhere affordable, earning some money—and the eternal girl search.

I thought often of the Lindens. They were probably lost to me forever. This greatly depressed me. It didn't occur to me that they were not through with *me*. I had not given them my return address, though they knew the junior college I would soon be going to. A week after I had posted my letter to them, I stopped by the college administrative office to pick up some material I wanted.

The gray-haired clerk looked at me sharply when I gave her my name. "You're the boy from England? There was someone here looking for you a few days ago."

"A young blonde girl?" My heart was pounding.

"No, an older lady. She asked for your home address. I didn't have it. Do you want to give it to me now?"

"Yes."

Was she tracking me down to tell me what she thought of me? I considered it again as I stacked dishes that night at Shadburn's Corner Café. And then it came to me: Ruth Linden had just learned from me that I had been friends with her son during the last months of his life. *Of course* she would want to talk with me.

I telephoned them from my rooming house and was amazed that Mrs. Linden was overtly friendly. She asked me over for the following evening. I could say I was busy: the coward's way out. But I knew I owed it to them to talk about their son's final days. I accepted, though I knew an emotional whirlpool was sure to develop.

I took the bus, despite their offer to pick me up. I told them I wanted to return by bus, as well, thereby setting a time limit on the visit. I had decided to set some ground rules of my own. I was taken aback when Ruth Linden hugged me at the door, even that Alex Linden was all smiles as we shook hands. At dinner we talked of President Truman's recent actions, the prospect that Colorado College would win their final football game and other neutral subjects. The Lindens were biding their time; after dinner they would want to talk of Rick.

I knew Ruth Linden liked to wash the dishes immediately after dinner, with Alex drying. Neither happened tonight. They asked me into the living room and drew up three chairs together. "Now, Rob, it's time to talk about you and Rick. It's amazing that you knew him." She didn't question why I hadn't mentioned it earlier. "We want to hear how you and he met, what you talked about, and, well, the whole story."

This was her right as Rick's mother. She didn't bring out the photo albums, the school pictures, the memorabilia of her son's life in Colorado Springs. That wasn't what this session was about. It was my turn to talk. And so I told them, clearly and with no great detail, of how we had met fishing, of our talks, of climbing Roans Peak, of the problems with my father, and how Rick's friend Major Burks had handled them. I told them how much I had liked and admired their son.

I said I had thought at the time (and even more so now) that Rick's mind was always working on how to solve the problems of the world, and that I had concluded that he would have made a difference in the world.

"But of course you know that," I said.

"We do know that," Alex Linden said, "but it is awfully nice to hear it from you, who knew him during the last few months of his life. How long?"

"Two months and 27 days."

A brief silence followed. My exactitude provided them an insight into just how close we had been. I knew, and they suspected, that there was more to be discussed. Such as: what was I doing in Colorado Springs now?

I plunged in. "Rick confided in me the things he wanted to do after the war. He wanted to give something of himself to the

169

world. First, he wanted to write and publish and influence people, if possible."

"He had a lifelong passion for writing," Alex said.

"Another important issue was world peace. He felt very strongly about that. Promote peace. End wars."

Mrs. Linden said, "He wrote to us many times on that subject."

"And then, education for everyone. Did he write to you about that, too?"

"Not so much in his letters," she said. "But we know education was important to him, especially for the poor and underprivileged. And he wrote a full chapter on the subject in his autobiography, *Trail of the Bombers.* We just received the published copy, sent to us by his agent in New York."

I had never caught up with his book. Jeanne, a friend of Ricks' in England, was supposed to have returned the carbon copy to Pat Morse after Rick's death. Presumably, it had been sent home to his parents who, I was just learning, had succeeded in getting it published.

"Do you mean it's a book now?" I was becoming emotional again, in a big way.

"You bet it is," Alex said. Rick's father, whom I'd found to be a quiet, introspective man, was now brimming with excitement.

"It's such a wonderful gift from a departed son—to leave his family and the world," Ruth added.

My heart was in my mouth; words were difficult for me to formulate. My careful control of my emotions was about to be smashed. "Could—could I read it sometime?"

It was Alex who responded. "Of course you can, Rob. Take it home with you tonight if you wish."

I was back in my bath—my favorite place to think. It was late; I was alone; there were no sounds except the splashing of tub water. Go to bed, Rob, m'lad, I said to myself. It's midnight, the hour of dead souls. Get back to your room now; go to bed. You don't need more emotion tonight.

But of course I ignored such logical thoughts. I could hardly wait to get back to my room, throw off my towel, and, snug in bed, start Rick's book. It was a beautifully-bound edition, published in New York a few months earlier in hardbound. The cover mesmerized me: a boy and an airplane and a distant horizon, with the book's title emblazoned in red letters across the top: *Trail of the Bombers*. Good title, but the best part of the cover were the words at the bottom: by *Richard P. Linden*.

The question I asked myself as I looked carefully at the title page, the credits, the photographs of a young Rick on the page facing "Chapter 1," is how much should I read tonight? A half-hour, I concluded. Get into it, get the feel of it. Then tomorrow, a Sunday and a day off, I would read more. I would take three or four days to finish it. That's called savoring, I thought. Good plan.

Two hours later I was halfway through, unable to stop. I tried to think of words to describe it: compelling? Emotional? Gripping? Yes, all of these and more.

I put the book on the floor, next to my watch, and turned over to sleep. I was tired, physically and emotionally. I would sleep soundly now. Two hours later, having tossed and turned over several times, I awoke with a start. I rolled onto my stomach and reached for my watch; it was after four. Without further thought, I began reading again. It took another hour and a half, and my heart was beating almost painfully in my chest. I had read Rick's view about flying in bombers and his developing take on the killing game, about universal education, about the futility of war, about the need for understanding, for compassion, about the universal need to work together to make the world a better place.

I felt as if I had a head cold, as I had had the flu, as if a giant had a grip on my larynx. My eyes watered as I closed the book; I had no tears left. I imagined I would come apart if I took a deep breath.

But such is the nature of youth that a few minutes later I was sound asleep. I stayed in bed until noon.

I made myself a tuna sandwich and poured a glass of milk in the rooming house kitchen. I sat at the table by the kitchen window, gazing out at fading flowers and a patchy lawn. I could just see Pikes Peak in the distance, enveloped in haze and mist. It was not snowing.

As I ate I said "Rick Linden" aloud several times, and the past came flooding back. It seemed that bits and pieces of my past floated by to become again part of my present. Very confusing.

The book seemed like a dream now, but I knew I could pick it up at any time if I needed strength or inspiration. Yet, I felt sad, as well, and helpless. I wanted to get out and do something, not sit here in the kitchen by myself. I wanted to see Rick again, talk with him, laugh with him. Those things not being possible, what could I do? I could read the book again, and then again, digest it, even attempt an outline. But for what purpose? I knew what was in it. I'd known the author. It was a time for action.

I walked briskly up the hillside towards the Garden of the Gods, the great natural wonder. I marveled that it was just yesterday that I had decided to put Rick and his parents at the back of my mind, that I would lay off for awhile on "The Rick Quest."

What a difference a day makes.

I walked six or seven miles until mid-afternoon, while the sun peered wanly through cirrus clouds. It wasn't snowing, but if it had been, I knew I would be there, anyway. My head had cleared, my stomach was reasonably full, and the resiliency of youth worked its usual magic on me.

I realized I had read Rick's book too fast, that I'd likely skimmed some important parts. I'd buy my own copy from the college book store, then return the Lindens' copy. For the book Rick had written was going to be my guideline for my quest; it would be the plan I'd never made.

As I stood at the high point of the Garden of the Gods overlooking my new city, it came to me with a startling vividness that I had known—and loved—Rick Linden without reading anything he'd written. A few letters, perhaps. I had known the flyer as a caring, compassionate, fun person, as well as a deep thinker. To realize now, two years later, that he was also a fine and convincing writer, was overwhelming. What a wonderful surprise. I felt strengthened by it, buoyed skyward.

I looked around; no one was in sight. I knelt in the rocky soil and lifted my eyes to the overcast skies. It would be better if it were night and bright stars were overhead, but this would have to do. I spoke to him aloud:

Rick, are you listening to me now? I'm speaking for myself—to understand where I am in my search for you. You have taken over my life, pal, and I intend to follow through with your passions,

I swear it by everything I hold holy. That's all I wanted to say, Rick. Sleep well.

I stared at the free-wheeling clouds in the pale gray sky and felt a longing so deep it nearly made me physically sick. No one had witnessed my vow, my prayer, except God and perhaps Rick. It was enough.

I ran the several miles down the hill, all the way to my boarding house, stopping only a couple of times to catch my breath. I felt ennobled, glorious, charged up as never before in my life. My mind was afire with the possibilities, the potential, the unlimited power of my commitment.

After my long walk and run, I radiated energy. I wanted to look in a mirror to see if I could capture the essence of how I felt. What I saw there mesmerized me: I had the look of wildness, my thick hair tousled, my eyes gleaming with energy, ready for whatever came my way. I recognized, perhaps for the first time, that my friendship with Rick, my adoption of his ideals, could be of unimaginable benefits for me. Not in getting ahead in the world—that was selfish and not the point—but in having great things to do, ideals to emblazon across the world, levels of the highest sort to attain. I was Rick's surrogate, his disciple, and I would go to places and accomplish things that I could never reach on my own. With Rick Linden as part of my persona, anything and everything was possible.

Lying in bed, my mood slowly deflated like a balloon with a slow leak. My high of the afternoon had been inspired by having read Rick's book, from my long run, from my prayer to him, and from an artificial, rosy-colored view of the future. I knew my quest to follow Rick would be long and lonely, filled with challenges I might not be up to. I deliberately willed Rick to invade my soul to give me the strength for the battle ahead.

24

STRANGERS IN MY LIFE

I was a busy lad: working, studying, dating when I could afford it, perhaps a movie with a friend from Shadburn's Corner Café. I was on the lookout for the perfect American girl. At last I had my priorities straight. I needed education, money, discipline, and plans. And I needed to develop ideas on how to live the new life I'd embarked upon.

I knew I took myself too seriously. I asked myself if there was room for dedication to a higher cause and fun in the same world. I didn't have much experience with the lighter side of my life, what with my early life at home and now the quest I had taken upon myself. But, I asked myself, couldn't I have fun, too? I didn't know. I didn't try very hard to develop close male friends. And I met no girl friends capable of lighting up my life. And then I met three people within a short time of each other, all of whom were to play a large part in my life. And not all necessarily positive.

Until recently I was the suspect new boy in town, with the pronounced English accent, and wandering around like a lost soul.

Now I had been accepted by Rick's parents and my own decisions about working/living/schooling were in harmony.

Most of the people at my rooming house were married couples in their 20s or 30s, with a few elderly men and women in the mix. My first-floor room was larger than most of the others. It just happened that way—it was the one available the day I applied. Now I thought there was room for another bed and dresser. I might be able to have company and save on rent, as well. I asked my landlady, Mrs. Marple, if I could look for a roommate.

I could see her calculating the situation. She was a tall, thin woman of undeterminable age, a venerable gold wedding ring on her finger, curly gray hair. I had heard that she was a war widow from World War I. "Hmm—you pay $45 a month now. I would need $65 for the two of you."

"Sixty," I said, quickly.

She wasn't used to fast decisions nor was she sure she wanted one more roomer to mess up her household. When she didn't respond, I smiled but said nothing. I figured she liked me and would trust that I would pick out someone as suitable as me. We waited each other out until she asked if I would take responsibility. I had no idea what this meant, but readily agreed. I observed she wouldn't have to advertise. She liked this.

At the college office, the same secretary I'd talked to about Mrs. Linden told me there were occasionally inquiries for rooms. "Only one enquiry in the past few days," she said.

"Oh. Can you give me his name?"

She looked in a file. "Charley Peek." She offered an address downtown.

"Thank you, Madam. I'll go and look him up now."

Her quick blush surprised me. "Oh. Mr. St. Clair. There's something you'll want to know. He's a Negro."

"Negro?" I repeated as if I didn't know the term. I had heard stories about how dark-skinned people had been segregated in the United States, even in the armed forces. It seemed peculiar to me. Not wrong, necessarily, just peculiar.

"Well, I said, uncertainly. "I'll go see him. He may not want to room with me."

She was looking at me with her mouth open as I left.

I went to the place he was working, a shoe shop in the center of town. I asked for Charley Peek and was directed to a back room. A young black man was putting heels on shoes. He looked up curiously as I approached.

"Charley Peek?"

"I'm Charley," he said slowly. He had a deep bass voice. "What can I do for you?" He seemed nervous, on the edge of embarrassment. I asked him right out. "I hear you need a place to live and I was wondering if you wanted to room with me. It's a large room and you'd have your own bed and dresser. You would pay $30 per month. There are kitchen privileges. Have you ever done any cooking?"

It seemed I was the one who was nervous, blurting out all the facts in a series of quick sentences. A slow blush crawled up my face. I looked him over for the first time. He was perhaps four

175

or five years older than me, a good-looking man with close-cropped black hair. I noted his biceps were well-developed. A faint smile hovered over his lips, and finally he broke into a half-grin. "Just a minute, guy. What's your name?"

"Rob St. Clair."

"You're not from around here, are you?"

"I am now. Originally from England."

"That explains the accent, and maybe other things, too. Just where is this room?"

"On South Crescent Street." I gave him the number.

"Do they know you're asking a black man to come live in their house?"

"Uh, well, n-n-no, I guess not."

"Check it out, Rob. I've been kicked out of places before where I wasn't wanted. I reckon I wouldn't want that to happen again. I'll be here until about seven tonight."

Mrs. Maple was cleaning the second-floor hallway. "Hello," I began. "I-I found a roommate. But I thought I'd better check with you first."

"Same rules apply to him as to you and everybody. No drinking, no smoking, no girls past eleven o'clock. If he understands that and you vouch for him, it's all right with me."

I could have left it at that, but I'd learned something in the past few weeks. "Uh, Mrs. Maple, well, there's something you might want to know. He's a—a Negro."

Her face blanched. "I've never had no Negroes here," she said. "Can't you find someone who's not—that way?"

If Rick had been faced with this situation, he wouldn't have let pass the opportunity to educate. "You know, Mrs. M, we just won a war that was fought to free the world from prejudice. Charley is a war veteran and he has not had an easy life." This was an assumption, but was probably warranted. "Just because he's black does not make him somehow undesirable."

"I've never had no Negro," she said again. "I dunno—why take a chance?"

"He's a clean-cut, likable young man. I really want him as a roommate. I've never known him to do or say anything that would cause any embarrassment." This last was not a lie but was a first cousin to one.

She still hesitated, so I decided to play my trump card. I hinted that I would leave if Charley Peek couldn't room with me. "I'd hate to, but I have my principles," I concluded.

What a dishonest, totally absurd thing to say.

There followed a long stare. I met her eyes with some difficulty, knowing that I had lied and exaggerated, and afraid that she'd see it in my eyes. Finally, she said she guessed it would be all right. Charley was in. I wondered why I had fought so hard. I hardly knew him.

Christmas was almost upon us and I wasn't surprised when Ruth Linden asked me to their home on Christmas Eve. "It'll be a small group. Our daughter Jane will be here, and her fiancé, Mark. Oh, Rob, is there anyone you would like to bring with you?"

She was probably being nice in case I had found a girl I liked. I thought of Charley Peek. Since becoming roommates we had moved slowly towards a friendship; the more I saw of him, the more I liked him. I think he liked me, but I wasn't at all sure. We both came and went at such odd hours that we hadn't spent much time together.

"Uh, I guess not, Mrs. Linden. I have a roommate, but I think he's been invited somewhere." The lie just lay there. The real reason, I thought, was that I just wasn't self-confident enough to take on another emotional upheaval just now. There would be enough going on in meeting Rick's sister, Jane, to test my fragile emotions.

Alex Linden took my arm and ushered me in. A large oak table dominated the dining room and the Lindens had decorated for Christmas in festive style. There were linen place mats, five small red candles, one for each guest, and an overhanging wreath of holly.

Alex and I joined the others in the kitchen. A young man was in the middle of a story; he stopped abruptly. As my eyes swept the small kitchen, my mind registered the expressions on each face. Mrs. Linden's held a welcoming smile, the young man a neutral curiosity, and the young lady—what look had I surprised there? It was certainly not benign; perhaps only a slight irritation that her fiance's story had been interrupted.

Ruth had told me Jane was three years younger than Rick. That would make her about 22 now. She didn't have Rick's coloring; her hair was a light brown with tiny curls at the neck line. She was tall, perhaps five foot seven. Her skin was clear and entrancing; she was a striking young woman

I was introduced as "Rick's young friend from England," and it was evident she had been briefed about me. Her skin felt cool and impersonal as we shook hands.

Mark, her fiancé, was also tall, with blond, wavy hair. He wore steel-rimmed glasses. He shook my hand without overt enthusiasm, as one will sometimes do with a stranger intruding on a family gathering.

The Lindens had told me that Rick and Jane had been close and for this reason I looked forward to meeting her. I wanted to ask about their "growing up" days.

The couple sat together at dinner with Mr. and Mrs. Linden at the ends. That put me alone, opposite Jane. More than once I caught a look from her that I couldn't define. Curiosity, of course. Questioning my presence, possibly. I let the older people do the talking—it was their family—but I answered questions put my way without asking any in return. I was not comfortable in my role as an outsider in a family holiday gathering.

Mr. Linden included Rick among his pre-dinner prayers. His words so closely paralleled my prayers that I felt tears welling up in my eyes. It seemed as if tears were part of my face whenever I was with the Lindens. My thoughts strayed to the lost member of the family who must have been about my current age when he had attended his final Christmas gathering in this same dining room.

Later in the evening we listened to Ruth play the piano accompanied by Jane on the flute. Rick had told me about these evenings of music; he himself played the clarinet. Mr. Linden told me his contribution was as a good listener, a comment which drew polite laughter. It was a pleasant time, but I didn't relax. Was Jane responsible for that?

When it came time to leave, Mr. Linden insisted upon giving me a ride home. I couldn't refuse without hurting his feelings. Then Jane Linden gave me the surprise of the evening. "I'll drive him." She said. "It will give us a chance to become acquainted." She even staved off Mark's joining us. "I know you've been wanting to play chess with dad," she said. No one argued the point.

In Mark's black Chevrolet which they had driven from California, she spoke first. "Just tell me straight or right or left." Her tone was pleasant, offering me no hint of what was to follow.

A block later, she spoke again, in a cool, impersonal tone. "How did you happen to choose Colorado Springs to live? All the way from England."

"Well, I like Colorado and I like your city, too. It's---." I ran out of ideas fast.

"How well did you know Rick? He was a special guy."

I know, Jane, I know.

"I got to know him well, although it was just for three months."

"All right, St. Clair, here's the real question: did your knowing him have anything to do with your coming to live here in the Springs?"

She didn't allow me to answer so anxious was she to make a point. I was glad; I would probably tell another lie. It was evident that the Lindens hadn't yet confided in Jane about my reverence for their son. Bless them. But they would soon, maybe during this Christmas weekend. In the meantime, here was Rick's unsympathetic sister probing my presence in her hometown.

"Whether you are aware of it or not, St. Clair, my parents took Rick's death very hard. It was a bad time for them." She paused and looked directly at me. "Now I can't tell you where to live, but what I will tell you is that it makes me uneasy to have you around. Not because I don't like you—you're just an English kid, after all. But your presence is a constant reminder of what they lost in Rick—and that's not a good thing. You'll never be a replacement for Rick."

That raised my hackles. "I never said that and I never thought that. Ever. And as for your parents, they seem to like me."

"That's because they're nice people. Rick is not here to speak for himself. I would give anything if he were with us now."

So would I, Miss Linden.

"But he's not and you are and I'm wondering what's going on."

"Rick and I were frightfully close, Miss Linden." I wouldn't call her Jane.

"In only three months of knowing him?"

"It was a magical relationship. He called it destiny. We hit it off so well from the beginning. If you could have seen—Oh, turn right, here."

"Well, I wasn't there and I can't even imagine you and Rick as close buddies. I have this feeling that your presence is not good for my parents."

I ducked an immediate response by having to direct her to park in front of my rooming house. I was still thinking of how to respond as she parked the car and turned to face me. Her face was in shadow, making her seem a formidable opponent.

"Just lay off. Refuse their invitations. Don't give them false hope that Rick still lives through you." I was amazed she would make that assumption although I had myself more than once. But for Rick's sister to say this, so soon after meeting me, surprised me. But it pleased me, as well.

"One thing Rick taught me," I said, greatly daring, "was not to be intimidated. Like you're doing to me right now."

It was a daunting thing to say but I was glad I said it.

She cast me a long, hard look, and was silent a moment. Then she surprised me again. "Well, St. Clair, I'm beginning to see what Rick might have seen in you. You're tougher than I thought. Okay, I came on kind of hard with you and I'm willing to call it a draw tonight. We'll talk again. I have some thinking to do. So get yourself out so I can get on home."

I had some thinking to do, too. I didn't care for Jane, but she might have a point. Perhaps my presence in the Linden's life was troubling to them at some deep, undefined level, a level they might not be aware of themselves.

I had no idea what my future with Rick's parents, not to mention his sister, was to be, but one thing I knew: not Jane Linden or anyone else would cause me to give up my vow to Rick made in a pub in Ridgewell two years ago the previous week.

25

A VERY SPECIAL STRANGER

I hadn't played the banjo since I had learned to strum at Aunt Bea's house in Manchester. She had said I had a natural talent (although she was probably just trying to buck me up) but now I thought I would take it up again. My nerves needed soothing. One Saturday afternoon I asked Charley if he wanted to go look for a used banjo at a music store or somewhere.

"Just what I wanted to do," he said.

In due course we found one. I had realized that when I was with Charley some people looked at me in a strange way, not antagonistic exactly—but, rather, enquiringly. Even the clerk at the music store asked if the other man was with me.

I told him he certainly was.

During odd hours I would strum notes I made up myself. Once in awhile I discovered a theme which carried me along with it. At times I recognized beauty in the making, and I ached to capture it, to preserve it. It made me want to leave my body here in my cheaply-furnished room and chase the music into space—or somewhere. I didn't know if I was happy or sad to have developed an interest outside of Rick Lindens'.

A notice on the bulletin board at school steered me into a new job possibility. Pikes Peak Ski Lodge was seeking bus boys. The ambience would be much classier than at Shadburn's Corner Café, and the tips would be much better. Still, I wouldn't have considered changing a permanent for a temporary job if I had been fairly treated at Shadburns. Three times I had received a call from Mr. Judson, the manager, that it would not be necessary for me to come in: there wasn't enough business that evening. This played havoc with what I laughingly called my budget.

I hitched a ride up the mountain the day after Christmas. My self-confidence was still low and my self-esteem, as well. I would have to undergo an interview. I was determined not to lie. I had no assurance that I could reclaim my old job after the ski season was over, but I wanted to do this. Rick's influence again?

I stood tall and straight in front of the Assistant Manager of the ski lodge, eight thousand feet on the slopes of Pikes Peak. His name was Mr. Cavanaugh. He told me they would be hiring about 15 boys for the next several weeks. "That interfere with anything in your life, young man? College? Love life?" He laughed and I smiled. "Okay, let's go, then. Name, please?"

Without even thinking, I answered: "Rick Linden." I had used my friend's name only on the cross-country bus, but it slipped in here as if by magic.

"Linden? Well, I'll be damned. We had a Rick Linden teaching skiing just before the war. Any relation?"

"Uh—no." So much for planning and basic morality.

"He was a swell guy, a student at Colorado College, as I remember."

Yes, I know, Mr. Cavanaugh.

"A top skier, of course. A real shame he died in the war."

Yes, I agree, Mr. Cavanaugh.

"And you have the same name. That is really quite a coincidence. Well, young man, be proud to carry that name."

I am, Mr. Cavanaugh, I am.

"How old are you, Linden?"

"Eighteen, sir." Lying certainly came easy to me.

"Tell me about your restaurant experience."

I told him I had worked at Shadburn's Corner Café for several months, and the reason I left. There was no problem there; he knew their tightwad reputation.

"Tell me about your accent, Linden."

"English, sir. I came over a year ago with my aunt and uncle. I moved to Colorado to attend college." And for other reasons.

We talked for a few more minutes about the demands and extent of the job. "It gets pretty hectic here," he said. "Skiers in by the hundreds, all wanting clean tables, fast service, and then back to the slopes again. You ski?"

"Yes, sir." Why did I tell lies when I didn't have to?

"Then you'll know how it is during the height of ski season. Can you handle pressure, Rick?"

"Yes, Mr. Cavanaugh. I'm as cool as they come. No pressure anywhere around." It was the fourth or fifth lie and by far my most outlandish one.

I relished the fast pace of the dining room, with athletic girls, some even pretty, on all sides. I made new acquaintances every day, pocketed the odd large tip, and had exchanges with sharp young college kids, most down from Denver or up from Albuquerque. I saw few familiar faces. There was seldom a chance to talk and this was fine with me.

I had been slow with girls in America. Perhaps it was my accent, or my youth, or—somehow—my obsession with Rick. I couldn't see how it could show, but I'd never had an obsession before. I'd had a few dates, but nothing memorable.

Now that I would be Rick Linden for several weeks, it might be that my luck would change. And, amazingly, it did.

As I walked briskly through the well-lighted dining room, a towel over one arm, an order form in my shirt pocket, I eyed every girl in the room, in particular those without an escort.

A table by a window was the clear winner: three girls there, two of whom I'd like to know better. A tall, willowy brunette made a quick impression on me; a winsome girl with straw-colored hair was a distinct possibility; only a washed-out blonde with large hands seemed out of the running. She reminded me of someone. Who? Ah, yes, Louise. Well, perhaps she was a possibility.

I had fun at this innocent pursuit, apparently a universal sport here in America. I hadn't been assigned their table but I worked it anyway, wiping away imaginary stains, filling water glasses, emptying an ashtray that had just been emptied. The room was filled with cigarette smoke.

My own tables were in good shape, and when my break came—a ten-minute affair—I strode out on the balcony, shivering a bit with nothing over my white shirt. I ambled close to the window nearest their table. It would be a casual but lengthy inspection of the young ladies. It came closer to a pure stare, I suppose, but I figured I could only be dimly seen from the way the light reflected off the window.

I couldn't hear their voices but I became fascinated with their gestures. The brunette waved her hands at nothing, blew cigarette smoke towards the ceiling and showed white teeth during frequent laughing spells. I named her the talker. The straw-haired one—the winsome one, I named her—spoke little and didn't smoke. She smiled frequently, though, and I noticed she fixed her entire attention on whomever was speaking, even their waiter, whom I felt dropped by too often. After a thorough look at the washed-out blonde, I didn't bother with a name for her.

After five minutes of undiluted staring, I opted for the brunette. I wished she would stand up so I could see how tall she was. As I headed back to the kitchen, I stepped aside for three young men. At the door of the kitchen, I glanced back. Damn. The boys had stopped at my favorite table, already in conversation with the threesome there.

By the time I had tied on my apron, picked up an empty tray, and relieved my reliever, the young men, no doubt college boys, had the girls on their arms and were headed out the main door. Double damn: why did it always have to end this way?

I was proud of the name embroidered on my shirt: Rick. My fellow bus boys called me by that name, most of the waiters did, Mr. Cavanaugh did, and some of the customers picked up on it, as well. Every time someone addressed me as Rick, I was thrilled. But there was another emotion there: embarrassment that I had appropriated—even for a time—Rick's name. But what harm could come from it?

My last table had been cleared and I was through for the evening. It was after nine o'clock and the last bus for the Springs departed at ten. I walked out on the porch to admire the night sky, fingering the name on my shirt. I was dead tired and although I couldn't afford many smokes, I lit a cigarette now and puffed away. I didn't inhale; I had never learned properly. Smoking was a sort of declaration of independence when I had turned 17 a few months earlier. I remembered Rick had been a casual smoker. He probably thought it was the thing to do as a fighter pilot.

Leaning on the railing, I looked upward at Pikes Peak, mostly obscured now by clouds. I blew smoke at the peak and knew intuitively that Rick had stood on this same balcony and communed with the mountain he loved.

"Do you enjoy smoking or are you just trying to impress everyone?"

I whirled around, ready to do battle, my mind slow in accepting the fact that it was a girl's voice.

"I enjoy it or I wouldn't do it," I said, which was about halfway between truth and lie. I met the steady gaze of the straw-haired girl from the dining room. I noticed a scattering of freckles, over her nose, her cheeks, and on the backs of her hands. I sported a few freckles myself, and I decided this brought us closer together.

"I guess that means you don't smoke."

"I don't, but hey, it's a free world."

I wanted off the subject. "I'm Rick. I waited on your table a while back."

"I noticed that. You seemed to be around all the time. I'll bet you had your eye on Illa. You certainly got an eyeful from your own private window."

I fought off a rising blush. In 30 seconds, perhaps 40, she had managed to inform me, somewhat less than tactfully, about my shortcomings: smoking and amateur peeping tom.

I took a deep breath. "I'm sorry I was that obvious. Did you all see me gawking at you? I suppose you had a great time laughing at me."

She laughed softly and delightfully. "Hey, a girl likes an admiring look—even five minutes of pure staring. But, listen, Illa and Joyce never noticed you. I was the one facing you and I got the full brunt."

"Full brunt. Hmm. Well, I deserve that. But there's hope for me yet. You wouldn't be talking to me now if you were sore about it? Uh—what's your name?"

"Sylvia. Cass for short. Like it?"

"I love it," I said, not to be outdone. "Hmm. You look cold. I know I am. Why don't I find some coffee and borrow a couple of coats and we can gaze at the moon."

I left her there, quickly poured cups of coffee from the huge pot on the stove, and grabbed two coats from a line of them on the rack.

For a long moment we sipped coffee and simply looked at each other. I broke first. "What happened to your friends? You had a boy on your arm a bit earlier."

"Illa and Joyce went off with the boys. They're on their way—somewhere."

"And you?"

"The boy I was with—I just met him on the slopes today—hinted at some things I didn't want to do. I just told him to shove off."

"I like your spirit, Cass. But listen, we don't have much time. Want to ride down with me on the bus?"

"I'm driving. It's an old Ford but it still operates, sort of. How about you? Want to ride with *me*?

She had said the magic words. I would see more of this frank, attractive girl.

I hoped she wouldn't ask me to drive, since most of my limited experience was on a two-ton army vehicle. She didn't.

The snow had frozen and we were driving mostly on ice. That didn't bother Cass. Once underway, she directed a smile my way. "Let's see. I know your name is Rick—from your rather dirty shirt. Do you have a last name? Are you in college? What else is there to know and admire about you?"

I liked her openness and her humor, if that's what it was. I nearly said "Linden" but stopped in time. That would certainly lead to complications if I wanted to see her again. So I told her my real last name. To cover myself, I said, "Some people know me as Rob, some as Rick." I was experiencing the sort of problem which comes with borrowing someone else's name.

I told her I was first year junior college, that I was English with my parents still living in the old country, and where I lived now. There were no lies anywhere around.

Of course I committed a lie of omission by not telling her more about the name thing. I would tell her soon, after our friendship was secure. Meantime, I decided I would just shut up.

I also learned about her. She was a high school senior at North Springs High School, that she loved skiing, dancing and iceskating. I groaned inwardly: none of these activities were in my repertoire. She would go to Colorado College, she supposed, but perhaps not until after a year at my junior college.

My heart gave a great leap.

I told her some more about myself, none of them lies.

Meanwhile, I decided I liked her pale yellow hair with a touch of brown showing through. I liked her face, she way she talked, the way her voice was low and sweet. And those freckles.

I liked her.

As we approached the Springs, I had to decide whether to kiss her. Do it: risky. Don't do it: not spunky enough. By the time she had delivered me to my rooming house, I had made my decision. I leaned over and kissed her quickly. At the last possible moment her lips parted just a bit. It didn't last half a second, but for that brief time the moon shown down with an unexpected benevolence and the stars brightened with promise.

I had her telephone number written in my wallet and we both knew we would see each other again. But my euphoria at meeting a girl I could really relate to was dampened by the ridiculous thought that she knew me by Rick St. Clair. There was no such person.

26

FIGHTING THE GOOD FIGHT

I lay listening to Charley snore softly on the other side of the room. Without any plan, I quickly threw the covers aside, slipped into my heavy wool coat, and, shoeless, crept out of my room and out the back door. Patches of snow on the lifeless lawn glistened in the moonlight. My eyes pivoted immediately skyward. I knew I was going to have a profound experience—whether positive or negative I didn't know. I shivered as much from exhilaration as from the cold, penetrating wind. There was my lovely, enigmatic sky. The wonder of it never ceased to energize me.

It was January 1, 1948, the fourth New Year's Day since Rick Linden had crashed and burned and left me alone.

Not entirely alone. I now could count Rick's parents as friends. I liked my roommate. I had met a scintillating girl, who might be in my future. There were a few others; I didn't attempt to categorize Jane Linden. I had launched myself in a new country and a new life; I was supporting myself; I was getting along. Would I say I was content? No, I wouldn't.

Content, you ask? How ridiculous. Rick's been gone now for two years and you, St. Clair, have done nothing towards fulfilling his goals. All right, you've begun the preliminaries. But hasn't the time come to take some clear steps to show that you are seriously *interested—and capable—of stepping into Rick's shoes?*

I was good at one thing: staring down the stars while making vows. Well, I would make another one: I would start the Rick Quest immediately. But where to begin? By the time I was cold enough to crave my bed again, I was no closer to listing or defining those steps.

Following my most recent vow, I had coffee downtown the next morning, pencil and paper in hand, ready to record what I had decided under the dark sky. I was a decent writer, but was I an inspirational one? Well, no. I needed to enroll in a course in creative writing. Can you learn inspiration? Then it came to me: use Rick Linden's book as your model. Re-read it along with anything else he had written, and become an authority on writing the Linden way. Read the best literature you can find in the school library. Check with the English department at Colorado College. They might have some of Rick's writings: term papers and essays.

Now, about education. How does one influence that huge subject while a college freshman? Did I need a master's degree, so that I could teach? I didn't know. Rick would have. It was my decision, I knew, whether I wanted to wait four or five years to finish my education before doing anything meaningful.

The final passion of my friend had been the most difficult: world peace, outlawing war. Get the message across to the politicians, the financiers, the military, the leaders of the country, of the world, that the waste and futility and degradation of war just had to be recognized by everyone. But—what an overwhelming subject. No one had solved the elimination of war in the history of the world. And yet…and yet. Rick had been an intelligent young man and he must have had a plan to get started. Rick's lost leadership was crucial. I was the disciple, not the leader. But since he was not here, it was up to me to take his place. Should I put this goal on hold, too, until I finished college, secured a master's degree, could write well, and had made valuable contacts along the way?

I knew Rick would not have waited for an advanced degree to get to work. That was not his style.

I *felt* a conversation with Rick. My eyes lifted to the ceiling of the restaurant—not an inspiring sight—while I mouthed the words I heard Rick saying and my responses.

"*Rob,*" he would say, "*you can't do great things until you're educated, wise to the ways of the world, and carrying at least a fair level of influence.*"

"But Rick," I responded, "would you wait that long?"

"*No, I wouldn't, kid. While I was finishing up education, I would be writing—and publishing if I could—and trying like the very devil to influence people. You do realize my anti-war goals are tied to the other two? Teaching and writing and lecturing would be my strategy to launch the peace message, loud and clear."*

"Would your crusade be put on hold until you had finished college?"

"No, Rob, no. I would not wait to start that campaign. Why waste those years? I'd start now, this month, this week, right there in Colorado Springs, whenever the opportunity arose."

"How, Rick?"

But Rick's voice was fading, his message becoming garbled. I picked up a few more words: *"By lecturing, writing, twisting arms, talking it up everywhere, fighting—the—good—fight."* His voice faded completely.

After Cass dropped me off that first night, I didn't follow up immediately. I'm not certain why not. Yes, I was. It could only be that she knew me as Rick, not Rob. I made a vow to tell her about the mix-up in names—ha, what a laugh to call it a mix-up—the next time I saw her. I put it off for nearly a week, while I worked out how I would broach the subject. She might drop me completely, unequivocally. Before I could decide when to call her and what to say, she called me. I was thrilled but nervous.

I took the call in the hall phone. "Hey, Rick, this is Cass."

"Hello, Cass. I was going to call you."

"Sure you were. I wondered if you wanted a ride to your job feeding hungry skiers. Tomorrow. Saturday, you know?"

I was excited about seeing her. But I vowed to tell her my real name, and this scared me right down to the bones.

We did some light flirting during the day. She was up with two girl friends. I had been working during the day but she came down from the slopes to lunch with me, and she quit at four o'clock and sipped coffee by herself. I made sure I handled her table.

I was off at six o'clock and we had dinner together. I was thrilled to be in her presence and delighted—and surprised—that she seemed to like me. Could she be the girl of my future? Time would tell, but of more immediate importance was the need to tell her who I was.

It went terribly. First she thought I was kidding, but then her eyes filled with doubt, incredulity, and something akin to

190

disgust. Whatever it was, she didn't disguise it. She had the whole story now and the next move was hers.

She was quiet a long minute. We had finished dinner and were still sitting in the busy, well-lit dining room. Then she said quietly, "I can understand that you idolized this Rick in England, given your pathetically unsympathetic family. I could possibly believe you would want to carry on with some of his goals, though they would have to be yours, too, or you'd lose any credibility with me. But, Rick—Rob, I cannot accept your following him to his hometown, and acting as if you really were his surrogate."

"But I am," I said, nearly inaudibly. "Rick wanted me to."

She didn't dignify that with a comment.

"Where I absolutely draw the line," she continued, "is in using his name on the bus and again here at the ski resort. Don't you realize you can only have one name in this life? That you've taken over something that doesn't belong to you?"

My voice was still barely audible. "Perhaps I should be contrite. I know I'm embarrassed. But this is something much bigger than me. It's—it's the biggest thing in my life."

"Then you need to get a better life, buster."

Thankfully, she didn't quite drop me. We dated four or five times over the next two months. There wasn't that spark that had been so promising at our first meeting. The spark was still there for me, perhaps smoldering. On her side, I sensed it was nearly out. It would only take a pinch of two fingers to extinguish it completely.

After the ski season was over, I returned to Shadburn's Café. They had actually missed me, or at least my bussing skills.

Mr. Judson surprised me by offering me a waiter's job. I was thrilled; thirty cents an hour more. Then to help Charley, and also to help Mr. Judson, I asked my roommate if he wanted to interview for my former bus boy's job. The pay was about the same as tacking heels on shoes, but a lot more social. He said to check it out—I knew what he meant—and he'd be open to it. "The only thing," he said, "is I'd have to clean up after you." Then he added something that pleased me greatly. "Perhaps we could work the same shift and have more time together."

Charley and I had been out together—to movies, or walks, to throw the football around in our front street, friendly things. I even taught him how to kick a soccer ball. During these times, we'd had our share of queer looks, even hostile ones. We ignored them.

He told me his race might disqualify him for the job. I said, "Just let me take care of it, Charley. By the way, do you have a picture of yourself at your high school graduation?" He was from Texas. "And maybe one in your army uniform, too." I had seen his army photo; he had gathered a few impressive-looking medals during the war.

He looked at me with puzzled eyes but went over to his dresser drawer and returned with a framed photograph and a snapshot. As I had hoped, in both pictures he looked handsome and intelligent, which of course he was.

"Okay if I borrow these?"

"Sure. Oh, ho, I think I see what's on your mind. But the boss is going to want to meet me, not just my pictures. Not unless you can teach my photos to bus tables."

"Oh, you're funny, Charley. But trust me. Let's try this my way. I'm headed for work now. I'll set up an appointment for you. Tomorrow noon okay?"

He agreed and I set off with more swagger than I felt.

Shadburn's Restaurant, in downtown Colorado Springs, was an old standby for students and townspeople alike. They served plain food in large portions.

I arrived before my four-hour shift was to start and found Mr. Judson in his office. I counted on what I hoped was true: that he considered me a good employee.

I knocked on his half-open door. "Got a minute, Mr. Judson?"

He swiveled around in his chair so he could face me. "Sure, Rob, what can I do for you? Do you have someone to recommend for your old job?"

I put on my brightest, most confident face. "I do, sir. His name is Charley Peek. He's my roommate and I know him well. He's a fine worker."

"Is he here now? Send him in."

"No, he's at work at a shoe shop. But I wanted to tell you a bit about him first."

Judson was slightly surprised, slightly vexed. He didn't like puzzles. Before he could respond, I pulled out the photographs of Charley.

192

"This is his high school graduation photo—five or six years ago. And in this one he is serving his country. Won a couple of medals in the Infantry. A real hero. Isn't he a fine looking lad?" Mr. Judson's frown had turned fierce. "St. Clair, I don't like to be tricked. Instead of just telling me he was a Negro, you shove photographs at me along with a lot of smooth words. Sure he's handsome, sure he's a war hero, if you say so. But it's what my customers will think that's important."

"Do you know what I think, Mr. Judson? Your customers will be happy to see you've hired a black boy. He's got the widest smile you've ever seen and in white coat and dark pants he'll make an outstanding impression on your customers."

Judson had steepled his fingers together in obvious thought. "Why should I take a chance, St. Clair? What's in it for me?"

"You'll be helping a war vet, you'll be giving a good guy a chance, and I think your customers will like you for it."

"We still segregate Negroes, you know," he said.

"Not in the armed forces," I said. "President Truman just signed a law that integrated Negroes into the military."

"I know that, Rob. But this isn't the military. I appreciate that you are trying to help him, but I don't like being a guinea pig and I don't care for your approach."

"There's one other benefit, Mr. Judson."

He had swung his chair around but now he turned it back to me. "What's that?"

"You'd keep me as an employee."

Judson sat up straight in his chair, as rigid as a lamp post. He said, slowly, "You mean you would quit if I don't take him on? You've just added blackmail to your sins, St. Clair. I'm learning a lot about you today, none of which I like."

"Respectfully, I do mean it, Mr. Judson. Try him for a week. If you're not perfectly satisfied with his work, and mine, we'll both leave with no hard feelings."

He sat there for at least thirty seconds, studying me. I kept my face impassive, not pressing any further, but not backing down, either.

Finally, he spoke. "Send him in for an interview."

"Noon tomorrow okay?"

"Yeah," he said, and turned his swivel chair back to his desk.

193

*　　　　*　　　　*　　　　*

After his third night at Shadburn's, there was no question Charley would stay on the job. As I had told Judson, without in the least knowing what I was talking about, several customers complimented Mr. Judson on hiring a Negro bus boy.

Charley and I walked home after his first night on the job.

"Thanks, my friend," he said, glancing in my direction.

"Good God, Charley, you're a better worker than I am."

"Blacker, not better," he said, and that's all either of us said about it.

I was feeling sky high. I felt I had done something which needed doing, I had stuck with my principles, and I had out-bluffed an experienced businessman. I thought I would build on this minor triumph. "Charley, as a war veteran, are you automatically a member of the American Legion?"

"No, but I'm eligible to join. I've never been interested. The war is over."

"Well, roomie, I'd like to go to the next meeting. Actually it's next Monday night." I stopped talking abruptly.

"You're pretty obvious, Rob. Make that devious. Okay, I'll go and you can come as my guest. We may find that they don't welcome dark people any more than Mr. Judson initially did."

"Seven-thirty then. Shadburns is closed Mondays, as you know. And that's a sign from the stars that the timing is right for this great endeavor."

"Great endeavor? What are we talking about? You're going to tell me what this is all about, aren't you?"

"Sometime, Charley. As much as you need to know."

Then, since that sounded sort of exclusive and I wanted to get off the subject, I added: "No more studying tonight, roomie. Get your guitar out and let's do some southern melodies. I'll be on banjo and we'll see how well we harmonize. Don't count on any great quality, but it'll be fun."

27

VISIT BY AN ANGEL

Charley and I were studying when the knock came on the door. It was Mrs. Maple, our landlady. She got right to the point. "This is really about you, Mr. Peek." Charley had risen from his chair, his face a study in apprehension. He had been around long enough to recognize trouble.

"There's been a complaint about your use of the bathtub." "It's from a gentleman on this floor. He's asked me to move you to another floor."

"But why?" This was from me.

"He doesn't want to share a bath with no Negro. Them's his 'zact words."

Charley spoke slowly but firmly. "Unless you're asking me to leave right now, Mrs. Maple, we want to stay in this room. We like it here."

"Why doesn't *he* move?" I asked, quickly. I could already visualize Charley and me out on the streets tomorrow, looking for other quarters. I figured Mrs. Maple would go along with the other resident, who had probably been with her for years.

She addressed Charley, not me. "I wanted your opinion," she said, "and you've already given it to me. I have a room comin' up vacant on the second floor, just opposite the hall phone. You can have it if you want it. But I ain't---"

"Who is this guy?" I asked. "I think I'll pay him a visit and maybe knock a little sense into him." I had heard of American prejudice but now it had hit me right in the gob.

"He's in his mid-seventies, Mr. St. Clair."

"Oh." I was deflated but still upset. I glanced at Charley and thought I detected a smile forming.

"But Mr. Peek, Mr. St. Clair, you don't have to move. Fact, I hope you don't."

This mystified me. "Why not, Mrs. Maple?"

For the first time she showed some embarrassment. "Well, because you've been good tenants and I don't want to force you into something. I'd rather force it on him."

"You mean---?" I could hardly believe it.

"I'm gonna ask him to move to the other room, or out the door. Either way."

I shook her hand, making a grand gesture of it. Charley came over and did the same. If I thought she'd stand for it, I would have kissed her hand.

It was a small enough incident, but both Charley and I felt triumphant, as if a victory over an old man was something special.

The older gentlemen did move, and I expect he had the last laugh. Because the room on the second floor was larger, sunnier, and close to the phone. If we'd been given a shot at it without the pressure from the man who didn't want to bathe in the same tub as Charley, we would have grabbed it. Such was life in a rooming house.

We had no difficulty getting into the monthly meeting of the American Legion held at the Elks Lodge on Nevada Street near the college. The uniformed Legionnaire at the door took Charley's word that he had been in the army, and I was allowed in, as well.

I had done some homework on the organization at the college library. It was chartered by Congress in 1919 as a patriotic veteran's organization. There were some million and a half members, some from as far back as the Spanish-American war. Many at the Springs Lodge were from World War I, but the vast majority were veterans of World War II. There were about 40 men in the lodge hall.

Charley decided to stay, having come this far. There were two other Negroes present, both older men presumably from World War I. Before the meeting began, I approached an older man on the stage. My heart was in my mouth. "Are you in charge, sir?"

"Yes, I am. I'm George Gullings. I'm Commander of the post. Post 426. What can I do for you?"

"I came to observe, sir. I'm English. In my country I knew a young man from Colorado Springs. He was a pilot and he was killed in action. His name was Richard Linden."

Mr. Gullings looked interested "I know of the family," he said. "We have at least a couple of members who know his parents." He thought a moment. "We have an open period after the break during which anyone is invited to comment upon any Legion affair. If you'd like to say a few words about your departed friend, I'll call upon you. We don't get visitors from England often."

I thanked him and Charley and I seated ourselves in the front row. This was so easy. Commander Gullings had been very friendly and I wasn't sure what to make of this. I figured the Legion was a war-honoring group. Perhaps not a war-*mongering* one, but an organization of people who met and talked and planned activities centered on the military, and war. Whether it was the right place to be, I didn't yet know. I was feeling my way. Rick never said it would be easy.

The business meeting lasted about 50 minutes and was followed by a break for coffee and doughnuts, courtesy of the Legion Auxiliary. Charley talked with the other two Negroes while I went over my notes on what I wanted to say. I was calm on the outside, but my insides were a mess. This would be the hardest thing I'd ever done.

After the break, it was time for testimony, time for anyone to speak of ideas, concerns, or simply to tell a story which needed telling. I listened closely. Legionnaires spoke of their relatives, dead or wounded, of the need for a strong Legion, of the need to squash the Soviet Union, and especially the need for a strong military.

"We must lobby Washington to budget more for the military," one man said.

"We must punish war criminals," another said.

"We must honor our veterans," others said.

"Too many men have left the services," another speaker said. "We need to build up our forces. We must not be caught with too few troops in case there is another war."

I listened closely: not once did I hear anyone condemn war, or even suggest that we work with the United Nations towards a world without war. The prevailing feeling seemed to be to prepare, prepare, prepare.

To prepare for what? Was another war inevitable? Should we just assume one was coming? Did we have to plan for continued killing? Wasn't anyone preparing for a permanent peace?

There was a brief silence, and I knew my moment had come. I held up my hand and the commander nodded at me.

"May I come up on stage, sir?"

"If you wish." His hesitation was brief but noticeable.

I glanced at Charley Peek; he looked apprehensive. He was probably thinking he wished he were home studying. I mounted the steps and walked to center stage, my heart beating painfully. I had never done anything like this in my life. But I had to speak; it was what Rick Linden would have done, perhaps before this very group.

I was nervous but as soon as I talked about their home-town boy and his contribution to victory in Europe, I relaxed. I would lull them for a few minutes, then let go with my big guns. Big guns? Who was I kidding?

I told them I knew Rick Linden in England and that we were friends. "Lieutenant Linden could have come home to Colorado Springs after flying in bombers," I said. "But he wanted to fly in fighters. And he died as a result."

There were nods, a "hear, hear," and several clapped hands. The regulars were appreciative of this English lad telling them about one of their own.

"It is my belief," I went on, "that if he had lived he would be here talking to you gentlemen. And he would say things similar to what I'm going to say now." I paused. No one seemed interested in my youthful opinions. A mesmerizing public speaker I was not.

"Many of you talked about building up the military"—I heard gentle murmurings of agreement—"and the need to spend more money on the tools for war." The group seemed to be listening more closely now. Go for it, Rob, go for it, Rick. "But I did not hear one of you—not one—speak about the need to take drastic steps to stop war, to find peace. You all seemed to be saying we should get ready for the next one. I heard about the *glorification* of war—and it makes me sick at heart."

"Now that's enough, St. Clair," the commander said.

I noticed Charley Peek had slipped low into his chair.

I wasn't finished. "Do you know what I think?" and someone from the rear yelled, "We don't care what you think."

Someone else yelled, "Let's see what the boy has to say."

Emboldened, I went on quickly. "I think this great organization should put peace at the top of your agenda. Stop war! Send the message to the president. And work through the new United Nations. But quit talking about glory and honor and building up more of your killing forces. Do something about preventing another war." Mutterings were coming from all over the hall now, and I quickly added, "And why are so many of you in uniform? You're civilians. So act like civilians."

It was the final straw. Two men from the first row bounded up the steps, each taking me by an arm. Commander Gullings was talking in my face, saying something blasphemous. Charley scrambled up on the platform and seemed to be wrestling with one of my attackers. Another man pushed Charley away violently, yelling, "Stay out of this, Nigger."

Then Gullings took charge and I was not surprised when I heard later that he had been a company commander in the infantry in World War I. "All right, men, quiet. QUIET. Everyone take their seats. You two Legionnaires on the stage, get down offa there. St. Clair, get back to your seat, and you, too!"—he indicated Charley.

He waited a long half-minute, then said, "Now then, let's talk this out. How old are you, St. Clair?"

"Seventeen." This was not the time for lies.

"And you think that at your age you have the smarts to know what is best for America—and you a Limey, to boot?"

I couldn't trust my voice; I looked at the floor.

"I want to tell you a few things about the American Legion. We all lost friends and relatives in one god-damned war or another, and I'll bet it's unanimous here that we don't want any more wars to come along. That's why we want our military to be built-up, to deter other nations from starting a war. Particularly with the atomic threat so huge."

I looked up at him with unseeing eyes.

"We believe in education and we raise money for scholarships. We support Boy Scouts of America. We have a children and youth program—rescuing our young people from poverty, a bad home life, that sort of thing. We sponsor blood drives. We provide drill teams for parades, and color guards, things like that." He trailed off. "Anything else anyone wants to mention?"

"We teach kids how to use guns properly," someone in the front row said.

I bit back the temptation to comment on that.

"Anything else?"

"That about covers it, Commander," another voice said.

"Do you have anything further to say, St. Clair?" Gullings was looking at me. The temptation was great to shake my head and get out of there. But I needed to leave on an up-beat note, if that were possible in this forum. I stood up and I noticed with pride that Charley did, as well.

"Maybe I was wrong to come here tonight. Maybe you're the wrong group. But—do you see what I'm trying to do?" I took a few seconds to gather my thoughts. "I'm trying to stop war. Forever. I'm trying to save lives. Can you help me?" My last few words were a plea, a prayer, a cry for sensibility.

"I'd like to, son," Gullings said. "The American Legion believes in raising the consciousness of all Americans towards the military and on behalf of all veterans. We won a major war a few years ago by developing the finest military force the world has ever known. If we hadn't done that, we'd all be speaking German now."

There were sprinkled laughs and one "Aye, aye."

"We believe we must have a strong force in the world. We know that Russia is the biggest new threat. So we can't afford to relax. That's about it, St. Clair."

I had no more words. I was played out, emotionally and physically. I lifted my hands in a slight shrug, to show my capitulation, if that was what it was.

The meeting ended soon afterwards and Charley and I joined the others filing out the door. Most of the veterans avoided me, but a few clapped me on the back. Just outside the door, an old man stood in my path. He was in civilian clothes and wasn't even wearing a Legion cap.

He looked me directly in the eye. "You—Robert St. Clair. I want to know you. I am Mathew Janzen. I want to say that you are on the right track. Don't give up, and don't believe everything George Gullings says. He can talk anyone into anything. He is merely protecting his turf—his Legion post.

"If you want to hear what someone from another generation thinks, let's talk. How about meeting tomorrow?"

His presence was like a tonic to my jangled nerves. Ah—someone on my side. But I had a test in the morning and another in the afternoon and work at six. "I have school and work tomorrow, Mr. Janzen. But how about right now?" I was fired up again.

We talked for well over an hour at a coffee shop on the Colorado College campus. Charley begged off; he said he had a test in the morning. I should be studying, as well—but I had to see what this man had to say.

He told me a bit about himself. He had been a pilot in World War I, flying Spads. This enthralled me. "After the war," he recounted, "I got a job as an electrician, but I quit my job in 1942 when my wife became ill." He paused.

When he didn't continue, I asked, "Is she well now?"

He looked up. "She died last year. I went back to work, but for myself this time. It's been more satisfying when I can set my own hours. With my wife gone, and with no more career goals to worry about, I have time for reading, studying, and thinking about the world. Which brings me to you. What you did at the Legion meeting was quite extraordinary. Taking on that group of older men, all pretty much set in their ways.

"That's why I wanted to talk to you. I wanted your perspective. I wanted to see if we could team up."

I was fascinated that someone his age—he had told me he was 55—felt as I did. His beliefs lined up with mine so well that I felt like hugging him, but of course I didn't.

I told him my story, even including my obsession with a dead flyer. He seemed entranced. By the time I'd finished it was nearly eleven. He was yawning visibly and I needed an hour to study for my exam tomorrow. We both stood up.

"Rob, do you want to meet again?"

"Definitely, Mr. Janzen. Let's exchange telephone numbers."

We did so, but he had something else to say. "Until we meet again, do you mind listening to a slogan I've gone by for years? It would make me happy to pass it along to someone your age."

Something rumbled in my chest and for a moment I had trouble breathing. "Sure, Mr. Janzen."

"Fine. Let's go outside—it'll be better there." He insisted on paying the bill, and we walked out to the cold street together. My heart was pounding for some undefined reason.

We looked upwards where a half moon peeked through thin clouds. As usual, I was enthralled with anything to do with the sky at night—moon, stars, even clouds. I held my breath as I waited for him to speak.

"Here it is then: *Somewhere in that dark sky the men of all nations will learn the true meaning of brotherly love.* Goodnight, Rob, my boy."

I would bet that I knew that slogan better than Mr. Janzen did. After all, he hadn't heard Rick Linden speak it under similar skies the night before he died.

Oh, Rick, that was a message from you, wasn't it? You were here tonight. You helped me to have the courage to stand up for what we both believe in. You helped me form the words, and never mind how little impression I made. Thank you, Rick, and God bless you in your heaven.

28

A HERO IN DUMMY'S GARB

I lay in my bath, my second-best thinking area after midnight under the stars, to put my prospects into perspective. Start with positives: steady-on at school and job, Charley as a friend, a good relationship with the Lindens. The negatives were fewer but huge: I had done little towards following Rick's goals; and I could lose Cass if I wasn't paying attention. Both disturbed me greatly.

A casual remark by Alex Linden had given me a new direction. He said Rick had begun his writing career in college; he had been editor of the Colorado College Tiger. I hadn't thought of that, a measure of how derelict I was as a planner. The next day I visited the small offices of the school newspaper and asked about a former editor named Rick Linden.

The staffer searched the files and handed me a thick bundle of papers. I read them at the library.

I had found a treasure trove. Rick had written a dozen or so articles about things he believed in or felt needed change. He poked fun at his fellow students, and he wrote about education:

An education should teach a person how to think, and what humility is, and try to get him to open his mind, and remind him there are all sorts of people with all sorts of blood strains and color phases, all pretty much like him. An education should teach him he is a part of mankind. Schools should be the best-built, most carefully-planned buildings in our society. They should be kept up better than banks, because there is a whole lot more wealth stored in them.

There was much more. I decided I would come back when I had more time. That evening I wrote an article on education. I used some of Rick's words, some mine. My goal was to raise an awareness in this one college town of the positive effect over a lifetime of a good education. I could easily distinguish the quality of writing between his and mine. But I didn't know how to merge the two without lessening the power of his article.

I re-read my attempt in the morning and was far from satisfied. I put it on a shelf in my bookcase; I'd read it again in a few days. I concluded that what I was trying to do was, if not impossible, very difficult. Certainly beyond the talents of a 17-year-old. As a writer and editor I was a nonentity. Perhaps Mr. Janzen could help; I didn't know if he was a writer.

My mood improved late that evening when Charley told me I was wanted on the telephone. "It's someone with a sweet voice," he added, winking.

"Hello, Cass," I said.

"All right, how did you know it was me?"

"Who else has a sweet young voice?"

She let it pass. "I want to see *Johnny Belinda.* It's on at the Roxie. Will you take me tomorrow night?"

"I was going to ask *you* to see it."

"Sure you were."

We held hands in the movie, an improvement over recent dates. I knew she had something on her mind, and she let me have it as soon as coffee and peach pie were in front of us at Shadburns Restaurant. "I hear you've been lecturing a bunch of men on war and morals," she said, cutting right to the quick.

"Gosh, Cass, did you hear about that? I was about to tell you, anyway."

"Sure you were. A friend of my father's is a Legionnaire. My dad told me his friend mentioned that some English kid told them off at the meeting Monday night. I figured it had to be my friend, Rob St. Clair, a nice sweet English kid. Or—just possibly—it could be Rick Linden, a ghost from the past."

"I don't want to think of Rick as a ghost. But let it go."

"That's another thing—you don't level with me. 'Let it go.' That's you, right down to your fingertips."

"If you'd just accept me like I am, we'd get along fine."

"Accept you like you are? Don't you see, you dummy, I don't know who you are?"

204

This was not my idea of a happy date. I guess I must have showed it, for she took my hands across the table and squeezed them tightly. "Whatever you are, immature, a dummy, indecisive, whatever—I like you." She paused while I digested these mixed messages.

"Rob, we're not going anywhere, you and me, unless you clarify what your life is all about, and let me be the first to know." She released my hands and smiled. "Otherwise, the only time I'll see you is when I need an escort to a movie."

That was the way it was with Cass; she was as serious as hell one moment and crazy the next. I think I was halfway to being in love with her, but I'd hardly kissed her—maybe six times in three months. What a Romeo I was. She had this obsession about *my* obsession and I'd better do something about it if I expected Cass to be any more than a casual movie date, if that. We had movies in common, thank God for that. Without a new show in town every week or so, I'd never see her. I remembered Rick loved movies, too, but I'd never mentioned that to Cass. I wasn't a *complete* dummy.

I met with Mr. Janzen for lunch Sunday, but I didn't mention that to Cass, either. He barbecued ribs on the small deck of his second-story apartment overlooking a grammar school. He added a green salad, rolls, and coffee.

He had not known Rick Linden or his parents. He was simply an anti-war man, and I was sure there were such believers in every city and hamlet in the country. The problem was they weren't organized. He wanted to do something about that.

"Rob," he said, sipping coffee, "you and young people like you are going to have to swing this. You have to be in a powerful position to do some good. State Senator. Governor. Congressman. Or President."

"President? Gosh, Mr. J, I'm a freshman in junior college. We're talking about years to get to that kind of position, aren't we? Even if I did have it in me to be elected to something. I'm still working on becoming an American citizen."

Later, he said, "I brought something for you. It's some material on the United Nations. I know you're aware of the UN because you mentioned them last week at the Legion Hall. Read it over. It might be you will decide, as I have, that they are our best hope of keeping the world out of another war."

"Thanks, Mr. J. I'll read it. But I can't just turn over the problem to some agency, even a peace agency. I need to be personally involved. When I last saw Rick I knew it was my destiny to follow him. I would have been good at that."

"Rick Linden, yes. That concerns me. Do you feel as strongly about this as he did? If you're doing this out of loyalty to his memory, then it won't work. You have to believe in those goals, yourself."

"I do, believe me, sir." I would have liked to have added, *Aren't I Rick the Second? Aren't I his disciple?*

"Okay, just checking. Listen, I have time on my hands, you don't. Do you want me to work out some sort of program?"

"Mind? I would be absolutely thrilled if you did. I don't have to be the leader. You can be."

"Don't misunderstand, Rob. Your job is as leader. I'm just offering my services now to help move us along."

"Thank you." I told him about my visit to the college library and reading Rick's editorials and opinion pieces. "I even wrote an article—well, I started it."

"I want to read it. Two heads are better than one. I'd urge you to follow through with the college newspaper, Rob. They're always looking for well-written material. Work with *The Tiger* and I'll work on town newspapers. We both need to get our opinions in the press."

My spirits rose; these were concrete ideas. I added, "We could run a series of articles about Rick in *The Tiger* and—using his own words—submit them to the college. Something with a title like "Stories from a Former Student-Editor, the Late Rick Linden."

"Splendid. That's the way to think. We might excerpt short sections of his book—"

"Trail of the Bombers."

"Yes. You would want to give him credit, of course. Well, now we both have our assignments."

"Righto. I'll skip some classes to get going on this."

"Wrong attitude, Rob. School is the bedrock you'll need. Where will you go next year? Boulder? Denver? Out of state?"

"There's time for that," I said, shortly, a bit peeved that everyone in my life was lecturing me on what Rob St. Clair should be doing. Then I shook it off. Mr. Janzen had expressed some ideas I should have thought of myself. We agreed that we should talk by phone, or meet, every Sunday.

I was glad I had made the pitch at the American Legion hall or I wouldn't have met Mr. Janzen. I told him that, but then he surprised me by saying, "Your speech at the Legion was a good start. If you want to build on it, I have an idea. Recruiters from the armed services are going to make a presentation at North Springs high school next week. There'll be a couple of hundred students listening to well-prepared pitches. Are you ready to offer them an alternative view?"

The thought of facing another hostile crowd was daunting. "Are you suggesting I give an encore there? They'd throw me out of their school."

He smiled. "Yes, I believe they would. But you'd have the chance to get a message across, albeit briefly."

"When is it?"

"Tuesday at eleven o'clock. In the auditorium. I'd offer to help except my age is against me. They should hear the truth from someone their own age."

I walked the two miles home in a daze. I was hanging on at school, and still held on to Cass, but in appearing before Rick's own high school speaking out against seasoned speakers, I was in way over my head. But, like the dummy Cass thought I was, I thrilled at the opportunity.

It was a special assembly in the auditorium. I noted the students, most about my age, and the platform at one end for the speakers. No one stopped me at the door. As Mr. Janzen had said, I looked like any other student attending a mandatory auditorium.

I sat near the front, off to one side, by myself. I spotted Cass, on the aisle on the other side, near the back. She hadn't seen me. There were at least 200 students, perhaps more, attending.

It was about what I expected. Each young man from the platform spoke for about ten minutes.

"Now we don't want any of you senior boys to choose a military career if you have immediate plans to attend college," the navy man said. "But I can tell you that if you want a life of travel and adventure, as well as to learn a trade you could practice the rest of your life, then I'll be happy to talk to you. Right after the

207

assembly, if you wish. Or you can visit us this week, right through Saturday. We'll be at a hotel right here in Colorado Springs." He named the hotel and its address.

The marine said, "We're especially proud of our service. Not that my three cohorts here don't have good outfits, too, but there's something special about the marines." The other servicemen put on false smiles and there was a bit of laughter from the assemblage. He went on to tell us about some of the splendid exploits of the marines during World War II in the Pacific.

And so it was with the army representative, a Master Sergeant. "The army is a multi-faceted unit," he began. "We serve in the trenches, man huge anti-aircraft guns, fight with tanks, and jump out of airplanes, too. Paratroopers. Any of you young men might find a home in the United States Army."

The final speaker wore the blue of the United States Air Force. "I'm the newcomer on the block," he said. "The air force was established as a separate fighting unit just this past September. In this case, we've saved the best for last." Light laughter followed, although no one could have said what they were laughing about. "By joining the new air force, you'll be making history."

There was applause for all four men and the principal told his students there would be time for about 20 minutes of questions. My heart was somewhere near my shoes, but I had to try again. I would let a few others speak first.

The questions came, most answered crisply and briefly.

My time came. I stood up and raised my arm. I knew the principal couldn't place me. He must have decided he couldn't know every student in his school. He waved me to go ahead.

"You recruiters have done a good job," I began, more loudly than necessary. "You described how each of your forces are trained to kill people. Have any of you thought why we condone war, why we send recruiters out to enlist 17 and 18 year old boys to be part of the killing game?" I spoke fast.

I could feel—right down to my fingertips, no, down to my toenails—the buzz of excitement sweeping through the assembly. This was not on the agenda. I only had a moment left and I used it quickly. I faced the students directly.

"And you boys. Have you thought how you would feel about killing a fellow human? Would you be able to live with yourself if you pulled a trigger and shot a teenager dead? And would you---".

The principal had heard enough. "Collins, Roberts," he called urgently. "Get him out of here." Two burly boys, no doubt from the football team, jumped up. Each grabbed an arm and dragged me to the main floor and then up one aisle. "Think about it, you young guys," I yelled, dragging my feet to slow my removal. They man-handled me towards the exit. "Think hard about it." Maybe one or two would think it over and change their future. If so, I was glad to suffer the indignities I had.

My escorts literally dumped me in the gutter on North Nevada Street in front of the high school. I couldn't decide whether to be happy or dejected. It came to me that I was getting pretty good at playacting. Maybe I had found my career.

Reality set in fast. I had done absolutely no good. And what kind of disciple was I to create a spectacle in the same high school Rick had graduated from?

I was a block away, walking fast, my spirits lowering by the step, when I heard my name called. No, it wasn't the cops to nab me for disturbing the peace. It was Cass. I quickened my steps. I couldn't handle her sarcasm now.

"Hey, Rob, wait up. I won't eat you up." I stopped and watched as she approached. I couldn't guess what came next.

I was embarrassed and defeated but I thought I detected something in her body language that gave me hope. I decided to act more up-beat than I felt, playing along with her apparent light-hearted mood. "Cass, you amaze me. I thought the boy walks the girl home in America. What's going on?"

"That's my way, Rob. Get used to it. And don't think you'll keep me off the subject of the little show you put on back there at my high school. And if you try to interrupt me before I'm done, or outrun me or something, then screw you."

"Another thing: your language."

"Maybe I should have been born a boy. But no, I don't mean that. For then I wouldn't be walking you home now."

It was the nicest thing she had said to me recently. This girl was always surprising me. I thought I might as well hear the worst. "So how did you think I did?"

"Well, for openers, I could hardly sit still listening to you make an ass of yourself."

I looked at the sidewalk. "I guess that answers my question."

"Hey, anyone would react like that. You were asking for trouble going in and you knew it. I still haven't decided whether you're one of the dumbest guys around, or just one of the most idealistic."

My heart gave a flip. I slipped my hand in hers. She didn't fight me off.

"You want my rating? You collect an A for effort and enthusiasm, about a C for the performance, and a straight F for the overall idea."

I took heart. "It's sort of hard to average that group of grades," I said. "So what's the final figure on the report card?"

"I make it a strong B." She stopped and faced me, holding both my hands in hers. Then this girl amazed me. She kissed me on the cheek.

"Heavens, Cass. We're on a city street here."

"Let's get serious. Your plan to speak at the assembly was ill-advised, you were reasonably prepared, and you delivered the goods—until they caught up with you. I'm just amazed, Rob. I'm going to have to give you more respect, I guess." Her eyes were bright with mischief. Suddenly, she reached up, pulled my head down to her level, and kissed me on the lips.

We walked in silence for a few minutes, then she said, "Want a hamburger?"

"Just what I want, Cass. My histrionics made me hungry. The same histrionics that make me feel like an ass. I get kicked off the school grounds and I suppose I can't show my face around there for a couple of years without getting jeered by one and all. So how come you're being so darned nice right now?"

"Because you're you. Because you stood up for what you thought was right, however misguided. Because you have such high ideals and are not afraid to speak your mind even if you look like an ass doing it."

"Boy, are those a group of mixed emotions. I *think* I came out all right in the end, but that's just a guess." I smiled at her, then decided to be greatly daring. "Does this mean we're going steady now?"

"Gosh, you beat me to it. A girl likes to lead on these important matters. Let's get that hamburger and shake before either one of us gets any more mushy."

At Murray's Drug Store, she bowed, opened the door for me, and said, "After you, you big shaggy-haired dummy. Are you a dummy in hero's garb or a hero in dummy's garb? I'll let you decide."

"I doubt if I win either way. But thank you, I think."

29

A LIFE IN TURMOIL

Charley and I drifted down to the Roxie after dinner for a new movie in town. Cass was busy writing a term paper. We watched Humphrey Bogart and Walter Huston emote in *Treasure of Sierra Madre*. I was in an expansive mood as we emerged from the theatre on El Cajon Avenue. As we turned the corner, leaving the lighted street behind, I put a hand on Charley's shoulder and said, "Did you ever see better acting? That Bogart, what a character, I'd like to be Bogart, Cary Grant and Gregory Peck, all rolled into one. What do you think?"

Charley said something in response, but our platitudes were interrupted by three boys of college age, who stood in our path. We were on a darkened street, around the corner from the Roxie's bright marquee.

"You like that nigger, don't you, fella?" the biggest of them said. "Well, just get down there and kiss his ass. Go ahead, right now."

Charley stiffened as tight as a board. I stood stunned for a moment, steaming, and then lost complete control. Without any plan, I hit the boy in the stomach as hard as I could. I yelled something unintelligible. At the same time, Charley came alive and smashed a second fellow on the neck with his large hand. Both boys were out of the fight for the moment. The third boy stood there irresolute, unwilling to tackle us both.

The big lout I had hit recovered quickly, straightened up and drew back a bulging arm, ready for a little payback. But he was still groggy which gave me the opportunity to kick him in the right shin as hard as I could. He howled and I kicked him in the left shin, beastly hard. He collapsed, yelling bloody murder. His two companions had had enough. They grabbed him under the armpits and dragged him around the corner. A minute later, we heard a car accelerating down El Cajon Avenue.

My roommate didn't say much as we walked to our rooming house while we kept a sharp eye open for the possible return of our antagonists. Once in our beds, he said, "What you did tonight was something, Rob. Thanks. I couldn't have handled them alone, and if the cops had come they'd take their side. Where did you learn to fight?"

"I never had a fight in my life," I said, "but that was so easy I might start thinking about turning pro. Some fun, eh?"

Charley just laughed a bit nervously.

"Gosh, Mr. St. Clair," Cass said when she heard about it. "I'm going to have to give you more respect. I knew you had courage but I didn't know you were a street fighter. I'm going to be careful not to antagonize you."

After my two abortive attempts at activism followed by a three-minute fight, my life steadied and summer stretched out invitingly. I worked nearly full time at Shadburns, I saved money, and I saw the Lindens occasionally. I considered a trip to California to see Bea and George, then decided on a long letter instead. Then, when I didn't receive a return letter, I put them on hold temporarily. I also wrote what I thought was a tender letter to my mum and added, "Say hello to father."

There were relaxing times fishing with Alex Linden, and a weekend camping trip with both Rick's parents to the Estes Park area. Dates with Cass, with no commitments other than "going steady." Sort of. I had hoped that we had arrived at the point of "going all the way," as my American schoolmates called it. I wanted to, but Cass let me know by body language that she wasn't ready—or maybe not interested? I didn't know. Frustration with girls had become a way of life with me. I was a virtual virgin, despite the night with Louise. I wondered if she had married Chuck.

I wanted to intensify learning the skills and interests of Rick—to bring me that much closer to him. I had tried skiing with limited success. Cass was an excellent skier. Tennis had been a trial. I had played with Charley several times but he was a fine athlete. I lost every time despite my roommate's attempt to take it easy on me. I had signed up for the tennis team at college, but I figured I would sit on the bench unless all six players ahead of me broke an arm or leg. I just didn't have the style or grace for tennis.

And writing. I could produce a serviceable letter or school theme which might earn me a B at best. But I was far from Rick's league. There were a few things: I fished and hiked well enough. But teams sports defeated me utterly: football, baseball and basketball. Well, I could out-cricket him, I thought.

Rick had loved to fly. I had not been up yet because of lack of money. But now I had some money in the bank and the weather in our part of the world, east of the Rockies, was perfect for aerial flight. I felt I had the concentration and coordination necessary to fly an airplane.

My double life suffered a crash landing one Saturday when Cass and I were returning from a movie. We walked past a book store on Cascade Avenue just as Mrs. Linden emerged, a wrapped book under her arm. They had not met. Ruth seemed delighted that I had a girl with me. It took only a few minutes for a dinner invitation to be offered. It would have been difficult to refuse. I had been wary about taking Cass to meet the Lindens because I suspected we would spend part of the evening talking about their son.

It was worse than I had imagined. It wasn't part of the evening; it was the entire evening. When Ruth realized that Cass knew little of her son, she brought out the photographs, the sports awards, the flying souvenirs, the works. It wasn't fair.

The key factor was that practically everything the Lindens said showed they were aware that their son had been a special friend to me. While Cass knew this, it apparently troubled her that the Lindens were so far into it, as well.

Alex Linden sat back in his easy chair before dinner, aware of my obvious difficulties. He gave me a wry smile and shrugged his shoulders slightly. I realized anew that he had always been on my side.

It was hard to read Cass' face. While she showed obligatory interest in what Mrs. Linden said about Rick, I thought I detected a message to me: *We've got some talking to do.*

It was more of the same at dinner. Ruth Linden steered the talk to what Rick would have done if he'd lived. This was a fascinating subject for me; I had thought about it often. It was impossible not to contribute to this conversation. By my side, Cass audited our conversation closely without contributing.

Alex Linden led off with "I think he would have been a foreign correspondent, combining travel and writing."

Ruth Linden added "He would have gotten a higher degree so he could teach, and continue his writing."

They both looked at me, the foremost non-family Rick expert around.

I was not comfortable; I did not dare look at Cass. "You are both right, probably. I talked about it with Rick. I believe he would have written, lectured, and done his best to change things he believed needed changing. He would have been a strong activist." I stopped talking abruptly as I saw Cass' eyes roll. I suppose I had been so obvious, so enthusiastic, so honest, that she knew I was a long ways from abandoning my quest.

"Great, great projects," Mr. Linden said.

"Rick would have worked at them with all his heart and soul," Mrs. Linden added.

So will I, so will I, Mrs. Linden. So explicit were my thoughts that I was surprised I hadn't said the words aloud.

Later, I said we should leave (claiming both our needs to study) but Mrs. Linden brought up a new subject. At first slightly resentful as one is when the host is seen as deliberately prolonging a visit, I quickly became enthralled. For she said, "We now have a copy of Rick's first book. Did you know about that, Rob?"

"*First* book?" I couldn't keep excitement out of my voice.

"It's not in the same class with *Trail of the Bombers*. He wrote the book, really more of a journal, while still in college. It's an autobiographical account of his first year here at Colorado College. We lived in Boulder then and Rick lived at his fraternity here in the Springs. He typed it himself on his trusty Corona." She added the magic words: "Would you like to borrow it? You can take it with you now if you wish. I don't mean to interfere with your study time."

Oh, it won't interfere, Ruth Linden. It will inspire and motivate me more than ever.

*   *   *   *

Mr. Linden offered me a ride home and I was glad to accept. I desperately wanted to avoid being alone with Cass just now. Cass lived north of me and he dropped her off first. She whispered to me, "Rob, we need to talk about you-know-what." Then she turned her graceful smile on Mr. Linden and said her thanks and good night without a further look at me.

Alex looked a question at me, so I said lamely, "I think she wants to talk about the chemistry exam coming up." Why I said chemistry was a mystery. Neither of us took the subject. I was getting back to the lying game I was so good at.

Charley was out. I cradled Rick's 100-page journal on my chest in bed. I read it straight through, finishing just as Charley returned from a meeting of the football team. I lay awake in the dark and thought how surprising it was that I now knew more of Rick's motivations, attitudes, and frustrations than I had learned while knowing him. It was going to be of inestimable help to me in following his footsteps with greater understanding. And then I balanced these thoughts with how I was doing with Cass.

I had held my emotions in check for months against the pressure coming from various directions: subtly from the Lindens, *Do you have a hidden agenda concerning our son?* Not so subtle from Cass, *I'll never take you seriously until you get rid of this fixation on a dead man.* Even my mother, *Why don't you come home, dear? Your father has mellowed and would welcome you.*

Even Charley, who knew little of my emotional life, noticed something. *You look like you're under a strain, buddy. Anything I can do to help? Maybe you can find some bullies to beat up on.*

Mathew Janzen was active in my life. He assembled a half dozen friends his age or older who believed as we did. I met with them a few times. At the Colorado College library, I read all of Rick's editorials and made notes of the best of them. Matt Janzen had told me to use Rick's actual words, a not-so-subtle hint from him that Rick wrote more powerfully than I did. He said he'd edit them if I wrote the first draft. I kept putting it off.

I wasn't receiving any pressure from Aunt Bea because we were out of touch. I had decided she must have left Morro Bay, but I had no idea why she hadn't contacted me. George was the important person in her life and she had probably followed him somewhere; she'd write when she had an address. But it left me wondering whom I could count on.

I awoke at two something in the night, sweating. I jumped from bed, threw a bathrobe over my naked body, and trekked to the kitchen. I drank another tenant's milk, promising myself I would replace it tomorrow. I had brought Rick's journal with me, and now I decided to re-read it although I'd just finished it a few hours earlier. It wasn't as well-written as his wartime autobiography. It was probably sophomoric in places—Ruth had said he was just 18 when he wrote it. Yet, there were passages which thrilled my soul. I marked them for later memorizing.

By the time I had finished it for the second time, reading by the dim light of the kitchen table, I was yawning. Before I rejoined my bed, I decided I wanted a session under the stars. Stare the night sky down. The yard was fenced; no one could see me. I threw off the robe and stood naked in the middle of the lawn, shivering violently, my head tilted skyward. My lips moved: *Somewhere in that dark sky the men of all nations will find the true meaning of brotherly love.*

What did I accomplish by these nocturnal visits with Rick and his magical sky? I didn't know and I was too tired to analyze it. I analyzed things too much, anyway. I rejoined my bed and slept through the rest of the night.

"So you're going flying?"

"Well, I'm going to try it, Charley. I hope the weather holds this afternoon."

"After you learn, I'd like you to teach me."

We were sharing a lunch of salami and mayonnaise sandwiches and canned apricots in our mutual kitchen.

"If I learn to fly. I may wash out, as a friend of mine once called it."

We heard the postal delivery man put mail in our slots. We jumped up to see who had written to us today, as if it happened often.

"A letter from my mother," he said, holding up a letter with a Texas postmark. He went off to our room to read it.

"A letter from my aunt," I said to his departing back. I had recognized Aunt Bea's handwriting. It was postmarked Santa Fe, New Mexico. I remained in the kitchen to read it.

30

JOURNEY OF TRANSFORMATION

The airport owner's name was Shadinger. I had told him on the telephone that I could afford perhaps five lessons. Could I solo in that time, I asked? He'd said not likely, that most students needed eight to ten hours translating to six or seven lessons. The field was 20 miles southeast of Colorado Springs, on the way to Pueblo. I had no idea whether I was going to be successful in this endeavor. I would have never tried if I hadn't known Rick.

I was driving a wheezy Ford pickup that I had borrowed from a man upstairs who said he couldn't keep it going. The small private field I was headed for was off Highway 25 on a dirt road leading from another dirt road. For a short time I was lost. My gosh, if I couldn't find a small dirt strip in the hinterlands, how could I find my way around the sky?

The letter from my aunt had told me how they happened to be living in Santa Fe. George had been offered a job in Albuquerque driving truck to various points in the Southwest. So they had moved to nearby Santa Fe, which had an appealing ambience that intrigued them. George still stayed out for days at a time, and she was afraid, she hinted, that he might be developing a network of women along his new routes. She didn't know whether to confront him or not. She asked me to advise her on that. I had a good laugh to myself. Bea asking my advice about an emotional issue? I was sorry to hear, though, that George was up to his old tricks. I thought it was a good letter, especially the way she ended it.

> Robbie, come on down for a visit. It's not so far.
> Let's trade advice. Listen, if you can swing the
> bus cost (please don't hitchhike) I'll take care of

all your costs here. But you may have to sleep on
the couch again.

I decided to take a bus to Santa Fe as soon as I could. I
needed an understanding aunt about now. Perhaps we could cry on
each other's shoulders.

Shadinger ran a one-man show; he owned only two airplanes and one was out of order. He told me on the telephone he
would like to see me learn on a Piper Cub but that this was in shop
for a week or two. "If you want to wait for the Cub," he said,
"that's okay with me. But if you don't mind flying a former army
training plane, come on out today." It was a Stearman—which
Rick had learned to fly on. That made it an easy choice for me.

The airfield owner came out of his shack to meet me. He
was a big man with a bushy mustache and a noticeable limp. He
might be 50, he might be 60. He had an accent that I thought could
be German.

"Mr. St. Clair?" I stepped out of my truck.

"Right," I said. "And you're Mr. Shadinger."

We shook hands. "What's your first name?"

"Rick." It was out of my mouth before I knew what I was
saying.

"Have you flown before?"

"No, I haven't. But I used to know a pilot and he told me a
lot about it."

"Oh, where was that?"

Careful, Rob. "Uh—in England."

The airplane waiting for me was the PT-13D, made by
Stearman for army primary flight training. This was the airplane in
which many if not most aviation cadets learned to fly. It was a bi-
plane powered with a 225 horsepower radial engine.

"I bought this crate from the army, surplus you know," he
said. "I like it. The plane is covered with fabric, as you can see,"
he said while giving me a personal tour. "Sounds flimsy, but it
really ain't. The engine is water-cooled which means nothing to
you, likely, but it's something to know."

"What's the top speed?" I asked.

219

"Why do all my students want to know that? This is not your fastest plane, but it is stable and a joy to fly. Maybe 110 top speed. About 50 on take-off. "You sit in front, me behind you. "We communicate by a tube called a gosport." I stared at the cheap, rubber tube and wondered what kind of a situation I had gotten into.

Any inhibitions I might have had about my adaptability to flying disappeared during that first flight. I paid attention, listened to what Shadinger said, and put my memory to good use. I wanted to be good at this; I *had* to be good at it. We went through all of the maneuvers my instructor had planned without any need to repeat any. This seemed a good sign. When I was holding the stick and throttle, I felt confident, in control, happy. Those feelings gave me a high I had not experienced in a long while.

Shadinger never chewed me out and never took the stick back. I thought this might be unusual for a first-time pilot, but I had no one to check with. We did climbs, banks, glides, and stalls, and I was with him all the way. He told me to keep my neck swiveling, looking for other aircraft. "I don't want no collisions at my age."

On the ground, he spoke again, "Next ride, we'll get into controlled spins, more stalls, power on and power off, more climbing turns, forced landings, and flying the pattern." He faced me directly. "Rick, you fly well, and I don't say that often, believe me. Are you sure you haven't flown before?"

"No, sir, but I learned from just being around Lt. Linden."

"Linden? Do you mean Rick Linden, by any chance?"

Warning flags took over my countenance. How could I be Rick occasionally if everyone remembered the original? Then it began to make sense. Rick had learned to fly in Colorado Springs He probably knew Shadinger. He might have even---.

"Did you teach Rick Linden to fly, sir?"

"Yes, I did. And he was a quick learner. How did you know him?"

Of course I had to go over the story. I certainly had his attention and only the arrival of another student kept me from having to go over every detail of our friendship. As we shook hands again, he said, "Funny you have the same first name," he said. "Is that a coincidence?"

Tell the truth or lie? "I borrowed his name." I felt empowered by my choice.

"Hmm."

*   *   *   *

Mr. Shadinger was talking to his next student, and I was surprised to see that he was Japanese. Hmm. Then I saw that Mr. Shadinger wanted to say something else to me, so I walked part way towards him. "Rick, come out again. I'd like to work with you." Did he say that to all his students? I didn't think so.

On the way home, I felt as if I were in a different world. I felt as high as the Rockies as I raised clouds of dust on the dirt road. I no longer had any doubt that I would solo; it was only the question of when. It was obvious that I'd passed this first test; I had pleased Shadinger, and he didn't look like one who threw praise around. Well, he hadn't exactly praised me—I didn't think any instructor would do that after one flight. But the lack of chewing out had been a tonic to me. And inviting me back: great.

Was it possible I was a "natural" flyer like I had always believed Rick Linden to be? I pounded the steering wheel. Yes! It was possible and I would prove it again on my next flight. I had found something I was good at—if only the money held out.

I was still on a high when I pulled in front of the rooming house just as the engine on the pickup died. I yearned to tell Charley—or someone—that I was a fledging pilot. He wasn't home, no doubt at the study hall. Cass? No, better leave her alone. I hung around for a half hour, waiting for my roommate. I soon got bored with inactivity and took off jogging for the foothills. I would feel better after strenuous exercise. At an elevation well above the town, I sat on a rock and took stock.

I was still feeling good about my exploits in an airplane. I wondered if my friend Rick had anything to do with it. I wouldn't be surprised. Sitting there on my rock as darkness threatened, reliving my afternoon's flight, something about it bothered me. It was at the air field—there was someone there—I couldn't come up with it. Then, abruptly, I remembered. Mr. Shadinger was of German stock, although he'd lived in Colorado for years. And—and, his next student—was Japanese. So what, Rob?

Simply this: Germany and Japan had been our enemies in World War II. My brother had died in a Japanese prisoner-of-war camp; my other brother Rick had died while fighting Germany.

Ergo, were Germans and Japanese deserving of my hate? If so, for how long? A lifetime? I would have to think on that.

I did think about it, all the way back to my rooming house.

By that time, tired, hungry and dirty, I had decided that it was war that was the real villain. The people who had been responsible for the deaths of my brothers were acting under orders from governments and for political reasons. How could I hate a person for the actions of a government or a nation? I couldn't. End of subject.

I felt better, although I was still a bit annoyed at Charley for not being home to hear my news.

I took two more lessons the next week, cutting classes both times. Mr. Shadinger took me through other maneuvers, including inverted flight, snap rolls, slow rolls, and more spins. After one dual spin, he said, "Okay, Rick, you do the next one by yourself. I'll touch the stick only if you get in serious trouble." I did a spin to the right, then one to the left, while he was true to his word. We practiced landings during both sessions and I learned the theory of short-field landings. He demonstrated how to pick a field for a forced landing, then did one himself before turning it over to me. I found a field to force-land three times in a row, and took the plane down to about 100 feet before leveling off and increasing power. I was lucky or I was good, I didn't know.

At the conclusion of the fourth lesson I had only four and a half hours aloft. As far as I knew I did nothing seriously wrong and, perhaps more importantly, I never made the same mistake twice. I began to think I could solo this Stearman right now. But my instructor had told me the typical student took eight or more hours—perhaps six flights. Well, he was calling the shots.

Rick, have you invaded my soul for the purpose of getting me through flight training? If so, thank you. In a way, I hope you haven't, since that would mean I can accomplish something important without your help. On the other hand, I hope you are involved since I want you in my life in any form I can.

31

SEARCHING FOR IDENTITY

I learned the next weekend that I was still on good terms with Cass. You never knew with her. I think she respected me— maybe loved me. In any case she was willing to give me the benefit of the doubt. She had decided to attend my junior college for a year. She also moved from her parents' house into a girls dormitory six or seven blocks from my rooming house. This was good news for me, but before I could make the assumption that Cass had made these choices to be closer to me, she told me not to read anything into this. "We're still going steady," she said. "That and ten cents will buy you a cup of coffee. No cream, though."

Her parents, whom I didn't know well, wanted to stake us to dinner at the Broadmoor, a ritzy hotel in the southwest part of the Springs. It would be our first "dressy" date.

It was late on Saturday afternoon, freshly tubbed and scrubbed, that I stood in front of the mirror in our bathroom. It was time for a check on R.J. St. Clair. The light gray blazer I had bought for $3.00 at a thrift shop looked surprisingly classy. My only slacks—dark gray—worn but with a crease still showing. No tie. And my face? Thick brown hair, needing a trim, perhaps, but I had no time, no money. Nose: a bit big possibly, but unfixable. Eyes light brown and shining now. I buffed my brown loafers with a flick of a towel and called it a draw.

It was classy, all right. Two bands to choose from, three dining rooms, an adjacent ice hockey rink, a small lake. We didn't have the funds for the cover charge on Les Brown's Band of Renown. We chose a small, crowded, smoky room where the lights were a dim reddish haze. I doubt if anyone present was even 25 years old. A five man dark outfit was on the stand, beating it out. We ordered beer, listened to them swing into something high and wild. My girl and I were almost a one-some, so close were we.

223

We let the music filter into our senses where it grabbed me by the lapels and carried me away.

The evening lay before us, glittering and filled with promise. Cass was enjoying the whole scene and I was enjoying her energy, her flickering eyes, her smell, her rhythm. Later, as we strolled through the gardens, held hands and watched the lights play on the lake, happy and carefree, I realized I had not thought of Rick Linden the whole evening. Then of course I did: Rick had probably danced right here at the Broadmoor many times.

Charley said to me the next Thursday night: "What time is your first class tomorrow morning?"

"Nine o'clock," I said, "*American Literature*. Why?"

"I told a friend at the Service Center that I'd serve breakfast tomorrow, from 7:30 until 9.00. They always seem to be short of help. Want to go with me?"

I usually slept in until after eight on Fridays, but I didn't hesitate. We had just taken over the payments on a 1940 Chevrolet sedan; we split the small monthly payment. Charley drove us about three miles to a seedy building in a seedier neighborhood. We served up scrambled eggs, bacon, toast and coffee to about 150 people down on their luck. Besides one cook and a helper, we were the only ones there. It kept us hopping. "I don't know how you would have managed it you hadn't talked me into this," I said to Charley as we stood in line serving.

"You didn't take much talking into."

Most of the "guests" were either Negroes or Mexican with a smattering of other nationalities thrown in. I noticed that a few people met our eyes and thanked us; but many others wouldn't meet our eyes and seemed to resent our presence. Did they think we were slumming it? This didn't seem right; I didn't own much more in the world than the great majority of them. It seemed to me Charley was accorded more respect than I was. Was this because of his race?

I asked him about it as we drove home. "I guess I get more respect than a whitey," he said, a twinkle in his voice. "They don't know what to make of you. They don't know if you're patronizing them or not."

"What can I do to appear less patronizing, assuming I am patronizing them?"

My roommate shrugged. "Just be yourself. Don't worry about it. Oh, Rob, sorry we were so late. Somebody had to clean up." It was nearly ten o'clock. I wasn't worried about my missed class; my grades were good and I could always make up for it by writing an extra paper.

"Want help next Friday?" I asked.

"Petey will be back then but if you came we could be finished in time for your nine o'clock. It was pretty clever of me to set up only ten o'clocks for Monday, Wednesday and Friday."

"You black guys are known for your cleverness."

He just smiled. I could make half-ass cracks like this now. He knew I respected him and he respected me because I did.

It was Charley who gave me a severe shock the following morning. Our budget called for oatmeal, toast, and coffee on Saturdays and we were sitting there reading the Springs' *Tribune* which an early-rising housemate had left on the kitchen table.

"Terrible murder and suicide down in Pueblo," he said, looking at an article on the second page.

My breath shortened and my heart felt like a giant had it in his grip. "What happened?"

"A guy shot a girl in her apartment, then turned the gun on himself. He was her former boy friend, I gather."

My throat was dry. "Any—any names given?"

"Louise something and Chuck something. Want to read about it? Not very pleasant reading."

So Louise had not been able to break off with Chuck, after all. I thought of her friendliness on the bus, of her tenderness at the YMCA, of her rough life as a waitress. She had made the error of taking up with the wrong man, not an uncommon mistake. I was quiet and introspective the rest of the day. I didn't want to talk to Charley about it except to say that perhaps I'd met her. He slowly nodded, although not understanding. I retreated into myself for the remainder of the weekend.

Cass and I spent a lot of time together. Since she lived so close now, we studied together, ate together when finances allowed, and hiked into the countryside in all weathers. We climbed in the Rockies where the brown-hued leaves of fall greeted us; we swam at the YMCA and I actually beat her in the 50-yard sprint. We saw movies and a play or two at the fall series at Colorado College. And we roamed the Garden of the Gods, one of our favorite places.

I had another letter from my mother, my father adding a note. Characteristically, he referred to America as a "developing country" as if it were the Congo or perhaps Liberia. My mother was emotional; I'm sure she feared I would be lost to them forever if I stayed in the United States. I was inclined to agree with her. I had taken the time to examine my relationship with my parents. They were themselves; they were all right. I knew the loss of Geoff and my move to America had hit them hard. To them, I was as lost as their older son was.

I had never been sorry I'd moved to America. I missed very little about England. Except mum. And Geoff. I wondered once in awhile about God: taking both Geoff and Rick from me.

I got along well enough with Mr. Judson and he seemed to like me, although keeping a wary eye open. He had long since accepted Charley as a good worker; he had been a bus boy for four months with nary a complaint. I decided to push my luck. I knocked on his door.

The instant I suggested that Charley be promoted to waiter he came down hard. "You're not pulling that stuff on me again, St. Clair. And if you tell me you'll both quit, then I'll fire you both before you can. I decide these things myself. Now get out of here, I'm busy."

As a liar I was in the top layer; as a blackmailer I had a lot to learn.

Still, the seed had been planted. For when an older waiter had a stroke a week or so later, it left Judson in a bind. He asked Charley if he wanted to try out as a waiter. Charley did and easily made the grade. Judson had his own 14-year-old son temporarily fill the gap as bus boy. Judson was getting to be a regular old sport: a black waiter and an under-age busboy.

The Lindens liked me; I could sense that. When I returned Rick's college journal they invited Cass and me to dinner a week later, on a Saturday night.

Walking home, I wondered whether Jane Linden had a point. I probably did remind them of Rick every time they saw me. But was that necessarily a bad thing? You don't want to forget lost loved ones, do you?

Cass and I had been bowling at the local alleys. Neither of us was any good; it would have been nice if I could have beaten her at something besides swimming. On the way home, my half-owned old Chevy had finally given out. It sputtered and died. Battery? Coils? Spark plugs? Who knew?

Being late on a Friday night, we decided to leave it on the street and walk home. "I'll get Charley to check it out in the morning," I said. "He's a mechanical wizard."

"You really like him, don't you?"

"He's a regular guy."

"I've just met him once."

I said, "Why don't we stop off at my place and you can meet him twice. Maybe I'd be clever enough to make coffee."

I quickly shaped in my mind the remainder of the evening: talk and coffee with Charley, then walking Cass to her dorm. She had to be in by eleven or she would be locked out.

We entered our dark room. "No Charley," I said rather unnecessarily. A different script for the remainder of the evening swept through my mind like a wind off the Rockies. There was a slip of paper on my bed. I swept it up and read:

Rob: I'll be out all night. Help yourself to anything you can find on our side of the ice box. I repeat: I'll be out all night. It was signed "C."

My temperature had risen three degrees in the past three minutes. Weren't you supposed to plan these things in advance? Could I pull this off without any plan, any build-up?

Cass was pottering around the room, pretending to find an interest in something, although there was precious little to look at. I put Charley's note in my pocket. My newly devised plan was quite simple: kill a little time so she would miss the eleven o'clock deadline and she would have to stay over. "How about that coffee?" I asked.

"Make it tea and you're on."

I demonstrated my kitchen abilities by preparing both.

Back in my room, I said casually, "Charley will be out all night." I showed her his note. "You could even sleep here if you wanted to. But—not in his bed. It has a hard mattress. But mine doesn't." I stopped abruptly.

I sat on my bed and crooked my finger for her to join me. I was taking a chance; she seldom responded to this kind of preemptive persuasion. This time, unaccountably, she did. My heart swelled. We sat side by side for a full minute, my heart saying, "Go to it, Rob," and my common sense replying, "Don't rush it." I gently kissed her on the lips, then just as gently moved her shoulders towards the bed. She had the choice of resisting or going with the flow. Her response was unmistakable. She simply disentangled herself, rose from the bed, and asked, "Want to walk me home, Rob? It's a quarter to eleven. We'll have to hurry."

I remained on the bed, stunned. I had been ready for love. I made no attempt to hide my disappointment and frustration. She didn't seem to notice.

We walked rapidly down the dark street. It was five minutes shy of eleven when we reached her door. Five minutes to make my case. "Cass---."

She took my hands in hers and spoke quickly and softly. "It wasn't the time or place, Rob. You have to take my word on that. But"—and her bright eyes bored into mine and her next words thrilled me. "I want to do it, Rob. I *want* to, with you. But I gotta go now. How much money do you have? In cash?"

My world had suddenly brightened, but it had deepened, as well. "Maybe seventy dollars."

"Wow, we're rich," she said. "I have about forty. I want to do my part. Are we partners?"

"You're moving pretty fast. What's this about money? And what is doing your part?" I had a suspicion but I didn't want to get my hopes up.

"I have two minutes to tell you. Enough. You and I are going up into the mountains tomorrow and stay all night at a neat little inn nestled there. One of the girls told me about it. So, to hell with studies. To hell with morals. There'll be you and me and the moon. But don't forget your seventy dollars. Not that we'll need all of that."

I walked home in the dark, my eyes on the sky, my head in the clouds.

It was a real inn, sixty miles northwest of the Springs, on the road to Aspen. We were in a small town surrounded by mountains, the air crisp with the anticipation of snow within the month, the sky clear, a hazy sun looking down on our stolen weekend. We were young and gay and looked it, but the innkeeper didn't seem to care. Our room was a corner one, affording us a magnificent view of shadowy mountains to the east and north, in a room decorated in pastels of brown and yellow. Comfortable, homey, romantic. Could I ask for anything else?

We found a narrow trail behind the inn, we crossed a stream or two and walked through a forest of fir. Then, above the trees, a mountain trail. We hiked fast, hand in hand when the trail was wide enough. When we were out of breath, we stopped and admired the scenery. I spied our little inn far below and my heart nearly stopped with joy. It was good to be stretching our bodies and souls. My body felt loose and oiled and glowing. Despite my own emotional troubles, power came in limitless waves from within my very being. I was a king without a kingdom.

We followed the trail to its end, at a minor summit. I walked closely behind her most of the way. I couldn't take my eyes from her, wondering if she knew how closely I studied her. I was ravished with the beauty of the world; it was as if I'd never known joy before. I felt wise, triumphant, victorious, immortal.

We found a large flat rock and sat in opposite directions, back-to-back, self-supporting. The view spread widely on all sides: forests, peaks, rivers, late-blossoming lupines in fields of purple. Cass described her view, painting a picture of beauty, her voice creating a different kind of beauty. Then I told her of my view, choosing words of poetic value when my brain was up to it.

My heart was light, my cares washed away, my whole being intense with anticipation for what lay ahead in that little inn below.

On the downward trail we talked. There was so much to tell each other about ourselves: memories, hopes, likes, regrets, fears, wisps of knowledge, hints of philosophy. The words and phrases tumbled out, laced with humor, sarcasm, seriousness, wit, nonsense, silliness. I was anxious to prolong the entrancing talk, yet increasingly longing for the adventure awaiting us as night approached.

Five o'clock. The cocktail hour for some, the witching hour for us. As soon as we closed the door, I encircled her in my arms and we kissed. She broke away in a minute, and said, "I'm frazzled. Me for a shower." This time, she crooked her finger at *me,* and I was enthralled. The beauty of her sent blood roaring in my ears.

She faced away from me in the shower; I gently turned her around. She put her arms on my hips and drew me to her. Her face glistened in the lash of water. I tilted her chin upward and kissed her on the eyes, throat, mouth. I never felt so needed, so strong, so invincible.

We dried each other from head to toe, using the inn's rough towels. My skin was tingling. A small smile, seductive and adventurous, hovered over her face. She cupped my face in her hands, then kissed me full on the lips. Her energy fired my blood. I hadn't known it was possible to feel so much alive.

Our love-making was in inverse harmony with the fading light outside. The warmth of her, her energy, her animation, filled every corner of the little room. Flesh against flesh; gasps of pleasure; stars in our eyes; fire in our blood.

Later, we walked hand in hand down the curving street of the little village, and found an old hotel with a dim restaurant inside. The interior smelled of dust and dishwater, and our waiter had a stained apron and a dispirited look about him. But nothing about the café or the meal could undermine the pleasure of the evening. Our meal was simple country fare, enormous helpings, liberal use of salt, pepper, butter, ketchup. Blackberry pie topped the feast. I gazed wonderingly at Cass during most of the meal; I ate my meal and presumably tasted it—but I couldn't have said later what it consisted of. Except for the blackberry pie.

Walking back to the inn hand in hand, amazed to find it wasn't even nine o'clock, we gazed skyward at a spangled banquet of stars. The moon was up there somewhere. We looked for it, didn't find it through shifting clouds, and decided we didn't need it this night.

I had always figured it would be easier to walk alone and I had always planned on it, but after that night with my girl, alone in a village in the wilderness, I knew I would never take the easy route while there was a girl named Cass in the world.

32

FALLOUT FROM A DINNER PARTY

And then it all came tumbling down.

Cass and I had looked forward to the Lindens' Saturday night dinner party. Then Mrs. Linden told me her daughter would be in town. Jane was in the Springs for the wedding of a high school friend. She was free for a short time Saturday evening, long enough for dinner. I asked Ruth whether Jane knew I would be present.

"Yes, certainly. She said she wanted to see you again."

It was fair warning. Jane wanted to see me, but for a different reason than her mother might imagine. Jane wanted to judge whether I had heeded her clear advice: no harmful influence on her parents. I didn't feel anything I'd done was harmful to them, but Jane would have a different perspective.

More exciting would be the presence of Pat Morse and his wife. Mrs. Linden told me about it on the phone. When she'd told him I was also in the Springs, she said he was very pleasantly surprised. Pat and his wife Julie had driven from Connecticut on the way to California, leaving their two young children with his parents.

As we gathered in the living room over glasses of plum juice ("from our own tree," Alex said) I sat on the edge of my chair. Would there only be casual family talk or would Jane bring up her brother's name to find out what I was doing? The presence of Cass complicated things. Despite our disagreements about Rick's influence, there was that wonderful Saturday night in the wilderness, just a week ago. Wouldn't that change everything?

I decided not to mention Rick's name tonight. Perhaps no one else would. I had just completed that thought when Alex Linden said, "Wouldn't Rick have been happy to be here tonight?"

Jane wasted no time. "He certainly would have, dad. With his parents and sister to fuss over. And with his old friend Pat here." She looked around. "And with a young lady like Cass, as well;"—she smiled at my girl—"Rick always had his eye out for a pretty girl."

I waited in vain for my name to be mentioned. "Rick would have been happy to have me here, too," I said, daringly, "He liked me hugely."

"You knew him for how long? Three months?" Scorn vibrated in her voice.

Every fiber of my being was inflamed by her unfair indictment. Passion and a sense of fairness loosened my tongue and the words came out fast and surprisingly lucid. "I knew Rick during the last few months of his life, at a time when he was in the middle of combat pressure you in America could only guess at. And yet most of the time he was relaxed and cheerful. And he took the time to get to know a 15-year-old English kid and make a friend of him. Me. I was naïve, I know, and over-emotional and some other things, too. He knew about my unhappy home life and that made our friendship almost inevitable. He wanted to help me. Our friendship was real, Jane."

Pat Morse had a puzzled look on his face.

Before Jane could reply, Ruth Linden spoke up. "Rob, you don't have to justify your friendship with Rick. You've convinced Alex and me of that long ago." She looked at her daughter. "What's gotten into you, Jane?"

I sneaked a look at Cass. She looked as if she were somewhere far away.

Jane said, "I just find it incomprehensible that Rick would devote so much attention to—Rob here—while he was risking his life in combat."

"Maybe that's when Rick most needed a trusted friend." This from Mr. Linden.

Jane cast an exasperated look at her father. "So a 15-year old from another country could give him something his fellow pilots couldn't? It just doesn't ring true."

"It happened just that way," was all I could say.

"May I say something?" Pat Morse asked.

"Of course," Ruth Linden said.

"I think Rob did offer things his fellow pilots couldn't. I was one of those pilots and I was a confidant of Rick's. Your typical pilot could not compare to Rick as a sympathetic listener. That's all I wanted to say."

I doubt if anyone enjoyed the dinner. It was well-prepared and well-served, but there was too much doubt and ill-feeling in the air. No one could relax. There was no further mention of Rick and it pained me that I had caused my friend's name to be taboo in his own house.

After dinner, with three women in the kitchen cleaning up, and Pat and Julie Morse looking at family photo albums, Alex Linden and I found ourselves alone in the living room. He took a moment to light his pipe. Then he cleared his throat, looked uncomfortable for a moment, and finally said, "I'm not done with talking about Rick tonight. How about you, Rob?"

His words cheered me.

"It's none of my business, I suppose," he went on. "But then perhaps it is." He had my complete attention. "Are you still pursuing Rick's goals? You described them so well to us, and he'd written to us about them. We told you that."

"Thanks for the vote of confidence, Mr. Linden. I haven't done much lately. School, work, sports, Cass, and now flying lessons. They take nearly all my time."

"And that's as it should be." He offered a crooked smile. "I did hear about your speeches at the American Legion Hall and North Springs high school. Anything come of them?"

"None that I know of," I said, with a sheepish grin. "A few people I knew told me I made an a--, joke, of myself, that's all. I need education, maturity, and a plan. At least."

"Then you will continue?"

Careful, Rob, the ladies might walk in at any time. "Yes, I intend to." I told him about my work with Mr. Janzen and my plan to read and excerpt from Rick's editorials from his college newspaper. "I don't have a lot of time, but I just can't stop indefinitely. It wouldn't be true to Rick."

My timing misfired. Cass, Ruth, and Jane heard the last sentence.

"Talking about Rick again?" Jane asked sarcastically.

"*What* wouldn't be true to Rick?" Cass asked.

All three ladies looked at me. Alex looked bemused.

I accepted the challenge. "I was talking about Rick's passions—education, world peace, and writing," I said. "He wrote to his parents about them and he talked to me about them in the last month of his life."

"What does that have to do with you?" Jane asked in her direct way.

"Just about everything," I said. "The anti-war message has to be addressed in every generation. I made a vow to Rick that I would try to accomplish things for him—since he couldn't be here. I'm too young and inexperienced to get much done yet, but check with me in two or three years."

It was a sarcastic and probably impertinent thing to say to Rick's closest relatives. Still, I was glad I had said it so plainly.

"What right do you, a kid from England, whom I heard is not even an American citizen, to take up Rick's ideals? Leave my brother out of this, damn you. Let him rest in peace."

I was speechless. Cass was looking at me strangely. I wondered whose side she was on. Why shouldn't it be mine?

Mrs. Linden stepped into the breach with her usual aplomb. She asked Jane to apologize to her guests for her tone and language, then told her, in a quiet voice, that she and dad knew about my desire to carry on for Rick.

Jane did not go quietly. Looking at me, she said, "Cass told me in the kitchen that you've been trying to master all of Rick's sporting interests. Skiing, baseball, football, tennis. I doubt if you ever tried any of those before you came to Colorado."

"I played a bit of tennis in England," I mumbled.

"Well, I don't like your obsession. At Thanksgiving last year I told you to lay off. Do you know we've talked about Rick all evening?"

"*And what is wrong with that?*" Alex said. "I like talking about my son."

I had never doubted I had the support of the Lindens. But Jane was a clear antagonist. What Cass was making of all this was still a mystery.

I was about to find out.

"Rob really has a greater case on Rick than you know," she said. "When I first met him he wasn't the Rob St. Clair we're talking to now. His name was Rick Linden."

They all looked puzzled. Then Alex said, "What do you mean, Cass?"

235

"When I first met him at Pike's Peak Lodge, he introduced himself as Rick Linden. He was a waiter there and he had 'Rick' stitched on his shirt."

"Is that true, Rob?" It was Mrs. Linden speaking. The expression on her face was painful to look at. I recognized the full effect of Cass' betrayal. Now I had lost Mrs. Linden and probably her husband, as well.

My days of lying were over. "Yes, it is true. I only used his name on a few occasions, but when I did it brought me that much closer to him. Don't you see, if I was going to carry on his great ideas, if I was going to be Rick the Second, I needed to use his name, too."

"*Rick the Second?*" Jane asked incredulously.

I went right on. "If I was going to attain his goals, I had to come as close as I could to thinking like Rick, *to being* him."

No one said anything. I needed to finish, to present the whole story regardless of consequences. "That's why I've tried to learn his sports, and I'm learning to fly, too. I needed to transfer some of Rick's force to me. He willed me the job of carrying on for him."

"That's it," Jane said, standing up quickly. "This guy has got all of you fooled, except I think Cass has him figured. If I were you, mom and dad, I'd kick him so far out of your life he'd bounce all the way down Cascade Avenue." She glared at me and I glared right back. How could this unsympathetic young woman be Rick's sister?

"I've got to get back to the wedding party," Jane said, picking up her coat. "Thanks for the dinner, mom and dad. I'll see you at the wedding. Nice to have met you, Pat, Julie, Cass." Without a glance at me, she went out the front door.

We weren't finished with the evening and we all knew it. Mrs. Linden spoke first, her face creased with lines of doubt and pain. "Rob, do you remember I once told you Rick and I used to talk things out at the kitchen table? I offered you the chance and you didn't take advantage of it. Now you will. Sit still and listen to what I have to say.

"You have some lovely traits, young man. Loyalty. Love. Compassion. But you're also overly persistent and, worse, possessive. Possessive about other people's lives and names. You've taken liberties you had no right to. The Bible preaches against obsessions and that's what you have—an obsession. So leave Rick out of this. He's ours, not yours. We knew him for 23 years, you for three months. We've always been understanding, Rob, but Jane has opened our eyes. Then using another man's name. The Bible has something to say about that, too."

I stared mutely at her.

"We're not shutting you out of our lives. You're too good a person for that. I wish you would think about all of this and then come and see us again."

I wasn't quite done.

"May I say one other thing?"

"It's late," Mrs. Linden said.

"Ruth, let the boy say his thing." This from Alex Linden. She looked bleak but nodded at me.

"It's my belief that Rick Linden rests more peacefully because someone—perhaps others as well as me—is carrying on for him back on earth."

Cass and I walked home; the Chevy was still ailing. There were still things that needed to be said. We walked two blocks in silence. Then I asked, quietly, "Cass, why did you betray me?"

She stopped on the sidewalk. "Rob, don't you see? You were forthcoming to a point. But you needed to get it all out. A part confession is not enough." She was silent a moment while I began walking again, my head down. Then she added, "Rob, Rob, I just want him out of our lives. Let him go."

I stopped again, facing her. "I don't want to let him go. Don't try to change me. I'm definite on this. By the way, you're getting pretty good at defaming me to all the wrong people. Why *did* you betray me, Cass?"

Her eyes bored into mine. "Because I must have the truth. I realized you weren't going to mention stealing his name, so I had to speak up. If we are to stay together, Rob, I want you perfect. So maybe you don't want to stay together. That's up to you."

I should have told her she was right, that I would drop the masquerade, that I would be a normal college kid without complications. Instead, I didn't answer at all, and we walked the rest of the way in more silence.

What a difference a week makes. Last Saturday night, heaven in a little mountain inn. Tonight, my world had come tumbling down.

33

A TIME OF NO DECISION

For once I hoped Charley was out or asleep. I didn't have enough energy for more emotion tonight. He was studying in bed. I tossed him a tired look but he didn't take the hint.

"I'm glad you're home, Rob. Just the excuse I need to give up on biology for the night. How'd it go at the dinner party? Have fun?"

I shook my head. "No, quite the opposite. Everyone hates me. I insulted my hosts and their daughter thinks I'm an asshole. And Cass—God, I don't even want to talk about it." I certainly had his attention. "First, she betrayed me, then she more or less kicked me out of her life."

"Shit, that sounds pretty bad, Rob. You managed to piss off all of them in one evening? That's my boy."

That startled me. "Is that as insensitive as it sounds?"

"I'm sorry how that came out. What I mean is, I guess, is that you can't please people all the time. I'll bet you were just being yourself. That's more important than being Mr. Good Guy."

"You just don't understand, Charley."

"I might if you'd tell me about it."

"Well, I'm not going to."

That silenced Charley and I lay down on my bed, fully dressed, and clasped my hands behind my head. My thoughts were jumbled and confused. I lay there for a few minutes, then sat up and faced my roommate. "I'm sorry, Charley, I was pretty short with you and I can't afford to lose any more friends. You're the only friend I have in the world right now. That is, if you are still my friend."

Charley offered me his wide grin. "You bet, fella."

At eight o'clock the following morning, Mrs. Maple woke me with a knock on the door informing me I had a phone call. Could this be Cass seeking to make up?

It was Pat Morse. "Good morning, Rob. Julie and I want to leave by noon. We're going to reach Salt Lake City by tonight. To see your marvelous West. But I'd like to talk with you. Do you have time to talk now? I'll take you to breakfast. Alex Linden gave me your address. How about 10-15 minutes?"

Where else but Shadburns? We ordered, then he sat back, looked me in the eyes, and plunged in. "I was sorry I was not able to help you last night. You did pretty well without me."

"You did help, Pat. Thanks for what you said about Rick enjoying talking to me. In the past two years I've made mistakes right and left. And poor judgments. I think they all hate me."

"Don't you believe it. The only lost cause is Jane. The Lindens will come around."

"I may have lost Cass forever."

We were sitting across from each other in a small booth, and there was room for Pat to reach across and put a hand on my shoulder.

"You'll have to work on that. It won't happen by itself." He smiled. "I'm buying breakfast, so does that mean I get to spout a bit of advice?"

I didn't return his smile. "I guess you're going to, anyway."

"I'll make it quick. Don't use his name as your own. Mrs. Linden was right about that."

I looked at the floor. After a moment he went on: "And give up Rick the Second."

I stopped messing up my scrambled eggs and put my fork down. "I can't let him go, Pat."

He laid down his own utensils and looked me directly in the eye. If I closed my eyes I could imagine it was Rick talking to me. "You've been his truest friend," he said, "you've given him loyalty galore, sacrifice, dedication. But---."

"I knew there'd be a 'but' at the end of the sentence."

"If you'll take my suggestion, you've got to stop thinking of him as a young god. Remember him as your lifetime best friend, a great guy who died before his time."

Despite my liking for Pat, I was tired of being lectured about my relationship with Rick. Last night it had been Jane and

Ruth and Cass. This morning, Pat continued the campaign. But I bit back my tongue; I didn't want to antagonize this man who had been Rick's friend for much longer than I had.

We talked a bit longer, then he stood up to go. I told him I'd walk back since I had some thinking to do.

"Well, then, I'll say goodbye. We'll meet again, I'm sure. And listen, my friend"—he put his hand on my shoulder again—"if I can help in any way, let me know. I mean that." He wrote out his address and telephone number.

Noontime on a Sunday. A beautiful day. I climbed up to the third story and through a small window to emerge on a flat portion of the roof. No snow had fallen, but it would soon. I looked at Pikes Peak visible over a couple of rooftops. I would talk Charley into climbing it with me. Sometime.

I stared at the peak for a minute, then deliberately swung my gaze around to the south where I knew there was an airplane I'd like to know better. I had been saving a bit towards a trip to Santa Fe. But first, was there any left for another hour of instruction? I didn't know, but the need to fly again was suddenly overwhelming.

Shadinger started me out by practicing landings. Then we reviewed climbing turns, spins, and forced landings. Mr. Shadinger asked me questions through the rubber gosport, and I did my best to be clear in my answers.

"Rick, before we even think about soloing, I'd like you to take me on a short cross-country. Take the controls and let's fly north—say a heading of 315 degrees. Climb to 2,000 feet. Use the appropriate power settings. Fly to Boulder, circle the city clockwise, then return here via Denver. Just don't overfly Lowry Field in Denver or you'll get shot down." He laughed. "Just kidding—I hope."

I concentrated as never before. After leveling off I was easily able to pick out highways and other checkpoints on the ground. I took the requested heading and just held her straight and level, keeping the Rocky Mountains on my left. Soon I saw a town which had to be Boulder, circled it, careful to exert back pressure to hold my altitude in turns, and headed for Denver. Mr. Shadinger said not a word. I flew over Denver, and figured a heading of due south would take me home. Close enough. I approached our field.

"Take her in," Shadinger said, talking for the first time in a long while. "Use left-hand traffic."

My heart leaped into my throat. I suddenly had several things to think about: losing a thousand feet to pattern altitude, flying the pattern correctly, monitoring engine settings, then the landing itself. I was Mr. Nonchalance as I went through the steps.

Five or six minutes later we were on the ground and I taxied to the hangar. Mr. Shadinger's voice was loud in my ears. "Nice job, Rick. You just soloed. Of course it wasn't a real solo. I was here with you." He laughed at his little joke.

"Don't cut the engine yet," he said as I neared the hangar. "You have five hours and forty-five minutes total, not a helluva lot. Even so, what I'm suggesting now is I get out and you take it around the pattern. Three times. Are you ready?"

"Yes, sir." My heart was somewhere other than my chest. Was I really going to do this alone?

He got out and grinned up at me. "Good luck, Rick."

Perhaps it was the use of my stolen name, or perhaps it was my lucky day, or perhaps Rick's force had begun to work on me. I offered him Rick's two-fingered salute and taxied off.

I made it around the pattern three times with a bounce or two but with no other problems. Shadinger was waiting for me with a cigar.

I shouted at the top of my lungs as I drove the Chevy home. "Whee—wow—holy smokes," I screeched. "I soloed an airplane. I did it! I did it! Holy Saint Christopher. I'm a hot pilot. I'm on my way." When I'd gotten over the shouting spree, still high on my flight, I thought of Ruth, Jane, Cass, and Pat. Who cares what they think of me? They can't fly an airplane. Only I can.

By the time I'd parked in front of our rooming house I had lost most of my high spirits. I had given Shadinger all of my cash and I had no money for the week ahead of me. I didn't know how I would eat tonight; perhaps I would find something in the ice box. I couldn't, but it didn't matter. About five o'clock I got a call from Matt Janzen. By any chance could I come over for dinner tonight? He wouldn't keep me long. Could I? An FM—free meal—just when I needed it. My luck was changing. I reluctantly pushed Cass further back into my mind.

241

I walked to Janzen's apartment. The Chevy had been steaming when I pulled in from the airport.

"I eat simply," he said, as we sat down to meatloaf, new potatoes, and carrots, with plenty of bread and milk. We ate rapidly. I waited for him to take the lead.

"I have a letter to the editor coming out next week in the local *Tribune.* And I've sent the same letter to the *Denver Post.* A friend of mine works in the editorial department. He phoned to say it would be in the paper at the end of the week."

"That's wonderful, Mr. J. I've copied some of Rick's editorials, but I haven't done anything with them. I brought them with me."

He scanned the material. "Pretty powerful stuff. When do you have time to work these over?"

"Right now?"

Two hours later we had edited Rick's college editorials and selected the best bits for publication. I read one paragraph to him: *"Parents: war is coming, and your sons are not exempt. Male students: take your girl out for that last ride in a convertible, and be sure to dance one final time at the Broadmoor. Don't forget to kiss her; it may be your last chance for a while. Or forever."*

"That'll go over fine." He looked at another of Rick's efforts. *"People say that peace is impossible, but that is a dangerous and defeatist belief. We think war is inevitable, that we the people are doomed, that we are in the grip of the madmen who run the world. Since the world's problems are man-made, they can be solved by man—by reason, resolve, and spirit."*

We planned future steps. I told him I was through facing down the American Legion and the high school, but that I was open to suggestions on other groups. We said goodnight and I walked home in the dark.

Ostensibly, it had been a good Sunday: breakfast with Pat, soloing an airplane, and a promising meeting with Matt Janzen. What would set the day off properly would be to talk to Cass. It was only nine o'clock. I jogged the last few blocks, so anxious was I to talk to her. I should have waited a few days, maybe a week. But I had to try; perhaps she would have mellowed.

She hadn't. "What do you want, Rob? Or is it Rick? I'm hitting the books pretty hard."

"I wanted to talk to you, to explain things, to---."

I had said the wrong words, and she lost it. "I thought you were sensitive, Rob. It was only last night that we disagreed about as much as two people can. I need time to figure out how to deal with your obsession."

At the word obsession, I lost it, as well. "I don't like that word," I said, then stopped talking before I said too much. "Cass, we have to meet sometime and talk. When?"

"Call me Saturday. I'll see how I feel then."

That was a nearly a week away. "All right, Cass. In the meantime, I'm going to see my aunt in Santa Fe." I had just made the decision that moment.

"Have a good trip." There was no discernible enthusiasm in her voice.

It was time to call Aunt Bea. I reversed charges with only a slight guilty feeling. She sounded delighted to hear from me. Would she be home tomorrow? You betcha. Just get yourself down here and I'll take care of you from then on. I had checked the bus schedule and found I could leave within the next 20 minutes, or else tomorrow late morning. The prospect of an overnight trip appealed to me. I told her my bus would arrive at 8:17—tomorrow morning.

Back in my room, I said a cheery hello to Charley, then asked: "Remind me, roomie, have I ever asked you for a loan?"

"No, but I have a feeling you're going to now."

"I need fifteen dollars. Just for bus fare to Santa Fe."

"Santa who? Christmas isn't for several months." Charley could be exasperating. But I took heart: he already had his wallet out. "How long will you be gone?" he asked. "What about school tomorrow? And you have a shift at Shadburns' Wednesday night."

"I'll be gone a couple of nights, Charley. I'll be back for dinner shift Wednesday. And if you see any of my professors just tell them I'm sick."

"You want me to lie for you?"

"It won't be a lie. I *am* sick. Sick of life. As my best friend, can you cover for me?"

Charley melted. "Not thinking of jumping in front of the bus, are you? Sick of life? Who isn't at times? Okay, here's a twenty. Now *I'm* broke."

"Charley, you're a saint. Uh—can you drive me to the bus station?"

"What, you going now?"

243

"Bus leaves in—let's see—fifteen minutes."

"Boy, you sure know how to disrupt a guy's studying. Listen, just leave the Chevy at the bus parking lot. I'll walk down and drive it home tomorrow."

Pulling my small bag from under the bed, it bumped against the banjo case. I hauled it out, as well. Bag in one hand, banjo case in the other, I headed for the door. I stopped abruptly and turned around.

"Charley?"

"Yeah, what now?"

"You're the best. Thanks loads. I'll pay you back and take you out for a hamburger when I get back."

"Sure you will."

I felt a pang; this was a term Cass was always using.

I gave a final wave and scooted for the door.

I sat awake on the bus, my thoughts convoluted: a lot of highs and one big low. There were only a few people on this late-night run. I yearned to strum my banjo. I moved to the last row of seats where I had the entire width of the bus to myself.

I strummed a few notes of *Jeepers Creepers*. Next I dove into *Louise*, then *Once in Love with Amy*. After that I didn't know where the notes came from. I started low and easy and built it up, went out into space for awhile, chasing a wild sweet dream. Other travelers could have their own dreams; I was enchanted with my own music. I slowly relaxed from the problems people in my life had caused. Or more correctly, I had caused.

Rick had taught me the words and music to the Army Air Corps song. Something pretty deep inside me made me strum the stirring theme, and after a moment I sang, low and sweet:

> *Off we go into the wild blue yonder*
> *Climbing high into the sun,*
> *Here they come, zooming to meet our thunder*
> *At 'em boys, give 'er the gun.*
>
> *Down we dive, spouting our flames from under*
> *Off in one helluva roar*
> *We live in fame or go down in flame. Hey!*
> *Nothing can stop the Army Air Corps.*

Music: the great healer. I propped my banjo at the end of the seat, stretched out my full length, content to turn my life over to an unknown driver for the rest of the night. I wondered how I, the hater of war, could have tears in my eyes over singing the fight song of the air corps that had killed my best friend.

I awoke after six o'clock; it was light enough to see the change of landscape. It fascinated me. The starkness of the desert, the flat-topped mountains in the distance—mesas I had heard they were called—the scrubby sagebrush and stunted trees. All were new to me. I wanted to get out there and hike across the desert, maybe meet a rattlesnake or a scorpion.

I wouldn't have to worry about my dual personality here in New Mexico. I would be Rob; Aunt Bea knew little of Rick Linden. Bea was a St. Clair herself, or once was. The irony that she had dropped the St. Clair name forever was not lost on me.

34

JOURNEY TO THE SOUTH

"Robbie!" My name rang out among a half dozen competing noises in the bus terminal. People were talking and laughing and shaking hands, a horn blared somewhere, and an amplified voice called off a 7:30 bus. I'd recognized Aunt Bea's voice when she screeched my name, but I couldn't spot her yet. Well, she *was* rather short.

"I thought that was you," she said, hugging me to her. "How you've filled out. You could out-wrestle George now, I'll betcha." She pecked me on the cheek and picked up my bag all in one motion. "Let's get out of here," she said, leading the way.

Meeting a friendly face, a dear face, in a crowded bus station had taken my breath away. Was it just two nights ago that I had battled four people in another world? Here I was loved for myself, *because* I was myself, no matter what name was attached.

She let me out through double-swinging doors on to the street. She turned left and strode rapidly towards the corner. I followed her like a pet poodle, meekly but happily.

"This is Plaza Square." She said, flinging an arm to one side. "We'll explore here tomorrow if there's time. You'll find lots of jewelry selling right here on the streets. I want you to take a few choice bits back to your girl. You do have a girl?"

"I'm not sure, Auntie."

"We'll talk of that later."

She took my arm and grabbed my bag. We approached a roadster, a 1936 Ford. She tossed my bag into the rumble seat and opened the door on the passenger side, again all in one motion.

"You have something big stirring in your life, I'll bet."

Laughing, I said, "Well, I did come down to see you."

"You'll stay a few days?"

"Two nights, Auntie. I have to be back Wednesday night."

"That first time in Manchester you stayed eight months. Then more months in San Luis Obispo. But now you've settled up in Colorado, right?"

"Well, I'm going to college, have a job, and maybe a girl."

"I want to hear about that. But just now I'm gonna show you a few sights of Santa Fe. I called in sick today and I just might have a relapse tomorrow."

"Oh, Auntie." After the bad feeling, lecturing, and scorn thrown my way recently, I was ready to be spoiled.

Bea drove the roadster like she still didn't realize that Americans drove on the right side of the road. She double-parked at the Kit Carson Monument so that I could read the inscription, pointed out the Santa Fe Trail marker as we drifted past, told a funny story, true or not, about Burro Alley, and finally parked in front of the Padre Gallegos House.

She turned to face me. "Want to go to Ciudad Juarez?"

"Ciudad---?"

"It's in Mexico. Just across the border. A fair drive, but it's worth seeing." We had breakfast downtown and I had my first taste of tortillas, tacos, chips and hot sauce. Then we drove to her small rented house in the south area near the University of Santa Fe.

"It's not much, Rob, just a cottage with one bedroom and a sleepable couch in the sitting room."

I said, "You remember I'm a couch guy, Auntie."

"Yes, I remember well. Meanwhile, you're tall, husky, brown-haired and handsome, too. I suspect the girls have caught on by now."

"That's part of what I want to talk to you about."

"We'll get to that at dinner, which I'll cook under the stars, New Mexico style. Can you believe a cold-country gal like me from northern England would catch on to Southwest cooking so completely? It surprises even me. And it's what keeps George on a short lease. Well, not too short at the moment." I suspected she needed some comforting, herself.

On the drive south she told me how she happened to be in Santa Fe. "George left California and headed down here, chasing his dream. A trucking friend told him there was an outfit here that needed drivers. Miracle of miracles, it turned out to be true. Then I came down and immediately missed the Pacific Ocean. Now that we're settled here, I like it best of all. The California coast and

Santa Fe are opposites, and of course both are nothing like Manchester. Some fun."

"Where's George now?"

"Off on a trip." She didn't look at me.

It became obvious Bea was upset about her husband. I didn't press her. But she took it out on her car; she exceeded the reckless. She slowed down not a whit during a dust storm, we skirted a police trap, probably for smugglers, we were passed on the right side by a fast-moving black sedan. We were both devastated by the sight of young children by the roadside, thin and dirty. "Makes me want to sweep them all up in my rumble seat and go buy some tacos," she said.

At Ciudad Juarez we drove through back streets so that I, a proper English boy, could see how people lived in a foreign country. Two old men played dominoes in the dust at a street-side table. A boy who looked seven but was probably ten watched us with his mouth open, a soccer ball glued to his hip. Several older men and a few women hunched up against a hot stucco wall, with no evident purpose in life other than to exist for another day.

On the way north again Bea, properly softened, stopped for a couple on the side of the road, a Mexican lad and his girl. She installed them in the rumble seat, their long black hair wild in the wind. With broad grins they accepted our invitation to tacos and chips and lemonade at a roadside stand.

"What do you want to do tomorrow?" she asked, on the road again after we'd dropped the two off at their uncle's house in Las Cruces.

"I don't actually know, Aunt Bea. You decide."

"I love that 'actually.' So British. Have you ever been sorry you left your country, Rob? Do you want to go back?"

I didn't hesitate. "No, I've done with Britain. You know, I'd heard that America was a paradise, that it was easy to find a job with limitless opportunities. Well, I've been here long enough to know that's not true. Still, I like the freedom, the chance to make your own way, the lack of—well, I guess I'd call it the class system. The only class system I've seen in America has to do with money. You go to the Broadmoor Hotel in Colorado Springs and you do see people with money. I guess that's the 'upper class.'"

"Close enough. Money and position will always separate groups of people, Rob. Well, you've seen a bit of Mexico. How about going into the mountains tomorrow?"

Deciding I'd had enough Mexican food for one day, Aunt Bea fired up the barbecue and cooked steaks for dinner. I helped her; it was my first experience in this American style of casual living. Roasted potatoes, barbecued shrimp, and a huge green salad took care of any perceived hunger pains.

After dinner she removed a sleek saxophone from its case. "Grab that banjo of yours and let's try a duet. I don't know if these two instruments are meant to harmonize, but we'll find out soon enough." We played into the night while she introduced me to tequila. "I hope I'm not corrupting you," she said as she poured. We both drank, toasting each other with our eyes.

"I'm not sure we're often on the same key," I said a bit later. Neither of us was particularly adept at our instrument of choice, but the time making music provided me with the most relaxing hour I could remember in a while.

Late in the evening, she said, "Let's talk. I want to know where you are in your young life."

"You go first, Aunt Bea. Start with George."

"I don't hide things very well, I know. In the past, George has been gone for as long as ten days. Several times."

"But he always came back---." I let the sentence hang.

"He always came back. But two weeks ago today, I received a card from Dallas. He wrote that he had found something that he had to chase, that he was headed East the next day. He's found a girl, Rob, the special girl he's probably been looking for ever since I've known him. He's headed in the opposite direction from Santa Fe. He's been gone longer than he ever has before. I don't think he'll be back this time."

"He didn't mention a girl. He just wrote---."

"Something he's got to chase. Who do you chase except a woman?"

"It's possible he's chasing a job."

Bea was bleary-eyed now and her voice deepened. "Thanks for putting a better face on it. Rob. But I know my George." She yawned. "Thanks for listening to me and I'll hear your story on the way to the mountains tomorrow. Here, I'll get you a couple of blankets. Need a sheet?" She couldn't stop yawning.

"Not really." I was a bit miffed that she had told me her problem but had left mine hanging. I fell asleep on the couch dreamily contemplating the knots and tangles of my life.

We hit the road about ten o'clock, heading northeast to the Sangre de Christo range. We lunched on a promontory about half way up the grade. From there we could make out the broad outlines of Santa Fe.

"It's quite a town," Bea said. "Unbelievably different from any other place I've ever been, much less lived." I stared at the distant city, twinkling in the midday sun and felt a longing so deep it shocked me. *Oh, to belong somewhere, to belong—and to be loved.*

Bea had divined my mood. "I don't want to lose track of you again. Leave your troubles in Colorado. Come on down and live with us. I'm the closest kin you have outside your folks. I could be mother, father, friend, confessor."

My face went soft, touched by her words. I hugged her.

At the summit we pulled into the turnout and soon perched on another rock. The view this time was easterly, from mountains to valleys and then more mountains. Rivers crisscrossed the valleys and a road the size of a string of pearls led to a town the size of an oyster. Smoke curled lazily up to merge with a gray sky. I longed for a little airplane to carry me deep into the valley and across to those hazy peaks.

She tossed me an opening line. "What do you think of Rob St. Clair now, kid?"

It was time to hear from Bea; I had already checked in with all the other people in my life. "Not too much," I began. "In England I gave up on the St. Clair kid. He was in the past, just a lad who had lived the first 15 years of his life on an island—but wasn't going anywhere. I found someone I'd rather be."

"You mean Rick Linden."

"Right. Ostensibly, I'm where I want to be. Colorado Springs, Rick's emotional home. I've been privileged to know his parents and his sister."

"You said 'ostensibly.'"

"Yes, I need to explain that." I stared over the beautiful desert, trying to put my words together. "Listen, Bea, Rick will live on if I do my job properly. His parents have their memories. Eighteen years of Rick living with them. I don't have enough memories of him. I need to create some more. Does that make sense?"

She put her hand on mine. "Not really, dearie. But do continue; this is fascinating."

When I didn't immediately go on, she had a thought. "Do you think he was asking you to be a reincarnation of himself? Is that possible?"

I leaped to my feet then kneeled by her side on the rock. "I never thought of it as reincarnation, but maybe that's what it is. He gave me his name, suggested I go to his home town, and even live with his parents. I've done all that. Reincarnation. Wow."

"You do have an imagination. I have a feeling what you just said ties in with your use of the word 'ostensibly' earlier."

"Hmm. Perhaps it does. I ended up in Colorado Springs, but all has *not* gone well. Ruth and Jane Linden, Cass, and Pat all feel I should be Rob St. Clair and that's all I should be."

"And now you want my take on the situation?"

"It's why I came down here."

Aunt Bea was silent a long time. Then she said, gently, "My first inclination is to agree with them"—I groaned and put my face in my hands—"but there's the other side to consider, too. You believe in what you're doing, that's quite obvious. The sensible course is to drop this quest, as you call it, for a couple or three years. But I ask you, Rob, is there some higher law that says we always have to be sensible? I've never followed that line, myself. If you want to indulge yourself—yes, indulge, my dear Rob—that's well and good. But the thing you must be very careful with is not to hurt anyone else with your indulgence."

I felt an immediate antipathy for the word 'indulgence.' Was she for me or against me?

She answered my unspoken question. "In the end, Rob, you have to decide this for yourself."

My aunt had let me down. She built me up, she let me down, she left me hanging. I was through with the subject for the day, but she came back to it as we drove to her house.

"You have three or four years of college ahead of you, just like Rick would have had. You can write, you can get into grass root politics, become an activist—they are always looking for young idealists—or, if you have the money, you can travel, teach, or do anything your education and interests leads you to."

"I'm not going to just sit back and wait three years."

"Keep active, then, as you already are. Take interesting classes, learn another language—Spanish would be my choice—learn about the American way of life. Get that citizenship out of the way—I've got mine now. Travel as your budget allows. And write and publish, if you can do it."

"So you're saying this gets me closer to Rick's goals?"

"That's just what I'm saying. You can't run until you can walk."

I didn't like her analogy, but I let it pass. "But then there's Cass. I love that girl so much it hurts all the time."

"My advice is to be patient with her, and honest, too."

"Like you're patient with George?"

"Hells bells, you can be sarcastic. Listen, I'm so romantic that if George doesn't come back, then he can go to hell."

"And if Cass doesn't come back to me?"

"Then it's her loss and she doesn't deserve you."

Although my couch was about eight inches too short for me, I went right to sleep. I awoke sometime in the early hours and I knew, as you do sometimes, that I wouldn't go right back to sleep. The battery of my soul cried out for re-charging.

I threw on my heavy jacket and, barefoot, I crept quietly out the back door. It was one of those lonesome nights I'd run into so many times. A million stars in a bright sky greeted me. It was impossible in this setting not to think of Rick. I stared at the sky, Rick's and my temple of wonder.

Rick, give me a sign, tell me what to do, who to believe, tell me to give it up or to try even harder. What about it, pal?

Back in the living room, I was wide awake. My eyes fell upon a news magazine on the coffee table. The cover was about the United Nations. I skimmed through the lead article, something about Eleanor Roosevelt's work with the U.N. My eyes skipped to the final paragraph and I read the italicized words there.

Somewhere in that dark sky the men of all nations will learn the true meaning of brotherly love.

252

I had asked Rick for a sign and here it was. But what could I do abut it? Finally, emotionally tired and frustrated, I turned off the light and lay on my back, hands cradling the back of my head. My eyes closed, then almost immediately opened again as I heard the air brakes of a truck or bus seemingly right outside Bea's cottage. Bright headlights were trained on her living room. I leaped off the couch, the blanket wrapped around me, ready to tell off a drunk or a careless driver.

Before I reached the front door, I heard Bea shriek and then watched in awe as she sprinted by me, opened the door, and bawled, "George! George. You came home."

A moment later a huge figure filled our doorway. George swept Bea up and swung her around and around, just as he had that first night in Manchester. Then he kissed her while ruffling her hair and swinging her around again.

Then, as in England, he condescended to notice me. "And what's this whipper-snapper doing here? Every time I go away, he shows up. And—look at that blanket around his body. I'll bet there's nothing on under there. Bea, you cradle-snatcher."

His big hand grabbed one part of my blanket and he tugged hard. I held on for dear life. We were having an arm wrestle of another kind. A moment later he gave up, laughing, and hugged Bea again.

All he said was, "There was this possibility of big money in New Orleans, Bea, so I headed down that way. There were two other guys involved. It was interesting for awhile there, but it all fell through. So I turned around and headed home."

Aunt Bea wasn't trusting her voice and he went right on. "I'm going to stay here, sweetie. This is my home. Hell, I'm 45 now and life can't get much better than you and Santa Fe and lots of Mex food." He looked at me. "And Rob can stay around, too, as long as he stays on his couch." He laughed and thumped his ample thigh with a huge hand.

Still, neither my aunt nor I seemed capable of speech, so he added, "Bea and I are going to bed now, Rob. It's time for you to put your ear muffs on."

Bea had to get back to work and so did I. She woke me at seven o'clock and we breakfasted together. I was reading the entire text of the news magazine I'd skimmed in the early hours of the morning; she fixed pancakes and tortillas. George was sleeping in; he had driven 12 straight hours from New Orleans the previous day just so he could sleep in his own bed, Bea at his side.

Bea noticed what I was reading. "That article is right up your alley," she said. "Did you note the U.N. has taken a stand on world peace and humanitarian matters? Eleanor Roosevelt just helped establish a Universal Declaration of Human Rights for the United Nations. She's a member of the first delegation to the U.S. General Assembly."

"I know. I've just been reading about it."

"Then you'll know that Eleanor's twin goals are education and world peace. Sound familiar? You're not alone, Rob. There's a sort of slogan at the end of the article which might interest you."

I said, "*Somewhere in that dark sky the men of all nations will learn the true meaning of brotherly love.*"

"So you know about it already. I might have known you would."

Yes, I know about it, Auntie. Rick was the first one to tell me, and there have been others since. But what am I supposed to do with it now?

35

SAVIOR OF A LOST SOUL

Toting my bag and banjo, I walked from the bus station to my rooming house. All was quiet there. It was mid-afternoon. There was nothing I felt like doing after my holiday. My down mood was paralyzing.

I lay on my bed watching the play of shadows on the wall cast by filtering sunlight through the aspens at the side of the house. Charley had left a message on my bed: he would be out for training camp dinner with the football team; and that Mrs. Linden had called. Twice, he thought. What they probably wanted, I concluded, was to inform me I was out of their lives forever.

On the bus ride north, my thoughts had rambled all over the place. I had heard from everyone; now it was up to me to decide my future. But a future without Cass was not to be accepted in such a cavalier manner. There had been no call or message from her; I hadn't expected any. I dozed, and was lucky to wake before five o'clock when I was due at Shadburns' Restaurant. I changed clothes and walked to my job with no discernable enthusiasm.

I had promised Cass I wouldn't call until Saturday and I held true to that. I attended classes Thursday and Friday, waiting for Saturday.

"It's me, Cass. I'm back."

"You're back. I'd forgotten you were going somewhere."

"Did you try to reach me?"

"No, I've been busy. Tests and things."

There seemed no answer to that. After a moment, I said, "Cass, it's no good talking on the phone. I'll take you to dinner." I had been paid by Shadburns, repaid Charley, and still had enough for dinner for two.

A long pause, then, "Well, I do have to eat."

It wasn't the most gracious acceptance, but I accepted it. I said I would walk by for her about six o'clock. Charley had our car out somewhere.

As I finished a bath, I remembered that I had vowed to call Mrs. Linden to apologize. I went directly to the telephone and dialed their number. There was no answer.

I watched her come down the steps of her dorm. Her hair had been newly cut and washed and her brown eyes, set in her round, freckled face, were serious. I longed to bring back that mischievous look she so often sported. I doubted I had it in my power to do so anytime soon. I loved to look at her trim little body, not forgetting for a moment the quaint little inn and what had happened there. Gosh, was that only two weeks ago?

For the first ten minutes it was like old times. The pasta, French bread and cokes were served while I told her of my trip to Santa Fe. "My aunt was awfully nice to me. She even took off a couple of days to be with me."

"And you took off three days to go down there."

I refused to be deterred. "Yes. My Aunt Bea did some right smart lecturing about my future."

"So what did you decide?"

"She was against my using Rick's name and I agreed with her."

That cleared up Cass' slight frown. "And the rest?"

"Still up for interpretation."

"Well, that puzzles me. Is this going to go on forever? I liked your honesty at the Linden's house, but it came pretty late. You were forced into it. Mrs. Linden was close to tears and we were about kicked out of her house. Have you telephoned her since that night?"

"I called her just before coming out tonight. No answer." It sounded pretty weak. "I probably should have phoned before going off to Santa Fe, but then I left in a hurry Sunday night."

"You couldn't find time to even write a note?"

"I guess not. Listen, Cass, let's not get hung up on Mrs. Linden."

"What part of the mess do you want to get hung up on then?" We were talking more loudly than normal; the jukebox was playing *You'll Never Know* over and over A hand-holding couple kept putting nickels in the machine to play their favorite song.

"Are you ever going to give up the whole identity thing? I need to know."

I chose my words carefully. "I reaffirmed something in Santa Fe, Cass. I know now that I believe in those goals as much as Rick did."

"Of course you'd say that. As if that justifies all of your past and future character defects."

I looked for a hint of a smile. There was none. "That's pretty strong language, Cass. Character defects. Do you really believe that?"

She didn't answer directly. "Listen, you talked the other night about trying to excel in his interests, to fly and write and ski and so forth. Don't you know you have a lot of interests that are not necessarily his?

"Think about it. You play soccer. Did Rick? Never tried it. You play banjo. Did he? You sing, did he? I know you serve meals to the homeless. Did he ever do that? Possibly, we don't know. Listen, don't get uptight. I'm not criticizing Rick. He had his interests and now you have yours. Let's keep them separate."

"Why can't I learn his interests as well as mine?" My tone was plaintive, and she rightfully didn't deign to respond.

Our bowls of pasta were getting cold, and I felt like telling her to eat more and talk less. But she was just getting warmed up.

"Then there's your sticking up for Charley. Segregation and desegregation are going to be big things in this country. That's a goal that Rick didn't think about. He would have, probably. But don't you see that's you? I don't think there's the tiniest bit of racism in your whole system. I admire you for that, Rob. That's the boy I could love someday."

I didn't like the 'some day,' but I could live with it.

"Meantime, grow up, Robert St. Clair. Get a life of your own."

That woke me up. "Grow up? To be what? As Robert St. Clair I'm a man without a country or a cause—or even a good solid reason to be on this earth. I need to finish being Rick so that someday I can be Rob." Cass had her mouth open to speak but I wasn't finished. "I've said over and over that I believe in Rick's goals, so what the hell's wrong with pursuing them, along with the banjo, the soccer, sticking up for Charley, all the rest?"

She said, sorrowfully and wistfully, "How different your life would have been if you had never met him. You'd be Rob St. Clair without any complications."

Still heated, I said, "I accept those complications as the price of knowing Rick. I'm glad I knew him. It was the defining moment of my life."

"Listen---."

"Rick didn't die in that airplane crash. His spirit didn't. A young lad named Rob decided he'd gladly—*gladly*—give up his own name and identity to follow his star."

"A lot of young men died without anyone volunteering to carry on for them."

"But this was Rick. He was special. And I gave him my word. And I *wanted* to do it. Don't any of those points count for anything with you?"

"Not much. I like my boyfriends to be all mine, not obsessed with a dead man."

At her door, I had to ask, "Will you go out with me next Friday night? A movie, a dance?"

She looked hard into my face. I wanted to hug her, to kiss her sweet mouth, to forget all this talking. I needed her comfort, her understanding, her love.

"No, Rob, it's obvious we're not thinking enough alike these days to spend another evening together. I'll see you around."

Soaked in sweat, with an aching head, I awoke with a loud gasp. For a long moment I didn't know where I was. I couldn't believe I hadn't awakened Charley. I had gone to bed in my clothes, and when Charley came in, he must have decided to let me sleep. I glanced at the clock: three o'clock, the witching hour.

I couldn't keep my thoughts off my girl. *Oh, Cass, Cass, my lovely lass who should be here with me now, in my bed, warm and loving. I was a fool to lose you, but what could I have said or done and still be true to myself?*

I got off the bed like an old man would. I walked into the hall and opened the front door. The moon was in that direction and I craved the moon. Seated on the front steps, I gazed skyward. I narrowed my eyes, focusing on a bright star in the northwest skies. *Are you there, Rick, watching over me, helping me to make sense of my life? If you are, you're not doing a very good job of it. Is*

*Cass right? Should I put you out to pasture? Give me a sign. Oh,
Cass, Cass.*

It had only been a week since I had soloed the Stearman. I
missed flying already. It had gotten into my blood. I slipped out
my wallet; there was a twenty dollar bill left. I didn't know how
I'd eat until next payday, but the only thing I wanted to spend that
twenty on was to fly solo again.

Shadinger told me he would prefer to give me another
hour of instruction before I flew alone again. I told him I didn't
have money for dual, only for an hour solo. I reminded him I had
had no trouble aloft, not even any close shaves. All right, he said,
let's take a quiz. He asked me a dozen questions: pattern altitude,
power settings, the proper attitude in power on and power off
stalls, stalling speed, and so on. I had memorized these variables
during my first flight and I had not forgotten them.

"Don't forget the pre-flight," he yelled as I approached the
trainer. "Stay up 45 minutes tops. And watch those clouds. They
may descend fast." I knew from the weather chart that the ceiling
was 4,000 feet above ground level.

My takeoff was perfection. I banked left, east, in order to
stay away from the Rockies' dominating presence. I did some
stalls and some climbing turns, but decided against a spin. I felt a
little light-headed to be flying solo under an overcast sky on a
Sunday afternoon. Forget personal problems. I was in my element
now.

After ten minutes flying east, I turned north for a few
minutes, then west again and overflew Colorado Springs. I picked
out my rooming house and Cass's dormitory, and was looking for
the Linden's home when the weather closed in. I was at 3,500 feet
above the ground. In the confusion of suddenly flying blind, I
forgot my last heading was 270 degrees, due west. I put the trainer
into a glide attitude to get under the clouds. It was eerie not to
have a ground reference. I watched my turn and bank indicator and
altimeter closely.

A vise seemed to grip my heart. I was still letting down in
a shallow glide when it hit me: I was headed west, into the
Rockies. I banked to the left in a gentle turn, then steepened it

sharply when a shoulder of the foothills loomed up in front of me. I fought panic; it was very close. Although still flying blind, I kept increasing my bank. I might spin in, but this was no worse than hitting a mountain.

Luck rather than good flying brought me out of the steep bank and flying straight and level again. I checked my compass: 85 degrees. I was flying east, out of immediate danger. My heart beat, racing a moment before, settled down a bit. I would be okay.

Are you crazy, St. Clair? How can you be okay if you are at 2,000 feet and lost in the clouds?

Fear gripped me again. What was I doing, a novice pilot, flying blind over unfamiliar territory? It was still a solid undercast beneath my Stearman. I must be well east of Shadinger's field by now, and it came to me: *I didn't know the ground elevation out there!* Should I make a 180 and fly west? No—I would be flying towards a 14,000-foot peak again. How much gasoline did I have left? I didn't know.

I fought panic; I knew it could be deadly. I was still riding along at 2,000 feet, blind and lost and getting mighty scared, when I saw the other airplane. How could I see another plane in the dense clouds? I don't know. It was flying formation with me, off my left wing.

I inspected it as well as I could from my cockpit. Could it be—yes, it was a P-51. I knew it was a Mustang; I had admired its sleek lines many times at Rick's base. Unbelieving, I stared hard at the other pilot. I could not see his face; he was helmeted. An astonishing thought hit me: *could it be Rick?* I was still staring at him when he pointed a gloved finger first at me, then in another direction entirely. His gesture was clear: I was to follow him.

He must have throttled well back because I was able to stay with him. He lost altitude steadily and I put my Stearman into a standard glide attitude and followed his tail. I glued my eyes to his tail. An eerie five minutes followed, both of us flying blind. We had lost a lot of altitude; my altimeter showed 800 feet. Would he fly us both into the ground?

No, Rick wouldn't. Because I had decided from the moment I had recognized the other plane as a P-51, that Rick Linden was at the controls and that he would never let me crash.

And then we were out of it. At 600 feet it was clear below and the airport was in sight. It would be a piece of cake going in.

The Mustang was flying formation with me again, and I had the mesmerizing thought that he might land with me. I would see Rick again.

He offered me a two-fingered salute, then pointed first at me then at the airport. He knew I had seen the field and that his work was done. In a final gesture, he pointed first at himself, then upwards, towards the sky, the heavens, the wild blue yonder.

I knew without doubt that Rick Linden was leaving me on my own, that he no longer would be a presence in my life, that he was bidding me a final adieu.

Shadinger was so relieved to see me drop out of the low clouds that he forgot to chew me out for getting into them in the first place. I didn't tell him I'd been lost and had missed hitting a mountain by a few feet. Nor did I tell him about the P-51, my savior, Rick the First looking after Rick the Second.

For my own peace of mind, I did ask him if he'd do me a favor. Would he check by radio with Peterson Air Force Base in Colorado Springs and with Lowry Air Force Base in Denver to see if they had a P-51 out on a flight? Shadinger looked at me strangely but did so. When he told me Operations at both fields told him they had no P-51 at their field at this time, I was not surprised.

Rick Linden's Mustang wouldn't be based at Peterson or Lowry or any other air force base. It was based in the heavens above, and it had come down to help a friend in need. I knew it in my bones that I would never hear from Rick again. Sadness engulfed me at first, but then I knew a kind of peace I hadn't known since a December morning in 1944.

Now I had some fence-mending to do, and I'd better get right down to it.

36

A LIFETIME AHEAD OF US
(REVISITED)

My lifetime record had shown I was not a good salesman. Now I was facing the toughest task of persuasion ever. I needed to see the Lindens and Cass together. Tonight. I didn't want to wait longer. I telephoned Cass as soon as I returned from my flight and asked her to go with me to the Linden's house for dessert. Very trusting of me: I hadn't yet checked to see if the Lindens would even be home, let alone would want to see me. But I had to call Cass first; she had to be present.

"Something the matter with your memory, St. Clair?" she asked. "Didn't we decide just last night that we weren't thinking enough alike to see each other for awhile—or perhaps forever? Now you want to bring up the whole stupid subject again." Her voice could have been filtered through an iceberg.

Time for persuasion. I begged her not to hang up on me; I pleaded with her to give me a final chance. I promised her I had a new attitude. I asked her for a leap of faith, this last time. We talked on. She wasn't convinced, far from it. But she didn't hang up on me, either. Ten minutes of talk, then a long minute of silence. I held my breath. Then, slowly, with a straining sort of grace, Cass said she'd cancel her plans to go to dinner with her roommates, put aside her studying, and go with me against her better judgment. She had taken the leap.

I called the Lindens and asked Ruth whether Cass and I could come over for dessert if we brought the ice cream. It was trite and presumptuous, but I could think of nothing better.

Her answer was typical Ruth Linden. "Ice cream will go well with the apple pie I baked this afternoon." She told me she'd left phone messages for me and written a letter asking for me to call them. "We wanted to see you," she said.

Good. I wanted to see them, as well.

The four of us sat around the dark pine dining room table, dessert dishes stacked in the kitchen. Ruth had fed our stomachs; now it was time for me to feed their minds. I thanked the three of them for this chance to talk again about my behavior, past and future. I wouldn't say anything about flying formation with Rick Linden that afternoon; that was between Rick and me, forever.

"My name is Rob St. Clair. It is *not* Rick Linden. I'll never call myself again by his name. It was his name and his alone. He's entitled to carry it proudly forever."

It was a positive beginning, I thought. I imagined Ruth's smile had a relieved quality, but it occurred to me that Alex Linden looked slightly crestfallen. Perhaps he would have welcomed another Rick around, even a pseudo one. As for Cass, she remained straight-faced. She wanted to hear the rest.

I next told them my days as 'Rick the Second' were over. Period.

Now Cass' neutral look tilted in my favor.

"Third point." I told them I would not pursue interests, sports and other activities that had been Rick's special domain. I mentioned football, basketball, baseball, and skiing. They were not my interests. I sneaked a look at Cass; were her eyes shining?

"I do have interests of my own," I told my rapt listeners. "Cass pointed them out to me the other night. I sing, play banjo, serve meals to the homeless, and play soccer and tennis." There were overlaps, I went on, things that both Rick and I enjoyed. That included tennis, fishing, writing, and flying. I told them about my recent solo flight. "As for tennis, I'm going to practice hard so that someday I might beat Cass. Just once." This brought a laugh and most of the remaining tension evaporated.

Cass' eyes were close to shining but I wasn't done and she knew it. "One other thing," I began, "I am going to continue in all my beliefs and causes." The Lindens looked expectant while a frown began to form on my girl's brow. "That's because I believe in them. Certainly they were Rick's interests before they were mine. But they are mine, also." I told them about the ideas Matt Janzen had, of the involvement of other followers, friends of his. I told them about the editorials written by Rick which we had edited for printing in newspapers in Denver and Colorado Springs. "And perhaps several other newspapers, as well," I concluded.

I told the Lindens I would take the time while in college to pursue the grand passions their son had told me about. I would earn a degree, but I would not give up on my causes. They would be a significant part of my life.

From their immediate smiles, and hugs when we left soon after, I felt the Lindens had become friends for life.

That left Cass. We walked home together and she didn't mention my monologue. When we had nearly reached her dorm, she stopped dead on the sidewalk and poked me in the chest. "There's a show on at the Roxie Friday night. *Casablanca.* How about if I take you this time?"

That told me all I needed to know how Cass felt about the new Rob St. Clair.

We were married two years later, in September 1950. I was just 21, she 20 with a birthday coming up. The ceremony was at the home of Cass' parents in the Springs. Charley came down from Casper, Wyoming, to be my best man. He was a scat-back for the University of Wyoming.

Surprisingly, my mother came over. She told me my father had mellowed in later life, but not enough to face a trip to the U.S. He loved me, she said, but I wondered how much. My mum got along well with Ruth Linden. Aunt Bea and George were there, the latter looking unique in a coat and tie.

We moved to Boulder where we both enrolled at the University of Colorado. We liked that small city backing up to the Rockies. I majored in Journalism and Cass in European History. Journalism offered me a mixture of reporting, writing, and editing. We thought we could move to another city in pursuit of bigger jobs or larger salaries, but we ended up staying in Colorado.

On September 9, 1951, we celebrated our first anniversary and my 22nd birthday by announcing Cass' pregnancy. I wondered about names if it was a boy. I would want to name him Rick. Cass would probably be against it. I almost hoped it would be a girl and put off the sweet question.

As editor of the college newspaper, I assigned myself coverage of a special meeting. This was a War Committee of the United Nations at the Stanley Hotel in Estes Park. The committee was to deal with how to discourage war as a remedy for international conflicts. "Discourage" seemed a weak word; I would have preferred "condemn." The festivities included a dinner speaker, a morning panel discussion, and a luncheon on the second day with another high-powered speaker. I was reporting on the two speakers for the college paper. The school's budget did not cover all costs, so I shared a room with the editor of the *Boulder Daily Camera*, a friend of mine.

It was a great opportunity: covering a meeting devoted to peace, especially with the Korean War a near reality. The program finished about ten in the evening. It was late September. The sky was clear but snow was in the air. The highway was dry and the traffic nearly non-existent. It was over 12,000 feet at the top, and I wanted, I *needed,* to commune with the dark sky.

It had been a wonderful summer of 1950. Pat Morse, on a business trip to California from Connecticut, stopped in Colorado Springs to visit Rick's parents—and me. Alex Linden telephoned me and I drove down from Boulder for the evening. At the Linden's house, I told Pat about the steps I was taking on behalf of Rick. After dinner Alex, Pat, and I visited Matt Janzen. The four of us spent a late evening at Mr. J's apartment. Two young men and two not so young. Pretzels, popcorn, and beer helped us relax and loosened our tongues.

We talked about the same subjects as Rick and I had done on the slopes of Roans Peak. I was thrilled that four people, three of whom had known Rick intimately, were discussing his passions over five years after his death. It was a magical evening, filled with good fellowship, memories, and ideas for spreading the word.

Alex and Mr. J knew most of the steps I'd taken in the past two years. But Pat didn't. "At the suggestion of my Aunt Beatrice, I wrote to Eleanor Roosevelt. And she wrote back. Not just once but four or five times. We shared our ideas about her grand passions: world peace and universal education. Sound familiar?

"I also wrote to Charles Lindbergh, Bernard Baruch, Al Smith, Mayor La Guardia, Wendell Willkie, Lloyd Douglas, let's see, to Grantland Rice, Christopher Morley, Edward R. Murrow, Dwight Eisenhower, Harry Truman, and a young war correspondent named Andy Rooney. And there were others. I asked for their ideas, for their support, for their plans for peace. It was gratifying that most of them responded and shared their ideas. I was thrilled that so many people in powerful positions were with us."

Rick's father spoke up. "These two did something else, Pat, that I was particularly proud of. They promoted Rick's book, *Trail of the Bombers*. They canvassed Colorado thoroughly. Driving, talking, book signings. They took me along for book signings. After all, I was the father of the author. Colorado has out-sold every other state. We've all written to the publishers, W.W. Norton, urging them to do the same in other states. There wasn't much response until someone in Hollywood wrote to the publishers and inquired about movie rights. Now Norton is pushing the book as hard as we are."

We were only four and our effect would be limited for now. And yet, I still believed that in the long run we could make a difference.

At the top of the divide, I parked my car in a turnabout, wrapped my wool coat around me, and walked up the trail a short distance to where a promontory offered a wide view. I felt like I was King of the World or at least Prince of the Rockies. The clarity of the night had been obscured in just the hour it had taken me to drive here from Estes. Filmy clouds partially veiled the sparkling sky. With no-nonsense Cass around, lovable Cass, I didn't often have a chance to talk to the sky and the special person residing there. Now I would.

On the last night of your life, Rick, you quoted a line that became part of me: "Somewhere in that dark sky the men of all nations will learn the true meaning of brotherly love." It's happening, Rick, I can feel it in the air, I read about it in newspapers, I write about it in my column. Your passions are still alive. It was slow at first—a lot of wasted time and dumb emotions. I was an unhappy lad most of the time, but you saved my life and then said adieu.

Marrying Cass was the right thing to do. She's given me balance, perspective, a "You're going too far" reality check occasionally, and of course, love. I lost you but I found Cass.

We now have working disciples—yes, disciples—of yours in Colorado Springs with the Lindens and Matt Janzen and his group; in Wyoming with Charley Peek; in Santa Fe with Bea and George; in England with my mother (yes, my mother): in Connecticut with your buddy Pat; and—yes, she's coming around—in Boulder with Cass St. Clair.

So goodnight and serenade, Rick. I've got to get back to Estes Park and get some sleep. I've got a job to do and I'm doing it for you, with you, pal.